# REASON, TREASON AND TYRINGHAM TEA

David A. Weiss

*This is a work of historical fiction set in the period 1772-1776. While events involving historical persons and places are incorporated, all of the dialogue and many of the characters and incidents are fictional.*

"Reason, Treason and Tyringham Tea," by David A. Weiss.
ISBN: 978-1-62137-852-5 (softcover).

Library of Congress control number on file with publisher.

# Acknowledgments

I GRATEFULLY ACKNOWLEDGE all of the following: the Schenectady Fiction Writers' Club, and particularly Joyce McCormick, Robert Conahan, Betty Pieper and Carolyn Houston, the members whose sage criticism aided me in this work; Dr. Richard Greene, physician, novelist and long-time Board Member of the Bidwell House Museum, who critiqued the manuscript and provided important historical background; Robert Hoogs, President of the Bidwell House Museum Board, for educating me about Tyringham roads of the 1770s; Barbara Palmer, Executive Director of the Bidwell House Museum, for furnishing helpful information (including a museum photograph by David Dashiell, Courtesy of the Bidwell House Museum, Monterey Massachusetts); Danielle Stavio, Lodgewood Mfg. Ltd., for allowing me to use the photograph of a Mid 18th Century Club Butt Fowler that appears on the cover; Jane Silver, for reviewing a draft and offering helpful ideas; Adrienne Weiss, my talented daughter-in-law, for proofreading and offering helpful recommendations; Linda Hoxie, a member of my Siena College tennis group, whose husband's ancestors were owners of the Sandwich Massachusetts Hoxie Saltbox (circa 1675), for proofreading this work and providing a wealth of astute and valuable insights and suggestions; my gifted and creative daughter Lori Weiss, for digital editing and design of the cover and diagrams; and my very dear and lovely wife Joyce who not only proofread this work, but also gives me endless support as I pursue my passion.

# Cover

THE SIGN DEPICTED at the top of the cover, "TYRINGHAM, 1739, A Hinterland Settlement," is located on Tyringham Road about two miles south of Route 20 in Lee Massachusetts. At the base of the cover is a photograph of a monument that stands in front of Town Hall in Great Barrington, Massachusetts. It identifies the spot where the first open resistance to British rule in America occurred on August 16, 1774, at what was then the site of the original Berkshire County Courthouse. The firearm that runs along either edge of the cover, a Mid 18th Century Club Butt Fowler Modified for Militia Use, is a reprint of a photograph authorized by and credited to Danielle Stavio, Lodgewood Mfg. Ltd. (website: lodgewood.com). The fowler so depicted was built by master builder Steve Krolick (*See* Endnote 114).

# Contents

# Preface

SET IN THE OLD TOWN of Tyringham, Massachusetts, *Reason, Treason and Tyringham Tea* takes place between 1772 and 1776. What was then Tyringham has long since been divided. The southern portion became the incorporated Village of Monterey on April 12, 1847, while the northern portion is still called Tyringham. The scenes of *Reason, Treason and Tyringham Tea* occur mainly in what is today Monterey, approximately fifteen miles from the southwest corner of Massachusetts.

As a youngster, at the ages of six and seven, I spent the summers of 1950 and 1951 at Camp Monterey. The camp, which is long gone, was located in the northern part of the Village along the shore of Lake Garfield. In the eighteenth century, Lake Garfield was known as Brewer's Pond and later Twelve-Mile Pond, the *twelve* referring to its distance from Sheffield, not its 1.5-mile length.

While *Reason, Treason and Tyringham Tea* is a novel and the main characters are fictional, numerous individuals who resided in Tyringham during the eighteenth century are sprinkled into the story. Among these are Captain John Brewer, one of the first settlers and the builder of the original sawmill and gristmill that eased the way for others to follow, [1] and Reverend Adonijah Bidwell, whose impressive home (*circa* 1764) with six large paneled rooms and four fireplaces endures as the Bidwell House Museum.[2] Although Reverend Bidwell's sermons were preserved, because he wrote them in code, their content remained a mystery for roughly a quarter of a millennium despite numerous attempts to decipher them. In 2012 a Museum intern cracked the code.[3] The Reverend's language, often in the form of notes, does not lend itself to a readable novel. His character, however, is too valuable to be ignored. I, therefore, opted to include him. While I have not incorporated the actual sermons or language he used, I have

1

tried to portray him in a manner consistent with the Congregationalist and American patriotic views he was known to espouse.

I considered writing *Reason, Treason and Tyringham Tea* in the parlance of the day but dismissed the idea for two reasons. The first, arguably a rationalization to avoid the challenge it engendered, was that it would render the work more cumbersome to read. The second was the risk, indeed likelihood, that I would create a bogus facsimile of eighteenth century speech.

Although the dialogue of *Reason, Treason and Tyringham Tea*, like its protagonist Thomas Webster, is fictional, I have endeavored to remain true to the history that preceded the Revolutionary War. More than any other region of colonial America, Massachusetts, particularly the city of Boston, provoked King George and the British Parliament. An inordinately large portion of the events leading up to the war with England occurred there. Among these were the Boston Tea Party, the siege of Boston, and the battles of Lexington and Concord and Bunker Hill. In the early 1770s, few in the American colonies anticipated that their demands for rights comparable to those of England's citizens would lead to war, but as 1774 wore on, the likelihood of armed conflict mounted.

Unlike the twenty-first century where information grows exponentially and individual expertise is often highly specialized, in the late eighteenth century, Renaissance men, well-versed in philosophy, science, architecture, economics and more, were far from rare. Such is the nature of Thomas Webster, the protagonist of *Reason, Treason and Tyringham Tea*.

Numerous scenes of *Reason, Treason and Tyringham Tea* take place at the "Hogshead Tavern," an establishment several miles northeast of the heart of Monterey along the Albany-Boston Post Road. While the Hogshead is fictional, in eighteenth-century America such taverns were commonplace. Locals gathered there, while those passing through sought respite. In nearby Great Barrington, approximately eight miles west of Monterey, there were several of these inns. According to some accounts, one in particular, the tavern of Josiah Smith, became the local depository of information. In early May 1775, roughly two weeks after the battles of Lexington and Concord, citizens of the Town of Great Barrington began taking turns riding to Tyringham and Sheffield to acquire daily updates regarding the so-called Siege of Boston. They would deliver that information for local distribution at Josiah Smith's tavern.[4]

In the 1770s the roads of Tyringham, like the town itself, were developing. As depicted on the map that follows this Preface, there were two main thoroughfares, the Albany-Boston Post Road and the Great Road. The former, which took a southeast course as it passed through Tyringham, joined the Great Road, which continued east to Boston. Traveling west on either of these routes, one could reach Albany, New York. While the Albany-Boston Post Road, the more northerly route to Albany, was shorter, its terrain was more difficult. The southerly route, the Great Road, went directly west through Great Barrington, where the Berkshire County Courthouse was located.

Open to debate is whether *Reason, Treason and Tyringham Tea* is a period piece or historical novel, a distinction that some would argue is replete with ambiguity. While the characterization is unimportant, not so the purpose: depicting life in eighteenth-century western Massachusetts amid the circumstances that culminated with America's Revolutionary War. Incorporated in the book are numerous documented events. Much as I have tried to relate them accurately, the work in no way purports to be authoritative, nor does it seek to unearth previously undisclosed details about the Revolution or subject those of long standing to a new microscope.

As reflected in the endnotes, I have employed a wide range of sources, some of which by their very nature beg scrutiny. A number of my sources come from organizations that openly grind political axes. Although one might question their use, they help capture the unreliability that plagued communication in eighteenth-century America. In an era when news passed by word of mouth, plus a small number of publications, and devices such as electronic media, photographs, films and DVD's were all but unimaginable, opinions and surmises, along with notoriously inaccurate eye-witness accounts, were the norm. Political leanings often skewed the accuracy of information. In

3

rural areas such as Tyringham, rarely the site of major events, accounts, generally $n^{th}$-*hand*, were even more unreliable. Newspapers did little to eliminate the problem. Not only were they dependent on unreliable eye-witnesses, but with journalistic standards in their infancy, even the best of periodicals were disposed to editorialize or twist the facts consistent with their agenda. In an effort to make biases more transparent, in addition to tapping diverse sources, I have armed my characters with countervailing information and arguments that invite thoughtful scrutiny. For the more curious, endnotes frequently shed light on ambiguities.

As is often true of history, particularly when related through the asymmetric lenses of victorious combatants, the American Revolution has been romanticized. Occasionally its chroniclers have allowed opportunities to perpetuate alluring stories to overshadow accuracy. Catchy quotes and quips, not the actual words of an alleged speaker, enhanced the tales. A prime example is Patrick Henry's 1775 "Give me liberty or give me death" speech. The famous, far-from-brief oration first appeared in print more than forty years later in William Wirt's "Patrick Henry: Life, Correspondence, and Speeches." Henry had died in 1799. Wirt's source was Judge St. George Tucker who was present when the speech had been delivered many years earlier. Wirt wrote to Tucker that he had "taken almost entirely Mr. Henry's speech in the Convention of '75 from you."[5] While there is no disputing that Henry gave an impassioned speech before the Virginia Convention, what he said remains open to debate. The improbability that Tucker recalled from memory a lengthy oration heard many years earlier suggests the storied rendition was to a significant extent the product of literary license.[6]

The extent to which such license has colored our patriotic history has been masterfully detailed by Ray Raphael in his well-documented book, "Founding Myths, Stories That Hide Our Patriotic Past."[7] Raphael not only debunks the myth of Patrick Henry's speech, but numerous others, including: the role of Samuel Adams; "Don't fire until you see the whites of their eyes;" Molly Pitcher, the legendary woman who, after her

4

husband was shot, dropped her water pitcher and supposedly took his place at a cannon; and even the role of Thomas Jefferson as the architect of independence.[8] Some might argue that such tales, despite being decorated with hyperbole and inaccuracies, have a redeeming purpose. Without heroes and noteworthy quotes, school children would absorb and retain far less than they do. Our communal awareness of our background would be diminished. Whether such contentions have merit or constitute convenient rationalizations is left for others to debate.[9] *Reason, Treason and Tyringham Tea* does not attempt to expose or explore the myths and legends surrounding the Revolution. Suffice it to say that insofar as license is tolerated, it should not be an excuse to whitewash history and open doors allowing past abominations to be repeated. Slavery, the economic convenience of treating people as chattel, is a prime example. So too is the Holocaust. Such horrors cannot be brushed beneath the pleasing patterns of a dense carpet. While some might deny the risk, American history proves otherwise. Far from an exhaustive list, consider the following: the sordid treatment of Native Americans; Nazi inspired eugenics (forced sterilization) statutes enacted in a majority of states; the internment of Japanese during World War II; the Tuskegee experiment; and "separate but equal," the Supreme Court doctrine[10] that perpetuated racial discrimination for nearly one hundred years after the Civil War. Not only did these seemingly unthinkable wrongs occur, but often decades passed before the iniquity they disguised was exposed. What other evils still lay buried, one cannot say.

When discussing the issues of the day, by design the characters of *Reason, Treason and Tyringham Tea* are prone to exaggeration, intransigence and inconsistency. Such foibles are alive and well in the twenty-first century. With the growth of communication media, agenda-driven positions bombard us with interminable distortions. Smooth-tongued demagogues at both ends of the political spectrum, displaying little regard for the truth, rant and rave, mainly to their respective choirs. Politicians give holier-than-thou exegeses justifying votes traded for contributions or, worse yet, kickbacks. Advertisers, using slick Madison Avenue techniques, not the least of which are sex, subliminal messages and misrepresentation, hock their wares. Infomercials backed with less than pseudo-science promise the impossible. Round tables replete with individuals interrupting and talking over one another are television's standard fare. Celebrities pontificate on issues about which they have no expertise. Propaganda, ranging from small distortions to total fabrications, remains rampant. That the characters of *Reason, Treason and Tyringham Tea* sometimes misstate the facts is to be expected. But as much as possible I have attempted to lay inaccuracies bare in order that the events of the period not suffer additional distortion.

Unlike my six earlier novels where the goal was to push the story forward, in *Reason, Treason and Tyringham Tea*, examination of mundane facets of daily life is equally important. Often the story and occasionally the characters yield to settings, community life and the development of a rural colonial settlement. At times the protagonist, Thomas Webster, equivocates as he struggles with the issues of the day. His desire to remain objective, coupled with a perverse propensity to play devil's advocate, pushes others, whether Patriot or Tory, to give more than lip service to views contrary to their own. Much as Webster's conduct sheds light on motivations and biases, it exposes him to criticism. Despite the temptation to resort to page-turning action, I have endeavored to remain focused on my primary purpose: exploration of life, frequently alone and unsure, for a rugged, sensitive and intelligent individualist in the hinterlands of colonial Massachusetts as he wrestles with both his day-to-day challenges and the political issues of the day.

David A. Weiss

Bidwell House Museum

Photograph by David Dashiell
Courtesy of the Bidwell House Museum
Monterey, Massachusetts

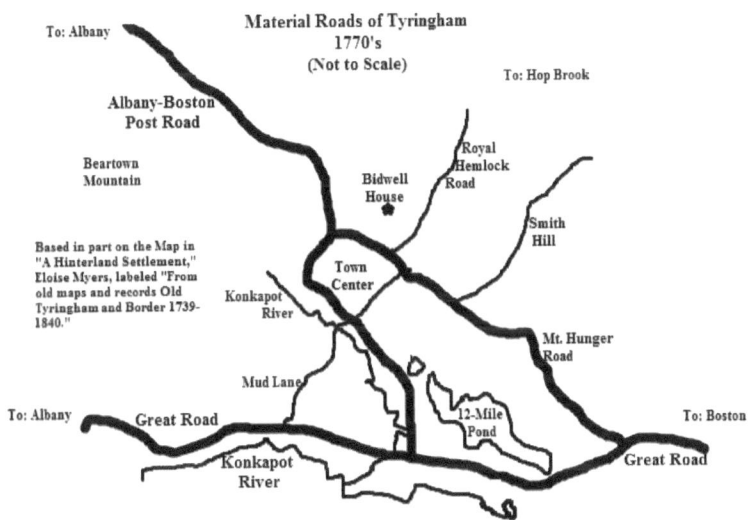

Material Roads of Tyringham
1770's
(Not to Scale)

To: Albany

Albany-Boston
Post Road

Beartown
Mountain

Based in part on the Map in
"A Hinterland Settlement,"
Eloise Myers, labeled "From
old maps and records Old
Tyringham and Border 1739-
1840."

To: Hop Brook

Royal
Hemlock
Road

Bidwell
House

Smith
Hill

Town
Center

Konkapot
River

Mt. Hunger
Road

Mud Lane

12-Mile
Pond

To: Albany

Great Road

To: Boston

Great Road

Konkapot
River

8

# Chapter 1

SEATED ON THE STOOP THAT FRONTED the home where he rented a room, Thomas Webster, mired in the depths of an agonizing depression, watched neighbors, dressed in their Sunday best, parade past to the wedding of Polly Winslow and Peter Blake. Thom contemplated what might have been. Little more than a year earlier, after Polly and Thom had professed their love for one another, Thom had asked Polly's father, a master silversmith from a wealthy background, for Polly's hand in marriage. In no uncertain terms her father had vetoed the proposed nuptials. The idea that his daughter would marry a common fellow like Thom with no formal education was out of the question. The Winslow family was highly respected in Berkshire County, and Polly would not be allowed to marry down. Little did Issac Winslow realize that before coming to America, Thom had spent more than a year in an English jail. That information, had Winslow known it, would have lent ample proof to his judgment.

Thom viewed it differently. Month after month he stewed. What right did any father have to interfere with his daughter's choice of a spouse? Though a far cry from the arranged marriages that had long plagued other societies, the antiquated vestige of parental veto had no place in the New World of the American colonies. In the more egalitarian land of which Thom dreamed, inequitable influences from a continent across the sea, long ruled by a self-indulgent aristocracy, would not be tolerated. He and Polly would have been wed.

Unlike Peter, who came from good stock, Thom grew up in rural England, the son of a poor laborer. His father, an alcoholic, was a cruel taskmaster with one abiding principle: Whatever Thom did was wrong. Thom's mother was caring, but cowed by her overbearing husband, she could do little to alleviate Thom's torment, and when she succumbed to influenza

9

during Thom's stint in jail, Thom had no desire to return to his father's abuse. Still seventeen, following his release from confinement, he signed on as a lowly boatswain's assistant aboard a ship bound for America.

Once he arrived in the New World, Thom undertook employment in Boston under the tutelage of an accomplished architect and home builder. Thom's rudimentary skills grew rapidly as he developed into a fine craftsman who took pride in his work. The influence of his mentor, a Renaissance man, did not end with skills of the trade. Into the wee hours of the night, aided by a single glass-chimneyed, whale-oil lantern, Thom's horizons expanded into the realms of science and history and philosophy. In the endless days of winter he devoured books and honed skills in furniture making. Intent on building himself a home in the mountains, Thom scrimped and saved, enabling him to afford the annual fees associated with a plot of land conveyed to him by the proprietor of a large tract in the western reaches of the Massachusetts Bay Colony. Thom's plot was located near Beartown Mountain in the Housatonic Township No. 1, one of four similar townships between Westfield and Sheffield, established by the Provincial Legislature of Massachusetts Bay on January 15, 1735.[11] It was a short distance from the Albany-Boston Post Road, a great trail linking the Massachusetts Bay Colony's economic center with Albany, the city in eastern New York that lay at the confluence of the Hudson and Mohawk rivers.

In 1770 Thom moved to the Berkshires where he rented a room in the rear of the home of Sarah Albright, a widow who had lost her husband a year earlier. In exchange for doing chores about the house and cultivating her farm-like garden, he received room and board. The arrangement enabled him to save much of what he earned assisting other settlers in the construction of their homes.

Not long after he had moved to the Housatonic Township, a friend sent Thom a letter indicating his mentor had passed away. Soon after Thom met Polly Winslow, and a romance blossomed. His plans to build a home, along with dreams of a wife and family to share it, seemed close to fruition. But all that came to an abrupt halt when he asked Polly's father for her hand in marriage. The emphatic veto squelched the relationship. While occasionally young colonial women ignored their fathers' dictates and eloped with suitors, Polly was not among those rebellious few. And much as Thom hated the thought, the possibility loomed that Polly, not her father, had spurned his proposal. Countless times Thom had replayed the sequence of events in his mind. There was the moonlit night when, seated on their favorite granite rock on the hill overlooking Brewer's Pond, he had proposed to Polly. She had seemed enthusiastic, but she had given him neither a *yes*, nor a *no*. Her father's blessing or the lack thereof would have to abide. That was how Polly had put it. Then came the painful paternal veto, the genesis of ineffable qualms that Issac Winslow was a foil, an easy way out for Polly. Just three months later Peter Blake began to court Polly. Their romance flourished, and with the blessing of her father, their wedding day arrived.

A part of Thom longed to despise Peter, but he couldn't. Everything about Peter, who was as strapping and handsome as Thom, labeled him a gentleman. The fact he came from good stock—his father was a pillar of the nearby Sheffield community—was secondary. So too were his degree from William and Mary and his professional reputation as a skilled surveyor. Comments that he was as fine a catch as was to be found in the southern Berkshire settlement of Tyringham were not easily dismissed. The fact that Peter treated Thom with utmost respect precluded Thom from disliking Peter. Rather than holding his academic credentials over Thom's head, Peter took pains to esteem Thom's ability to educate himself. When they talked about philosophy, government and economics, particularly France's Rousseau, Montesquieu and Voltaire and England's Smith and Locke, Peter lauded Thom's self-acquired knowledge as if elevating it above his own. As Peter put it, "Letters acquired from self-induced thirst are more admirable and lasting than those procured with the threat of exams and the lure of a degree." Peter never threw up his family background and economic status in Thom's face. With undeniable sincerity he applauded Thom's independence and courage to leave his home and family in England at the age of seventeen and sail across the Atlantic in search of a new life. To Peter, such

11

youthful audacity was remarkable. Much as Thom enjoyed the recognition, he viewed his past through very different eyes. Had he come from a background and family like Peter's, he would not have signed on for a squalid bunk in the bowels of a ship bound for the unknown.

Although far from wealthy, Thom was better off financially than folks in Tyringham suspected. From his long hours of work back in Boston, he had salted away more than one hundred pounds of silver coinage, mostly from Spain and the Netherlands. With his savings he could pay the annual proprietor's fees associated with his land, as well as purchase materials, not otherwise available on the tract, needed to build his home. He also had the skills. But ironically he lacked the very element that had enabled him to acquire those prerequisites. Thom's motivation, his drive, was gone. Without Polly, the love of his life, he had descended to the depths of an emotional abyss.

Thom gazed at the Berkshire Mountain canvas, hoping the season's beauty might lift him from the cloistered realm of his thoughts. Beneath a bright October sun, maple leaves of gold and crimson glowed. With hints of reddish brown the foliage of giant oaks, slower to succumb to the autumnal conversion, swayed resolutely like sheets of ancient parchment carrying distant biblical messages. The more diminutive yellow leaves of birches and poplars quavered. Their vitality waning, their demise inevitable, a mere zephyr could propel them helplessly dancing to earth. Soon enough the colorful palette would turn drab. All the deciduous trees would be barren.

Thom closed his eyes. A vision of upcoming cold, gray days emerged. Why, he wondered, did he choose to move to the Berkshires? He could have traveled south to Charleston, or, better yet, Savannah or St. Augustine. Perhaps he still could. But what of his contractual obligations? When granted his forty-acre tract from the Tyringham proprietors, in accordance with the laws of the Provincial Legislature, he had given his word, his bond and promise, that he would thereupon "build and furnish a dwelling house" and "improve five acres by plowing or mowing or planting same with English grass" and that the premises would thereafter be occupied by him or his assigns.[12] Whatever his faults and limitations, Thom had always been true to his word. But emotions, dismal and devouring, were challenging his most steadfast convictions.

~~~∽ᵔᵔᵔᵔᵔ~~~

Day by day, the nights grew longer. October yielded to November. November streamed into December. New Year's Day came and went. Indoor activities, not the least of which was increased sleep, predominated. With time on his hands, indeed too much, and wood of many types abundant, furniture-making offered Thom a means to varnish vexing thoughts beneath a glossy veneer.

"You have a minute?" he said, as he poked his head into the kitchen where Sarah Albright was drying a fry pan. "I'd like you to come into the parlor."

"Something the matter?"

"Just come and see."

The fifty-something, slim, graying brunette hung the pan onto a wall hook and trailed him through the dining room to the parlor. As she reached its threshold, she stopped. "What's that?"

"What does it look like?"

She stepped into the room. "Where did it come from?"

"I made it...for you." He put his hand on the upper panel of the rocking chair and swung it back and forth several times. "C'mon—try it."

She stood motionless.

"What's wrong?...Don't you like it?"

"I love it. I...I'm just overwhelmed." Eyes moist, she negotiated her way across to the black rocker. She ran her hand over one of its polished arms and seated herself. She gingerly pressed her toes to the floor allowing the chair to sway. Moments later she increased the force, vigorously propelling it to and fro. "It's wonderful. It's absolutely wonderful." She pumped it several more times, giggling as she did. "You really shouldn't have."

"And why not?"

13

"You already do far more than your room and board requires."

Thom shrugged.

"Thanks to you, my garden, in the past a weed-begotten mess, yields a magnificent crop of fruits and vegetables."

"Just enough rain at the right time."

"And I suppose the shelves in the cellar appeared on their own?"

"Maybe."

"And creaky doors fixed themselves?"

"A little whale oil."

Sarah continued to rock. "When did you find the time?"

He went to the window and drew back the curtain, one Sarah had woven from thread she had spun from sheep's wool. He pointed out at the drifted snow. "In case you haven't noticed, we get long, cold, seemingly endless winters here in the Berkshires. Finding time for indoor activities is hardly a challenge."

"Where did you make it?"

"In my room...at least all the pieces, spindles and arms. I kept them in the barn and assembled it there."

She rocked some more. Her horizontal lips shifted into an arc of contentment, one that filled Thom with a warm feeling. When he had labored on the chair, it had helped distract him from dark thoughts. Seeing her joy was a wonderful bonus.

14

# Chapter 2

JANUARY...FEBRUARY. WINTER RAGED. Drifts climbed the sides of Sarah Albright's home. Howling winds slithered through invisible crevices. The two large fireplaces, impressive though they were, often were no match for temperatures that occasionally reached no higher than zero by day before plunging at night. Thom did his chores, none more important than keeping the fireplaces aglow. Mainly, however, he sought to hide from the long, harsh season. Unfortunately, he could not escape himself. Depressing thoughts bedeviled. Downcast spirits deepened. Meals were skipped. A few were consumed in the dim confines of his eight-by-ten room. Try as Sarah did, she found it hard to drag Thom from his cloister. Having faithfully performed his responsibilities, fewer in winter, he was free to spend the bulk of his time languishing in all-consuming isolation.

"Thom..." A rap at his door. "Thom."

Half asleep, he rolled over in bed. Rays of sun squeezing through the translucent curtain of his room's one small window greeted his eyes. "Uh...yeah."

"You awake?"

"Well...sorta." Thom's internal clock told him midday was but an hour or two away. He had gone to bed at nine o'clock the night before. Though long stays in bed, replete with hours of tossing and turning, had grown commonplace, the fourteen hours spent since the preceding night was extraordinary.

"I'm a little short on flour. Would you mind taking a sack of wheat from the cellar, and maybe one of corn, over to the mill for grinding? It's a good day for it. Best we've seen in months."

Thom read between the lines. Most times when Sarah needed flour ground at Brewer's Gristmill,[13] the gregarious lady would fetch it herself. Asking him to go was her way to draw him out of hibernation.

"Uh...let me get myself together, and I'll go." Thom pushed back the thick quilt of his hay-stuffed rope bed and climbed out.

A half-hour later, a bever[14] in his stomach, he stepped out the front door. The unexpected warmth of the mid-March sun greeted him. With calm winds and a temperature hovering near sixty, spring's inevitable victory over winter was at hand. No doubt the frosty season would breathe a few late gasps, but nature's rebirth was on the doorstep. Though banks of drifted snow remained, much of the earth, albeit muddy, was face to face with the firmament above. Soon enough trees would bud and grass would green.

Thom hitched his equine companion Lodestone to Sarah's wagon. It was less than a ten-minute ride from her homestead to the mill. She and her late husband had arrived in Tyringham before the midpoint of the century, about a decade after its founding. Sarah often reminisced to those days and spoke of the changes as the population gradually swelled to four hundred.[15]

With rich valleys lining the mountains of the western Berkshires, the Housatonic settlement offered opportunity, along with scenic beauty and tranquillity, ideal for Thom to start a family and build the life of which he had dreamed. Polly was the perfect woman to complete that dream. But like the logs that burned in the fireplaces of every home, it had gone up in smoke the day her father had denied his request for Polly's hand. And when Peter had begun courting her, even faint hopes of resurrecting the relationship had vanished. Intellectually Thom had accepted the verdict. Emotionally was another matter. He avoided places where he might cross paths with Polly. If by chance he spotted her in the distance, he would detour. Meeting her was too painful.

That warm, March day in 1773, with sacks in the wagon, but Polly on his mind, Thom negotiated the muddy grooves that lined the road leading down to Brewer's Mill along the Konkapot River. Upon reaching his destination, he circled to the back of the wagon to the sacks of unground grain. A hand on his shoulder turned his head. His closest friend, Richard Thorn, had come up from behind.

"Great day. Looks like Ole Man Winter is on the run."

"Hope so." The prospect of extended days in the warm outdoors served a shot of elixir.

"I'm on my way to the Hogshead. Care to join me?"

16

Thom gestured at the sacks. "Uh...like to, but duty calls."

"C'mon, don't be a stick in the mud." Richard gave Thom an amiable shove.

"Well..." Thom's reluctance yielded in the face of a determined look. "Okay, once I've got my flour."

After leaving the flour and wagon at the Albright homestead, the duo reached the Hogshead, a popular stop along the Albany-Boston Post Road, located a couple miles northeast of town center.[16] The establishment was unimpressive, but it did a fine business owing mainly to two factors, a want of competition and its location on a main thoroughfare connecting Boston and Albany. Two years earlier, in 1771, the owner, Daniel Heath, following the death of his wife during pregnancy with what would have been their first child, had converted his home into the tavern. The enterprise was hardly a tribute to his former wife who deemed alcohol a tool of the Devil, but alcohol, particularly beer and ale and home-distilled rum, was popular throughout the colonies, and weary travelers on the trying east-west road welcomed a restful spot where they could imbibe.[17] Several booths and tables and a long bar, plus a loft with second-rate sleeping quarters for travelers, and a small annex attached to the left side of the structure, turned Heath's home into a profitable business.[18]

Richard and Thom were about to seat themselves when Orville Crane, the town's stocky, but muscular blacksmith, called out: "Well, Jehovah be praised! If it ain't the long lost thrall of Tyringham. Ain't nobody seen you since back when the colony was payin' forty pounds for a Penobscot's scalp."

While the reference to a time roughly two decades earlier when the bounty had been offered was absurd, it underscored for Thom how long it had been since he had frequented the popular haunt. His last visit dated back to the preceding fall, several weeks before Polly had married Peter.

"C'mon, join me," said Crane, gesturing at the opposite side of his booth.

Richard nudged Thom onto the bench, seating himself alongside. He called to the barmaid, "Mary, a couple of amber ales for my friend and me. And bring a dish of your custard flummery." He looked at Thom. "One for you too?"

"Uh...not for me." Were his tongue not quicker than his brain, Thom might have opted for the delight. Still he was missing nothing. At the Hogshead the flummery, typically a fruity blancmange thickened with isinglass and sweetened with sugar, was little more than flavored oatmeal. Apart from beverages and the communally served standard fare of the day, the flummery was all that Heath offered. Regardless, he deemed the flummery a bragging chip. He was quick to remind any who complained that most taverns, especially those away from cities, offered no food other than their fare of the day. Patrons could take it or leave it.[19]

"Ya know," said Crane, "things with England are startin' to look better."

Thom felt his eyes widen. Perhaps Crane knew something Thom didn't, but more likely the blacksmith, his frame more Herculean than his mind, was echoing Tory propaganda.

"What makes you say that?" said Richard.

"Parliament took back the 'Townsend Acts,' didn't they?" The Townsend Acts, among other things, suspended the New York Assembly and imposed duties on colonial imports of glass, red and white lead paints, paper and tea.

"Lord...help us," muttered Richard, rolling his eyes. "The Townsend Acts were repealed three years ago, soon after the Boston Massacre. Parliament continues to treat us like second-class citizens."

Crane turned to Thom. "Your pal don't appreciate our Mother Country." He pointed at the ales the barmaid had just placed on the table. "Without England protectin' us, we'd be like the mash they used to make these brews. Unfortunately, some folks got short memories."

"What's that supposed to mean?" said Richard.

"Hell, it ain't been but a decade since England fought the French and Indians. Eight years they battled. Without the Redcoats fightin' for us, ya know as well as me, our bacon woulda been fried."

Multiple reasons kept Thom from challenging the half-truth: his emotional state was ill-equipped for the fray; he was careful with whom, how and when he voiced criticisms of England; and he could count on Richard to attack the spurious arguments.

"Big deal...England fought the French and Indians. It wasn't for us. They were protecting their investment here. And as for the repeal of the Townsend Acts, they kept the crummy tax on tea."

"Well, a British soldier who was passin' through says they're gonna lower it."

"So I heard," said Richard. "But you know why?"

A blank expression appeared on Crane's globular face.

"They want to kill the competition...enable their damn British East India Company to undercut the smugglers. Then they'll milk us for all they want."

Crane snatched his brew and took a gulp before looking at Thom. "I suppose you agree with your buddy."

"What do you want from me?"

"An opinion about our Mother Country. And don't get me wrong. I ain't no fan of taxes, but fair's fair. Colonies cost a bundle. Ya can't expect a free ride."

"Maybe so, but that doesn't mean England should treat us like dirt." Thom bit his tongue. Determined to steer clear, he had been drawn into the debate.

"That's a crock," said Crane, "and ya know it. I'm all fur rights, but we're a British colony...and lucky to be."

"Yeah—sure," said Richard. "For over a century the greedy English bastards let us languish while they pillaged our raw materials. Now that our economy shows life, they're plundering that too."

Crane opened his mouth, but Richard was quicker. "What about the stinking 'Trade and Navigation Acts?'"

"Uh...what about 'em?" Another blank look gave Crane away.

"For your information," said Richard, "they limit our trade to English ships and ban us from exporting tobacco, cotton, sugar, and you name it, to anywhere but England. Not that anyone worth his salt obeys the damn restrictions." Richard looked Crane in the eye. "Of course, you being a blacksmith, your business is local. You don't give a damn."

19

"No call to get nasty." Crane stood up. He tossed several coins onto the thick wooden table. "Unlike some, I got work to do." He marched away.

"Good riddance," said Richard. He turned to Thom. "Well...say something."

"Like what?" Thom sought the refuge of his brew.

"Sorry...but the dolt infuriates me. He's as hardheaded as the damn iron he forges, and I don't mean after it's been fired in the oven." Richard hesitated, appearing to study Thom. "Don't tell me you disagree?"

"No...but debating with Orville is a waste of time. Most of what he says is nonsense. At best he parrots Ezra." Ezra Jenkins, the local attorney, as well as the local tax collector, was a strong supporter of England. "Of course, unlike Ezra, Orville has only half a brain. Regardless, I wouldn't tell him anything I didn't want repeated, especially when it relates to the trade acts. A word to Orville is a word—"

"I know—a word to Ezra." Richard got up. "Be back in a minute."

Alone with his brew, Thom silently debated whether he was making much of nothing. Was it really risky if Ezra knew how one got his goods? Back when the Stamp Act was in effect, no one paid the tax when buying a newspaper or pamphlet or when signing a legal document. But the Stamp Act hardly proved the point. The day it went into effect, the radical Sons of Liberty had forced the stamp agents to resign. There was no one to collect the tax. The same could not be said for the Townsend Acts. But it was common knowledge, or at least widely reputed, that John Hancock had made his fortune smuggling,[20] and England had done nothing to him.[21] Thom found it hard to deny that disregard for the trade regulations posed little danger. Still he would exercise discretion when flouting Parliament's unjust dictates. Prudence could do no harm.

Richard returned, sliding into the opposite side of the booth.

"Where do you think we're headed?"

A furrow rippled Richard's brow. "What the hell does that mean?"

"Don't mind me," said Thom, conscious that musing had his thoughts adrift. "I was referring to our relations with England."

"Oh...that." A groaning voice suggested the assessment would be pessimistic. "They're bound to get worse before they get better."

Thoughts of the damned "Declaratory Act"[22] in which Parliament had proclaimed its absolute power over the colonies made it impossible for Thom to adopt a rosier view. "I...I guess you're right. Unless and until England gives us a voice, antagonism will run high."

"One thing sure—we won't get our rights if we aren't steadfast. As long as the muckers in Parliament think they can treat us as second class citizens, they'll continue their get-rich at-our-expense mercantile policies. England may be our Mother Country, but...even in the best of families, some refuse to play fair."

The analogy reminded Thom of his abusive father. He kept the notion to himself. He had no desire to share information about his English past. Even if it were otherwise, he would have skipped the point because of its unseemly implications. No matter how hard he had tried, no matter how long he had waited, his father would never have relented. He was the master, and Thom, nothing. Leaving home had been the only way to escape relentless abuse. Circumstances between the colonies and England would never grow that bad. Frictions existed, but an amicable resolution would surely eventuate.

~∂∂∬∭∿

By the time he left the Hogshead, Thom had imbibed double his usual two or three ales. How many, he couldn't say for sure. Meandering home with an unsteady gait, in small part attributable to the ruts of spring, he breathed in the fresh March air. After months of being cooped up in the frigid New England winter, the sunny rays warmed more than his body. Perhaps his ample alcoholic consumption was equally responsible for an improved mood. His frame of mind was better than it had been

21

in many a day. He wended his way southeast on the Albany-Boston Post Road. As he approached the intersection of Royal Hemlock Road, he diverged again, enough to avail a view up the slope that led to the home of Congregationalist Minister Reverend Adonijah Bidwell. Yale educated, the Reverend, who came from a family of means, owned one of the most impressive homes in Tyringham. Thom counted the windows that decorated the front of the gracious saltbox. Rectangular arrangements of four on either side of the center entrance, plus a window several feet directly above the door, brought the total to an impressive nine.[23] Even in the depths of winter, his home, with its southern hillside exposure, was cheery. Thom knew that firsthand. Though he had never joined the congregation—religion was not high among Thom's priorities—several times he had attended Sunday services at the Reverend's home. Owing to its size and imposing fireplaces, it was an ideal venue, particularly when winter's bite was especially harsh. And too, the Reverend owned an amazing number of chairs. Word had it the tally approached fifty.[24]

With the impressive structure dominating his thoughts, Thom headed down the hill toward Mt. Hunger Road and the home of Sarah Albright. As he neared Morse Corners, an inspiration, one that turned his head one hundred eighty degrees, caused him to trip and nearly fall; arguably, however, alcohol's influence was the primary reason. He reversed course and started back up the hill in the direction of Beartown Mountain where his own plot lay. The time had come to build his house. He had the land. He had the skills. He had sufficient funds. He had loads of timber, virgin trees, and a plentiful supply of stone on the rockier portions of his acreage. And he had the obligation, the bond he had given to the General Court when granted his lot.

A surge of adrenaline, the likes of which he had not felt in many a fortnight, engulfed Thom. Reverend Bidwell's home, its image still fresh, emerged from his brain. Alluring, yes, but far too daunting, and much too expensive. Thom shifted his gaze toward the northerly corner of the Morse intersection where the modest house of Deacon William Webster stood. A pillar of Tyringham, Webster had occupied the home, one of the town's oldest frame structures, for approximately twenty-five years.[25] Webster was hardly a dime-a-dozen plebeian. He was descended from one of New England's original settling families. If the humble abode sufficed for the likes of Webster, then Thom, a bachelor, had no need for something more pretentious. Whether he would settle for the minimum required by the General Court, "18 foot square by 7 foot stud,"[26] was another matter. Such dimensions, representative of a one-room cabin, were not unusual in the rural settlements of western Massachusetts, but an imagination running free, easily conjured something more ambitious. What Thom wanted was a saltbox, so termed because of its resemblance to the lidded box used to store salt. Both bore an extended rear roof that ran closer to the ground than its front counterpart. Thom knew the design well. During his days in Boston he had helped build several. With a flat front façade, chimney rising in the center and symmetrically placed windows, saltboxes put one-room cabins to shame. Challenging, no doubt, but worth the effort.

Thom headed back up the hill to his plot on Beartown Mountain. He strolled back and forth, up and down, over the wooded acreage until he came upon the perfect spot, a small plateau on the otherwise sloping land. He closed his eyes. His imagination took over. He was standing on the stoop of his new home. There on Beartown Mountain, facing downhill, with timber cleared for an open view and exposure to the southern sun, he reveled. Stately trees rising beyond a yard of English grass stretched upward, their peaks touching an evening sky streaked with hues of pink and gold and topaz. Thom turned and lifted the latch and opened the door, crossing the threshold of the chimerical edifice. To his left and right were rooms of roughly equal size, each with its own hearth and fireplace, placed back to back on either side of a stalwart chimney. A stairway led to a loft. Across the rear of the house in the shed-like section where the roof hung low ran a neat kitchen and buttery, complete with a door leading to a garden laden with fruits and vegetables.

A chirp of a robin, the first of spring, stirred Thom from his reverie. He opened his eyes and peered upward at an oak from whence the sound emanated. The feathered warbler tweeted

23

before disappearing in woodland flight. Fanciful goals could vanish as quickly. Thom bristled at the intrusive thought. With the sun on his shoulder and an ample supply of alcohol down his gullet, his dream, like flint striking granite, had sparked. Ablaze, it would not be quelled.

# Chapter 3

THE NINTH OF MARCH 1773. Thom was up at the crack of dawn. His linen shirt, which stretched down to his over-the-knee stockings, was in place. It had been a month since the shirt/nightshirt had been off, not that others did differently. Once winter's chill was fully banished, more frequent changes and washings would be in order. As he slipped on his breeches, the patched pair that he used for work, he tucked the long shirt into the crotch, diaper style. He donned one of his three waistcoats, a sleeveless one, which, like the others, had many buttons, more than were necessary to keep it closed. Buttons in large numbers had become fashionable, and though Thom was an individualist, the stylish look appealed to him. Before buckling his shoes, he noted that the horseshoe-shaped heel protectors were in good condition. Unfortunately some of the hobnails on the soles were worn. He hated the thought of replacing them, what with the high cost of nails, but delay would only magnify the expense with a trip to the cordwainer for new soles. Following a quick, but hearty bever, he put a sandwich of bread and apple butter into his haversack, already loaded with a folding knife, flint, a rag and other small necessities. He donned his frock, along with a black felt hat, and, after filling his canteen at the pump and fetching a broadax and spade from the Albright barn, wended his way up the hilly roads to his Beartown Mountain lot.

Nearly four decades earlier, on January 15, 1735, in an effort to promote the settlement of the western portion of the Massachusetts Bay Colony, the Provincial Legislature, using land purchased from the Stockbridge Indians,[27] had voted:

*"That there be four townships opened upon the road between Westfield and Sheffield, each of the contents of six miles square and that there be sixty-three home lots laid out in a compact and defensible form in each township, one of which to be for the*

*first settled minister, one for the second minister, one for the school, and one for each grantee which shall draw equal shares in future divisions.*[28]

Tyringham was among the four townships. When the number of Tyringham proprietors increased to sixty-seven, seventy lots of roughly forty to eighty acres each were laid out, including those for the ministers and the school. The lots were arranged on a strip of land approximately three miles wide extending northeast along the hills between the valleys.[29] Lot No. 25, a prime property, was reserved for the first minister; Lot No. 21, for the second; and Lot No. 20, for the school. The rest, except for one plot of seventy acres that was reserved for the mills, were drawn by lot among the sixty-seven proprietors, and the remainder of the township was divided into larger lots, called town lots.[30]

Thom had arrived in Tyringham near the end of 1770. Under his contract he had almost three years of the permissible five to build a house on his lot, one he had acquired from an original proprietor. But that fine March morning in 1773, Thom had no need for such a lengthy allowance of time. He was primed to begin.

Dating back to the prior October, not once until March had he visited the rectangular, forty-acre site. While weather provided a partial explanation, despondency was the primary culprit. When first he had moved to Tyringham, he fancied a parcel overlooking Brewer's Pond. Instead he had opted for a lot along the southerly slope of Beartown Mountain. Reflection and hindsight had validated the choice. True, portions of the parcel were steep, but the plateau gracing its upper reaches provided the ideal spot for a home.

Thom headed up to his site where he laid his broadax and spade next to a granite boulder. He gazed in a southerly direction down Beartown Mountain. Though trees obscured his sight, his mind trimmed the forest, painting a marvelous view. He strolled back and forth, around and around the area where he would construct his house. There were ash, oak, birch, maple, elm, hickory, pine and fir, and despite knowledge gained

26

both homebuilding and woodworking, some he couldn't identify. That didn't matter. He had all the various woods he would need to fashion a quality structure. He toured the slope picking out potential candidates. Oaks, strong and durable, were perfect for the exterior. Maples garnered consideration for the supporting beams, but firs, likewise strong, but less dense and, therefore, more manageable, drew favor. Maples gained attention again for the flooring, but pines, softer with their signature knots, were in the running. Both took stain well, yielding an outstanding finish. Thom left the decision, along with his framing choice, for another day.

He took time to check the surface of the hillside. Beartown Mountain was renowned for its abundance of dense rock, particularly granite, ideal for the foundation. It also had its share of limestone needed for plaster that, along with the wooden lath strips, would fill the area between the exterior clapboard and the interior walls. His parcel was well suited to both the project and a settler's life, not that his land was so different from many that dotted the hills of Tyringham.

Thom rewalked the acreage of his property, finally returning to the plateau where he planned to build his house. He wandered amongst the trees that graced the section. The area included oaks, firs and pines. Maples were absent. The area would have to be cleared of trees, and it was easier to use that lumber rather than cut more elsewhere. Pine flooring had grabbed the edge over maple, though the final verdict awaited future deliberations.

He returned to the boulder where he had left his tools. He took a drink from his canteen and laid it down, along with his haversack. He picked up his broadax and headed to a nearby pine. After studying it from every angle, he began to chop, carving a wedge on its southerly side in order that it would fall down the hill. Hack after hack, he pounded the tree until it tumbled toward earth, grazing the outer branches of another pine before crashing into terra firma. Thom eyed the fallen timber, circling it several times. A feeling of power and triumph seized him. He had begun the long process of building his home.

Thom hurried to another pine and hacked again. For several hours he labored before he headed back to the granite boulder. He took his apple butter sandwich out of his haversack and, interspersed with healthy drinks from his canteen, devoured it. A short respite and he was back to work. It was mid-afternoon when he stopped. He might have continued, but there were chores to be done at the Albright home. He gathered his gear and, after pausing to appreciate how much he had accomplished, headed downhill. The morrow, with its opportunity to go forward, would arrive soon enough.

⁓ᴓᴓ⑁ᴓᴓ⁓

Once Thom returned to the Albright homestead, he went directly to the cellar and carried up a fresh supply of kindling wood. He was about to fetch another batch when Sarah poked her head around the corner from the kitchen.

"Thom, did you hear about the fire today?"

"Fire?...Where?"

"The schoolhouse."[31]

"The kids...everyone okay?"

"I think so."

Thom laid his wood by the hearth and joined Sarah where the kitchen and dining room met. "Awful," he said, picturing the small structure, located southeast of his own plot, not far from town center.

"Thirty years we had women, mostly teaching in their homes, before the town had a real schoolhouse. Six years later, and we're back to square one." Sarah heaved a sigh. "It's not fair. It's just not fair."

"What's the town gonna do?"

"Build another, I suppose." She gazed somberly into space. "Sure to cost us landowners, but no mind. We gotta have a school. Truth is: we need more than one."

The point, one Thom had heard from others, made sense. People in the town seemed to support education, but the young community in the wilderness had lots of needs, and given the costs, it was a matter of choices. "What do you think they'll do in the meantime?"

"Probably go back to holding school in folks' homes. Don't mean to knock those who teach, but it's not the best way to get our young educated."

A decade earlier, before his Boston mentor supplanted Thom's mediocre childhood English education with a thirst for knowledge, he might have disagreed. But expanded horizons, the kind that enabled him to design and build a home, as well as logically cogitate the social, political and philosophical issues of the day, had convinced him of the value of academics. He said, "What about Mr. Mahoney?"[32]

"Don't know. But I doubt he'll continue to teach, certainly not at the Orton house where he boards." Sarah shook her head. "The whole thing is a can of worms."

"Any idea how the fire started?"

"Don't know whether anybody knows, but one thing sure, if it isn't clear, there will be lots of speculation, and the way folks are, there'll be finger pointing as well."

⚬⚭⚮⚯⚬

The following morning Thom was up and out early. On the way to his property he checked out the school, what remained of it. Any hopes that the charred structure might be saved vanished. Once he arrived at his plot, he resumed felling trees. The downed timbers needed to cure before they could be cut. The sun, climbing higher with each passing day, along with the downward slope of his property, would accelerate the process, but still it would take at least two months. The sooner Thom chopped the trees, the sooner they would dry and be available for construction. In the interim there would be plenty to do, digging up the earth and laying a stone foundation.

With efficiency exceeding expectations, for more than six hours Thom chopped and trimmed. Whether he could fashion an enclosed and roofed structure by mid-November remained to be seen. Owing to early winter snows, failure to meet his self-imposed deadline would be problematic, if not disastrous.

Though all the interior work, even the lath and plaster, could be left until winter and on into the following spring and summer, his Boston experience dispelled any illusions that his eight-month goal for a completed exterior would be easy. From his parcel he headed down the hilly roads that led to the mills of Captain John Brewer along the Konkapot River, not far from Twelve-Mile Pond, or what many still referred to as Brewer's Pond. The plucky and wily entrepreneur had come to Tyringham in 1739 pursuant to an agreement with the town's proprietors under which he received a mill lot of seventy acres and L60 in bills of public credit based upon his promise: "To build a good sawmill in said lot, and complete the same in six months...and also to build a good gristmill on the said lot and finish it within the space of two and one half years next ensuing..."[33]

Word had it that Brewer, the town's first settler, had slept beneath an ox-cart the first night he had arrived. By the second he had constructed a shelter of logs and bark, and in a short time he had the required sawmill in operation.[34] His choice of location, like much in Tyringham and other towns, was a matter of geography. Vigorously flowing water was required to power the mill. Accordingly he built in the lowlands near the turn of the Konkapot River. The town center developed a mile or two to the north. That too was a matter of geography, the need to be close to the Albany-Boston Post Road, a key route of commerce, thereby facilitating the flow of materials and goods, as well as people, to and from the new wilderness settlement. The Provincial Legislature had this all in mind when in 1735 it had authorized the town's creation. With three adjoining lots reserved for the first clergyman, second clergyman and a school, all located close to that key highway,[35] the town center naturally developed nearby.

Massachusetts, as well as the other colonies, differed from Thom's boyhood English homeland. Across the Atlantic, labor was plentiful and cheap, while land and wood were expensive. In the colonies the situation was reversed. Land and wood were readily available, but rugged individualists generally depended upon their own labor. Despite some inherent disadvantages, on balance the distinction was beneficial to the colonists.

Sawmill owners who were close to main rivers, like the Hudson that flowed into the Atlantic, developed lucrative mercantile operations shipping cut lumber to England and the West Indies. In contrast, most mill owners who were located on smaller streams in the hinterlands, men like Captain Brewer, ran custom sawmills. In exchange for turning a customer's logs into usable timbers and boards, they generally kept between one-eighth and one-quarter of the wood.[36]

As Thom wended his way to the sawmill, he mapped a strategy. Brewer's ability to come to the area when it was raw and achieve success convinced Thom that his project, far less ambitious, though certainly daunting, was doable. But he realized that Brewer, one of Tyringham's most skillful card players, was a savvy businessman. If Thom wished to avoid a losing hand, he would need to play his cards close to his vest. Cool patience would be important. With that in mind, he approached the sawmill. He found Brewer stacking lumber.

"Afternoon, Captain."

"It's a fine one." Brewer gestured toward the sky. "Good to have the winter behind us. If you ask me, they get tougher every year."

"I know what you mean." Thom welcomed the chance for agreeable small talk.

"You still renting from the widow Albright?"

"Yup. But I've got a plot and—"

"You gotta build a house on it."

Thom shrugged. "Yeah...but I got five years."

"Sounds like you're in no hurry."

"Not really. But when the time comes, I'll let you know, cause I'll need some timber cut and trimmed."

"What you thinking—a one-room log cabin?"

Thom shook his head. "Wanna do a saltbox."

Brewer's eyes widened, perhaps from surprise, or maybe opportunity...more likely both. "Gonna need a lot of lumber cut." Brewer gestured at his sawmill. "This is the place. Been so for more than three decades. And we're reasonable."

Nothing Thom had heard suggested otherwise. On the other hand, Brewer had the only game in town. "Well...down the road when I decide to build, I'll keep you in mind. And by the way, I've got lots of nice timber. I could help you out. Bring you some extra logs in exchange for the milling."

"I suppose you do. Of course, around these parts everyone does."

"Yeah, I guess so." On the way to the sawmill Thom had done his homework. He had asked around to learn if Brewer had recently expressed a need for any particular types of wood. The sawmill operator had been trying to get mahogany and red spruce. Mahogany, great for furniture and shipbuilding, was a west-African wood. None grew in the chilly Northeast. In contrast, red spruce could be found in the Berkshires, but only in rocky, upper elevations. Thom's land on Beartown Mountain fit that bill, and indeed some red spruce grew there. He said, "About a week ago a fellow from Albany was passing through. Said he was in the business of making musical instruments—violins, harpsichords and the like. Wanted to buy my red spruce. Said they—"

"You got red spruce on your land?" Brewer's eyes were wide once more.

"Yeah. The fellow told me red spruce have incredible resonance. Make great instruments. Said he'd pay a pretty price for my trees."

"How much?"

"We didn't get into numbers. In about a week, on the way back to Albany, he'll be coming this way again. Wants to talk more then."

"Tell you what," said Brewer. "Bring me the logs for your house, and I'll cut all the boards and timbers you need to frame it, along with clapboards for the outside, in exchange for a pair of forty-foot red spruce."

The offer was attractive, but Thom made a conscious effort to appear unmoved. "Well, I'll keep you in mind when I decide to build...in a couple of years."

"A couple of years?" Brewer folded his arms and stared off into space. "Suppose I sweeten the offer, might you change your mind?"

32

"Doubt it. But..." Thom heaved a contrived sigh. "The least I can do is hear you out. So, what you got in mind?"

"I'll trim your interior boards."

Thom squeezed his lips together.

"What kind of expression is that?"

"Sorry, don't mean to hard time you, but don't think I'm ready to build, not without a roof."

"A roof! You expect me to cut lumber for a roof too?"

"Well, I can't see myself diving into this, 'less I've got all the lumber needed for the job. But I'll tell you what—you cut all the lumber, and I'll throw in a third red spruce, provided you cut the spruce and haul them away. I'll do all the chopping and hauling for my wood."

"Glory be. Your generosity staggers me." The inaudible mumbling that followed underscored the frustration conveyed in Brewer's sarcasm.

"I understand," said Thom. "Not easy to do business when one fellow (Thom gestured at himself) prefers to put it off to a different year. But doesn't mean–"

"Hold on. You made me an offer, and I'm taking it. Three forty-foot red spruce, I cut and haul, and you get all the lumber for your house cut."

The deal, a great one, was done, but Thom remained expressionless.

"Now, now. Don't start backtracking."

"You're right. I said it, and I'll live with it. Last thing I'd want is a reputation as a welsher. But next time we deal, I'm gonna be a whole lot sharper."

"What's that supposed to mean?"

"C'mon. You talked me into building two years sooner than I wanted, just so you can get my red spruce. Aren't many guys foxy enough to pull a trick like that."

Whether Brewer's expression reflected self-satisfaction or puzzlement was hard to discern. Thom didn't care. He said, "See that. You know you got the best of me."

Brewer patted Thom on the back. "Don't look at it that way. You have to build a house, and the sooner you do, the sooner you can enjoy it. Having all your wood cut is hardly the pit of a peach."

Thom laughed.

"What's so funny?"

"You're still selling. 'Course, that's what you do. You're a businessman...an entrepreneur. Isn't that what they call it?"

Brewer shrugged. "Well, I'm glad we were able to do some business." He held out his right hand.

Thom shook it. Brewer was right. They had done some business. And it had been a pleasure.

∽᷂ᴔᴔᴔ᷂∾

Along with the two or three hours he spent on daily chores at the Albright homestead, with the dawn of April, Thom was putting in nine, ten and even eleven hours at his property chopping trees and trimming branches. Using his knowledge of leverage, with the aid of his sorrel stallion Lodestone, a wagon and other equipment from Sarah, he stacked felled trees across two large, downed oaks. Raising the wood off the ground provided maximum exposure to the air, accelerating the drying process.

Seven days a week he labored. While most folks in Tyringham reserved Sunday for the Lord, Thom couldn't afford the time. It was a matter of pragmatics. He had nothing against religion, not that he had a whole lot for it. There was a possibility, though remote, that after he was more settled, his attitude might change. If so, the conservative Congregationalist Church of Reverend Bidwell, the only option in town, wouldn't be bad. Like other Congregationalist churches, it was not part of a larger organized religious structure. It existed independently and solely for its members. For Thom, averse to dogma, especially when dictated by a distant authority, the independence of the local Congregationalist Church was a plus. The equality of all members was another. These principles harmonized with the political views he had acquired from his readings of the French philosophers back in Boston.

When Thom had first arrived in Tyringham, he had attended several of the church's meetings. He had considered joining the congregation, if only to integrate himself into the community. Folks had seemed welcoming, and, like him, most were practical individualists. But one critical factor, though arguably an excuse, had kept him from joining. Congregationalist churches, including Tyringham's, were all founded upon a single abiding principle, the gathering of two or more people in Christ's name. Thom did not believe in Christ, at least not in the manner of his churchgoing neighbors. To Thom, Christ was a very learned man of utmost character, but nothing more and nothing less. Though he never voiced the view, lest he become an outcast in the Christian community, Thom refused to yield one day of his week to a gathering grounded upon a tenet he did not embrace. And so, Sunday was for Thom like the other six days.

The first Sunday in April, he had begun work in the early morning, and by mid-afternoon he had laid out the last of his chopped trees for drying. The first phase of his project was complete. The following day, Monday, would be soon enough to begin digging the foundation. Thom climbed aboard Lodestone, who, like most days, transported him to and from the site. Riding was easier than walking, and Lodestone, along with his harness, was needed to haul the timber. Thom wended his way from his homesite along the Albany-Boston Post Road. As he approached the point that adjoined the property of Reverend Bidwell, up ahead he observed a number of the townspeople departing the lengthy Sunday service. Reluctant to display his irreverence, he slipped off the roadway about fifteen yards into the adjoining woods where he tethered Lodestone to a tree. He waited until the last of the neatly dressed parishioners had gone on their way. Though his detour screened him from the censure of his neighbors, it failed to offer safe haven from his thoughts. Spindly poplars reminded him of the bars of his cell in an English jail. The expansive ocean and thousands of miles that separated his former prison home from the mountain wilderness evaporated amidst the vagaries of his imagination. Common sense urged that likening Tyringham's spacious woods to the four walls of a distant lockup was absurd. Nevertheless, haunting recollections of loneliness and confinement bubbled forth. Thom waited several minutes until the coast appeared clear. As he was about to poke his nose out, he spotted Polly and Peter Blake entering the road from the Reverend's property. Thom ducked back behind the trees as the pair headed down the road in the opposite direction. On foot, they would need a big head start, lest he soon catch up. Thom gazed at the poplars again. The bars were unmistakable. The prison of his mind was patent. Through the depths of the long winter months, he had languished, unable to face the loss of Polly's love. Diving headlong into the construction of his house, he had repressed the pain, but still it lurked, waiting to rear its odious head. A structure, a new home, could shield him from rain and wind and ice and snow. He could fend off the harshest of elements. But even with a rock foundation, one of solid granite, and a frame of hard oak timbers, no matter how thick, the structure could not shield him from that which lay within. Slamming the shutters and barring the doors would accomplish nothing as well. Worse than a ghost that could slip through otherwise impenetrable barriers, the ineluctable enemy remained omni-present.

Back amongst the trees, a bit deeper in the woods, he leaned against an elm. Anything but a poplar. From his haversack he removed several roasted chestnuts. Though better hot from the fireplace, they were preferable to nothing. He washed them down with water from his canteen; a flask of apple brandy would have suited him better. After several minutes he trudged out of the forest. Were it not Sunday, he would have gone to the Hogshead. Tavern owner, Daniel Heath, an observant Congregationalist, honored the Sabbath. Thom guided Lodestone out to the road and saddled up. He had gone but a hundred yards when a female voice drew him to a halt. Off to his left, Juliette Chandler was coming down the path connecting Reverend Bidwell's property to the road.

"Good afternoon," he said, as he reined Lodestone to a halt.

"Is at that." She gestured down the roadway. "Appears you're headed my way. Might I bother you for a ride?"

"Gladly." As he climbed down, he noted that the widow, in her early forties, about fifteen years his senior, looked smart in her black cape and hat. "You just getting out of the church meeting?"

"Oh no. It ended an hour ago. Ruth, the Reverend's new wife, gave me a few pointers about candle making. She's mighty good at such things. Maybe even better than Theodosia and Jemima." Theodosia and Jemima, Reverend Bidwell's first two spouses, had died in 1759 and 1771 respectively.[37] Juliette glanced back in the direction of the Bidwell property. "Seems like the Lord ought to do better by the Reverend. Really tough, losing two wives like that. Of course, if they'd been anything like my Sam, it would have been a blessing. He chased anything in a petticoat. Not long before he died, he ran off with a little minx from Sheffield."

Thom helped Juliette onto Lodestone and climbed on in front of her. She wrapped her arms around him. He tugged the reins, encouraging Lodestone to move at a comfortable walk. With two aboard, a faster pace on the rough road would have been difficult, especially for Juliette who had no stirrups.

"Mighty solid frame you have. Nothing but muscle." Juliette squeezed tighter. "My Sam was your height, just about six feet on the nose, but after we got married, he developed a paunch. No fat on you." She moved her interlocked hands down from Thom's chest to his waist as she seemingly verified her observation.

Lodestone's pace remained constant. Thom's heart rate accelerated. Juliette's provocations, coupled with the press of her breasts, had captured his full attention. He wondered if she could feel the pounding in his chest.

"You're awfully quiet."

He wanted to respond, but nerves spawned a blank. "Uh...yeah, I guess I am."

"Well...ain't nothing wrong with the strong, silent type. Lot better than those little woodchucks who run off at the mouth." She leaned her head forward, so close that he could feel her warm breath on the back of his neck.

From what Thom had heard, Juliette Chandler manifested penchants similar to those she attributed to her late husband. Just as he was prone to chase anything in petticoats, she stalked anything in breeches, though arguably her standards were higher. At that moment, given her prey, Thom was happy to concede that point.

It had been a long, hard winter, and there was no denying Juliette was an attractive woman. She was also well endowed.

Thom's back confirmed that, not that it was ever in doubt. "Did the Reverend deliver a fine sermon today?" he said in an effort to make some conversation.

"He surely did. Said community and fellowship are important. That the Lord wants us to help our neighbors. Appears you got the word without attending the meeting."

Whether she had delivered a compliment or a rebuke for impious ways was hard for Thom to discern. Self-flagellating propensities notwithstanding, he told himself it was the former. "Well, it's no big deal, me giving you a ride. I was going your way." The comment echoed, its reverberation sour. "I didn't mean that the way it sounded. Just the opposite. Having company as pretty as you is mighty nice."

"Why Thomas Webster." Her embrace tightened. "Good thing you can't see my face, 'cause you're making me blush."

Her flushed cheeks, an appealing accompaniment to her flowing red hair, were a spontaneous product of his imagination. Such quixotic creations of his mind were unnecessary to capture the intoxicating scent of her perfume. "That's a wonderful fragrance you're wearing."

"I'm glad you like it. I made it myself last spring from the lilacs alongside my house."

Thom inhaled deeply imbibing the alluring scent. What had begun minutes before as an innocent gesture of civility on a familiar road was becoming a seductive excursion down an uncharted trail. With unconditional trust in the surefooted Lodestone, Thom briefly closed his eyes. The stallion's smooth gait stirred them in a rhythmical dance, its ebb and flow an enticing aphrodisiac. With senses heightened, silently they rode through the still spring air.

When finally, though too soon for Thom, they approached Juliette's home near the south side of Twelve-Mile Pond, she said, "Yesterday, I made an apple pie. Would you like to come in and have a piece?"

A mental image of the delightful dessert, enhanced with thoughts of potential accompaniments, whetted Thom's appetite. He was about to accept the invitation when Mary Goodrow and her eldest daughter came strolling around a curve in the road ahead. Thom brought Lodestone to a halt. He could read Mary's face. "Good afternoon, ladies," he said, as he climbed down.

"Thom was kind enough to give me a lift home from the church meeting," said Juliette, as Thom helped her down.

"Meeting ended the better part of two hours ago," said Mary. "I should know. I was there from start to finish."

"Yes, I saw you," said Juliette. "Afterwards Ruth gave me a few pointers about candle making. Thom happened by when I was leaving."

Thom kept an eye on Mary, watching for a reaction. Though she gave no clues, he knew the busybody would turn the situation into a titillating tale worthy of unremitting repetition. "Well," he said, "I got lotsa chores that need doing. I should be getting along."

"Thank you again for the lift."

"Anytime." He turned to Mary. "Nice seeing you ladies. You enjoy your walk. It's sure a fine day for it." He mounted Lodestone. A tug of the reins and the trusty horse had him on his way. Thom inhaled. He could smell the splendid aroma of fresh apple pie. "Damn," he muttered. He had missed a great dessert. But with a little luck, and perhaps a bit of planning, opportunity's lusty embrace would engulf him again.

*⁓⁓⁓*

By the light of a whale oil lantern, with pen and ruler and paper, Thom sat at the small table that, along with a chest of drawers and a rope bed, furnished his small room at the rear of Sarah Albright's home. The time had come for decisions, how the exterior of his saltbox should be designed. He had made several freehand sketches, experimenting with various possibilities. Though their differences were small, they were important. Once he excavated his site and put in the foundation, there would be no turning back. But even that phase required a plan, and that was what Thom was committing to paper.

As a youngster in England, Thom, good with numbers, recognized the value of arithmetic. Folks needed to count their pence and shillings. They needed to add and subtract. Multiplication and division came in handy. But when as a teen he was forced to endure geometry, his view differed. With its many theorems the abstract mathematics was tedious. Its principles, seemingly superfluous, were quickly forgotten. The ability to use a ruler and draw rectangles and other shapes was enough. Such was Thom's view until he moved to Boston. Under the tutelage of his mentor, geometry took on a new character. It was power, the ability to design a structure on paper with complete knowledge of every dimension.

Long before he had come to Boston, Thom knew what a triangle was, but the secrets that had been unlocked many centuries earlier in ancient Greece and Egypt, the magical aspects of right triangles, were a foreign concept. The right triangle helped him advance from novice to journeyman in the world of structural design. It unlocked the key to roofs, especially the kind found in a saltbox. With the Pythagorean Theorem, $c^2 = a^2 + b^2$, he could calculate the length of diagonals. And two special right triangles, the ones Thom repeatedly used, allowed quick calculation of their two shorter sides. The first, the isosceles right triangle, Thom's favorite, provided the perfect 45-degree roof. The other, the 30°-60°-90° triangle, could be used for a very sharp peak or a shallow one, depending which side was selected as the base. But the transcendent aspect of both the isosceles right triangle and the 30°-60°-90° right triangle was that once a length was chosen for one side, the other two could be determined immediately. Armed with these tools, coupled with a decision to use an isosceles triangular roof, Thom began to design his saltbox.

Planning the front façade of the house was easy. Zeal, an appetite for the challenge, had cajoled him to make his house twenty-three feet across the front, far above the eighteen-foot minimum. He opted for a height of eleven feet from the top of the foundation to the point where the front roof commenced; seven feet from floor to ceiling on the main floor, plus an additional four for the loft at its shallowest point adjoining the base of the front roof. The rectangular front frame up to the roofline was set. Ruler and pen in hand, he drew a diagram, a sketch of the house on which he specified the dimensions of the front façade.

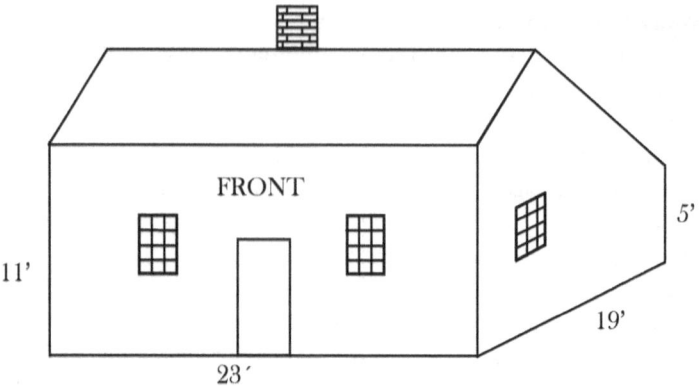

FRONT

11'

23'

5'

19'

Next Thom embarked on plans for the asymmetric sides of the saltbox. Thanks to his geometric knowledge, inscrutable transformed into intelligible, frustrating into satisfying. He had already established an *eleven-foot height* (seven plus four) to the base of the roof where the side frame met the roof truss. He had flexibility in terms of the depth of his two front rooms. He opted for *thirteen feet*. For the narrow kitchen and buttery that ran across the entire rear of the house, he chose a width of *six feet*. Together that gave a depth to the house from front to back of *nineteen feet*. He drew a diagram, as he prepared to calculate the remaining, more complex dimensions of the asymmetric, pentagonal-shaped sides of the house.

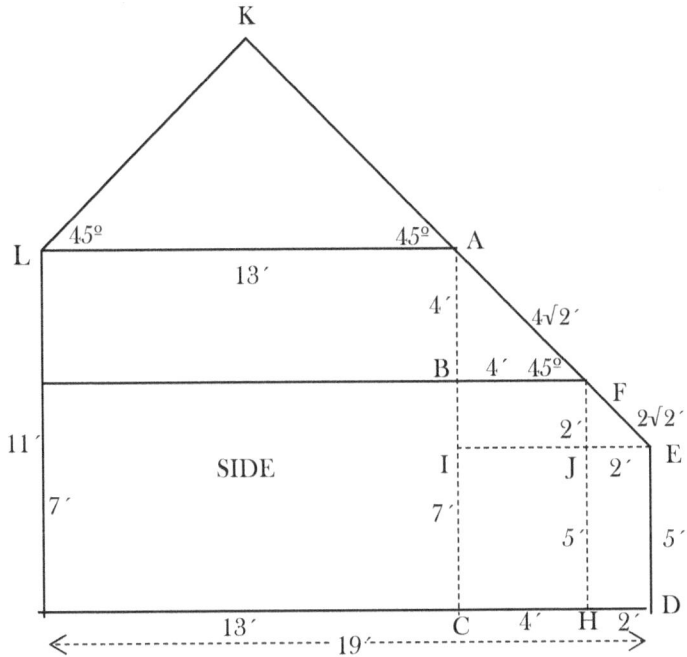

Step by step, he reasoned. Like triangle KAL, triangles AFB and FEJ were isosceles right triangles. AB was four feet. Since triangle AFB was isosceles, BF was also four feet. And CH, the opposite side of the rectangle, was also four feet. He already knew CD was six feet, implying DH was two feet (six minus four). And EJ, the opposite side of the rectangle, was also two feet. Since triangle FEJ was isosceles, FJ was two feet. Therefore, HJ was five feet (FH minus FJ; i.e., seven minus two). And, therefore, *ED the opposite side of the rectangle was five feet.*

IJ, the side of a rectangle opposite BF, like BF was four feet. Thus, EI was six feet (IJ plus EJ; i.e., four plus two). But triangle AEI was an isosceles right triangle, so both its sides were six feet and its hypotenuse AE, per the Pythagorean Theorem, $c^2 = a^2 + b^2$, was the square root of $6^2 + 6^2$, or the square root of seventy two or 8.49 feet.

With that last calculation Thom had completed the design of his saltbox. The front façade was twenty-three feet across and eleven feet high. Excluding the isosceles section supported by the roof truss, the sides were pentagons with dimensions as follows: nineteen feet along the foundation from front to rear; thence upward perpendicular five feet at the rear; thence upward at forty-five degrees for 8.49 feet; and thence parallel to the base thirteen feet; and thence perpendicular eleven feet down to the point of beginning on the ground. The rear of the saltbox was a simple rectangle, five feet high and twenty-three feet wide. A ruler in hand, he completed his scale model showing the side view of his house, after which he drew a diagram of the rear.

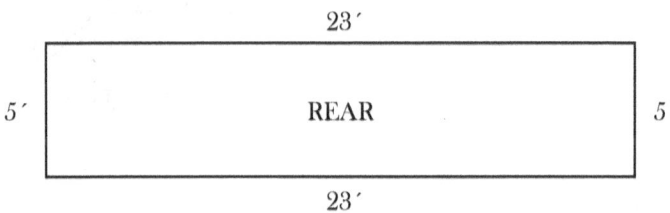

Thom gazed at his drawings, each marked with their calculated dimensions. They were by no means what a skilled architect would have drawn. They failed to take into account the thickness of the connecting beams and girts and sills and posts. He would need to do that in the course of construction. For example, to fit a beam between two posts, he would measure the actual space between the posts, cut a beam with a minute excess and then gash, trim and file the beam so it fit precisely. Men like Reverend Bidwell or Thom's Boston mentor would never have settled for such inferior techniques. Thom's drawing would have fallen short of their lofty standards. Architects would have voiced even harsher criticism, but that was of no concern to Thom. His pragmatic approach worked, and that was all that mattered. And too, when compared to the rudimentary methods used by many settlers when building simple log cabins, his drawings and methods were masterful. In less than two hours he had completed drawings of the front and rear of his saltbox, along with one of the two matching sides.

Thom sat back, conscious of the smile that enveloped his face. There was great satisfaction in what he had done, but there was also a broader appreciation of what his mentor had done for him. The thoughtful Renaissance man had taken Thom, a common English bloke, fresh off the boat with minimal knowledge and no skills, and turned him into a capable, thinking adult. His mentor started Thom out as a building worker. Gradually he piqued Thom's curiosity for the how and why behind what they built. And so Thom learned the principles of Euclid's geometry. Next his mentor encouraged Thom to explore Descartes' world of Cartesian coordinates and analytic geometry, the link to Sir Issac Newton's equations explaining the interrelationship of constantly changing variables. The goal was to teach Thom the principles of calculus, mathematics' crowning achievement. Matters, however, failed to go as planned. Thom found it hard to get his arms around the abstract theory underlying calculus. On the other hand, Descartes' philosophical theory of rationalism and mechanism intrigued Thom. Never receptive to dogma, he welcomed writings that rejected the theological bias of the past in favor of reason.[38]

Having whetted Thom's appetite, his mentor, rather than pushing calculus, encouraged Thom to explore the political and social philosophies of Descartes' successors. Thom delved into the theories of men like Thomas Hobbes, whose "Leviathan" depicted the state as an all-powerful monster. But Hobbes' conclusion that people give up everything in exchange for security troubled Thom. While preferable to past doctrine proclaiming that kings derived power directly from God, tenets that continued to embrace the omnipotence of kings were troublesome.[39]

A rugged individualist, Thom longed for principles that respected the common man. In the philosophers of the Enlightenment, particularly the French, his yearning found support. Voltaire's advocacy of free speech, his castigation of the church for branding people as heretics, was sweet music. Then came the day in 1768, when his mentor gave him a copy of Baron de Montesquieu's "The Spirit of the Laws." Written only two decades earlier in 1748, Thom was in awe. Montesquieu harmonized what for Thom had been a hodgepodge of confusing and seemingly inconsistent ideas. The three types of government, despotism, monarchy subject to laws, and republican (elected government ruled by laws), became clearer. More important was the concept of separation of powers: an executive, be it monarch or elected official, to enforce the laws; a legislature to make the laws; and a judiciary to interpret the laws. No longer could Thom only voice objections to the powers of the past. He could comprehend the abstractions of a viable alternative. And despite an overreaching royalty, Great Britain, with its Parliament and courts, had elements that took the concepts beyond mere abstraction.[40]

Thom loved the democratic concept of the town meetings of the Massachusetts Bay Colony. They were suited to a rural, largely self-sufficient place like Tyringham. Unfortunately, they were inherently impractical when applied to large numbers of people spread over a vast area. But Montesquieu allowed Thom to bridge the gap between despotic kings and town meetings. The French philosopher convinced Thom that a government fashioned upon a fair and workable middle ground was possible. And more than anything, what appealed to Thom, the individualist, was Montesquieu's view of liberty. He relished the idea that laws should concern only threats to public order and security. Unencumbered freedom, provided it didn't violate the rights of others, had great appeal.[41]

Back in Boston when he was with his few close friends, Thom was comfortable voicing his philosophical and political leanings. Religion was the one glaring exception to that rule. Unlike Thom, who was secular, most with whom he fraternized were religious. Where Thom favored Montesquieu's view that church and state should be separate,[42] his friends thought otherwise. They rejected the philosopher's argument that because God needed no protection, laws should not address purported offenses against God.

When Thom moved to Tyringham, the dangers of espousing his religious views magnified. Congregationalist principles were founding elements of the town and basic to everyday life. Like many other rural Massachusetts communities, the legislation creating the town had set aside two prime lots for two Congregationalist ministers. The town paid their salaries. Thom recognized the need to keep his views about religion private.

45

Despite qualms, on balance Thom accepted Tyringham's link of church and state. In silent self-debate, he reasoned that individuals of a common religious persuasion should be able to travel to a wilderness like Tyringham and establish a community built upon their values. Why should an interloper, a *Johnny-Come-Lately* like himself, be entitled to demand change?

The logic, however, had its limits. What if a community required that all the inhabitants join and regularly attend their church? That would be unfair. The inconsistency was troubling but far from insurmountable. Balancing the rights of society and those of the individual invariably necessitated lines, some of which were not altogether satisfactory. If nothing else, Thom's ventures into the realm of philosophy had taught him that even the greatest minds had struggled with such difficult questions. Disagreement was inevitable. Over the centuries clerics and secularists had battled endlessly. Rationalists, like Descartes, and empiricists, like Locke and Hume, had argued whether the road to knowledge was through reason and logic or, alternatively, experience and evidence, especially sensory observations. Those debates were apt to continue forever. Ontological arguments purporting to prove the existence of God furnished the quintessential example. Their undeniable brilliance was exceeded only by their futility.

While such unanswered questions caused some to throw up their hands, thanks to his mentor, Thom found comfort in them. They encouraged him to think. They aroused his curiosity. Where first his mentor had taught him a few everyday skills, those talents soon opened doors to knowledge both practical and abstract, concrete and esoteric. The more Thom learned, the more there was to explore, and the greater, his thirst. Just as his future home was destined to grow from a two-dimensional Euclidean drawing on paper to a real three-dimensional structure existing in Descartes' XYZ Cartesian coordinates, so too was Thom's knowledge. Already drawn to woodworking, mathematics, architecture, science, political and social philosophy, other areas remained to be explored. And for all Thom knew, their dimensions might expand beyond Descartes' three.

# Chapter 4

FOLLOWING A FULL DAY clearing brush and rocks from his homesite, on his way back to the Albright homestead, Thom detoured north on Royal Hemlock Road. His purpose was a stop at George Whitaker's place. Whatever one required could be had from the bearded man with the deep voice. Whitaker didn't actually run a shop. He was a Yankee Trader. Between house and barn, he had a huge inventory. Jars, candles, nails, kerosene lanterns, tools, seeds, dolls, wheels, spectacles, knives...you name it, and Whitaker carried it. But few of his wares were new. Mostly he acquired what people didn't need. Sooner or later he found someone who did, and in the process he managed to make a healthy profit, not that the gain was necessarily in cash. More often than not, he traded for something better. His business was akin to arbitrage, except intangibles, bills and stocks, were not what he offered. As much as anything, the key to his success was his large, diverse stock. His location, just north of the intersection with the Albany-Boston Post Road, didn't hurt. Whenever the folks of Tyringham needed something, especially when the need was immediate, Whitaker was ready.

As Thom approached, he spotted Whitaker, along with Johnny Woodstone, a mason by trade, standing in front of the barn. Thom tethered Lodestone to a hickory tree and started toward the two men.

"You believe this guy?" yelled Woodstone. "I offer him a fine quilt for one crummy axe, and he demands more."

"I didn't put a gun to your head. If I recall, you came here wanting an axe. And about that quilt of yours, it's seen better days."

"Your damn axe ain't new either."

Whitaker folded his arms across his plump torso. "As I told you, if you don't like the deal, keep your stinking quilt."

Whitaker turned to Thom. "You tell me. Does it look like I'm twisting the man's arm?"

Immersing himself into the middle of the bickering was the last thing Thom wanted. "You mind if I go into the barn and look around?"

"Suit yourself, though you could help me out."

"Yeah, I suppose I might...but then again, I might not." Thom hurried into the barn before his vacuous response could be challenged. Apart from a stall in the corner with a horse and some adjacent hay and tools, the structure was loaded to the gills. On hooks and shelves, on the ground, on and under tables, even hanging from the ceiling, there were wares. Thom had to squeeze his way between a couple of wagon wheels and a table. He climbed over a butter churn. He caught his foot on a loom, nearly tumbling to the ground. He made mental notes of what was available, not that he was there to negotiate. Come the following spring, once his home was built, he would need lots of things. Scouting the available merchandise, especially items for which there might be excess supply, seemed a good strategy. On the far wall there was a wide selection of hammers, chisels and files. Once Thom moved out of Sarah Albright's home, he would need tools of his own. He could get them new from Orville Crane, but a deal with Whitaker might work out better. And too, pitting one against the other might provide negotiating leverage. There were some nice tables, chairs, a desk and a hutch, but they were of little interest. Thom had the skills and plenty of wood to make whatever furniture he needed. He checked the tools one more time before heading outside.

"Okay, two candles, along with the quilt." Woodstone turned to Thom. "Damn, he drives a nasty bargain."

A hint of a smug smile on Whitaker's face belied the otherwise blasé reaction by the man with the big brown beard. "How about you, Thom? Something in the barn strike your fancy?"

"Nope." No way would he show an interest in the tools.

"Wuzn't that terrible 'bout the school?" said Woodstone. "Especially after it took so long to get it built."

"If you ask me," said Whitaker, "it was a torch job."

"What makes you say that?" Were the claim coming from someone less prone to rash remarks, Thom might have been less skeptical.

"Maybe the Indians did it."

"Who—the Stockbridge Indians?...Ya can't be serious," said Woodstone.

Thom had the same reaction, though unlike Woodstone he contained it.

"And what does that mean?"

"Need I spell it out?" Woodstone gave Thom a glance, one begging confirmation that Whitaker's allegation was absurd.

Thom remained impassive, as if unaware of the invitation.

"Why would the Stockbridge Indians, our friends, burn down our school?" Woodstone pointed at the Yankee Trader. "And before you make a bigger fool of yourself, George, remember—they fought with Rogers' Rangers when the French and other Indians invaded from Canada."[43]

"Big deal. That was fifteen or more years ago."

"So, they're still our friends, and with good reason. Ever since they moved to Stockbridge back in the thirties, we've helped 'em. That John Sergeant guy is a perfect example, not that I'm enthused about his English missionary group."

"You mean the Church of England Society for...for the Propagation of the Gospel...or something like that?" said Thom.

"Yeah, some such thing." Woodstone shifted his focus to Whitaker. "Anyway, he built 'em a school and taught 'em agriculture and science and ways to earn a living.[44] And after him, that other guy...Edwards...Jonathan Edwards made treaties with 'em. There's been peace ever since." Woodstone gave Thom another look, but its self-satisfaction required no confirmation other than approval for a debate won.

Thom showed nothing. Chances were, the shrewd Yankee peddler, not prone to go off half-cocked, had a basis for his position.

"Thanks for the history lesson," said Whitaker. "But some of us who came here way back when...recall that not all the Stockbridge Indians were thrilled with the deal that moved them off this land to their current home. And as for the wonderful

49

Mr. Edwards, some of the Indians didn't take to an outsider changing their way of life."

"So what," said Woodstone. "The missionaries expelled the trouble makers."

"From Stockbridge maybe, but not the entire region. And who knows, maybe they came back and got even."

"Sure." Woodstone rolled his eyes. "Thom, kindly tell our pal that he's suffering from nonsensical notions."

"Don't stick me in the middle."

"What—you agree with George?"

"I didn't say that. And no, I don't agree with anybody. I don't know who burned our school. I don't even know it was arson. But—"

"That's my point," said Woodstone. "When ya got no evidence, it's crazy to blame the Indians for the fire."

"Well, buildings don't burn by themselves. Someone or something has to be the cause." Whitaker folded his arms. "Maybe King George himself sailed across the ocean and torched the place."

"Speaking of King George," said Thom, more than happy to change the subject, "he's probably a greater concern than the Stockbridge Indians."

"Is that so?" said Whitaker.

Thom heaved a sigh. Altering the conversation was less welcome if it meant stepping into the line of fire. "I was referring to the fact that our benefactors across the Atlantic have hit us with heavy burdens."

Whitaker groaned.

"What's that mean?" said Thom.

"Just this. I'm sick of indolent whiners who expect a free ride. How fast they forget that England spent itself silly defending us in the French and Indian War. But for our Mother Country, the colonies, Massachusetts included, would have been routed."

"George has a point," said Woodstone.

Thom did a double take. The familiar Tory argument had made him odd man out.

"Do you object to Parliament's exercise of authority over us?" Whitaker's tone was non-confrontational. If past experience were a good predictor, his succeeding comments would bear increasing rancor.

"Well...yes and no," said Thom, trying to weigh the pros and cons of immersing himself in a probable polemic. The unreceptive looks that greeted his equivocal answer pressed him to explain. "I don't object to them governing us, only that we have no representation."

"That's a matter of debate."

Woodstone displayed a puzzled look.

Thom, better versed, recognized the distinction that Whitaker was drawing. In Britain the prevailing view was that representation was a matter of class. Nobility enjoyed representation in the House of Lords, while every commoner was represented in the House of Commons. As for the colonists, they enjoyed *virtual* representation, at least according to philosophers like Thomas Hobbes and John Locke. Thom didn't buy it. His readings had convinced him that representation had to be real. It also should be geographical. He was reluctant to get into an argument.

"Representation," said Woodstone. "Fancy word. Uppity folks, the kind who like to hear themselves talk, use it. They call it politics and philosophy. If ya ask me, they're rabble-rousers, just lookin' to complain. I don't care who makes the rules as long as they stay outta my hair...and that includes my pocketbook." He looked at Thom. "You agree, don'tcha?"

Thom might have resorted to another *yes and no*, had his use of that insipid response not evoked an unreceptive reaction a minute earlier. He said, "Take the Trade and Navigation Acts, for example. Shouldn't we have had a say when Parliament stuck us with those restrictions?"

"Big deal," said Woodstone. "So cotton and tobacco can only be exported to England. Let the folks in Georgia and South Carolina worry 'bout that."

"The Acts also restrict us to trade on English-owned and English-built ships. What about that?"

Woodstone shrugged.

Thom turned to Whitaker. "I would think that someone in your business, George, must have been miffed when they put those rules into effect."

Whitaker laughed.

"You telling me you don't care?"

"Not really...all things considered."

If Thom were speaking with a dunce like Orville Crane, the response might have made sense. "C'mon, you can't be serious." He gestured at Whitaker's barn. "There's lotsa stuff in there that came from across the ocean. The Trade and Navigation Acts had to make it more expensive."

"Occasionally, but it's a fair price for protection." Whitaker leaned in closer. "And about that stuff in the barn, a fair bit arrived on Dutch ships that come up the Hudson. Albany's a whole lot closer than Boston, and when its price is better, that's where George trades. Anyway, when it comes to the Acts, I've got a pretty good relationship with the fellows who do the enforcing. A few shillings in their pockets, and everyone is happy." Whitaker smiled.

The disclosure came as no surprise. Whitaker was crafty. His byword was *principal*, not *principle*. But Thom couldn't blame the Yankee Trader. As long as Parliament gave the colonists no voice in the rules, they had reason to bend them. He said, "Some folks, like the Sons of Liberty, believe if we press Parliament, they'll give us representation."

"The Sons of Liberty...those damn radicals. They want a helluva lot more than representation. As far as getting it, icicles got a better chance in a blazing hearth." Whitaker laughed.

Thom chuckled, but only to himself. Whitaker was a cynic, but, like Thom, pragmatic. Very pragmatic.

"Well," said Whitaker, "this has been an enlightening discussion. It's good to know where your neighbors stand." He shook his head, and, seeming to chide himself, added, "And it's wise to think twice about what you say to whom."

Whitaker had a point, perhaps the best of the entire discussion. But it was after the fact, and none of them had followed it. People often didn't. The propensity to gossip was tempting, especially out in the hinterlands. As Thom bid the two goodbye and rode off on Lodestone, he chastised himself for imprudence.

Frequent early spring rains, often wind-driven, coupled with the melting of mountain snows, riddled roads with ruts and puddles. While some cursed gray, damp days, Thom relished their bright side. Wet ground eased the task of digging the area where his saltbox would rise. With Sarah Albright's sled-like draw-bucket harnessed to Lodestone, earth moved from the site. The big stallion pulled up stumps of downed trees, not that prior digging and hacking could be avoided.

By the time May dawned, Thom had excavated the area on which his home, twenty-three feet wide and nineteen feet from front to back, would stand. Ambition, memorialized in his carefully drawn plans, far exceeded Tyringham's minimum. Thom had dug the area to a depth of five feet, well below the harshest winter's frost line. With the living space of the structure raised the better part of a foot above the ground, it allowed for a cellar in which he could stand, though admittedly with difficulty. The bare earth substructure would provide ample storage, along with a cool place for food stocks.

Abundant sunshine and mild temperatures reigned near midday. Thom had completed the excavation of his cellar earlier in the day than he had anticipated. A half-hour break, during which he ate the sandwich he had packed in his haversack, was more than enough to re-energize him. The fine afternoon was too good to waste. Were the weather otherwise, likely he would have made the same decision. He began gathering fieldstone for his foundation. Lodestone, harnessed to the draw-bucket, was the prime mover.

Rock by rock, stone by stone, big and small, Thom gathered material for his foundation. Load after load was deposited into the excavated area, but always leaving space where the exterior wall of the foundation would rise. Beartown Mountain's rich supply of limestone and granite aided the process, but many a boulder refused to be moved until sledgehammer and chisel had reduced it to manageable pieces. The task was arduous, and the days, long. Eight elapsed before Thom had gathered a sufficient supply.

Weary, but pleased, he stood in the late afternoon sun along the rim of his excavation. He surveyed the oval-shaped pile of rocks that awaited placement. He closed his eyes and pictured them neatly stacked along the rectangular border of his digging. His imagination stretched further as he conjured the completed saltbox. Months away, with much to do, the vision brought a conscious smile to his face. The goal, still incredibly distant, was growing more plausible. He unhitched Lodestone from a nearby birch, but, rather than climbing aboard, led him out onto the Albany-Boston Post Road. Like Thom, Lodestone had put in a hard day's work.

With the sun to his back, his senses heightened, Thom worked his way southeasterly on the Albany-Boston Post Road. Buds and incipient leaves on trees lining the road garnered his attention. Puffy white clouds interspersed in the blue firmament provided a blissful canopy. A gentle zephyr from the south caressed his cheek. Thom soaked it in. The glorious days of late spring and summer lay ahead. His efforts, his accomplishment and nature's blessing had elevated his spirits.

"Hello Thom." The call came from Thom's left.

Halfway through the intersection of Morse Corners, Thom recognized the dulcet voice even before he looked. It was disconcerting. The best part of a year had passed since he had spoken to Polly. On a couple of occasions he had seen her, but not face-to-face. His mind raced. Might he continue on, pretending he didn't hear? Having stopped in his tracks and glanced her way, the flawed solution was absurd. Civility dictated a single option. He turned and said, "Hi Polly. It's...it's nice to see you."

She continued into the intersection and joined him. "And it's good to see you. How have you been?"

"Fine...thanks. And uh...you?" A child caught with both hands in a cookie jar would have shown less discomfort.

"Been a while since I've seen you."

"I...uh...guess it has."

"I understand you're building yourself a house."

"I'm trying." His terse answers, hardly the fountain of lively dialogue, contrasted with the ease he had felt when they had courted. An engaging question about her would have been

54

appropriate, but asking a second time how she'd been, hardly met the criterion.

"Well, with your skills and determination, I'm sure you'll succeed."

Whether the compliment was sincere or a polite reply to his visible disquiet was difficult to judge. Eye contact was harder yet.

"Seems like this must be today's place to meet. Maybe as good as the Hogshead or Brewer's Mill." She appeared to study him. "Don't mind me if I don't make sense. But on the way up to the Bidwell's place—Ruth showed me a new recipe for apple-spiced fritters—first I bumped into Amos Heath, and then your pal Richard Thorn showed up. And speaking of him, he was a favorite topic of the ladies the other day."

"Only good things...I hope."

"Very good. As a matter of fact, they couldn't name a more eligible bachelor in all of Tyringham."

"I noticed you said *they*. Does that mean you disagreed?"

"Thomas Webster—are you putting words, inaccurate ones, into my mouth?"

He found it hard to tell if she was playacting.

"Just to set the record straight, I think Richard is a fine man. Any woman would be lucky to snatch him up." Her eyes showed a twinkle.

Histrionics or not, Thom knew the praise would not have been expressed were her regards for Richard not high. A twinge of envy stirred. "Yeah...he's a great guy."

"As are you."

Thom shrugged...uncomfortably. He longed to tell her she was beautiful and sweet and compliment her with a litany of other attributes sufficient to outlast the lengthiest of Reverend Bidwell's sermons. He said, "It's...it's a lovely day."

"It is indeed. And better yet, it's the time of year when we have many better ones on the horizon."

The ease with which she returned his awkward conversation did little to alleviate his self-consciousness. As for yearnings, they only mounted. He said, "It's been really nice to see you."

"You too." The words were barely out of her mouth, and she was on her way.

He headed in the opposite direction, glancing back several times until she disappeared with the twist of the road. In recent weeks he had done an excellent job of staying busy and hiding from vexing emotions, but the brief encounter laid bare vulnerability owing to suppressed feelings. Thom knew of no way to deal with his dilemma. Back when they were courting, he had placed Polly on a pedestal. With the passage of time the pedestal had grown taller. Other women, mere mortals, could do no better than gaze upward at her feet.

Thom stopped. He stared down the deserted road. That old embers rekindled was hardly shocking; the same, however, could not be said for the rapidity with which they stirred. Even harder to fathom was his jealousy of Richard.

Another week had been spent laboring at his homesite. It was after six on a Friday night when Thom prepared to call it a day. A break in his routine was needed. He could have done without it, but a comment by Sarah suggesting that he had become obsessed, perhaps possessed by demons, forced him to prove otherwise. Though he knew the gibe had been made with his best interests at heart, she had a point. He was pushing too hard.

Before leaving the site, Thom admired his handiwork. Precisely laid fieldstone, dressed with hammer and chisel, attested to the skills he had learned from his mentor in Boston. The foundation of his home was taking shape. One more small stone squeezed between adjacent rocks, and he was on his way to the Hogshead, but not before considerable vacillation. Of all evenings, Friday was the one he could always find several of his favorite regulars there. Saturday was popular, but less so because Sunday services required some, especially those with families, to rise early, unencumbered by the after-effects of over-indulgence.

Thom tethered Lodestone to the rail outside the Hogshead. As he approached the door, he observed a bulletin posted on the adjacent wall. The town was expanding its core of Minutemen. Like all able-bodied men ages sixteen to thirty in the Massachusetts Bay Colony, Thom was required to serve in the militia. It had been that way for well over a century. Training, especially after resolution of the French and Indian War, took only a couple of days, generally twice per year. The always-ready Minutemen, chosen from the militia based upon enthusiasm, political reliability and strength, underwent more frequent and rigorous exercises.[45]

The moment Thom entered the Hogshead, his good friend Richard Thorn stood up. Since his wife had died in childbirth, along with what would have been their first child, Richard had become among the surest of the Hogshead regulars. Tall and handsome, with his own home, he had also become one of Tyringham's most eligible men. In a culture where family was emphasized and premature death was commonplace, widows and widowers often remarried after a short time. Folks assumed it a safe bet a pretty maiden would snatch up the sinewy, blond-locked Richard.

"Well, lookie here," said Richard. "The hermit of Tyringham ventures forth from the woods." He motioned with a pewter mug as he slid over making room for Thom on his bench. On the opposite side sat George Whitaker and Paul Cooper.

"An ale for my buddy," called Richard to the tavern maid.

"How's with the house?" said Paul, the local cooper, who had a stomach resembling the barrels he made. Few in Tyringham were fat, but Paul fit the exception, mainly owing to a strong bent for ale. With seven children and a wife, who, like many spouses, worked harder than most indentured servants, Paul devoted his time to his business, leaving chores around his home to the rest of his family.

"You mean my hole in the ground?" said Thom.

"Hey, you gotta start somewhere." Cooper gazed into space. "Brings back memories when I built mine. Tougher than making barrels."

"That's not what you say when you come to my place looking to trade them," said Whitaker.

Thom chuckled. The shrewd Yankee Trader with the glib tongue was always looking for the upper hand. Whatever someone needed, he had, but with little interest in what they had to trade. With Whitaker one could expect the short end of a deal. While most Tyringham wives spun their own thread and made the family's clothes, even with five children, George's wife could concentrate on other pursuits, thanks to his argle-bargle.

"How far along are you?" said Whitaker.

"Cleared the site, dug it, and I'm laying the foundation."

"Movin' right along."

Coming from Whitaker, Thom was unsure whether the remark might be sarcasm. Then again, there were probably times when the words that flowed from Whitaker's facile tongue befogged the Yankee Trader as well.

"When it comes time to raise the timbers and put the frame in place, you can count on all of us." Richard gestured across the table as he spoke.

Thom, who anticipated that he might need assistance, welcomed the nods that greeted his eyes, not that he expected otherwise. Folks in Tyringham were quick to assist in a house or barn raising, and Thom, who had aided others, had ample justification to expect reciprocity. Whether pride might prevent him from soliciting it, remained to be seen.

The barmaid delivered Thom's ale.

"A toast to our neighbor's home...to be," said Cooper.

The four men, three already bearing the influence of alcohol, rapped pewter mugs, one against another. Thom guzzled a healthy portion of his brew. His Hogshead visit was being validated.

"Did you catch the notice on the board out front?" said Cooper.

"The one regarding the need for additional Minutemen?"

"We could use a strong, smart guy like you." Cooper looked Thom in the eye.

Were he not preoccupied with his home, Thom would have jumped at the opportunity.

"It's a darn side easier for a single fellow like you than someone like George with five kids and a wife with health problems."

"Paul has a point," said Richard. "And being in the Minutemen isn't all bad. Besides training, we have some great camaraderie, plus an ample supply of tasty spirits."

Thom looked around the table. Refusing would be difficult. Richard, like so many others of the Minutemen, had served when his wife was alive. And many, struggling farmers, had children as well. But knowing he needed to complete walls and a roof before winter, Thom could ill-afford to spend time training.

"What do you say?" said Cooper.

*What do I say?* Thom took a drink in an effort to avoid the question. Moments earlier he had commended his decision to stop at the tavern. Getting together with friends was great, but not at the price of guilt. "Between my chores at Sarah's place and building my house, for now I've got a full plate."

"Everyone does," said Whitaker.

Hopes that the candid refusal might end the matter had been dashed. And who was Whitaker to apply pressure? The Yankee Trader wasn't a Minuteman, not that the elite group would want the rotund guy with the quirky personality. Thom said, "Come next year, after I get my house built, maybe I'll reconsider."

"Seems I've heard similar refrains from others," said Cooper.

"C'mon," said Richard. "Give him a break. Building a house is no stroll in the woods." He looked across the table. "All of us have our homes. We know what it entailed. Anyway, it's not like there's a crisis looming. Whatever the Indians may be doing in parts of Connecticut and up north, around these parts we've got good relations."

"What about the school?" said Whitaker.

"Don't tell me you're back on your Indian kick again." Richard shot him a look. "Anyway, there's no proof it was arson."

At that moment Thom didn't care about the cause. That the topic of discussion had changed was enough.

"Well, Jenny Casper told me that she heard someone say that one of the kids saw an Indian boy hanging out evenings near the school before it got burned. Saw him there twice!" Whitaker held up a pair of defiant fingers. "What's the matter? You don't believe me?"

"Not that," said Richard. "But you have to admit that second-hand gossip about a kid's supposed observation, itself of little moment, doesn't count for much."

"Fine. Then go talk to Jenny Casper yourself." Whitaker scowled. "Regardless, the thing seems mighty suspicious. You ask me...it's gotta be arson."

"If it was," said Richard, "I can't imagine anyone from Tyringham setting it. And as for the Indians, I doubt they're responsible. Though I have to admit, among the bunch there might be a bad apple."

"I guess," said Whitaker. "And that's why I didn't join the Minutemen."

The logic, if any, escaped Thom and, apparently, the others as well.

"Save your peculiar looks. I'll explain. Out here in the wilderness, far from Boston and New York and Albany, our problems don't require a legion of ready fighters. Now and then we have an isolated incident. But if you ask me, keeping all these Minutemen on call is a damn waste. If and when trouble brews, it's not gonna start here, and if it should spill our way, the British troops will have plenty of time to protect us."

"They damn well oughta, what with taking our trees and the taxes they levy on us," said Richard.

Thom echoed the sentiment, but silently, lest the conversation refocus on him.

"Well, I for one appreciate Britain's position," said Whitaker. "They spend a fortune protecting us."

Thom suppressed a groan. The Yankee peddler was like a myna bird, always with the same chatter.

"Big deal," said Cooper. "They do it for their own benefit. Hell, they force us to buy their goods, trade using their ships and pay taxes on paints, glass, tea, paper...you name it. They protect us only to line their own pockets."

"Unlike you, I try to be objective. Unfortunately—"

"Sure, you're objective, George." Richard's bark was laced with sarcasm. "But that's because you trade for everything, never paying the duties that are owed."

"Keep it down." Whitaker looked around the tavern.

"Afraid the tax collector might be listening?" Cooper jabbed an elbow into Whitaker's side. "The truth hurts, doesn't it?"

"All I know is that I'm thankful for our Mother Country's support. Without it, you better believe the French and the Dutch and, for that matter, the Spanish would be down our ever-loving throats."

"Admittedly our British benefactors, like a parent, deserve regard," said Richard, "but it has limits."

Recollections of childhood abuse back in England stirred Thom to abandon silence. "A colony, like a child, is not chattel. It has rights, not the least of which is representation."

"We have representation."

"We do?" said Richard. "Then please, enlighten us about this wonderful representation."

All too recently Thom had been down the same road with Whitaker, but that discussion had halted before the Yankee Trader's fatuous argument had been dispelled.

Whitaker folded his arms. "Representation of the House of Commons extends to all citizens of the British Empire, not just those of England. And folks in England can be taxed like us."

"Maybe so, but they're not," said Cooper. "And unlike our English brethren, we don't get to choose who sits in the House of Commons."

"C'mon, a vote isn't all that important," said Whitaker. "One more this way or that doesn't change a goose egg into gold. What matters is that folks like us pick those who sit in the House of Commons."

"Not quite," said Richard. "Not when Parliament hits us with trade restrictions and taxes that don't apply to English citizens. To paraphrase Sir William Blackstone, the people of England *care not one two penny damn* what taxes Parliament places on the colonies."

Thom curtailed the urge to point out that the phrase was attributable to the Duke of Wellington. He also let it pass that Sir William Blackstone deemed the power of Parliament absolute, a concept codified seven years earlier in the Declaratory Act of 1766.[46]

61

"The people of England aren't the only ones okay with our taxes," said Cooper. "Chaps like George, who dodge them, don't give a two penny damn either."

Bearing a smug grin, Whitaker stood up. "Some of us need to get home to awaiting families." He fondled his scraggly beard before tossing nine pence onto the table. "You gentlemen take care." He headed for the door.

"You think he may have been pleased with himself?" said Richard, ever the master of understatements.

"Maybe so, but I don't like it."

Richard shot Cooper a look. "C'mon, be honest. All of us duck and dodge those lousy taxes."

"I wasn't referring to taxes."

"Then what?" said Thom.

"Just this. If push comes to shove, if relations with England sour into real hostilities, my money says George will side with them."

Richard shook his head. "I know we have our disagreements, but if war broke out, not that it will, George will be with us."

"Don't you wish?" Cooper turned to Thom. "Apparently we have a difference of opinion. You know George as well as we do. What do you say?"

The middle was a spot Thom preferred to avoid. "It's an academic question. There won't be war."

"Really. What about the Boston Massacre, three years ago? If recollection serves me, British soldiers killed five of our Massachusetts brethren for throwing snowballs and debris at them. But rather than debate the issue, humor me, and answer my question about George as a hypothetical."

Hoping to get off the hook, Thom glanced at Richard. A shake of his pal's head convinced Thom he could not ignore the issue. He said, "Just because George shows some sympathies for England, doesn't mean he'd do so if guns replaced words. If you ask me, his would be aimed at the British troops."

"Much as I disagree," groaned Cooper, "I asked, and you're entitled to your opinion. Anyway, I hope you're right." He turned to Richard. "Looks like the deciding vote went your way."

Richard shrugged. "Unfortunately there are some in Tyringham about whom I'm less confident. Seeming Patriots...behind the scenes, spies. One who fills that bill—we all know him well—our local buffoon...excuse me, I meant blacksmith...Orville Crane."

"On that we agree," said Cooper.

Thom recalled the quality job Crane had done fixing a wheel on Sarah Albright's wagon the preceding autumn. "You have to admit his work is good."

"Fair enough," said Cooper. "But he's still a buffoon." Cooper raised a hammer-like fist. "And buffoons, especially those wielding a hammer, can be dangerous."

Whether Thom concurred, he didn't know. But that wasn't the point. He made a mental note to be wary of the burly blacksmith. He glanced at Richard in an effort to glean his friend's assessment. The move sparked a disconcerting realization. Too often he was looking to others. Months of depression had whittled away at Thom's self-confidence. A lone wolf had transformed into a bashful sheep.

"You hear that John Woolman passed away?"

Thom, about to lay another log onto the fire in Sarah's parlor, halted. He knew of most folks in Tyringham, even if he didn't know everyone personally. He turned toward the rocker where Sarah was stitching a sampler. "Who?"

"John Woolman." She drew back in an incredulous pose. "You're familiar with him, aren't you?"

"Uh...not really...Is he from around these parts?"

"No, he was from Pennsylvania, though I understand he died in England. It happened last autumn."

With the all-dayer in his arms outweighing curiosity, Thom placed the log into the fireplace before refocusing on Sarah. "Now that I've shown my ignorance, you mind telling me who this Woolman fella is?"

He was a Quaker preacher who traveled the colonies speaking out against slavery. He even came to New England, though that was a long time ago."[47]

"Can't imagine he was popular here in Massachusetts, at least among the slave-holding folks."

"I don't suppose he was, but that doesn't mean he was wrong." Sarah looked Thom in the eye. "How do you feel about slavery?"

Thom hesitated. It was one of those controversial issues he avoided. A part of him believed it was morally wrong, but the arguments on the other side managed to silence his tongue and, arguably, his conscience. "I don't have strong feelings."

Sarah shot him a look. "How can you say that when we claim to be a society of equals...a democracy?"

"True, but many of our democratic principles are grounded on the teachings of the ancient Greeks. They had slaves. And how about your own Congregationalist teachings? They proclaim us superior to Negroes. None other than Cotton Mather taught that the Lord punished Negroes with slavery because they were the 'miserable children of Adam and Noah.'[48] And what about 'The Massachusetts Body of Liberties?' It expressly allows slavery. It's been the law of our colony for over a century."[49]

"Misguided excuses for inhumanity don't merit a response."

Thom pointed to the shelf on the far wall where Sarah's Bible held a prominent spot. "Lest you forget, the Holy Book was the basis for the The Massachusetts Body of Liberties."

"Let me rephrase your explanation. The Bible, or should I say an abominable excuse for an interpretation of the Bible, was invoked to justify The Massachusetts Body of Liberties. In fact we both know the real reason."

Though the remark bore an obvious predicate, it escaped Thom.

"Economic convenience. Many profit from slavery. For the slave traders it's big business. So too for the ship builders and the loggers who supply them. And the sailmakers and tanners and ropemakers. And of course, you have the thousands of seamen who work the slave ships. And don't forget the lawyers who arrange the deals and do the contracts, not to mention those who insure the ships. And then we have the entire business of rum that finances the slave trade."[50] Sarah paused long enough to shake her head. "I could go on and on, and mind you, I've only talked about the commerce relating to Massachusetts. The South is another story...Anyway, the bottom line is greed...big, big money. As for the references to the Bible, as I said, they're nothing more than devices to perpetuate evil." Sarah folded her arms in punctuating silence.

The hiatus offered Thom the opportunity to debate. He thought better of it. His propensity to play devil's advocate, a practice that enabled him to see both sides of an issue, from time to time turned out to be his Achilles heel. This was one of those occasions.

"I know...there are those who are quick to point to slave owners who treat their slaves well. They're in the minority, not that benevolence makes them right. A perfect example is Colonel John Ashley of Sheffield, as rich and important a man as one can find in Berkshire County. Last month, Harriet Chadwick was praising him for such kindness."[51]

"How'd you react?"

Sarah bowed her head. Her answer, "I bit my tongue," was barely audible.

Thom reached for some small kindling wood, not that it was needed. He tossed it onto the fire. The blaze, a rich amalgam of ever-changing hues, contrasted with the blacks and whites that dominated his thoughts. "It's really strange..." His utterance trailed into silent reflection.

"What's strange?"

"Oh...I was thinking...it was a few months ago—January, I believe—when Colonel Ashley led the committee that issued the Sheffield Declaration.[52] How, when declaring that men have the right to 'their lives, their liberty and property,' can he own slaves?"[53]

"That's my point. Folks here in Massachusetts, as well as the rest of the colonies, are living a lie...talking out of both sides of their mouths."

65

"Money...self-interest has a way of doing that." Thom's response, spontaneous, caused him to gag. Sarah had made the point earlier, and she had done so more effectively.

# Chapter 5

THOM HID AMIDST THE TREES that adjoined the path leading to the home of Reverend Adonijah Bidwell. He had made certain to arrive early for the Sunday meeting but waited for others to enter before he made his move. As he stepped through the doorway, the Reverend greeted him.

"Thomas, what a pleasant surprise. Please come in."

"Thank you." Thom shook the hand the Reverend offered. Out of the corner of his eye he caught a glimpse of another couple approaching the door. Their arrival was a welcome excuse to move into the parlor where the chairs were arranged for the Sunday meeting. Since Thom had moved to Tyringham, there had been lots of talk about building a new meeting house, but other priorities had forestalled progress. And with the school, often a site for religious gatherings, having fallen victim to a blaze, the Reverend's home had become the place of choice. Even before flames had consumed the school, in the depths of winter the impressive home had frequently been used. Besides owning an amazing number of chairs, the Reverend had four large fireplaces that in winter kept his home warmer than the school, though not necessarily comfortable. On bitter days parishioners came armed with foot warmers laden with hot coals.

Thom went into the parlor where six rows, each with eight chairs, awaited. He seated himself on the far end of the last row. Good sense told him that revivification of his self-confidence demanded he get out into the community. Self-consciousness stirred second thoughts. He might have left, were inertia, remaining in his seat, not easier, especially when leaving posed an embarrassing alternative.

He gazed around the neatly appointed room. Like the home he was building, it was a Georgian saltbox. But there were saltboxes, and *there were saltboxes.* Reverend Bidwell's impressive home dwarfed what Thom was constructing. Straight ahead on the parlor's front wall hung a portrait of King George. Reverend Bidwell was known to criticize the autocratic interference of the Mother Country, but the painting was not a contradiction. Many who railed against the tyranny of Parliament held the Crown in high esteem.

"Isn't the green of the entryway splendid?" said a woman to her husband, as she seated herself in the row ahead of Thom.

As he had come through the front door, the expensive green paint had caught Thom's eye. The luxury stirred recollections from days in Boston when, while adorning finer homes, he had mixed his own verdigris.[54] Impressive and fashionable though the shade may have been, Thom preferred subtle, translucent stains. Eclipsing wood's natural grain beneath a costly opaque mantle was garish, not beautiful. On the other hand, the two perfectly carved hearts that decorated the upper portion of the open door to the parlor generated a different reaction. The manifest symbols, a popular Tyringham embellishment, struck him as apropos of a loving home.[55] He knew that view was not shared by all. George Whitaker had labeled the custom tacky. That green paint and carved hearts produced diametric reactions among different persons intrigued Thom. How boring if everyone were the same. Unfortunately, differing views, even on seemingly minor matters, gave rise to disputes, sometimes violence, even war.

The esoteric reflection, not uncommon for Thom, lent credence to his decision to attend the meeting. Though religion, particularly dogma, had scant appeal, allowing a clerical perspective could be an interesting addition to his secular views, not that a clergyman's axioms could supplant well-reasoned analysis. History had proved that trusting a glittering golden calf was fatuous.

"Thomas...Thomas Webster."

The sound of his name roused him from his reflections. He jumped from his seat. "Uh...nice to see you," he said, unable to recall the name of the wife of Ezra Jenkins, attorney and town tax collector. "And you too, Ezra."

The bald-headed lawyer with the bulbous jowls shook Thom's extended hand. "This your first time here?"

"No...but uh...it's been a long while."

"You'll enjoy the Reverend's message."

"I...I'm sure I will." Thom struggled to summon the name of the lawyer's wife. Chances were she knew he had forgotten it. Worse yet, perhaps she thought him a self-centered boor.

The couple circled around to the near side of the second row. Thom sank back into his seat. The urge to leave was rearing itself again. But folks, nearly twenty, had filed in. They would all see him leave. His strange behavior might become the talk of the town. And he would need to walk past Reverend Bidwell. Staying was the lesser evil. He lowered his head, trying to remain inconspicuous. The scene conjured a distant memory. He was back in Mr. Rhoden's grammar school class in England. The strict schoolmaster, the man the youngsters referred to as the ugly ogre, had it in for Thom. Whenever Rhoden posed an impossible question, Thom was the target. The moment the question was asked, Thom would dip his gaze. Frozen, he would try to remain invisible. Sure enough, Rhoden would call his name. Thom would draw a blank. An anguishing silence would ensue, after which Rhoden would berate Thom. Eyes focused on the floor of Reverend Bidwell's parlor, Thom sat motionless, hoping no one would call his name. He had no answer to the obvious question: What was he doing there at the meeting of the Congregationalist Church?

Another seven or eight or, maybe, ten minutes passed before the Reverend closed the front door and stepped behind his lectern desk to address the gathering. Thom remained low in his seat behind the burly man in the chair ahead. The possibility, unlikely though it was, that the Reverend might single him out, if only to welcome him, was reason for Thom to seek cover.

Mellifluous phrases streamed from Reverend Bidwell's lips to Thom's ears. His brain, its focus distant, failed to apprehend their content. He leaned to his left, gaining a glimpse through the front window of the bright May day outside. Instead of coming to the meeting, he could have worked on his saltbox. Stress could have been avoided. Stones supporting his chimney, the linchpin of his house, could have been laid. He stole a glance to his left at the large, finely crafted brick fireplace that dominated the adjacent side of the parlor. People in Tyringham had spoken of the basement's masterfully laid fieldstone arch supporting the massive chimney that rose through the center of the structure. Were it possible, Thom would have sneaked down to the cellar to examine the arch. Like saltboxes, there were arches, and *there were arches.* No doubt Reverend Bidwell's fell into the latter category. With art and science merged in perfect harmony, the semi-circular centerpiece, without one iota of mortar, would support an otherwise maintained home for centuries.

On and on the articulate Reverend spoke. Whether the quality of his message equaled the oratorical skill with which it was delivered, Thom couldn't say. He remained entranced in his own world. Instead of images fashioned from biblical scripture, he envisioned tongue and groove connections that joined the floorboards; lath and plaster that lay between the interior and exterior walls; and the sturdy timber sills that supported the walls. Even when his gaze was drawn upward, his thoughts were not directed to God. Images of the rooftree supporting the rafters occupied his imagination. Now and then he observed the other parishioners. All seemed attentive, even the children. Perhaps, they, like him, masked distant reflections with the appearance of heeding the Reverend's words.

At long last, the seemingly endless sermon concluded. Following the lunch break there would be another. Some had brought packed lunches, while others, those who lived in close proximity, went home for the noontime break. Thom, who had a sandwich in his saddlebag, slipped out the door. Apart from several spinsters, there were no singles. Families were the norm. George Whitaker, one of Thom's Hogshead cronies, was there, but naturally his wife and children were at his side. Thom debated whether to hop onto Lodestone and ride away. The thought revived memories of English school days, particularly the time he played hooky. Rhoden, with ten sadistic lashes of his switch, made Thom regret it. Might the Reverend, when next their paths crossed, deliver a harsher punishment, a diatribe laden with guilt? Thom delayed another half-hour before going back inside to the parlor. Spending the break alone outside was easier than standing ill-at-ease among the gathering. When he finally returned, he took the same seat he had occupied earlier.

The Reverend commenced his afternoon preaching. Thom tried to listen, but his mind constantly wandered. At times his eyelids grew heavy. The stones he dragged about his homesite seemed light by comparison. After more than two hours, the Reverend finished. Temptation cajoled Thom to make a dash for the door; discretion slowed him. From his seat in the last row he waited for the opportune moment. Some departed. Others moved through the entryway into the dining room. Once the Reverend joined them, Thom bolted for the door. Just as he opened it, the Reverend called out: "Thom, please wait a moment."

With the Reverend but a few feet away, pretending not to hear was out of the question. Thom stopped in his tracks.

The Reverend approached. "I'm glad you came today." He gestured toward the dining room. "Please have a bite. In a few minutes I'll be free, and we can talk."

"Uh...thank you." Reluctantly Thom stepped into the dining room and poured himself some tea.

Soon after, with only a few stragglers remaining, the Reverend came Thom's way.

With time to prepare, Thom was ready, at least more so than before. "That was an inspiring message you delivered today."

"Why thank you."

Though it may have been his imagination, Thom thought he spotted a skeptical cast on the Reverend's face. Perhaps Thom's faraway look throughout the meeting had been evident. He was glad the Reverend accepted the compliment without pressing for specifics.

"I understand you're building a saltbox."

"Well...I'm trying. Of course, it'll be much smaller than yours. Not nearly so impressive."

"How far along are you?"

"I've laid the foundation, and I'm about to build an arch to support my chimney." Thom motioned toward the large hearth and fireplace. "Folks tell me that the arch buttressing your chimney is a masterpiece."

"I wouldn't go that far, but...would you like to see it?"

"I'd love to," said Thom, the unexpected offer eclipsing his desire to depart.

Reverend Bidwell led the way into the basement. Thom's jaw dropped the moment the arch came into view. Lofty expectations were dwarfed. He estimated the structure to be seven feet high and thirteen feet wide. An archway about Thom's height bisected the center. The passageway extended the entire depth of the structure, a distance that Thom judged at an unbelievable sixteen feet. The impressive home was big, but the rectangular stone edifice in the cellar could have supported far more than that which lay above. On either side of the archway, relatively flat stones were precisely laid, but the key to the support was the masterfully set wedged-shaped stones that occupied the curvature surrounding the opening, especially in the area of its apex. Each was wider at the top than the bottom. Tremendous lateral pressure pushing them together made the enormous weight of the chimney, fireplaces and surrounding structure seem a trifle.[56] Lessons from his mentor, complete with vectors explaining the forces behind the architectural concept that had emerged from the Roman Empire, popped into Thom's head. But they were a blur. Like the Romans, Thom understood nothing beyond the practical aspects of constructing an arch. When his mentor had detailed the physics behind the concept, Thom struggled to follow the theory. But he knew the pragmatics, and the paradigm that greeted his eyes was an invaluable instruction manual. "Incredible," he said, his eyes transfixed. He turned to Reverend Bidwell and repeated the word, "Incredible."

The master of oratory responded with an abashed shrug.

"Did you build this?"

"With help...considerable help." He gazed upward.

Around Tyringham, the Reverend, a Yale graduate, was renowned for his diverse talents. Like Thom's Boston mentor, the Reverend was regarded as a Renaissance man. Any doubts Thom harbored whether the reputation was deserved were dispelled by the arch. He said, "Do you mind if I examine it more closely?"

"Feel free."

Thom touched the stones, first delicately as if they were fragile flowers, and then more firmly. He slipped his fingers between the tiny spaces, imagining the huge forces pressing the wedge-shaped stones against one another. He noted the skill with which the horizontally laid stones on the sides had been dressed. He moved to the center and, awestruck, stared at the magnificent keystone. His decision to attend the meeting had proved worthwhile. He said, "Where did you learn to do this?"

"Books...college..." Reverend Bidwell looked upward. "And mainly from God."

Whether the Reverend was suggesting the arch was the product of divine guidance, Thom was unsure. He followed the Reverend upstairs. As they headed to the front door, the Reverend said, "I hope to see you at future meetings."

An hour earlier the possibility would have been unlikely, but given the preceding few minutes, Thom could no longer rule it out. Reverend Bidwell seemed a decent man and far more interesting than Thom had imagined. As for his sermons, Thom had heard too little to form a judgment. His qualms about organized religion remained strong, but if he were to give it a try, Tyringham's Congregationalist Church would be a good choice. A congregation that owed no allegiance to any other and afforded all members equal status was preferable to a church that was part of a huge hierarchical structure.

⟋ⳑⳑⳑⳑ⟍

A week had passed since Thom had attended the church meeting. Day by day he had diligently labored on the centerpiece of his home, the arch. With the image of the Reverend's masterpiece indelibly stamped in his mind, Thom's high standards elevated. Aided by Beartown Mountain's ample supply of limestone, for two days he stacked flat-layered stones on either side. Gradually he created the curved connection in the middle by means of wedge-shaped stones. When at last he arrived at the center, he pressed the final wedge into place. The key had been turned, and the archway, locked. Whatever the height and breadth of his chimney, Thom had no doubt the arch could shoulder the load.

73

He went over to his haversack and removed a slice of marbled bread. He would have preferred something more substantial, but it was all he had, having eaten his midday meal several hours earlier. He took the bread, along with his canteen, and seated himself on the wall of his fieldstone foundation. He felt the caress of the late afternoon sun as it slipped through the upper portion of trees whose leaves neared full growth. Eyes focused on his arch, a sense of the pride that the masons of Rome must have enjoyed centuries before engulfed him. The project was becoming a labor of love. From his canteen, filled with clear, thirst-quenching Konkapot water, he took a drink. He inhaled the fresh Berkshire air. The enormous physical undertaking, changing the face of the primeval domain, was showing signs of progress. Perhaps the equally difficult and, in some respects, more complex process of rebuilding his emotional life was taking a step forward as well. Experience from his days working in Boston had taught him that building a house included bumps in the road, but they were nothing more than bumps. Setbacks were also certain to accompany an ascent from the depths of a dark winter. Whether they would be minor snags or free falls back into the abyss was unclear. Such was the nature of paths traveled in virgin territory.

♒︎

"C'mon...You're going." Richard Thorn tugged at Thom's arm.

"Give me one good reason." Thom had already said *no* twice. "And don't tell me that it's my duty, because we both know folks will get along without me."

"Damn...if everyone had your attitude, there'd be no one at the town meetings."

"You know that's ridiculous. Most folks are eager to attend."

"Sometimes you're impossible."

Stubborn as he was, Thom conceded the point, but with satisfaction. Like so many of his rugged and individualistic New England neighbors, he persevered under trying conditions.

"With mules like you, Tyringham ought to make attendance at town meetings mandatory."

"That would be absurd. And I don't care that some towns have the asinine rule."

Richard heaved a sigh. "Okay, let me put it another way. As a friend, I'm asking you to go."

Richard had struck a chord that had Thom reconsidering.

"And more important, you need to get out and be with people...Why the look?"

"You were making progress appealing to me as a friend. Lecturing me on what I need to do for my own welfare won't work."

"Fine, ignore my last comment." He slipped an arm over Thom's shoulder. "As a favor to me, your friend...please, come to the town meeting."

Thom squelched the urge to mention that Richard's real motive was to get him out. "If it'll shut you up, I'll go."

"Damn, if—"

"I can change my mind."

Richard ran his fingers across sealed lips. He led the way outside the Albright home to their horses. They rode to the Hogshead. By the time they arrived, the booths around the outer rim, as well as tables and chairs in the middle, were packed. Extra benches in front of the bar were also full. A few seats remained on the benches along the front wall. Richard and Thom squeezed in. Many were enjoying a brew, and for some it was not their first.

"Can we have quiet?" Deacon William Hale, whose ancestors were among the first settlers in America,[57] rapped a mug on the bar that stood behind him. "Quiet!" He waited a moment and rapped his mug again. With others reiterating his call, the din subsided. "We have much to discuss, and many who wish to be heard. Accordingly, let me turn matters over to our brother and neighbor, the learned attorney Ezra Jenkins."

The portly, bald-crowned lawyer strode to the center of the bar. "First on our agenda is the matter of replacing our school."

"One was never enough anyway," yelled a man in a booth off to Thom's right.

"Oh yeah!" barked someone from the far side. "We did just fine back when Mrs. Hale and Whaples and Heath and the others kept school in their homes."[58]

"Pipe down...One at a time," bellowed Jenkins. "All you freeman and male inhabitants will have your turns.[59] But we'll do this in an orderly way." His flabby stomach overhanging his waistline, he moved his eyes over the throng as if underscoring his determination to maintain decorum. "Understand—we're not going to waste time debating the merits of having a school. For those who think otherwise, let me remind you that for more than a century, since 1647, the law of this colony has required that every community with more than fifty householders have a school where the catechism and reading, writing and arithmetic are taught."[60] The supercilious Jenkins, ever one to put his erudition on display, studied the gathering. "I recognize Amos Garfield."

Garfield stood up. "A number of us have been discussing the matter. Tyringham is growing. People have been settling from one end of town to the other—down near Brewer's mills in the south and all the way to the northern marshes in Hop Brook. Our town, six miles square, is too large for our children to meet in one place, especially during winter. A single schoolhouse requires them to travel distances that are excessive and dangerous. I propose that we build four schools laid out in equally proportioned districts."

The proposal drew outcries both positive and negative. Jenkins banged his mug on the bar. "Quiet. You'll have your turns." He pointed at Hiram Bates. "The floor is yours."

"Our learned attorney tells us we must have schools. Fine...but let the costs be paid by those with children."

"We live in a community—"

"Mr. Blake, please wait to be recognized."

Blake, already standing, shot an irritated hand into the air.

"Mr. Blake, proceed."

"As I was saying, living together in a community, we all must pay taxes for the common good. Our children must have adequate schools. Education is important. I make the point, although my wife and I have no children."

"Yet!" yelled Bates. "That's because you're newly married. Soon enough you'll have little ones. And you'll want single men like myself bearing the cost."

76

Individuals began calling out. Jenkins tried to regain order. Thom's mind wandered to the philosophical readings inspired by his Boston mentor, particularly Rousseau's "Social Contract." The curious approach to governing, people coming together and relinquishing freedoms in exchange for the benefits of civilization made sense, but it was not simple. And if complicated in a tiny rural locale like Tyringham, how would it work if thousands of people from diverse communities spread over a huge geographical domain tried to unite into a single society? In theory the concept was easy to embrace. From a practical perspective, it was as manageable as clouds drifting in the sky. Thom's musing continued until finally the men voted to have four one-room schoolhouses in districts of equal size.[61] The outcome was no shock. Most were married with children. They voted their interests. They voted their pocketbooks. Democracy was great, provided one was in the majority. Still it was far better than a Mother Country across the ocean arbitrarily imposing onerous rules and taxes.

"'Scuse me," said John Woodstone, before Jenkins had the opportunity to move to the next order of business. "Has anyone figured out how the fire at the old school started?"

"Sure as cows can't fly, the Indians did it," bellowed Orville Crane.

"You have proof?" said Jenkins.

A voice from the rear called out, "A couple of the youngsters, Janey Miller and the Clark boy, said they saw an Indian kid near the school in the days before the fire. Of course, given the remains—you all know the school was fried to a crisp—no one could tell how the blaze started. Coulda been a spark from hot coals or lightning or arson. Nobody knows."

"Maybe you don't," said Crane. "But I do. It was an Indian. And if ya don't believe me, ask one of our leadin' citizens, Deacon Hale, 'bout the killings in Stockbridge."

"What about that William?"

Hale got up. "Yes...I...uh did move my family away from Tyringham to Enfield, Connecticut back in '47, but that was two and a-half decades ago, and, anyway, I returned here three years later.[62] But even if the stories about the Indians were true then, it

77

doesn't mean they're responsible for the fire at our school. Keep in mind that they helped us in the French and Indian War."

"The good ones did," said Crane. "There are others I don't trust. And don't forget the Deerfield Massacre."

"Forget?" rang a voice from the back corner. "How could we? It happened nearly seventy years ago, before we were born."

The comment stirred a smattering of laughter.

"Go ahead. Make fun," yelled Crane. "But don't come cryin' to me when a Redskin scalps your family."

Jenkins gestured to his right. "Homer, you investigated the fire. Is there anything you can add?"

"Not really. Like Morgan said, the school got fried. As for the cause...sparks from the fireplace, arson, lightning or whatever...it's anyone's guess."

"Fine," said Jenkins. "Then let's move on to Reverend Bidwell's salary. As you know, he's expressed some concerns about arrears. Others have urged his salary be reduced."[63]

Orville Crane was back on his feet. "We should cut the Reverend's pay. Rich as he is, he don't need the money. His home proves that."

Thom doubted Crane would have been so brash had the Reverend, normally present at town meetings, not been away in Westfield for a few days.

"The Reverend's home and wealth are irrelevant to his salary," said Richard. "The fact he comes from a well-to-do family doesn't mean he shouldn't get what he was promised. Remember, he left an established community in Kinderhook, New York to help build ours. We should be grateful, not spiteful."

"That wuz more than twenty years ago," said Crane. "Anyway, it wuz his decision. No one forced him to move. But fine, ya wanna pay him what's due, be my guest...but goin' forward, he oughta get a cut."

Richard turned to Thom. "Crane's as hardheaded as the nails he makes."

"If only he were as sharp."

Richard smacked Thom on the back. The discussion continued. The matter, however, remained unresolved.

Apparently Reverend Bidwell would not soon receive his back pay. The town had swept the floor clean of the issue.

For another hour the meeting continued until finally Jenkins sought to bring it to a close.

"Excuse me," said Paul Cooper. "I believe we should discuss Parliament's intentions, including those affecting our colony's legislature."

"I hardly think that's the business of Tyringham."

A voice from the rear benches called out, "Since when do you decide who can be heard and on what matters?"

Arms folded over his portly torso, Jenkins glared at the heckler. "Ever since I was asked to preside."

Someone else yelled out, "But everyone is entitled to be heard."

Numerous others voiced the sentiment.

"Fine," said Jenkins. "If you want to go on until doomsday, so be it." He turned to Cooper. "Let's hear what you have to say."

Cooper stood up. "In recent months we've been hearing rumors that Parliament plans to limit the authority of our colony's Assembly. Apparently our dear governor, Thomas Hutchinson, supports the idea."

"And?" said Jenkins.

"And we don't like it."

"Mr. Cooper, isn't that a matter for the Assembly and the British government?"

From the far wall a voice bellowed. "Not when it affects our rights and lives!"

"Mr. Slade, I believe I asked Mr. Cooper." Jenkins laced the words with sarcasm. He turned to Cooper. "You referred to rumors. Don't you think you should get your facts straight?"

"He's got his facts straight," barked Slade.

"I see," said Jenkins. "I take it you have first-hand knowledge."

"As a matter of fact, I do. I read about it in the Boston Gazette last month."

Jenkins turned away from Slade. "Our friend read about it in the newspaper. He calls that first-hand knowledge." Jenkins turned back to Slade. "Others of us—moi, to be precise—were

79

present at the Assembly when Governor Hutchinson addressed the issue."

"Great—so give us your version," said Cooper.

"My version?" Jenkins indignant interrogative was peppered with condescension.

"Just tell us what happened," said Cooper.

Jenkins cleared his throat. "Governor Hutchinson is on our side."

The comment drew groans and catcalls.

Jenkins waited stoically. "The Governor needs to walk a fine line. He has the interests of our colony at heart, but he knows we need Britain's protection. Without it, we would fall victim to France or Spain, or even the Dutch."[64]

Thom found it hard to dismiss the familiar point. Given the opportunity, the powers of Europe would grab what they could in the western world.

"In January when Governor Hutchinson spoke to the Assembly, he indicated that either Parliament rules the colonies or they must be independent.[65] There is no middle ground."

"Why not?" said Slade. "Why can't we enjoy the same rights and privileges as the people of England?"

"Because we're a colony."

This time Thom found the lawyer's point less convincing. A pervasive buzz suggested that similar reservations were widespread.

"The Gazette claimed that Governor Hutchinson is more interested in protecting his personal position than ours," said Slade. "Anyway, it's unfair that we're ruled by Parliament's whim. The new Tea Act that went into effect on May 10th is a prime example."

"What's wrong with it?" said Jenkins. "It simply preserves the three-penny per pound import tax that's been in effect for six years."

"Sure," said Cooper. "One that was arbitrary from the outset. And one that gives the British East India Company a virtual monopoly over the sale of tea. They sell to us without paying the taxes imposed on our merchants. There's no way our merchants can compete."

"But the action was necessary or the East India Company would have gone bankrupt. In the past two years their stock plunged nearly fifty percent on the London exchange. The loss of revenue has the British Treasury in serious financial difficulties. They had to do something. Otherwise—"[66] Jenkins grabbed his mug and banged it on the bar as rising voices began to drown him out. "We'll have decorum, or I'll halt the meeting." He waited a moment until a semblance of order returned. He pointed at Peter Blake who was on his feet motioning for recognition. "Mr. Blake, the floor is yours."

"Like the Stamp Act in the sixties, it's 'taxation without representation.'"

The familiar phrase drew hoots of support, but also another rap of the lawyer's mug.

Thom heaved a sigh. Blake had missed the point. East India's monopoly on the tea market was the real danger. Tea merchants in the colonies had no way to compete. If Parliament could create a monopoly with tea, then why not any import?

Jenkins waited for the din to subside. "You decry the tax, but you'll slit your throats just to shave the tiniest whisker. Back in '67, Parliament hit us with the Townsend Acts, taxes on glass, paper, paint and lead, as well as tea. Our objections have eliminated all but the tax on tea. Let them save a little face. Recognize that we won the war."

Thom stood up with hand raised. He was determined to expose the fallacy in the argument of the smooth-tongued lawyer.

"Mr. Webster, you wish to be heard?"

"I do." Thom took a deep breath. "We...uh...here in Tyringham...and...uh for that matter, all of us colonists who live in the woodlands far from the ports of trade should be concerned."

"Concerned...you contend we should be concerned." The disdain on the lawyer's face was as biting as his tone. "Parliament enables us to buy tea from the East India Company at a reduced price, subject to a mere three-pence tax, and you act as if they struck us with the plague."

The comment drew some favorable cries. Jenkins did nothing to quell them. "Tell me, Mr. Webster, why should we be concerned?"

There was a time when a confident, well-read Thom would have responded with an articulate comeback, but crushed emotions and crippling self-doubts tangled a once talented tongue. Like tea from the Far East, self-assuredness was a foreign commodity. He said, "I...I just thought that maybe..." Nerves frazzled his brain. Logical thought succumbed amidst panic. For several interminable seconds he stood motionless, while the onlookers, abuzz throughout the meeting, drew silent. They afforded Thom their undivided attention. Confused and embarrassed, he sank down into his seat.

Across the way someone rose to carry the ball. Back and forth the debate continued. The details passed vacuously through Thom's ears, not that he cared. What mattered was that he had made a fool of himself, and he had done it in front of the entire community. For several minutes he sat with head bowed. When he finally looked up, he spotted Issac Winslow, Polly's father, seated near the front. In all likelihood the pillar of the community was applauding his decision denying Thom's request for Polly's hand. If only Richard had not dragged him to the meeting. But coming wasn't the problem. Democracy, that wonderfully egalitarian concept, had afforded Thom the opportunity to speak. If only he had not availed himself of that freedom.

Thom glanced at Issac Winslow again. The middle-aged gentleman provoked thoughts of his own father. Though far across the sea, the browbeater's influence was still at work. Since leaving England, Thom had learned many things. From jail to boatswain's assistant to worker in Boston, he had grown into adulthood. He had gained confidence, a whole lot, but not enough to vanquish the emotional shackles of his harsh childhood. Intimidation, compounded by a lost love, had subdued him.

82

The springtime sun had worked its magic. Timbers chopped in March, resting on a southerly slope, gradually dried. With the advent of June, logs were well seasoned. With the aid of Lodestone and Sarah Albright's wagon, Thom hauled the wood—oak and fir and maple and pine—down from Beartown Mountain to Captain Brewer's sawmill. Each of the first two days, Thom brought two loads. Beginning with the third day he reduced that to a single delivery, after which he brought a load of cut timbers fit for framing back to his site. Though he had promised only to furnish, not deliver, three red spruce, on the last three days he helped haul those trees to the mill. Whenever Thom gave his word, being equal to it was the least he did. Something extra was not uncommon. In that respect he was not unique. Integrity was commonplace among the folks of Tyringham. Brewer, despite being a shrewd businessman, was cut from that mold. The timbers he delivered to Thom were well trimmed.

Alongside his homesite, Thom laid out two felled pines parallel to one another. He stacked each load of cut boards across the pines where, following any rain, they could drip dry rather than rest on the wet ground. With the last of his timbers arranged, he stepped back and studied his excavated site and supply of lumber. As he often did, he closed his eyes, taking a moment to picture what was yet to be. He imagined the frame of his house rising up from the ground. His mind, as if capable of a journey through time, envisioned his completed home. Ebullience surged, but just briefly. Thom opened his eyes. He had come a long way, but the road ahead was far, far longer, and getting ahead of himself was foolhardy.

An urge to begin framing the structure inveigled him. Thom looked back over his shoulder off to the west. The sun still reigned well above the horizon. Three hours remained until the long days of June yielded to the darkness of night. He glanced at the wood again. Good sense prevented him from getting carried away. Soon enough a new morn would dawn.

# Chapter 6

THOM RAN THE BACK of his sleeve across his brow mopping away beads of perspiration. No doubt the temperature was hovering close to ninety degrees, and with the humidity high, summer was beginning to reveal its true colors. A few were complaining about the late-June heat, but not Thom. Seventy-five or eighty degrees would have been preferable, but compared to the dark, bitter days of winter when wind-driven snows coated faces with an icy mask, summertime heat was heavenly. Regardless, in the Berkshire highlands any swelters were short-lived.

"Take a gander at this," said Richard, who was examining one of several papers on the board outside the Hogshead. "It proves you were right." Richard made room for Thom to read the sheet, a resolution, dated March 12, 1773, bearing the seal of the Virginia House of Burgesses, appointing a committee of eleven to communicate with the other colonies about complaints against Great Britain.

"Right about what?" said Thom, as he contemplated what he had read. "And anyway, it's old news."

"Well...sure, it takes time for documents to travel from there to here. But that's not the point. The leaders of Virginia are concerned about what's happening here in Massachusetts, specifically Boston. If folks in Virginia think it's important, those of us in the hinterlands of Massachusetts have to as well. That was your point several weeks ago at the town meeting. Jenkins, browbeater that he is, turned a deaf ear.

Thom recalled the scene. His recollection differed, and to the extent it did, he preferred to leave it buried. Jenkins may have been a browbeater, but Thom's inability to convey his views had occasioned his downfall.

"You don't remember?" Richard waited a moment. "So, why the puss?"

"I recall, all too well. I opened my mouth and made a fool of myself."

"You did not!"

Thom looked his friend in the eye.

"Well...maybe you didn't give the best account of yourself, but that's not important. What matters is that you were right."

Thom contemplated the nicety, albeit unenthusiastically.

"C'mon...being right is more important than winning."

"Not when you're a defendant in a courtroom."

"Jesus!" Richard threw up his hands. "You were at a town meeting. You weren't a defendant. And don't give me a look."

Discretion kept Thom from pressing the futile argument. "Not to change the subject, but were you able to finish staining your barn yesterday?"

"I...uh...got sidetracked."

Thom waited, anticipating Richard would be forthcoming. When he wasn't, Thom said, "With what?"

"Uh...just a wagon that lost a wheel in one of the ruts on Smith Hill Road, not far from my house."

"Whose wagon?"

Richard hemmed and hawed.

"A damsel in distress, perhaps?" Waiting, again unproductive, amplified Thom's curiosity. "Who?"

"Uh...Polly...Polly Blake."

The response explained both Richard's chivalry and his reticence. "So, how did she look?"

"You really want to know?"

"I asked, didn't I?"

Richard heaved a sigh as he looked away. "C'mon, there's not a prettier woman this side of the Connecticut River."

"Sounds to me like you could fall for her."

"Jeze...That's not fair, not after you asked...And anyway, she's married."

"But if she weren't, you could."

Richard fidgeted with his tri-cornered hat. He remained mute.

The reaction erased the need for Thom to press the issue. Still there was no way he could blame Richard for finding Polly attractive, not given the pedestal on which Thom had placed her. He said, "I have to admit, you have excellent taste."

At the crack of dawn Thom was back to the security of his homesite. Having laid a granite foundation, the top of which was precisely dressed to provide a level base, he was primed to attack the next phase of his project, the wooden frame of his post and beam saltbox. The comfortable morning, ideal for work, would soon yield to the strong, mid-afternoon sun, but Thom, rife with enthusiasm and blessed with stamina, was equipped to labor through it.

All morning, with axe and hammer and chisels and knife, he hand hewed four eight-inch-square oak timbers, a pair to the length of twenty-three feet and a pair to the length of nineteen feet. At either end of the two longer pieces he chiseled away a small section, half the timbers' thickness, on their upper side. Relying on the indispensable Lodestone, along with ropes and small logs for leverage, together they pushed and pulled, tugged and dragged the two longer pieces atop his rock foundation, roughly a foot above ground level. He chiseled away carefully-measured sections at the ends of the two shorter timbers, again equal to one-half their thickness. With Lodestone and leverage he laid the shorter timbers on the rock foundation running from front to back, this time with the notched-out section to the bottom side. The timbers fit together like embraced lovers, forming a magnificent twenty-three by nineteen rectangular sill on which his home would rise.

Thom stepped back and admired his handiwork. He walked foursquare around the masterpiece. He gazed skyward. The blazing, early summer sun, still high, had shifted a bit to the west. It had to be past two. He had been working eight hours with no sustenance apart from an apple and occasional drinks from his canteen. He went to his haversack and pulled out his usual sandwich. Seated on the sill, he gobbled it down, all the time delighting in his work.

Soon enough he was back to the task. With hammer and chisel he carved a square mortise in each of the four corners of

86

the sill. Tenons he would carve at the bottom of each vertical post would fit into those mortises, locking the sill in place. Tired though he was, Thom hewed two more beams, along with the first of the joists that would support the floor of his house. Once the beams and joists were in place, the frame could begin to rise. The thought stirred a familiar, disquieting notion. Raising a frame required lots of hands. Neighbors always helped neighbors. But doing it alone was the paradigm of rugged individualism. Thom imagined the glorious feat. The image shattered amidst visions of a side of the frame crashing to earth. Common sense demanded he accept help. But could he? Would he?

⁂

From the front sill to the rear sill Thom placed his two eight-by-ten inch summer beams, separating them by sufficient space to more than allow his chimney to rise in the middle. He considered chamfering the edges but suppressed fastidious tendencies in favor of the need to move forward. One by one he began laying joists between and perpendicular to the summer beams. He was about to install another when the sound of a female voice calling his name drew his attention. He turned and saw Juliette Chandler, a basket in hand, coming up the hill.

"Morning, Miss Juliette." He glanced at the sky. "Afternoon...I guess."

"Tis...and please, it's simply Juliette."

"What brings you up here on the mountain?"

"I wanted to see how your house is coming along. That, and I thought you might enjoy a nice lunch." She stepped closer and gestured at her basket. "According to Sarah Albright, you've been working long hours."

"I hope she doesn't think I've been ignoring my chores."

"Not at all, though she can't imagine how you do both. She says you've been pushing yourself too hard. It got me to thinking—you could use a good afternoon meal."

"Mighty thoughtful, but I packed a lunch." Thom pointed at a boulder where his haversack sat. "Got it right over there."

She shook her head.

"What's the matter?"

"Nigh onto one o'clock, and you haven't eaten. Somebody better keep an eye on you." She gestured at the haversack. "What have you got?"

"Couple carrots and a jam sandwich."

"You call that a lunch?" She opened her basket. "In here is sliced venison, cinnamon apple sauce, sweet potatoes and mince pie." The look she gave him was an exclamation point.

"You've convinced me." Recollections of the day he had given her a ride home aboard Lodestone triggered thoughts of other more tantalizing delights. "My table here is none too fancy. That rock is the best I can do." He noted her smart polonaise gown and petticoats. The outfit, not atypical for a woman out and about in Tyringham, merited dining facilities better than he could offer.

"Before we eat, I'd like to see how your work is progressing."

They walked the short distance to the construction site.

"You did all this by yourself?"

He nodded.

"Impressive...very impressive. The foundation looks excellent."

She was the first to see what three months of arduous labor had produced. He was glad she had come.

"You have your floor plan in mind, I assume."

He nodded. "Two rooms in front." He gestured to his right. "A dining room here and over there (he motioned left), a combination parlor and bedroom. Across the entire back, a kitchen and buttery, along with some storage." He pointed near the center. "Right here, there'll be stairs leading to a loft. And who knows, once it's set, I might consider an addition across the back or side...or maybe, build a barn."

"Sounds like a lot for one person."

"I suppose but..."

"Enough about building. You must be starved."

He led the way to the boulder. She spread a small cloth over the center and served the meal, complete with a previously unmentioned jar of slightly fermented apple cider.

"It's a veritable feast. A far cry from my usual."

She poured the apple drink into two tin cups. "A toast to your new home." She tapped her cup to his.

He took several gulps before digging into his food. "It's as good...make that better than the Torchlight Tavern in Boston." Thom had sampled its savory fare shortly before moving to Tyringham. "You're a terrific cook."

A smile, but one tempered with abashment, etched her face.

The look, more apropos of a girl in her late teens, made the forty-something woman seem much younger than her years. It was as if the gap in their ages had been reversed, and Thom, the lion, was stalking a young, unsuspecting doe. And too, on what had been an empty stomach, the sweet, intoxicating libation was sparking a buzz. "You're very pretty."

She laughed.

Her reaction took him aback. A few words of thanks or a smile would not have surprised. A coquette's demure uneasiness would have been predictable. But she had effectively deflected his compliment. She was hardly flirtatious. She was not the Jezebel some proper women in Tyringham had labeled her. She was unassuming and natural. And damn, she was attractive.

They continued to dine with little conversation. But unlike the disconcerting silence spawned of faltering tongues, a comfortable silence prevailed. Still the mood was anomalous. It was as beguiling as it was halcyon. And indeed, Juliette Chandler was beguiling.

Thom was savoring his last bite of mince pie. Juliette said, "I've kept you from your work long enough."

"Not at all. You've served me this extraordinary meal, not to mention providing such wonderful company."

She packed up her basket with utensils and cups.

"I must repay your kindness."

"No need. It was my pleasure."

"Perhaps some task at your place could use a man's hand." His brain questioned his tongue. Between the demands of his house and chores at Sarah's, he was overburdened. How could he take on anything more? But accepting gifts and kindness without reciprocity was out of the question. And too, he wanted to see her again. "No doubt, there is something."

"Well...we'll see. But if so, you'd have to stay for dinner." She got up and started to leave.

He jumped up. "Thank you. Thank you so much for this wonderful surprise." He watched through the trees as she disappeared on the path to her home. He had misjudged Juliette Chandler. She was a fine woman. A very fine woman.

An icy chill draped the warm summer day. From the rear of the gathering, roughly half of Tyringham, Thom stared at the dark earth that surrounded his shoes. He had no desire to watch the pine box housing the body of the Miller boy lowered into the ground. Eight-year-old Jacob had been the third of the family's five remaining children. Just two years earlier, the Millers had lost a daughter to diphtheria. Thom found it hard to accept the illogic of such youthful deaths. Everyone was entitled to live, learn, do, love and procreate. Such was the nature of life, at least in Thom's mind.

Thom shut his eyes. Though lowered eyelids afforded an opaque mask, the scene remained crystal clear. The image of little Jacob lying motionless with hands folded across his chest was inescapable. Thom had spoken no more than a dozen words to the youngster while he was alive, and yet Thom felt he knew the boy well. Polite, indeed shy, he was a tintype of his father. Had he lived another decade, he would have been the strong silent type.

Thom shifted his feet several inches wider as Reverend Bidwell, extolling the youngster's short life, sought to comfort his grieving parents. The words passed through Thom's ears as easily as the gentle breeze drifted through vacuous space. Thom opened his eyes. He focused on the marks the hob nails and horseshoe heel protectors on the bottom of his shoes had left in the dirt. The next rainfall, or, likely sooner, the steps of others would obliterate the indentations. Against the vast eons of time, life was no less fleeting. Thom detested funerals. Where others found closure, solace and strength, Thom felt emptiness.

Reverend Bidwell uttered the final amen. The Millers led the way from the gravesite. Thom started to slip away.

"Sad...very sad," said Wendell Dinsmore.

"Very," said Thom. "He was a fine boy."

Dinsmore nodded. "Smallpox is the Devil's curse. If you ask me, it's as bad as that Black Plague that swept Europe in the fifteen hundreds."

"You're right," said Thom, recalling stories he had heard in Boston of how a smallpox epidemic had killed thousands a half-century earlier.

"Wasn't a month ago it got Harold Weaver...God rest his soul. I feel bad for Nancy, being a widow at thirty-one, what with six children. Can't be easy."

"I'm sure it isn't."

Dinsmore looked Thom in the eye. "You being single and all might wanna give her a thought."

*And I might not.*

"It'd be a fine deed, not to mention that she's a fine lookin' woman...Don't you think so?"

"Uh...yeah."

"Course ya might wanna wait till fall before callin' on her."

The last thing Thom wanted was Dinsmore starting a rumor that he planned to court the recently widowed woman. Admittedly she was attractive, but six children was more than Thom was prepared to face. He said, "I'm sure there are others who are better suited than I. And too, she needs much more time to grieve."

"Not so. She needs a husband." Dinsmore gestured at Reverend Bidwell. "When our good Reverend's wife Theodosia died, he married her cousin a year later. And when she died eleven years later, with children to raise, it wasn't no time before the Reverend married Ruth."[67] Dinsmore hesitated. "Yeah, if I recall right, the Bible says that when death robs the spouse of a good man or woman, the neighbor who marries the widow or widower doeth a good deed."

Despite little expertise when it came to the Bible, Thom doubted that such a scripture existed. He said, "When Nancy is ready, surely one of her neighbors will do that good deed."

With joists to support the floor in place, Thom was in his third day of cutting, hewing and trimming the lumber that would frame his house from sills to roof. Much of the work had already been done at Brewer's sawmill. Oak logs had been cut into fine timbers for the four vertical corner posts, as well as the girts that connected them. Fir trees had been turned into strips perfect for framing. But there was plenty to be done before a frame could be fashioned. Pieces had to be cut to precise lengths, including jambs and headers that would allow for installation of the front and rear doors and five windows, two in front and one each on the back and sides. Mortises and tenons and pins that would lock the timbers in place needed to be carved.

Diagrams, a product of the geometry his mentor had taught him in Boston, had been made and reviewed, but one major unknown, raising the frame, continued to loom. Thom had convinced himself, or at least he had tried, that with ropes and pulleys he could go it alone. Whether he and Lodestone would be up to the task would remain unknown until the moment of truth. Assuming he got the sides up, might they fall before they were interlocked? Thom believed he had a solution. Temporary corner braces nailed to the sills could keep everything in place until the adjacent side of the frame was up. The braces and nails could be removed and re-used once the sides were locked together. The concept was excellent. Pulling it off, another matter.

It was mid-morning when the sound of hoof beats, a rare interruption, drew Thom's focus from his work.

"Had to see your progress," said Richard, as he climbed down, tethering his horse to a small birch.

"Be my guest."

Richard ventured closer, his gaze traveling the fieldstone wall that framed the interior of the pit. "Nice work. A fair bit more than the eighteen-foot-square minimum. I know you told me, but how much exactly?"

"Twenty-three across the front by nineteen deep."

Richard circumnavigated the land bordering the excavation, pausing several times to survey the work. "Impressive arch," he said, as he completed the entire three hundred sixty degrees. "Not many around Tyringham that good."

"Reverend Bidwell's is a darn side bigger and more precise."

"That you dare compare it to the Reverend's proves my point."

The detail, one that had escaped Thom, was gratifying. Like Richard, who was standing back and evaluating the work, Thom became an observer, divorced from his intimate involvement. He liked what he saw.

"So, when would you like me to get the fellows together to raise the frame?"

"Well...I...thought I might do it myself."

"Sure, and I'm going to build a bridge across the Westfield River, just where it's the widest."

"No, I'm serious."

Richard studied Thom for a moment. "Damn. You are crazy."

Thom nodded. "Being around you, it was bound to rub off."

Anticipated repartee was not forthcoming. Richard displayed a reflective countenance. "You're building a nineteen by twenty-four saltbox. Right?"

"Nineteen by twenty-three."

"Fine...twenty-three." Richard groaned. "My point is: It's not a cabin with eight-foot studs. Yours will be..."

"Only eleven feet. Seven for the first floor, plus four additional where the loft meets the low point of the front roof."

"A frame eleven feet high...by twenty-three feet across." He eyed the nearby pile of lumber. "Heavy timbers and studs, and you intend to raise that yourself?"

"Well...I have Lodestone and ropes and—"

"And a screw loose."

Thom shrugged.

"If by chance you get one side of the frame up—not that it's going to happen—how in God's Kingdom do you plan to keep it in place while raising the next? A sky hook, maybe? And don't tell me Lodestone, because he can't be in two places at once."

Already with misgivings, Thom felt hard-pressed. "I plan to erect temporary corner braces when I put the first side up. I'll nail them to the frame."

"You plan to waste nails on temporary corner braces?"

"Of course not. I'll take them out and save them when I remove the braces. I really—"

"You really are crazy." Richard threw up his hands. "Enough, Mr. Martyr. Like it or not, your neighbors are gonna help raise your frame."

"Well...uh...okay, if my plan doesn't work."

"No—not okay!" Richard stared Thom in the eye. "Since moving here, how many times have you helped others raise a frame? Seven or eight? Maybe more. It's time your neighbors help you. And don't dare say another word."

The look on Richard's face, even more emphatic than his voice, told Thom the discussion had ended. The result was welcome. At best, raising the frame without help would entail enormous work and aggravation, and, at worst, a catastrophe. Visions of the heavy timbered skeleton crashing into his excavated pit had provoked trepidations. Though he had managed to push unnerving images aside, beneath the surface concerns gnawed. Stubbornness, a combination of pride and uncompromising independence, died hard. Were it not for Richard's persistence, Thom could not have overcome himself. Self-reliance was nice, but occasionally judgment was better. The concept was easy. Heeding it, a different story. Thom was conscious of the distinction.

⚭

Seated by the window in Sarah's parlor, Thom leaned back contemplating what he had read. He had completed the entire pamphlet, more than forty pages, and he had done it without resorting to the oil lantern that stood on the adjacent hutch. The extended daylight hours of early summer were welcome, almost as much as the felicitous weather. According to what he had heard, folks in the South took comfortable warmth for granted but complained incessantly about the heat. If they had to endure Tyringham's bitter winters, perhaps their view would have differed. Endless weeks of heat and humidity were hard to bear, but minus twenty was a helluva lot worse than ninety-five.

"You finish the pamphlet?" said Sarah, who, in the adjacent corner, was sewing a sampler with the Golden Rule.

"Yup...Read it front to back."

"So, whad'ya think?"

Thom stared at the cover page of Samuel Adam's handiwork, "The Rights of the Colonists." Since its publication the preceding fall, about six hundred copies had been spread throughout the colonies.[68] Thom's copy had come to Tyringham in early spring. Richard had given it to Thom the day before, but with instructions to return it after a couple of days because others were anxious to read it. "It makes sense. We in the colonies oughta have rights. Having Parliament fix rules with us having no say is outrageous."

"My sentiments exactly." Sarah lowered her sampler onto her lap. "For a time I wasn't sure. I figured that out here in the Berkshires it didn't matter. Just as our congregation is independent of other Congregationalist churches, I rationalized that our community is too. But when I heard Reverend Bidwell discuss it—his knowledge of the subject exceeds mine—my thinking changed. The way things stand, our property isn't secure. Parliament could pass legislation confiscating what we own. Though I have to admit, that's highly unlikely."

"Perhaps not as unlikely as you think. They tax us however they please. They take the best trees in our forests, simply by marking them with the King's arrow.[69] And they claim absolute authority over us. Anytime, day or night, they could search your home."

"I suppose...but out here...in Tyringham?" Sarah hesitated as she seemingly contemplated the possibility. "Do you think Governor Hutchinson might heed the pamphlet and grow more lenient toward us? Maybe even solicit Parliament to redress our concerns?"

Thom chuckled.

"Thomas Webster, are you laughing at me?"

"Sorry...and no. And no also to your earlier questions." Thom flipped to the final pages of the pamphlet and pointed at it. "Appended to his work, Sam Adams attached a communication from Governor Hutchinson. It's dated November 22, 1772. It proves our wonderful Governor has no intention of soliciting Parliament on our behalf. He claims he has the power to adjourn or even dissolve our General Assembly. He even denies the Assembly's right to meet regarding our grievances."[70]

"And I thought he was on our side. At least that's what Orville Crane told me."

"Crane? You must be kidding! The anvil he pounds in his blacksmith shop has more brains." A chuckle from Sarah had Thom contemplating the need to give credit to the witticism's author. But he could not recall which of his buddies merited recognition. "And speaking of an anvil, I could throw it farther than I trust him."

"You don't trust Orville?"

Were Thom not speaking to one of a few close confidants, he would have kept the sentiment to himself. Living in a rural town like Tyringham, he knew better than to badmouth folks. Reverend Bidwell preached against it because it was wrong. A more compelling reason counseled Thom to avoid the practice. A reputation as a backbiter was easily earned but impossible to shake. "Well, if you ask me, Orville has too many sympathies for our Mother Country. If push comes to shove, I wouldn't want him watching my back."

"You think our squabbles with England might spiral out of control?"

Thom had contemplated the issue loads of times. He had heard about the extremists in cities like Boston and Philadelphia and Virginia who were advocating independence, but they were far from the mainstream. He said, "I'm confident we'll find a peaceful solution to our disagreements. Regardless, we can't let Parliament take advantage of us."

Sarah's brow furrowed.

The look made it difficult for Thom to deny the folly of his response. "Well, it's important that we assert our rights." He thumbed through the pamphlet, searching for language that termed the status quo as *slavery*. The highly charged rhetoric would help make his point. Once he found the page, he said: "Here, in Appendix No. 1, 'The Message of the Town of

Boston to the Governor' says in regard to the Committee's Report:

*"This Report has spread an Alarm in all considerate persons who have heard of it in Town and Country; being viewed as tending to compleat the System of their Slavery, which originated in the House of Commons of Great Britain, assuming a Power and Authority to give and grant the Monies of the Colonists without their Consent, and against their Remonstrances."[71]*

"Sounds to me like more than just a cordial request," said Sarah.

Thom eyed the word *Slavery.* "Yes...I'd say you're right."

⁂

Thom arrived a full half-hour early, concealing himself among the woods that adjoined the pathway to the house. Only after numerous others had entered, did he approach the doorway. His discomfort was palpable.

"Hello, Thom. Glad to see you."

"Good morning, Reverend. It's...it's nice to be here." The disingenuous comment made Thom nervous. If an all-knowing God was listening, Thom had chosen an inopportune time and venue to lie. He hurried to the end seat in the last row of Reverend Bidwell's parlor, the same spot he had chosen the last time he had attended services. He looked around the room, studying the main timbers and the walls and ceiling they supported. Two reasons, both practical, had brought him to the meeting. One involved finding his place in the community; the other, construction.

In Tyringham, Protestants of all denominations enjoyed toleration, but genuine acceptance was reserved for Congregationalists. Like England where the 1689 Act of Toleration had granted freedom of worship to all Protestants, including dissenters such as Congregationalists,[72] Massachusetts

97

Bay's Congregationalist communities tolerated other Protestants, but not without subjecting them to political and social disabilities. Non-Protestants, such as Catholics, Jews and atheists, were not even tolerated.

Thom's religious views were ambiguous. They were also in flux. To the extent he was anything apart from secular, he was a Congregationalist, if only because of where he lived. At times he was unsure he even believed in God. He wanted to, but in his heart of hearts skepticism remained. His past readings of philosophy had an anomalous effect. Ontological arguments from the world's most brilliant minds purporting to prove God's existence had magnified his doubts. Their categorical conclusions were predicated upon assumptions of that which they sought to prove. On the other hand, disproving God's existence was equally futile. If there were no God, from whence did the universe, the world included, come? Thom had no answers. Regardless, he knew better than to express such thoughts to his Tyringham neighbors. Discretion counseled that he appear to share their Congregationalist beliefs.

Thom's second reason, his more important one, for attending the meeting was to re-examine the skillful manner in which the Reverend had built his home. In Tyringham one might find its equal, but nothing superior. The parlor, where Thom was seated, evidenced that fact. He eyed the marble slab at the base of the hearth. His skills included masonry, but shaping stone into a perfect, polished rectangle exceeded his proficiency and, perhaps, potential. He noted the closet door adjacent to the fireplace. During his last visit he had observed another in the dining room. His recollection was that its door opened to an access beneath the stairway leading to the upper level. Someone had told him there was even a third closet somewhere in the structure. Interesting as closets may have been, Thom was not including the uncommon indulgence in his plans, certainly not for the foreseeable future.[73]

People continued to file into the parlor. Most chose the front rows. Thom's gaze shifted to the planked floor. Self-consciousness, the need to be unobtrusive, was the motivation. Nevertheless, the broad wooden boards offered a welcome, albeit unplanned, thought-provoking distraction. Thom's mind delved beyond the stained surface. He speculated that the boards' concealed connections were loose-tongue joints.[74] In Boston Thom had installed that type of floor in several finer homes. It required that both boards be grooved and a thin strip of wood inserted into the grooves. Such quality workmanship was nice, but practicality dictated simpler half-lap joints when the time came to lay the floors of his saltbox.

The parlor was nearly full. Only a pair of seats immediately to Thom's left and a couple of single ones in the next to last row remained vacant. He was preparing for the long ordeal when Peter and Polly Blake entered. A moment later, with the chime of the exquisite English Brass Lantern clock on the wall, Reverend Bidwell followed the Blakes into the parlor. As the Reverend took his place behind his lectern desk, the Blakes hurried to the last row. Peter slid past Thom, and Polly followed, seating herself next to Thom.

"Good Sabbath," she said.

"And Good Sabbath to you," he whispered.

Reverend Bidwell began the meeting. Thom had promised himself that unlike the last time, he would heed the sermon. His best of intentions fell by the wayside. His heart thumped. His mind swirled. He interlocked his hands in his lap in an effort to contain a quiver. Earlier that morning he had consumed a mug of coffee. Caffeine could be the culprit, but Thom knew better. Coffee never agitated him. The better part of two years had passed since he had sat that close to Polly. He took several deep breaths, hoping to calm himself. The intoxicating scent of her perfume filled his head. The rosy fragrance was as familiar as ever.

Frozen in his seat, head facing forward, Thom's eyes drifted down to his left. Polly's polonaise gown, open in the front, revealed a silk petticoat. He moved his head a fraction of an inch. The petticoat appeared to change from gray to pink. The permuting hue was unmistakable. It was also familiar. Numerous evenings, Thom, with book in hand, had sat alongside Polly as she had adroitly woven, pink in the warp and gray in the weft. Or perhaps it was arsy varsy. No matter. Lost-love rekindled, bearing the same vibrant shades that shone beneath the flickering candlelight when first the petticoat was woven.

99

Thom closed his eyes, picturing Polly standing before him in her familiar dress. He took her into his arms. The embrace was magical. The imaginary world was exquisite. Fear that Reverend Bidwell would think him napping forced him to open his eyes. The light of day, unwelcome though it was, failed to quell his imagination. Beneath Polly's lovely face—blue eyes, soft lips, high cheekbones and radiant complexion—her inveigling curves beckoned. He wondered if, perhaps, beneath her whalebone-stiffened stay, she might be wearing the wooden busk, complete with two small hearts, that he had lovingly carved for her many fortnights earlier. She had no need to wear a busk. Her posture was impeccable. But as unlikely as it was that she had come without her busk, the possibility that Thom's meticulously sculpted handiwork stood vertically pressed adjacent to her heart was far more fanciful. One from England or a gift from Peter was likely. Still there was the chance that hidden away she had saved the one Thom had made.

Deep into Reverend Bidwell's sermon, Thom, his mind ever-focused on Polly, felt the touch of her sleeve against his. In all likelihood she was unaware of the contact. But there was the possibility, albeit remote, that she too was taken by the glorious connection. Perhaps Polly was as focused on him as he, on her. The idea was tantalizing, even if unrealistic.

On and on Reverend Bidwell continued. His protracted preaching extended beyond its usual exhausting length. From Thom's standpoint many there deserved the masochism. The very parishioners who complained of the endless tedium reproved anything shorter. At times what they deemed an acceptable maximum seemed shorter than their version of a satisfactory minimum. The appropriate length lay somewhere in the non-existent world of impossibility.

Regardless, Thom had no desire that the sermon end. He basked in his world of fantasy. From time to time, invoking his peripheral vision, barely turning his head, he stole the tiniest glance at Polly. From all appearances she was engrossed in the preaching. But the possibility remained that she, like him, was savoring their closeness. Common sense told Thom he was engaged in wishful thinking. He dismissed the reasoned appraisal, preferring to indulge in an enchanting scenario.

At long last, though arguably too soon for Thom, Reverend Bidwell concluded his sermon, his first of the day. The second was set for one o'clock, following the midday meal.[75]

"It's nice to see you, Thom," said Polly.

For an instant her eyes met his. He was glad she broke the ice. "You too." He was as nervous as the day when, at the age of twelve in England, he had knocked on the door of Martha Gray, his first foray into the world of courting.

Peter reached out and shook Thom's hand. "Good Sabbath."

"And Good Sabbath to you."

"Wonderful sermon," said Polly.

"It was indeed." Thom held his breath for fear his thoughts on the homily might be solicited.

"I knew forgiveness was important, but after listening to the Reverend, the reasons are more manifold that I had imagined." Polly's gaze begged a discerning response.

"They are indeed." The insipid reply, nearly a duplication of his words a moment earlier, echoed in Thom's ears. "I...uh...mean the reasons for forgiveness." Thom observed the tiniest furrow in Polly's brow. Whether it was real or a product of his own self-consciousness, he was unsure.

Polly turned to Peter. "Dear, we best be on our way, lest we be the last to arrive for the afternoon sermon." She looked back at Thom. "We'll look forward to seeing you later."

"Likewise." Before coming that morning Thom had left open the possibility he might skip the afternoon session. That alternative had vanished. He headed out to Lodestone and the sandwich packed in his haversack. He wandered into the woods where he dined in the solitary comfort of a fallen log.

When Thom returned to the Reverend's parlor, the seats were more than half-filled, mainly with those who had brought their lunch. His chosen seat on the far end of the back row was vacant, and he went directly there. Minutes later Polly and Peter returned. They took seats in the third row, roughly on a straight line from Thom to the Reverend's lectern. From time to time Thom surveyed the workmanship of the floor and ceiling and walls. Occasionally he directed his attention, both visually and mentally, to Reverend Bidwell. For the most part he remained transfixed on the shiny blond locks that draped the back of Polly's head. Unlike the morning when he had rhapsodized that her thoughts might be of him, he assumed her mind lay elsewhere. By the end of the afternoon he was struggling to push her out of his head, if only for a few moments. The harder he tried, the more her charms consumed him. Her grace and class and indefinable magnetism bedeviled.

# Chapter 7

SUNDAY NIGHT, IN HIS ROOM at the rear of Sarah's place, Thom climbed into his bed, a hay-stuffed linen resting on crisscrossed ropes connected to a wooden frame. All day his mind had remained focused on Polly. Judgment told him that such obsession could steer him back into prior doldrums. Unfortunately emotions superseded judgment. Common sense urged that any feelings she once had for him had long since faded; flickering hope beat back logic. Perhaps Polly had left the Sunday meeting as fixated on him as he on her. Deep down he knew the tantalizing idea was absurd. Thom pulled the coverlet up to his neck and closed his eyes. He could see Polly, her well-proportioned shape and beautiful, soft-skinned face. He gazed into her blue eyes as he took her into his arms and drew her close, his hand caressing her silky blond hair. Their lips met, tenderly at first, but quickly with increasing passion. The line between reality and fantasy blurred as Thom drifted closer and closer to sleep. Imagination became dream. And dream for all intents and purposes was reality.

They were in a meadow overlooking an unfamiliar lake, one even more idyllic than Brewer's Pond with its zigs and zags and mountain backdrop. The radiant summer sun shimmered on the tiny ripples, stirred by a pleasant breeze. Bodies enmeshed in a tight embrace, they sank down into the lush emerald grass. Rapture, certain and enduring, reigned. Passion, persistent ardor, prevailed.

A crack of thunder shook the earth. An ominous gloom painted the sky. Polly was no longer in Thom's arms. She was nowhere to be seen. The flowered lea turned rocky, its only vegetation, unsightly underbrush. Burrs, countless prickly brambles, enveloped Thom's clothes, piercing his skin. From beneath the ground, black, slimy mud bubbled forth. A gray mist materialized. Eden transmogrified into a grotesque landscape.

"Thomas," roared a voice as loud as the earlier thunder.

Thom looked around but saw nothing.

Again the voice bellowed, "Thomas!"

The ground shook. Trembling in fear, Thom elevated to his knees. Uncertain if he could maintain balance, he dared rise no further. He kept his palms to the shaking earth.

"You have sinned, Thomas. Broken the Commandments. Retribution is at hand!"

A bolt of lightning flashed, striking the ground but a few yards to Thom's left. Another crashed on his right.

"Who are you?" said Thom, his meek voice an apt mate to his cowering posture.

"Your Judge."

"God?" Thom hunched lower yet. "Are you God?"

"Nay, transgressor."

"Where am I?"

"Rest assured...not Heaven."

Fear gave way to panic. "Please...please don't say it's Hell."

"Not quite."

Good news, but only minimally. "Then where?"

"Half-way between Heaven and Hell."

"Am I..." Trembling lips struggled to utter the terrifying word. "Dead?"

"You're not alive." A diabolical laugh punctuated the response.

Thom's stomach knotted. He had more questions, but a gagged throat could enunciate nothing.

"You know why you're here?"

Thom managed a tiny shrug.

"You coveted another man's wife. Far worse, you committed adultery. What say you?"

Thom was without defense, not that his lips would have been up to the task if he had a justification.

"Your silence bespeaks your guilt." An extended pause ensued. "Is there nothing you can say on your behalf?"

"I...I'm sorry." The hollow retort echoed in Thom's head.

A huge bearded face, vaguely outlined, appeared in the fog. It hovered several yards above the ground. The manlike apparition, the same voice Thom had been hearing, spoke: "Sorry is far too lame."

Thom longed to do better but could not imagine how.

"I appreciate your attitude." The face smiled.

Thom had no idea what he had said or done to please the ghostly judge, but the clement reaction was welcome. "Thank you."

"Apparently you misunderstand." The voice turned caustic. "Otherwise you would not be thanking me. I like your attitude because it simplifies my task. With no defense your destination becomes inevitable."

Thom's stomach was in his throat. "You mean I'm...I'm bound for Hell?"

"Where else?" Again the diabolical laugh.

"Is it as bad as they say?"

"Worse...much, much worse."

A part of Thom wanted to know the details. Another was too afraid. "Is there a way...any way that I might get into Heaven?"

"Frankly, I doubt it, but...I suppose if you could convince me that you did enough good deeds while you were alive...you never know."

Even before Thom could search his brain for examples that would prove him worthy, the apparition continued. "You spent a year in jail in England, did you not?"

The apparition's familiarity with Thom's past was disconcerting. What else did the ghost know?

"You rarely attended Sunday services in Tyringham. True?"

"Yes, but I went yesterday."

"That you did. But there, in the face of God, rather than pray and cleanse yourself of your sins, you turned deaf ears and a closed mind to the messages you should have been embracing. Instead of worshipping the Lord, you coveted the same woman with whom you now have committed adultery. What say you to that?"

Thom swallowed hard. The apparition knew everything, even his innermost thoughts. No doubt the apparition could read his mind at that very moment. The revelation was suffocating. Thom was afraid to think, for fear the thought be hurled back into his face. He wanted to shut down his mind. It raced, its precipitate fits and starts, a darting hummingbird. For an instant Thom envisioned Hell, an abominable inferno of molten slime, ghastly demons and ubiquitous anguish. Polly appeared before his eyes. His brain, its usual stoic cool overwhelmed with feral rabidity, stripped Polly's clothes revealing her voluptuous charms. He wanted to erase the image. Instead he seized Polly and, consumed by carnal instincts, enveloped her.

A mien of disdain, coupled with a furious lateral shake of the apparition's head, dispelled any possibility that Thom's thoughts enjoyed privacy.

Thom longed to deny the sordid visions, but to do so would compound the disaster. A philosophical discussion Thom had shared with his mentor popped into his capricious brain. He could see the two of them standing over a book bearing a sketch of Voltaire, the man who abhorred restrictions on speech. "Rightly or wrongly," said his mentor, "that which is uttered aloud can be met with repercussions. Thought, however, is absolutely free from limitations." Thom deemed the point self-evident. But face to face with the apparition, the categorical imperative was evaporating. Bad enough that every notion that came into his head was transparent; worse yet, he would be held accountable. He gazed up at his judge. The nebulous figure, its countenance menacing, drifted closer. Thom tried to step back but could not budge. His hob-nailed shoes had transformed into iron boots, each as heavy as Crane's ponderous anvil. They were mired in an ever-rising, black quicksand. With all his might Thom struggled to lift one foot from the quagmire. It moved not an inch. He tried to pull the same leg out of the boot, but, molded to his leg, the iron sheath locked tighter yet. The ghost drew within a few feet. A brief pause, just long enough to sneer, and it began enveloping Thom. He struggled to thrash his arms over his head. Nothing moved. Not one iota. He was all but swallowed in the all-consuming terror when...suddenly he awoke.

A cold sweat draped his body. His limbs weighed heavy. He was out of breath, totally spent. Amidst the darkness, Thom lay there motionless, unsure if he was lying in bed or if he had been transported to Purgatory. He moved his fingers ever so slightly, allowing the tips to feel the surface of the hay-filled linen bed on which he slept. He took a deep breath. And then another. His stomach churned. He convinced himself he was still alive. He had been dreaming, but whether it was a product of his mind or precipitated by an outside force was unclear. He longed to believe the former, but physical effects, an enervated body, suggested otherwise.

The night still reigned, dawn's distance unknown. Thom couldn't fall back to sleep. A part of him wanted to, if only to escape persistent fear. Another part urged he stay awake, lest the horror return. For hours he lay there, fettered by the shackles of horrific ruminations.

⌒⥩⥩⤜

Light testifying to Monday morning's advent began creeping through Thom's lone window. Exhausted, he dragged himself from his bed and dressed. Compared to the night he had endured, the hardest day, fourteen hours clearing trees or lugging granite at his plot, was leisure. His bever, a bowl of porridge, a chunk of bread and a noggin of beer, was mindlessly consumed.[76] Except that it was gone, he was unsure he had eaten it. Efforts to shun the night's vivid images were fruitless.

Almost never did Thom look to the Bible for comfort or guidance, but desperate as he was, he was willing to imbibe any elixir that might accord relief. He went to the parlor shelf where Sarah kept the Holy Book. He flipped the pages. Forward and backward he shuffled, glancing at a few words here and a few words there, hoping to hit upon something to ease his mind. His limited familiarity with the Gospel, coupled with his chaotic state, rendered the process no better than random. After several minutes of searching, he came upon a passage in Matthew, 15:19-20: "For out of the heart come evil thoughts, murder, adultery, sexual immorality, theft, false testimony, slander. These are what make a man unclean." A second reading of the words exacerbated his angst. He shut the Bible and returned it

107

to the shelf. What lunacy possessed him to presume the holiest of books would condone his lecherous thoughts.

Thom headed outside, if only to distance himself from the sacred text. The early morning summer air was comfortable, not that he could appreciate it. Rather than ride Lodestone to his plot, he went on foot. He was willing to try any method of distraction. The strategy failed. Halfway there, he contemplated turning back. Perhaps Lodestone's company would help. He dismissed the idea knowing the only effective one, leaving his mind at home, was impossible.

Once he arrived at the site, he began fashioning the posts that would support his saltbox. Owing to lack of focus, the labor progressed slowly. Thoughts, his ability to deal with them, ebbed and flowed. At times he was vexed; others had him panicking. Around midday, while carving a mortise, an image of Polly, dressed in a Polonaise gown, its silver weft and pink warp glowing under a moonlit canvas, popped into his head. No sooner did the entrancing fantasy emerge than it transformed into a sojourn of terror. The apparition was back. Thom's heart raced. The beats bore no hint of amour. His stomach knotted again. Work halted. Bad enough that month after month, the ache of unrequited love had consumed him. Did it need to spawn a fountain of dread?

The rest of the day, Thom struggled with his ruminations. Soon night was at hand. He climbed into bed, determined to adopt a more comfortable bearing. He closed his eyes and pictured a carefree childhood day. He and a friend were racing up a hill in the English countryside. They giggled as they approached the crest. A stone bench graced the peak. A younger version of Polly sat on the bench. An instant later she vanished, replaced by the apparition.

Thom opened his eyes. Panic, its physical effects, seized him. What was supposed to be a period of revivification deteriorated into another sleepless night. The need to alleviate affliction grew desperate, but Thom was short on solutions. Daytime focus on work had proved ineffective. Pleasant thoughts had failed as well. For hours he anguished. Finally, in the wee hours a strategy emerged. He would pay Reverend Bidwell a visit. If anyone in Tyringham had a link to God, it was the Reverend. Thom weighed the possibility of speaking to the Reverend after the next Sunday meeting. The approach failed on two counts. Getting a moment alone with the spiritual leader would be difficult. More important, Thom could not endure five more torturous days and nights until Sunday.

Tuesday morning, Thom was up at dawn. After dressing and a quick bever, he killed more than an hour fixing a fence post next to Sarah's barn. He would have gone to the Reverend's home immediately, but arriving earlier than eight o'clock was indecorous, especially for one who rarely attended on Sundays. The moment the clock on Sarah's mantle struck eight, Thom saddled Lodestone and rode up Mount Hunger Road, past town center and the point where the Bidwell property adjoined Royal Hemlock Road. Thom walked Lodestone up near the house and tied him to an elm. Nerves taut, he approached the front door. Gingerly he tapped the brass lion-head knocker. A minute later Ruth answered.

"Good morning, Thomas."

That she knew his name was pleasing. "And good morning to you, Mrs. Bidwell."

She gestured into space. "Certainly is a fine day."

"I...I was wondering if I might speak with the Reverend."

"You'll find him out back in the garden."

Thom thanked her and went around the house where he found the Reverend on his knees pulling weeds. "Good morning, Reverend."

The clergyman looked up. "And a good one to you, Thomas."

"Can I give you a hand with those weeds?"

"Thanks, but I'm nearly done." He displayed a handful. "I suspect the Lord put them here to remind me to get down onto my knees and thank him for the bountiful crop. I try to do that while I'm weeding. Of course, sometimes I ask if he couldn't give birth to a few more tomatoes and carrots and a little less ragweed." The Reverend tossed his handful of weeds into a nearby pile and stood up. "It was nice to see you at Sunday's meeting."

"You delivered some wonderful messages." Thom told himself the comment was probably accurate, even if his concentration on Polly had prevented him from absorbing what had been said. The possibility that the Lord, as well as the Devil, might be monitoring his disingenuous discourse was disconcerting.

"I hope we'll see more of you in the future."

Despite anticipating the overture, Thom had not forged a satisfactory response. He said, "I'll try."

"Fair enough."

The Reverend's beneficence, letting him off the hook without demanding a commitment, was welcome. "I was wondering," said Thom, "if I might bother you with a personal matter."

"Always glad to listen."

"In part it has to do with the service Sunday."

"I hope nothing I said caused you consternation."

"Oh no. Not at all." Broaching the delicate subject was even harder than Thom had expected. "It's about me. I mean what I did or...should I say, shouldn't have done."

The Reverend put a hand on Thom's shoulder. "Let's go sit over there." He led the way to a bench that rested beneath a giant live oak. "When troubles get the better of me, it's a good place to think. It's also a wonderful place to talk...So, tell me. What is it you wanted to discuss?"

Thom took a deep breath. "This past Sunday...during the meeting...I was seated next to Polly Blake."

"On the end of the last row, if I recall."

The unexpected detail, the possibility that the observant clergyman had noticed more than Thom had realized, was unsettling.

"Relax. I don't keep track of who was seated where. Less familiar faces make more of an impression. But that's neither here nor there. Let's get back to your reason for coming today."

"It has to do with Polly. All through the meeting my thoughts were on her. To uh...tell the truth, I didn't hear much of what you said."

110

"Well, much as I hate to admit, there were others adrift in similar boats. As a matter of fact, I know of one in the second row. I shant mention his name, but he nodded off more than once." The Reverend hesitated, looking Thom in the eye. "But if I gather correctly, your concern relates more to Polly than not listening."

Thom nodded.

"Before she married Peter, you courted her, quite seriously, if I recall."

"I did. I asked for her hand, but her father refused."

"You still have feelings for her...don't you?"

Thom nodded, though with a lowered head. "For the rest of Sunday, my thoughts, very amorous ones, remained on Polly." Thom glanced at the Reverend, trying to gauge his assessment. The clergyman gave no hint. "Sunday night when I went to bed, my mind ran wild with fantastic images of the two of us together." The suggestive, though far from graphic disclosure, kept Thom from further eye contact. "In the middle of the night a horrific apparition visited me. Whether it was a nightmare or something more, I couldn't say. The ghost, perhaps an emissary from God or the Devil—if so, I don't know which—condemned my unchaste conduct."

"You didn't commit adultery, did you?"

"Oh no...except in my mind."

Reverend Bidwell nodded.

"The apparition said I was somewhere between Heaven and Hell, but likely bound for the latter. I awakened, exhausted, in a cold sweat. I couldn't get back to sleep. Yesterday, while I worked, the thoughts consumed me. They made for another dreadful night. I'm at my wits' end."

Reverend Bidwell gazed into space.

"What do you think?" Thom's tone, unlike his matter-of-fact words, begged that the Reverend embrace the plea for relief-giving dispensation.

"Before answering, let's talk about your actions. You coveted another man's wife. That violates the Commandments. But—and this is important—you did not commit adultery. Lusting is wrong, but acting on that lust, far, far worse." The Reverend leaned back. "Before telling you what I think, I'd like to hear your assessment."

"I...I don't know. That's why I'm here."

"I understand, but no doubt you've thought about it. As you said, it has consumed you."

Indeed Thom had numerous thoughts about the matter, some of which were inconsistent. Others were downright terrifying. His preference was that the Reverend gives his analysis first, but that wasn't going to happen. Thom took a deep breath. "I assume my conscience is behind my thoughts, but that begs the more important question: Is God, or even the Devil, at work in my conscience?"

"If you had to guess, what would you say?"

The question forced Thom to confront his worst fear. "My dreams, my images and thoughts, are so vivid, and the apparition, so real. It feels as though forces from without have invaded my mind."

"The conscience has a way of doing that. And unfortunately, to be candid, I don't know for sure." The learned clergyman hesitated, his mien pensive. "I've pondered the question, but...whether God gave us a conscience to discern right and wrong, or it's His means to communicate with each of us...I don't know."

The ambiguous response fell short of Thom's expectations, further yet from what he had hoped to hear. "Do you think the Devil might intrude into our thoughts too?"

The Reverend lowered his head, running his foot through loamy earth. "I can't say for sure. But based upon my study of the Bible, I believe he does. In the New Testament, Peter warns us: 'Be sober; be vigilant; because your adversary, the Devil, as a roaring lion, walketh about, seeking whom he may devour.'[77] I suspect that Satan uses many tricks to lure us into sin, and that includes encroaching on our thoughts." The Reverend looked up. "We speak of Heaven above." He lowered his gaze. "And Hell below. They're polar opposites, separated by an enormous divide. But great as that gulf is, it is also remarkably small."

On one level Thom understood the concept, but more than likely the Reverend's message demanded deeper analysis. "I'm uncertain what you're saying."

"Let me explain." The Reverend took a deep breath. "Suppose we start with *evil*. Turn the letters around, and what do you get?"

Thom silently mouthed the letters in reverse order: "*l-i-v-e*. It...it spells *live*," said Thom, unsure what to make of the seeming anomaly.

"Suppose we now look with hindsight, adding a *d* to the word *live*, giving us the word *lived*. Turn that around, and see what you get."

Once again, Thom recited the letters in reverse order, this time aloud: "*d-e-v-i-l*." The unexpected outcome prompted him to check a second time. Sure enough, the same result. He said, "It spells *Devil*."

The Reverend nodded.

"Is it a coincidence?"

"I'll let you answer that. But before you do, think about it. What are the chances?"

The logic was hard to deny. It had to be more than a coincidence. "I see your—" Thom clipped his tongue. No doubt there was more to the Reverend's point than Thom had discerned. "What are you telling me?"

"In everything we do, the Devil is nearby...lurking. Even when we are close to God, we must be wary. For example, consider your own circumstances. On Sunday you came to the meeting, God's holy service. There, in the midst of your supplications, the Devil tempted you. Your prayers were turned upside down into lust, a violation of one of God's fundamental Commandments."

Thom thought to ask how he should protect himself from the Devil's inveiglements, but the Reverend had already told him he needed to remain on guard, and, regardless, a more compelling question was on Thom's mind. "Considering my lust and dreams, my entire situation, what do you think?" Thom suspected his entreaty, a renewed plea to ease his distress, was obvious.

Reverend Bidwell placed a hand on Thom's shoulder. "Your lust went no further than the confines of your mind. You won the battle. Continue to resist temptation, and I'm confident you'll frustrate the Devil and win the war." He patted Thom on the back. "Sleep better tonight."

Thom smiled. Whether the Reverend's words were an expression of kindness rather than theological expertise didn't matter. They were what Thom longed to hear from the one man in Tyringham who knew best. Though less than a panacea, they helped calm stormy waves on a sea of rack and panic. "Thank you, Reverend," said Thom. "Thank you so very much."

⟨⟩

By six the following morning, Thom was back at his site fashioning the pieces that would frame his home. With the skill of an artisan he worked his knife and chisel and file. So fine was his craftsmanship that diverted thoughts could not thwart quality. Vex, however, they did. Thom was wrestling with two dreams, both in their own way monstrous. The one, a saltbox, was rife with formidable challenges from ground to chimney top and everywhere between. Familiar though he was with every facet of construction, building a home by himself was a new world. Nevertheless, experience, skill and indefatigable determination were winning the battle. The other dream demanded none of the capabilities he brought to his construction project. No expertise. No practice. Not even determination. Yet the struggle was the harder of the two. Yearnings for Polly's love had to be silenced. Allowing covetous desires to re-emerge was perilous. Moments of imaginary pleasure were forerunners of dire reverberations. Thanks to Reverend Bidwell's compassionate words, the intervening night, while not anxiety free, had been better than its predecessors. Full attention to his saltbox had become the formula or, perhaps more accurately, diversion by which Thom hoped to regain an even keel.

One by one, with unmitigated persistence, he fashioned the large oak vertical posts that would rise up at his saltbox's corners. At the bottom of each he carved a thick tenon which protruded for a perfect fit into the mortises he had chiseled into the sill. For each mortise and tenon, he made a hole and corresponding pin that would lock the connection in place. He fashioned horizontal girts that connected the posts, along with

114

the huge 8" X 10" summer beam, chamfered with stops, that would run through the center of the house from front to rear. He labeled the pieces, and, propping them onto rocks to avoid ground moisture, he set them adjacent to the side of the foundation where they would rise. Thom hewed the vertical studs of fir that would stretch from sill to girt and from girt to girt, including all those needed for three parallel frames. The first, the front, once raised, would be eleven feet tall. The second, which ran across the low back of the saltbox would be just five feet high. The third and last of the three parallel frames, the middle section, which like the front had a height of eleven feet, would be located six feet from the rear of the house. For two weeks, Sundays included, Thom labored, turning raw wood from the sawmill into what would frame the four sides of his home. Off and on, thoughts of Polly bubbled forth. Thom fought to suppress them, but their gnaw persisted. As he chipped and filed wooden surfaces, the ruminations rasped.

⁓⁕⁕⁕⁕⁓

Mid-August found Thom fashioning the two trusses for the roof. They needed to extend thirteen feet back from the front of the house. The rear portion of the roof, which would rest directly on the frame, required no separate support. Because Thom had opted to make the slope of his roof forty-five degrees, his trusses needed to be isosceles right triangles. While many preferred to build roofs that were less steep, with the heavy snows that fell in the Berkshires, greater slope helped reduce the ongoing accumulation and its resulting weight. Familiar principles told Thom that the height of each isosceles right triangular truss, its perpendicular bisector, was half its base or six and one-half feet. He had planned to employ a simple King Post Truss design, a triangle with a single vertical support in the center. Local knowledge deemed it sufficient for up to a sixteen-foot base, considerably more than the thirteen he would have. After hewing the timbers, he decided to add two oblique supports that fanned out from the center of the base to the

115

center of the roof supports. The resulting Queen Post (fan) Truss had considerably more strength.[78]

It was late afternoon on the 20th of August when Thom finished the trusses. He seated himself on the boulder where he generally ate his lunch. Squeezed between some puffy clouds in the southwestern sky, the filtered rays of the dipping sun were a lighthouse beacon on the construction site. Thom closed his eyes, the after-image of his handiwork fresh in his mind. The three vertical sections of the frame rose and, with pins pounded at mortises and tenons, the sections interlocked with enduring indestructibility. Thom took a deep breath. The trusses slipped into place. The framework of his home was more than a drawing on a piece of paper. It was more than piles of timbers and boards lying aimlessly on the ground. His dream of a saltbox, enhanced by his imagination, was becoming a reality. He inhaled again, pleased with his efforts. He no sooner began to exhale when from the depths of his insides the torment of love lost bubbled forth. The painful thought prompted him to open his eyes. The gap through which the sun had come was blocked. A dark cloud lay on the horizon. Good sense urged that Thom rejoice in what he had accomplished and push aside that which could not be. Unresolved emotions got in the way. Unlike sturdy timbers, good sense was powerless.

*⁓᷼᷼᷼⁓*

Temptation lured Thom to raise the frame of his house alone. He might have tried had he not given his promise to Richard. Going ahead without help would be a slap across the face of his closest friend. Thom was stubborn, extremely stubborn, but he was not stupid. Like so many young colonial men, he was independent, at times to a fault, but he valued friendship. The decision whether to construct the frame without help had been irrevocably made the day Richard had come to the site. Thom's word was his bond.

Days of hard work making the frame and trusses had proved rewarding. Nights had been more difficult. In the wee hours his thoughts bounced back and forth between the construction of

116

his home and images of Polly. Often the two coalesced. Thoughts of Polly living with him in the finished saltbox were seductive. Inevitably they spiraled him downward. Dreams of Polly were also frequent. Some were glorious, at least until he awakened. Others were less benign.

Saturday evening, his trusses completed the preceding day, Thom headed to the Hogshead. He tethered Lodestone to the rail outside and pushed through the big oak door.

"My, oh my...if it isn't the hermit of the hills," called out Orville Crane, voicing one of his vapid utterances.

Richard, who was seated at a table with Crane, along with several others, turned and pointed. "You look familiar. Don't I know you from somewhere?"

Thom shrugged. He often resorted to the gesture. More times than not, it reflected the lack of a comeback or unease, rather than the absence of a view.

"C'mon...pull up a chair," said George Whitaker. He motioned to the barmaid. "An ale for the stranger."

Thom took a seat next to Richard. Warm smiles lifted his spirits.

"So...how's the house coming?" said Paul Cooper.

"I finished the framing and trusses."

"Don't you dare tell me the frame is up."

Thom thought better of teasing his friend. "Relax. The sections are lying on the ground just waiting to be raised."

"That's what I like to hear." Richard looked to the others. "Monday morning we have a frame to raise. Everybody in?" He surveyed the faces. "George, I didn't hear a *yes* from you."

"Well...I had planned to weed my garden and harvest my corn."

"You can do it tomorrow afternoon," said Paul. "Anyway, it's no big deal. What have you got...twenty stalks?"

"More like thirty-five. And in case you didn't know, the morrow is the Sabbath."

"Suddenly our Yankee Trader is very religious." Crane, who was seated next to Whitaker, looked across the table. "He didn't have a problem one Sunday last month taking my bushels of potatoes for his used corn broom."

"I didn't hold a gun to your head, and maybe you forgot, but you're the one who came looking for the broom."

"Broom...potatoes...who really cares? You in or you out for Monday?" said Paul.

Whitaker, whose hand was at the base of his beard, squeezed the tangled mass. "I'll be there."

Richard called over to the booth across the way. "Woodstone, we're raising the frame on Thom's house Monday morning." He glanced back at his tablemates. "At seven?" Once he got their okay, he redirected himself to Woodstone. "Seven A.M. You and Deacon Hale wanna help us?"

Woodstone flashed a thumb up. "I'll bring my ropes and poles."

"Count me in," said Hale. "I'll check with Peter Blake and Johnny Whaples."

From the other side of the room Amos Garfield called out, "Me and Zac 'll be there too."

"Appreciate that." Richard turned back to his own table. "Between now and then, we'll round up a few others. The more the merrier." He looked at Thom. "You're all set."

"Thanks to all of you." Thom's voice nearly cracked. He grabbed his tankard and took a swallow. Rugged men didn't get misty-eyed. He kept the tankard to his lips long enough to regain composure. He had lent a helping hand to others. The role reversal, foreign, felt good. Independence was nice, but allowing pride to yield to a helping hand, especially one laden with camaraderie, was nicer yet.

⌒⁓ᑭᑭᑭᑭ⁓

Monday morning, the 20th of August, found Thom at his homesite shortly after sunrise. Over the weekend he had gone through the painstaking process of examining every piece and ensuring that all the mortises and tenons were perfect. Miscalculation would bring the frame raising to a halt. It would leave his helpers disgruntled as well. Once Thom had established that everything was in order, he numbered the pieces and laid them out with the utmost care. A barnwright, had Thom engaged one, would have done no less. Meticulous preparation, guaranteeing that the process went off without a hitch, was imperative.

Even with everything set, on the morning of the 20th, Thom checked again that all the wooden pins needed to lock the tenons into their corresponding mortises were conveniently stationed. The last minute preparations were admittedly obsessive. It reminded him of the day he had asked Polly's father for her hand in marriage. For more than an hour he had paced in the woods rehearsing what he would say. He wanted to come across just right. As it turned out, the words didn't matter. Rejection was a foregone conclusion. Thom wasn't superstitious, at least less than most of his Tyringham neighbors. Still he could not help worrying whether the resurgence of the unpleasant memory might be an omen. He gazed upward at the gray sky. The likelihood the sun would show itself seemed dim. High clouds were a doubled-edged sword. A shield from searing August heat was a blessing, but a thickening overcast could be the forerunner of unwelcome precipitation.

The night before, Thom had checked his 1753 edition of "Poor Richard's Almanack." Whether the publication had accurately predicted the weather twenty years earlier, Thom had no idea. Using it for later years made no sense, but it was Thom's only book, assuming one could term a pamphlet with thirty-two pages as such. Regardless, he thought of it that way. It put him on an even plane with the typical Tyringham family. They too had a single book, the Bible. The difference, however, Thom was far better read than the vast majority of his neighbors. Thom had acquired his copy of Poor Richard's Almanack several years earlier, and experience, perhaps colored by wishful thinking, had lent credence to its prognostications. The old Almanack indicated "rain" on the 16th of August, "then more" on the 18th, and "temperate, clear and fair" from the 21st through the 23rd.[79]

Shortly before seven, pounding hoof beats from the direction of the Albany-Boston Post Road interrupted Thom's musings. A dozen riders pulled up and tied their horses to trees at the base of the clearing. Thom met the group halfway.

Richard, at the forefront, waved a salute. "First brigade of the house raisers reporting for duty. Reinforcements due to arrive before the hour tolls."

The group headed to the site and began inspecting the layout. Within minutes another half-dozen joined them.

"Whad'ya think?" said Thom.

"No problem," said Deacon Hale. "Compared to the barn we raised for Dopson, this is a flummery. Heck, that monster musta been twice the height and length of this."

George Whitaker rolled his eyes. "The Deacon's a bit prone to exaggeration."

Hale gave Whitaker a look. "The Yankee Trader is so used to chiseling, he can't let conversation be."

Whitaker started to retort, but Peter Blake cut him off. "We're here to work, not bicker. I think we can agree this one is straightforward, a lot easier than Dopson's barn."

A queasy murmur stirred in the pit of Thom's stomach. Accepting the assistance of a former rival was unsettling. Of course, Peter, having prevailed, may not have viewed Thom as a rival. And perhaps he wasn't. Polly, wanting an easy way out, may have importuned her father's veto of Thom's marriage proposal. It was possible that Peter might have declined to help raise Thom's frame had he known how Thom had lusted when seated next to Polly at Sunday services.

"We gonna stand around, or we gonna get to work?" Richard turned to Thom. "You got your hammer ready. Cause you're among the pin men today."

Thom might have balked at the idea of escaping the heavy lifting, but he knew the local tradition. The one whose structure was being raised stood ready, along with others, to drive the pins into the mortises and tenons. It was an easy job, but it was also symbolic of responsibility. If down the road, things didn't hold together, the property owner would have to point a guilty finger at himself.

Once the front section of the frame was assembled on the ground, with ropes ready, a half dozen men pulled it up to a vertical position allowing the tenons at the bottom to slip into the mortises in the sills. Ropes connected to pegs driven into the ground held the section in place. Six men raised the middle section of the frame, fitting its tenons into the mortises of the sill, thirteen feet from the front. Three men raised the summer beam that ran seven feet above the sill from the center of the front frame to the center of the middle frame, while another six raised the two girts that connected the two sections at either end. The moment all the pieces were fitted together, four men, Thom included, hammered pins locking the three horizontal beams to the front and middle frame. Pins were pounded to secure the middle frame to the sill.

Two parallel sections stood tall. Movement toward or away from the front of the house was precluded. But the sections were still vulnerable to sway on a line parallel to the front. The addition of horizontal girts, supported by angled braces, connecting the sections together, eliminated the potential sway. The morning was young, and the entire center core, the support for much of the saltbox's weight, was in place.

"We've got it made," said Richard, as the entire group stepped back to admire their handiwork.

Several slapped Thom on the back. The hardest part of the task was behind them. The crew of six that had raised the front section moved to the rear frame. Raising it just five feet and adding girts at either end that connected to the middle section was easy. With three sections erect, men grabbed the studs that Thom had meticulously labeled and laid out. They fitted the stud's tenons into the appropriate mortises. By shortly after noon the exterior of the house was framed up to the level of the roof, complete with headers for the front and rear door, as well as headers and sills for the five windows, two in front and one each on the sides and rear.

Ten women, a combination of wives and daughters, among them Polly Blake, arrived with two rounds of beef, corn on the cob, mashed potatoes, cow-cumber pickles and plenty of peach cobbler. Tea and beer were in ample supply. Thom thanked each of the ladies, but when it came to Polly, his eyes met hers for no more than a fraction of a second. The men dined and sang and celebrated their efforts before returning to the task. The afternoon was easier than the morning. By four o'clock two trusses stood erect at either end of the frame, along with three intervening pairs of rafters, to support the roof. In less than a day the group had raised the frame, taking the structure from a foundation and sills to a completed shell.

"Thom, c'mon over here," said Paul Cooper. "Last pin. You do the honors."

Thom climbed the ladder that led to the final pin. The others laded their tin cups with beer, warm though it was. Thom slipped the wooden pin into the hole in the beam. He pounded it through the tenon that penetrated into the beam's mortise. It locked tightly.

"Hear... hear," shouted the throng with tin cups raised. "To Thom and his saltbox."

He descended the ladder. The moment he reached the bottom, Richard handed him a cup of beer. Thom downed it nonstop to rousing cheers. He gazed upward at the frame. "Thanks guys." He would have said more were he not wrestling with capricious emotions. One by one he shook the hands of his compatriots. He had misjudged some of his neighbors. At times Orville Crane was a buffoon, but the blacksmith offered his ample skills when needed. George Whitaker was a shrewd trader, but he was not above lending a helping hand, even if it required arm-twisting from others. And leading citizens like Deacon William Hale, descended from the colonies' first settlers,[80] and John Chadwick, one of the original founders of Tyringham,[81] had joined in the project. They had no need to help a relative newcomer like Thom. And Peter Blake was there as well. Peter had built his home before Thom had come to Tyringham. If it were being raised in 1773, Thom wondered if he could bring himself to join in. For Polly he would do anything, but helping Peter might be too painful.

Another cup of beer or two, and the men left. Last to depart was Richard.

"Looks like you're gonna have a fine house. Solid from top to bottom."

"Thanks to all of you."

Richard shook his head. "A good frame is the result of carefully measured, well-hewed timbers. The man who wields the chisels and knives determines that. Raising is an art, but whether a house is sturdy has been determined before the frame rises." He patted Thom on the back. "You, my friend, are a craftsman."

"Nice of you to say, but you fellows did one helluva job. And if it weren't for you, stubborn here would have tried to go it alone." Thom looked Richard in the eye. "You've already got your place, but down the road I intend to return the favor."

"As a matter of fact, I have a job for you. Muffin, my mule, is kinda old and worn out. Another year or so, when she needs replacement, I'll slip her yoke onto your neck." Richard slapped Thom on the back. "Not the best specimen of wagon-pulling beef I've seen, but...you'll do." He smiled broadly before pouring one last cupful of beer down his gullet.

Thom watched his pal ride off. He turned and gazed at his neatly framed saltbox. The sun, which had made an appearance, remained high enough to light all but the bottom. The big oak summer beams and girts were a rich brown. The fir studs and rafters sported a golden glow. Back in Boston, Thom had dreamed of one day building a home of his own. In the woodlands of Tyringham on Beartown Mountain, that dream was moving toward fruition. And too, he had visible evidence that Tyringham was a good place to live.

⌒⟋⟋⟍⟍⌒

When Thom had negotiated his deal with Captain Brewer for cutting his timbers, he had anticipated returning when the time came to build a chimney. Few people paid the Captain in cash. Wood and food were the most common items bartered, but there were often others, among them bricks. As a consequence, the Captain generally had a good supply. Thom had assumed the wily entrepreneur would be his source.

Months earlier Chester Buckley had moved to Tyringham and begun building a home. Buckley had the necessary timbers and bricks, as well as glass panes for the windows. But he abandoned the project and offered his materials for sale when, after his wife's father died suddenly, he and his wife moved into her father's home, a structure superior to what Buckley had planned. Thom seized the opportunity. He bought the unused bricks and windowpanes, all at a bargain.

123

The day after his frame was raised, Thom began building his chimney, including the two fireplaces that would face east and west on either side. He might have taken a day or two off from the project save two factors: he was compulsive, though he preferred to characterize it as conscientious; and time was imperative. He had determined how much needed to be done before winter. While exterior work could be continued after the advent of snow, that would be incredibly arduous. Thom was hardy, but he was also pragmatic. Until December, snow, if any, was generally short-lived. After that, typical daytime highs would begin dropping into the thirties and only get colder. A check of his twenty-year-old edition of Poor Richard's Almanack conformed to what he knew about November weather. The outdated publication indicated for the 4th, 5th and 6th of November, "then turns cold rain or snow." For the 12th and 13th, it said "pleasant."[82] Absurd though it was to rely on the old periodical, Thom forsook no opportunity to use the prized possession.

Chances were he had the best part of three months of acceptable weather. During that time he needed to build his chimney and install the roof and exterior siding in order that the structure was fully enclosed before the snow began to accumulate. In the winter months, with a fire roaring in the fireplace, he could work on the interior at a leisurely pace.

All week he laid bricks, backing them with a stone filling up to the top of each fireplace.[83] By Friday evening a chimney, complete with a fireplace on either side, one for each of the two front rooms, rose up from his fieldstone arch to a height just above the apex of his frame. Nearly a half-year had elapsed since he had begun work. He was ahead of schedule. His goal was both doable and in sight. He put his trowel away and headed for the Hogshead, confident he would find a number of the regulars there. Sure enough, seated to the right of the entranceway, were Richard Thorn, Paul Cooper, George Whitaker and Orville Crane.

"C'mon," said Cooper, motioning Thom to join them. "You're in time for supper." He pointed at the slate board next to the doorway. "The Bill of Fare is beef stew."

"Is it ever anything else?" said Whitaker.

"Last week we had hog stew," said Crane.

Whitaker shot him a look. "As if you can taste the difference." The Yankee Trader displayed a nauseated expression. "Heath has a damn nerve charging a shilling for his slop."

"Well, John Chadwick told me he paid a shilling and eight pence for stew in Boston last year."

Whitaker gave Crane another look before turning to the others. "Our iron-headed blacksmith compares Hogshead swill to the fare in a Boston tavern, a real establishment. The man has no—"

"Damn," said Richard, "instead of carrying on like a cackling goose, you could make room for Thom. But forget it." He grabbed a chair from an adjacent table, and, shifting his own, motioned Thom to sit.

"A shilling is hardly chicken feed, especially for a second-rate hotch-pot. Hell, that's a third of what they paid me for a day's work back when I helped build the branch roads to the north part of town."[84]

"That was twenty years ago," said Richard. "As for the price of the stew, if you don't like it, go home and eat with your wife and children."

"Well!" Whitaker folded his arms.

When Thom first came to Tyringham, more than once he went out of his way to assuage the Yankee Trader's wounded sensibilities, but repetitions of the sulking routine led Thom, like others, to ignore the behavior.

"A few weeks back, I seen you at the meeting at the Reverend's," said Crane. "You startin' to hear the word, Thom?"

Thom shrugged.

"Didn't get a chance to talk to you none. You disappeared during the midday break. That plus the wife gotta have more attention on Sundays."

"Sure," said Cooper, as he gestured with his mug at Crane. "Orville has to wear his petticoats."

Crane bristled.

"C'mon, Coop," said Richard. "You better lay off. We got one sullen mister here already."

"I'm not sullen," said Whitaker.

"And I won't get like him," said Crane. "Though I might pop my barrel-making friend in the mouth."

Though Thom knew that alcohol was behind the talk, Crane had a point. Unlike Whitaker, who was prone to moodiness, Crane was more apt to lash out.

"You never answered my question," said Crane. "You hearin' the word, Thom?"

"Well...the meeting was nice." With religion such an integral part of Tyringham life, Thom preferred to remain non-controversial, and the last thing he wanted was to publicize his private tête-à-tête with the Reverend regarding his dreams about Polly.

"So, you like the Reverend's sermons?"

"Yeah...I guess so."

Crane shook his head. "Just like the rest of the damn sheep. Afraid to tell the truth. Not me. The way I figure, God knows when ya lie. So, ya might as well spit out what you're thinkin'."

"Fine, then tell us," said Whitaker. "How would you rate the Reverend's sermons?"

"Look whose back from pouting," said Richard.

"Leave him be," said Crane. "And no, I don't care for his sermons."

"What's wrong with them?" snapped Whitaker.

"For starters, I got a hard time followin' 'em. Worse yet, he does two, one long and the other, longer."

Whitaker turned away from Crane. "Orville wants the Reverend to preach at his level. Simple enough so his anvil can understand."

Crane ground his teeth. "Just cause ya think you're smart, ain't no call to badmouth me. Anyway, at least I learned enough from my prayin' to know the Golden Rule. More than you can say."

"Touché," said Richard, pointing a finger at Whitaker.

With others laughing, Thom joined in. He wondered if the Yankee Trader might revert to sulking.

"Look...I ain't takin' nothin' away from the Reverend. I know he got his education at Yale College. But going on and on for hours with three-shilling words ain't the best. Few years back

126

I was in Northampton. I heard that George Whitefield fellow preach.[85] That man put on a helluva show. Jumped around and shouted, all the while convertin' the sinners." Crane looked around the table. "Any of you fellas ever seen him?"

Thom nodded.

"Where'd you see him?" said Cooper.

"In Boston, at the Commons. About four or five years ago...not long before he died. He drew a crowd of ten thousand, at least that's what folks claimed. He never used a single note."

"I heard he drew more when he preached in Philadelphia, supposedly the biggest gathering in the history of the colonies." Cooper took a gulp of his brew.

Richard turned to Thom. "So, whad'ya think of him?"

"Orville's right. He put on a helluva show. Worked the crowd into a veritable frenzy, but one that drove many to silence." Though the description accurately reflected Thom's recollection, the seeming contradiction prompted him to add, "If that makes any sense."

"But what did you think?"

A decade earlier in England, Thom would have voiced controversial views without hesitation, but a loner with a criminal record recovering from a long bout of the doldrums, he was reticent. He said, "Whitefield was interesting, but personally...I didn't buy into his *new light* preaching with its highly emotional appeal." Thom paused just long enough to verify that his comments fit the mainstream of traditionally Congregationalist Tyringham. "The evangelical idea of accepting Jesus and suddenly being reborn understandably has great appeal. Just like that, a sinner with years spent on a path to damnation is on the road to salvation. If you ask me, it seems too easy."

"Exactly my sentiments," said Whitaker. "That whole Great Awakening, the born-again evangelical stuff, was a bad scene. The good news: the fad—I'd lay odds it's just that—seems to be fading. Unfortunately, like a smallpox epidemic, it had to get worse before it ran its course."

"Just whad'ya mean by that?" said Crane.

Controversy had been stirred, but Thom didn't care because he was not at the center. Whitaker and Crane were welcome to debate the proper path to salvation.

"I'll tell you what I mean." Whitaker folded his arms, a familiar signal that he was about to talk down to Crane. "In the early part of the epidemic—excuse me, I meant movement—you had men like Jonathan Edwards.[86] At least he was a scholar. Matter of fact, for a time he was President of Princeton University."

"Big deal," said Crane. "What about him?"

Whitaker gave Crane a look before turning to the others. "The anvil can't tell when someone is giving credence to his argument." He heaved a sigh. "Anyway, as I was saying before I was rudely interrupted, at least Edwards studied before he preached. I heard him at Northampton when he delivered his legendary 'Sinners in the Hands of an Angry God' sermon."

A quick mental calculation had Thom doubting whether Whitaker had witnessed the renowned oratory. The Yankee peddler, who was in his early forties, would have been barely a teen when the preaching had occurred.

"Much as I disagreed with Edwards' claims that salvation comes from total subordination to God's grace rather than good deeds, his preaching had strains of logic. His ability to stir fear with his threats of eternal damnation made him both effective and dangerous. Whitefield, on the other hand, simply rants and raves with fire and brimstone. A charlatan, if ever I saw one."

"What the hell is that...somethin' ya find in a mirror?" Crane, his brew assisting, laughed raucously.

"Orville gets a kick out of showing his ignorance."

The exchange of jibes, not uncommon for the Yankee Trader and the blacksmith, amused Thom. Remarkably, Whitaker's hauteur sometimes turned him into the bigger fool.

"I understand why Orville prefers the likes of Whitefield to our own Reverend Bidwell," said Whitaker. "Shouts with simple solutions fit him far better than reason. No doubt Orville also prefers the easy way." Whitaker turned to Crane. "Right, Orville?"

"Hey, if it gets me where I wanna go, I say okay. 'Course, I don't get why you buy into Reverend Bidwell's stuff about us bein' bound for damnation 'less we do enough good deeds. Seems to me that a fox like you, flimflammin' your neighbors, would be thrilled to get born again."

"Who you accusing of flimflamming? Folks come to me looking to trade, not the other way around. And when it comes to your *new light*, born-again hero, George Whitefield, do you know where he got his training, Orville?"

Crane shrugged.

"In his father's tavern in England. That's right. He's a barroom rabble-rouser with no education. You know what Connecticut does with his kind? They strapped a muzzle on his mouth. They've got a law barring itinerants like Whitefield from preaching on the streets. Our General Assembly ought to do it too."

"Sure," said Cooper. "Just like our ancestors did in England. Steal away free speech."

Whitaker glared at the barrel maker. A moment later, when the barmaid delivered a large trough of stew, he snarled, "That took long enough!"

"Just because you're angry, don't take it out on Mary," said Richard.

"I wasn't and...forget it." He waved his tankard at Mary. "Bring us another round." Along with the others, he dug his spoon into the trough. After a single mouthful, he said, "Now you see what I mean!"

Thom didn't, and other blank faces revealed he was not alone.

"The damn stew...and I use the term loosely." He looked around the table. "Heath calls this watered-down garbage *beef stew*. He's gotta be kidding. There's not enough meat in here for...whatever. And what's here...is mystery meat."

"If you don't like it," said Cooper, "don't eat it."

"What—and starve?" Whitaker gestured at Thom. "You're awfully quiet, Webster. What do you think of the stew?"

Thom shrugged.

"See," said Whitaker.

"Give him a chance to speak," said Richard.

"Well...it's not like Sarah's...but it's edible."

"Edible!" Whitaker shook his head. "You guys have no clue when it comes to food. That's why Heath is able to get away with slop like this."

129

Thom took another spoonful. Good? Not really. But good enough, especially with a ravenous hunger. Regardless, it was a helluva lot more palatable than Whitaker's disposition.

Quiet occupied the table for several minutes as the five men ate, Whitaker consuming as much as anyone. They were near the bottom of the trough when Thom felt a tap from behind.

"Aren't you Thomas Webster?"

Thom turned to see a slim fellow in his twenties standing behind him. "Yes...but I don't recognize you."

"Not surprising, but I remember you."

"Well, since you obviously have the better of me, you'll have to refresh me where we met."

"We didn't actually meet."

Thom studied the stranger but was unable to make a connection. "So, how is it that you know me?"

"Southampton...England. About nine, maybe ten years ago."

A knot gripped Thom's stomach.

"Something wrong, Thom?" said Richard.

Thom shook his head, but sensed that facial tension contradicted the gesture.

"Who are you?" said Richard.

"Me?...Nobody...just a guy who drives a wagon for folks that want stuff taken here or there. Stopped on my way from Sheffield to Boston."

"So, how do you know Thom?"

"He spent time in jail in Southampton while I was doing repairs there."

"Is it true...what the fellow says, Thom?" said Whitaker.

Thom swallowed hard. He had hoped that by crossing the Atlantic to the colonies, he could bury his unseemly past. He had contemplated how to address the issue if and when it arose. He lacked an answer. A wish that the matter would never come up was all he had, and that wish had just been squelched. He looked around the table. Everyone was awaiting his response. He said, "I spent time in jail in England...about a year."

"What for?" said Whitaker.

Thom doubted Richard would have pressed him. Paul Cooper was also the type to respect his privacy. But not the Yankee Trader. Regardless, if Whitaker hadn't pursued it,

Crane would have. Thom said, "I assaulted a fellow, but with what I considered legitimate cause."

"The court in Southampton didn't see it that way." The stranger laughed.

Thom lowered his head. His self-serving declaration flew in the face of the time he had served. Additional protestations would provide more fuel for gossiping vultures like Whitaker and Crane.

"Let me guess," said Crane. "You came to America to hide your past."

Thom shrugged. The implicit admission seemed preferable to a futile attempt at an explanation.

Whitaker turned to the stranger. "You got more details?"

"Not really." He chuckled.

"Why you laughing?" said Whitaker.

"Oh...I was recalling when I was patching the hallway at the jail. From behind the bars the prisoners constantly complained to me. Basically they had two gripes: lousy food and claims of innocence. From what I could tell, the first was true, but not the second. Of course, I didn't take their word on either. The guards said the food was garbage. As to whether they belonged behind bars, I believed the judges and juries, not the jailbirds." The stranger looked at Thom. "Appears you're doin' fine now. Glad things are workin' out." He glanced at the pendulum clock that hung on the far wall. "About time I get a move on. Supposed to meet with a fellow by the name of Captain Brewer down at his mill." He patted Thom on the back. "Been real nice seein' you."

*Can't say the same*, thought Thom, as the stranger disappeared out the door.

"So, give us your side of the story," said Whitaker.

"Keep your nose to yourself!" said Richard. "If and when Thom has something to say, he'll let you know."

Whitaker glared. "I merely wanted to give him a chance to clear his reputation."

Richard returned the look. "I know exactly what you were doing. Mind your own business!"

"Well!" Whitaker proceeded to grumble inaudibly.

131

Richard looked around the table. "Apart from the five of us, no one around here knows about Thom's past. Let's keep it that way."

"Won't matter," said Whitaker. "Not after that fellow visits Brewer's mill. Plum pudding to a cow-cumber pickle, the word's gonna spread."

Whitaker had a point. But Thom would have given much longer odds—mincemeat pies, a half-dozen of them, to one lousy pickle—that neither Whitaker, nor Crane would keep their mouths shut.

# Chapter 8

WITH HIS LAND YIELDING an ample supply of wood and stone, nails were the biggest expense of Thom's saltbox. In recent weeks he had wrestled with the idea of fashioning his own. He had calculated how many he needed and extrapolated their total cost: six-penny nails, two inches long, what he needed mostly, were six pence per hundred, while four-penny nails, a half-inch shorter, were four pence per hundred. Most folks got them from Orville Crane, but now and again, a frugal, self-sufficient soul forged his own. Walter Barnaby had his own iron swage block with holes of various sizes into which a fired nail could be inserted and the head hammered into shape.[87] Others borrowed the swage block or, more accurately, rented it in exchange for a few pounds of nails. The idea was good, at least in theory, but where could Thom build a fire hot enough to melt iron? Sarah's fireplaces were doubtful, and even if they worked, asking her to turn her parlor or dining room into a nail-making factory was out of the question. And there was another complication. If Thom sidetracked himself with nailmaking, his ability to enclose his house before winter would be jeopardized. Relying on Crane, who could fashion nails faster, would leave Thom free to continue work at his site.

Thom mounted Lodestone and rode past Brewer's Pond to Crane's place, not far from the Konkapot River. He found the blacksmith in his barn.

"Afternoon to you, Orville."

"And a fine one at that." The muscular smithy poked his head out of the structure and glanced up at the sky. "Not many left before the snow flies." He refocused on Thom. "How you doin' with your house?"

"It's coming along. Soon I'll be ready to install the doors. That's why I'm here. I need two sets of hinges and six staples for the bolts."

"Ya goin' with H hinges or the H&L?"[88]

"H&L."

"Just what I suggest. The extra metal strip on the door gives better support." Crane pointed at a sample on the wall. "I make seven and nine inch."

"Nines for the front...and sevens...No, make it two sets of nines. Both doors will get plenty of use." Rarely rash, the last minute turnabout surprised Thom. He rationalized that creatures of habit, like himself, needed occasional spontaneity, lest they become too predictable. He said, "In addition to the six staples, I'll also need nails."

A smile draped Crane's face. And why not? He was about to do some serious business. "What size ya want?"

"Six-penny." Thom held his index finger and thumb a couple inches apart. "I'm going with the extra length so I can clinch them. For the roof I'll need four-penny."

"Good choices. Clinching pays in the long run. Better lasting." Crane grabbed a nail. "You want Rosehead? They're the same price."

"Yeah...I guess."

"So, how many ya need?"

Experience had taught Thom that flooring, roofing and siding required about four hundred nails per one hundred square feet. In addition to 437 square feet of flooring, he had approximately 750 of sides to clapboard, 400 to roof, making a total of nearly 1600 square feet. Altogether he needed sixty-four hundred nails. He said, "I need forty-eight hundred of the six-penny and sixteen hundred of the four-penny."[89]

"Yeah, I recollect from when we raised your frame that it wuz more than eighteen-foot square, the town's minimum. Refresh me on the size."

"Twenty-three by nineteen."

"Nice...especially for a single fellow." He moved to a nearby table where he grabbed a quill pen and paper. He scribbled briefly before muttering just loud enough for Thom to hear. "Yup, sixty-four hundred sounds like a good number." He jotted some more notes and resumed muttering. "Forty-eight hundred at six pence per hundred...that's six times forty-eight...is two hundred eighty-eight pence. Plus sixteen hundred at four pence per hundred...is sixteen times four...is sixty-four pence. Let's see...altogether that comes to three hundred fifty-two pence." He went back to writing, mumbling as he did. A minute later he said, "That equals one pound, plus one hundred twelve pence...or, let's see, exactly one pound, nine shillings and four pence." He walked back over to Thom and displayed the calculation. He said, "Altogether it'll cost ya one pound, ten shillings. That includes a shilling for the door hinges and staples. I dropped the four pence, nice guy that I am."

Thom had done the arithmetic and, with the exception of the door hardware, knew the cost.

"Ya got that kind of money?"

"Yeah...if I dig deep." Thom had no desire to reveal his assets, especially to a blabbermouth.

Crane folded his arms and gazed off into space. "That rockin' chair ya made for Sarah is right nice. Might like one. Plus I could do with a writin' table like what she's got in her parlor."

The idea of bartering for furniture was enticing, but a Queen Anne Secretary, likely beyond Thom's skills, would exceed a fair trade, especially when coupled with a rocker. He laughed.

"What's so funny?" said Crane.

"What I suspect you're thinking." The indignation that greeted Thom's eyes had him re-evaluating the matter. Crane's demands were unreasonable, but killing the trade was foolhardy. "Tell you what: I could make you a writing desk...a very simple one. I'm talking flat-topped, straight-legged and no drawers...and it would be walnut."

"Walnut?" An unenthusiastic groan ensued.

The hardwoods already available on Thom's land would burden him with no additional cost. "You want mahogany...imported wood, you provide it."

"What size we talkin', not that I like what you're offerin'."

Thom spread his hands apart. "Oh...thirty inches wide and...and twenty deep."

Crane shook his head. "Nah...you want the nails and hardware, I'll take my one pound, ten shillings. With that kind of money, I suspect I could buy a rocker and desk and maybe have a couple shillings left over."[90]

Thom wanted to barter, but bidding against himself was a trap. He said, "That chair I made for Sarah is awfully nice. Come over and try it. It'll change your mind."

"Already did. Proud as she was of it, she insisted when I brought her the kettle I made for her a couple months back." Crane pawed at his chin. "Ya throw in a three-legged stool to go with the rocker and desk, and I'll make your nails."

"And my door hardware?"

Crane groaned. "Yeah, your door hardware."

"Let's shake on it." Thom started to extend his hand but stopped. "Understand—I won't be able to deliver your furniture until sometime in the winter."

"No problem. I'll keep your nails till then."

"You gotta be kidding. I need the nails to enclose my house."

"Fine. Deliver the furniture and ya get your nails."

Thom struggled to contain exasperation. "C'mon, you know full well that between now and the end of November, I gotta enclose my house from the elements. After that I'll make your furniture."

A scowl on his face, Crane looked away.

"What's the matter?"

"How do I know that once ya got my nails ya won't welsh?"

The question took Thom aback. All his life his word had been his bond. His handshake, once given, became a promise fulfilled. "What do you mean—welsh?"

"Exactly what I said. You ain't no saint." Crane looked Thom in the eye. "Ya didn't serve time for nuttin'."

"It had nothing to do with my word. I've never broken that."

"Maybe so, but sixty-four hundred nails ain't bird feed. I need security."

A law allowing a contractor or materialman to file a mechanic's lien for an unpaid bill would have provided the security Crane was demanding, but Massachusetts, unlike some colonies, had no such law. And Thom had no solution.

"Earlier ya hinted ya had the money to pay for the nails. Tell ya what. Give me a pound and ten shillings to hold, and as soon as you deliver the desk and chair and stool, I'll give you back your dough. Fair enough?"

Thom ground his teeth. He forced himself to swallow pride. "I'd want it in writing that you'll return my money when I deliver the furniture."

Crane pointed a finger. "Now who's the distrustin' one?"

"What do you expect after the way you've treated me?"

A look of disgust came over Crane. "Fine, ya want it in writin'. I'll put it in writin'...not that we're alike. Only one of us did time."

Thom did a slow burn, as pride, its inhibiting force, tempted him to turn and walk. Judgment overcame emotions. "We have a deal?" He extended his hand.

Crane shook it. "I'll sign your damn paper when ya bring the money."

"Fine!" Thom's tone contradicted the agreeable word. He untied Lodestone and climbed aboard. The deal, nails and hardware in exchange for a desk, rocker and stool, was a decent one. Regardless, Thom was anything but pleased.

⚬⚬⚬⚬⚬

Eight o'clock the following morning, Thom returned to the home of Orville Crane with one pound, ten shillings. Crane signed a note guaranteeing the return of the money upon delivery of the furniture. Immediate delivery of two thousand six-penny nails that Crane had on hand ameliorated Thom's ire and enabled him to begin work on the roof of his saltbox. For the better part of the ensuing four weeks, with the exception of Sundays, which Thom reserved for chores at Sarah's, he labored. He applied hand hewn, white oak boards to the roof and overlapped them with pine shingles, eight inches broad and twelve inches long. In Boston he had used more durable shingles of northern white cedar, but the long-lasting lumber, prevalent in swampy areas, was not among the hardwoods and softwoods common to the Berkshires. Like others in the wilderness, Thom made do with what was available.

Days after the autumnal equinox, Thom had finished the roof. Ahead of the schedule that would enable him to complete a fully enclosed shell in advance of the snowy season, he had every reason to take a break, if not for a day or so, at least the remainder of the day. Instead he immediately began hewing the oak clapboards that would side his house. The possibility he might be compulsive stirred ambivalence, but censorious thoughts were fleeting. In Congregationalist Massachusetts, with its strong work ethic, only a ne'er-do-well would disparage dedication.

Leaves had already begun to hint that the fall spectacular was near. Maples tinged with red and gold and lobster shell, and oaks painted with rust and brown, along with beige pine needles that dotted the ground, attested to the glorious palette that soon would drape the landscape. Cool days with temperatures rising no higher than the low sixties, a far cry from the dog days that had prevailed weeks earlier, enabled Thom to work harder than ever. Months of strenuous lifting and hauling and hacking and sawing had toned his muscles and increased his stamina.

"Webster!"

The shout of his name turned his head. He spotted Richard guiding his dapple gray up the hill.

"For a moment I thought you were deaf."

"What are you talking about?"

"I called your name three times before you finally reacted."

"Pounding away, breeze in my ears, I kinda get lost in my work."

Richard tied his horse to a nearby tree. "I was afraid you had vanished from the face of the earth."

"I've been working." He gestured at the house. "Gotta enclose it before the snow flies."

"So, you can't spare a few hours now and then...a Friday evening maybe? It's not like winter is imminent." Richard gave Thom the eye. "Let me guess. It's the time you served in England. The disclosures at the Hogshead have turned you into a hermit."

Thom looked away. For months he had been pushing himself. True, he couldn't dawdle, but he could afford a few hours each week. Others with large families to house and feed managed to reserve Sunday, the Sabbath, for the Lord. Much as Thom hated to admit it, his house had become an excuse to avoid facing his friends and neighbors. Work had become a crutch. Although the preceding winter's despondency, the need to escape himself, had diminished, he remained holed up in a saltbox frame, trying to hide from the outside world.

"It is the time in jail." Richard leaned around and forced eye contact. "Big deal. You had a problem on the other side of the Atlantic. It's in the past."

"Is it?" said Thom. "Folks here don't take to jailbirds."

"C'mon...this is a new world. Look at Georgia, Oglethorpe's colony. They welcome debtors there."

"Maybe I should move to Georgia. I'd fit right in." Thom shook his head. "Folks in Massachusetts, especially out here in the mountains, are mighty traditional. Criminals are about as popular as rattlesnakes."

"You're blowing it out of proportion." He grabbed Thom's arm and tugged. "Mister, you're coming with me to the Hogshead. No ifs, ands or buts."

Thom might have resisted were Richard's resolve not obvious. Ten minutes later they arrived at the tavern. Motivated by a desire to stay in the background, not gentility, Thom reached for the door, allowing Richard to enter first.

"Over there, against the wall," said Richard. He motioned toward a booth occupied by Orville Crane and Ezra Jenkins.

A quick glance forced Thom to concur. The alternatives, joining men twice Thom's age or strangers stopping on the long road from Albany to Boston, had no appeal.

As Richard and Thom passed through the center of the room, Polly's father, Issac Winslow, who was seated with Deacon Hale, looked up. "Hello there, Thom."

"Good evening, Mr. Winslow." Thom would have preferred to slip by unnoticed. The possibility that Winslow had heard about his stint in jail made him self-conscious. Thom told himself he was overreacting. Logic failed to quell uneasiness.

Crane and Jenkins slid over as Richard and Thom approached. Richard seated himself next to Jenkins, while Thom took the spot adjacent to Crane.

"You have to try the flip," said Jenkins. "Along with the usual hot cider and beer, it's got spiced rum and eggs. Heath's food may be slop, but now and again he delivers a mean drink. Even the bigwigs from Boston would have to salute this stuff." He took a gulp and then motioned the barmaid for two more.

Crane jabbed Thom in the side. "The way you've disappeared, I thought ya might be back behind bars."

Thom's stomach, already tense, knotted. Evidence substantiating his earlier concern had been immediate. Chances were most of Tyringham knew about his criminal record.

"Ignore him," said Jenkins. "Orville's just being himself. That plus he's downed two mugs of flip."

"No big deal," said Thom, pretending to be unaffected.

"How's your house coming?" said Jenkins.

"The roof's on. Once I finish clapboarding the sides and add the shingles, the exterior will be set."

"Do you plan to move in for the winter?"

"Haven't decided for sure." Thom anticipated he would spend part of the winter boarding with Sarah. Hints she had dropped made it clear she hoped he would stay. He wanted to accommodate her.

The barmaid brought Richard and Thom their flips. Amidst a potpourri of small talk, they imbibed. A second round, and Thom grew more relaxed.

"Some months back at the town meeting," said Jenkins, "you seemed concerned about the tax on tea. Now that you've had a chance to mull it over, any change in your view?"

Images, reminders of the scene where Thom had sunk down into his seat unable to enunciate his thoughts, stirred. Were the flips not suppressing inhibitions, he might have remained mute. Instead he said, "It's not about the three-pence tax."

"Oh really?" said Jenkins with a furrowing brow. "Please, enlighten us poor mortals, what is it about?"

"East India's monopoly."

Jenkins leaned back, folding his arms over his ample stomach. "East India's monopoly. Is that so?"

"Yup...that's so," said Thom, armed with alcohol's emboldening power. "Under the Tea Act, East India can export straight from its warehouses to its agents here. Our merchants, even those who smuggle tea, can't compete, especially if East India chops its prices. Faster than a jackrabbit snatches carrots from a garden, they could drive our colonial merchants out of business. What's to say—"

140

"It's—"

"Ezra, for once keep your trap shut!" barked Richard. "Thom's making sense. So, let him finish." He motioned Thom to continue.

"Very simply—if Parliament can grant East India a monopoly with tea, what's to prevent them from doing it with any commodity? Our merchants won't be able to compete, and once they're out of business, the monopolists can jack prices sky high." Thom looked Jenkins in the eye. "As I said, it's not about a three-pence tax. It's about Parliament subjecting us to a ruinous monopoly. It's about the survival of our colonial economy."

"Damn it," said Hale from the adjacent table. "I've been listening, and you're right, Thom. A fellow from Sheffield claimed this was about more than a tax, but I didn't get it. I do now." Hale called to several others. "Come over here. I want you to listen to Thom. He's got some important thoughts about East India and their tea."

As a half-dozen converged around the table, Richard whispered, "When Deacon Hale tells folks to listen, they do."

Thom, with the full support of the flips, reiterated what he had said. His message was well received by the congregation. A moment later the barmaid delivered another mug. Thom took in a satisfying swallow.

⁓⁓⁓

Fresh from a full day at his homesite, Thom stepped through Sarah's back door. The heavenly aroma of baked delicacies filled the air. What exactly Sarah had made, Thom wasn't sure, but brown bread, a couple of pies and baked beans were good bets. Every week Sarah burned dry wood in the brick beehive oven until the bricks were fiery hot. She brushed out the ashes, shut the chimney's draught, and laded the oven with ready-to-be-baked delights. Hints of cinnamon, apple, nutmeg, blackberry, maple, pumpkin—the list was long—transformed her home into an aromatic Eden.

"Glad you're back early," said Sarah. "We have company for dinner."

141

"Who?"

"A couple from Albany. They're on their way home from Boston and need a place for the night."

That strangers would be staying was no surprise. Like people throughout the colonies, folks in Tyringham often invited visitors into their homes, and no one was more welcoming than Sarah. Whereas most homes in Tyringham had large families residing in cramped quarters, Sarah lived comfortably. Even with Thom boarding in the downstairs bedroom, with two more upstairs, there was always one free.

Thom washed up and joined Sarah, along with the visitors, at the dining room table. "Thom Webster," he said, extending his right hand. "Please...don't get up."

The man did anyway. "William Acre." The robust gentleman, about forty, shook Thom's hand before gesturing to the woman seated across the way. "This is my wife Rachel."

"Pleased to meet you, Ma'am." Thom seated himself at the end of the table farthest from the kitchen, leaving the place at the opposite end for Sarah.

Ordinarily supper was a light meal, but whenever there was company, Sarah outdid herself. A glazed Holland board-cloth covered her Hepplewhite style table. Though only a copy of the noted English cabinetmaker's work, for a Tyringham home, where a three-foot wide board laid across two trestles was the standard, it was impressive.[91] At each of the four place settings sat a heavy pewter charger, polished with horsetail rush from the nearby marsh,[92] along with a silver knife, spoon and split-spoon. The last, a three-tongued utensil, which had been gaining popularity across the Atlantic, had begun to make inroads in the colonies. Sarah, always the gracious hostess, delighted in providing company with a fashionably tasteful table.

Sarah brought a large wooden bowl of pottage, a mixture of carrots, sallats, cow cumber and cabbage, doused with sweetened vergi.[93] After delivering a healthy serving to each place, she fetched a warm loaf of Indian cornbread. William Acre was already enjoying a tankard of Santa Cruz rum and his wife, a noggin of homemade blackberry cordial. Thom, thirsty from a long day, opted for cider beer.

They no sooner finished the pottage than Sarah delivered a large platter of mutton, followed by two bowls, one of parsnips and the other, corn. Conversation remained light, even through second helpings. Thom had barely cleared the dishes when Sarah brought out a fruitcake, along with an apple pie made from the apples of two trees her late husband had planted adjacent to their vegetable garden. She heated a teakettle on the crane that swung from the fireplace. Reluctantly she permitted Rachel to distribute the pewter saucers and wooden noggins for the beverage. Once served and maple syrup sweetened to individual taste, Sarah reseated herself.[94]

"Mighty good," said William, following a sip of his brew. "I understand the East India Company is shipping six hundred thousand pounds of tea, part to Boston and the rest to New York, Philadelphia and Charleston. Heck of a lot."

"Sure is," said Thom.

"I hear it stirred up a hornet's nest here in Massachusetts."

The comment about the politically charged issue piqued Thom's curiosity. "You mean because East India has a monopoly on the tea market?"

"Well, folks are worked up about that. But I was referring to the actions of your governor, that Hutchinson fellow."

"You mean the Hutchinson letters, the ones Sam Adams published, encouraging Parliament to get tougher with the colonies?"

"Uh...more than that."

Thom waited for details. None were forthcoming. "Seems you know something I don't."

"You folks aren't partial to the Governor...distant relations or something?" He glanced at Sarah.

She shook her head. A moment later she fetched the teakettle. The spoon that lay in William's saucer indicated he desired more tea. His wife's spoon, in her cup, confirmed she had consumed enough.[95]

William turned to Thom. "I don't know your politics and don't want to offend, especially with the kind hospitality, but what I've heard doesn't speak well of East India or your Governor."

"They enjoy no sympathies here. I assure you," said Thom, his curiosity wheedling him to avoid circumspect habits. "So...feel free to speak."

William glanced at his wife, who nodded ever so slightly. He said, "While in Boston, we heard that two of Governor Hutchinson's sons, along with his nephew, are consignees of East India's shipment there."[96]

"That no good—" Thom clipped his tongue before the expletive spilled forth in the presence of company.

"And to make matters worse," said William, "I understand they're all members of a firm in which Hutchinson is a partner."[97]

Thom's jaw clenched. "Not only is our dear Governor two-faced, apparently he's corrupt as well." Thom eyed his spoon standing tall in his cup. He didn't want a refill. No amount of maple syrup could make it sweet enough to drink. Had Thom known about the Governor's conduct sooner, he would have skipped his first cup. The beverage had fed the pockets of East India and the Governor, not to mention the three-pence tax for Great Britain.

~~~

October in the Berkshire Mountains was decidedly fickle. Temperatures were known to sneak past seventy, but snow flurries were also possible. As Thom installed white pine clapboards on the sides of his saltbox, the month was benign. His sawn boards of varied length, generally five to six feet, about seven inches wide and an inch thick, were planed smooth on their exposed exterior side. Armed with Crane's second installment of nails, twenty-eight hundred, Thom attached the clapboards from bottom to top, each succeeding layer overlapping the last. At the bottom he began with a lap of more than four inches and exposure of less than three. As he worked his way upward, he decreased the lap and increased the exposure by a fraction of an inch. The technique, which he had learned from his Boston mentor, reduced the number of clapboards required while giving maximum protection where it was needed most, toward the bottom. It also created the illusion of greater height. Thom carved a notch into the end of every board. He cut each at an angle so it overlapped and fit the notch of the next board forming a weather-tight scarf joint.[98]

Clapboarding experience in Boston had made him efficient. Still the process was more arduous than he had anticipated. Fashioning and installing his five windows, two in the front and one each on the sides and back, slowed him down. In his original design all the windows were double-hung 6X6, but the bricks and glass he had gotten from Chester Buckley's abandoned construction included only fifty-one panes. Five 6X6 windows would have required a minimum of sixty panes, assuming no breakage. Thom opted to do the front and sides. He covered the window frame in the rear with boards. The following summer would be soon enough to install panes there.

October had but a few days remaining when Thom nailed the last of the pine clapboards to his saltbox. From foundation to roof, the structure was complete, save for the doors. He still had about three hours of light in the ever-shortening days. But daylight was not the issue. He lacked the hardware. He called it a day.

*⸏⸏⸏⸏⸏*

Thom was up with the sun, but with the calendar deeper into autumn, dawn was arriving later and later. By eight o'clock he had dressed himself, consumed his bever and was arriving at Orville Crane's place. As he tethered Lodestone to a small tree, he could hear the banging of the blacksmith's hammer. Thom went directly to the barn.

"Morning, Orville."

"I guess," he growled. He continued to pound.

Thom waited. The blacksmith failed to look up. "Did I get you at a bad time?"

"Ah, don't pay me no mind. Just havin' one of them lousy mornings. That bumblin' son of mine, Elmer, spilled ink all over my good breeches. Damn things are ruined."

145

"Maybe you could dye them black?"

Crane glared. "If I wanted 'em black, I woulda had Hannah dye the cloth that way before she sewed 'em."

Hannah should soak you in black dye. Thom bit his tongue.

"I oughta have the rest of your nails, the last sixteen hundred, in another week. In the meantime, I got the hardware for your doors, the hinges and staples." Crane went over to a bench by the far wall, returning moments later. "Two sets of nine-inch hinges, along with six iron staples. 'Course, if ya ask me, doors are a lot classier, not to mention safer, with latches. But...ya want staples...ya got staples."

"I'm trying to keep my costs down."

"Jeze, it ain't like ya gotta do it on the cheap. Unlike me, ya ain't got a half-dozen mouths to feed. And I know ya got the money, 'cause I'm holdin' yours. Well...sorta."

"What do you mean—sorta?"

"I used it to buy stuff."

"You what?"

"Ya heard me. And don't get ornery." Crane pointed a finger. "I coulda made ya pay cash money for the nails. Instead I took your IOU."

"Took my IOU? The hell you did! You made me deposit a pound and ten shillings as security. And apparently your memory isn't too good. You're the one who suggested the trade for furniture."

"Yeah, and if ya gave it to me then and there, we woulda been done. As for your lousy money, you'll get it when ya deliver the stuff. Give me two weeks notice."

"Two weeks. That wasn't part of the deal."

"Jeezum...if I knew ya wuz gonna be a damn crab, I woulda sent ya elsewhere for your stinkin' nails."

*You double-dealing snake.* Thom did all he could to keep the vituperation from his lips. "Fine, I'll give you two weeks notice before I deliver the furniture."

"So...how soon can I expect delivery?"

"Early in the winter. I'll let you know two weeks before the stuff is ready."

"Ya mean to tell me you've been makin' all this fuss, and I gotta wait the best part of two months." Crane punctuated the comment with a protracted groan.

Thom gazed at the blacksmith in disbelief. Reminding the arrogant buffoon that he had received and spent cash money sufficient to cover the nails and hardware was useless. Crane was too dumb to comprehend anything inconsistent with his own self-righteous utterings. Thom picked up his hinges and staples and started to march away.

"Least ya could do is be civil."

Thom glanced back over his shoulder. "Good day, Orville." The moment Thom's head turned forward, he muttered under his breath, "You crummy bastard." He untied Lodestone and rode off to his homesite.

Mounting the doors on the hinges was easy. To each he added a wooden handle. Inside both the front and rear doors he installed three iron staples, one on each doorframe and two on each of the doors. He slipped wooden bars through the staples and tested their operation. They were adequate, at least for the time being.

Thom stood on a board he laid across the joists that would support the floor of his saltbox. The home was fully enclosed—four walls, including four of five windows, a roof and dirt-floor cellar, framed by a fieldstone foundation. He gazed at the chimney rising upward beyond the peak of the roof. The entire interior was undone. Lots of work remained. But the hardest portion was complete. He slid back the wooden bar, opened the front door and stepped outside. He closed it behind him. He couldn't lock it, not from the outside, but that didn't matter. In Tyringham many folks never locked their homes. In any event, Thom's saltbox contained nothing worth stealing.

Thom circled the structure in a clockwise direction. As he came around the rear, near the northeast corner, along the edge of the woods he observed what appeared to be berries. He drew closer. Sure enough, it was a raspberry bush. Its few berries were past their prime, but healthy stems at the base suggested the next summer might yield an ample crop. He finished his loop around the structure. He headed back around, this time counterclockwise, meandering in and out of the adjoining

147

woods. He passed the west side of the house and headed down the hill to a spot where he had previously observed a few roses. Just above ground level, growing from a long, thorny, crescent-shaped stem, whose tip sagged under its own weight, were the wilted remains of two tiny red roses. Further examination revealed more stems and another bush several feet away, though no more roses. Nearby stood a maple, a birch and another deciduous tree Thom could not identify. He gazed up at the all-but-barren branches. He imagined them full of leaves. In spring and summer, little sun, the kind needed for blossoms to flourish, would find its way to the roses. The following spring he would transplant them. He turned and looked at his home. Red roses about eight feet from either side of the door would be perfect.

He strolled through the edge of the woods that ran along the southern margin of his clearing. A squirrel with an acorn in its mouth darted past. It charged up a giant oak, disappearing among the limbs. Apparently the bushy-tailed critter, his pre-winter schedule more pressing than Thom's, had much to do before snowdrifts draped the mountainside. Thom looked around the wooded area. He inhaled the still air. A rustling off to his left caught his ear. He peered between the trees toward some bushes from which the sound had emanated. A deer, a fox or...whatever. He watched and waited. Most times he would have gone about his business without a second look, but now and then he put work aside, taking time to savor his surroundings. These weren't merely some woods. This was his home, and the animals with whom he shared it were his neighbors. Some, such as chirping birds, were gregarious. Most, like him, were very private.

A minute, maybe two elapsed before Thom finally stepped out of the trees. He gazed at his saltbox. Compared to the impressive Georgian homes he had helped fashion in Boston, it was second-rate, but that wasn't the point. On primeval Beartown Mountain it was majestic. He counted the months on his fingers. In less than eight, his lofty goal, a vision imaginable only with closed eyes and fatuous optimism, had been accomplished. A surge of adrenaline underscored his satisfaction. He walked over to Lodestone and patted the big

148

steed. From his haversack he removed a flask of Santa Cruz rum, an extra he had packed for the occasion. He took several swigs. A smile he could all but see enveloped his face. He had come a long way. Where once, across the ocean, he had resided in a crowded and squalid cell of an English jail, in the New World he had forty acres and a home of his own, a fine one at that.

# Chapter 9

"SURPRISED YOU AREN'T working on your saltbox," said Richard, as he poked his head into the barn adjoining Sarah's house.

Thom shrugged.

"Haven't seen you lately. I stopped at your plot twice. Couldn't believe you weren't there. By the way, your house looks great. You did a helluva job."

The compliment, a ray of sunshine on a gray November day, had Thom beaming.

"While I was up there, I went inside. I hope you don't mind." Richard peered at the chair on which Thom was working. "You making that for Sarah?"

Thom shook his head. "Matter of fact, I made her one already."

"You know she favors you."

Thom shot his friend a look.

"Damn, I don't mean that way."

"That way...this way. What the hell are you jabbering about?"

"She really likes you. You know, like a mother. She'll hate to see you move out. That's what she told Ella Miller." Richard waved his arms theatrically. "Makes no sense why a fine woman like Sarah would want the likes of you around. Well, only goes to prove there's no accounting for taste."

"You know..." Thom scratched his head, the gesture even more theatric than Richard's. "You're right."

Richard's eyes grew wide.

"Think about it...I associate with you. Talk about a lack of taste."

Taut lips quickly yielded to laughter.

Thom joined in the guffaw.

Richard gestured at the nearly completed chair. "With all you still have to do on the inside of your house, isn't it premature to be making furniture?"

"It's not for me."

"Juliette Chandler, maybe? From what I hear, she also favors you, and I don't mean in a motherly way. And in case you haven't noticed, she sports some sweet curves."

"I've noticed, and...Juliette is nice, but speaking of mothers, she's almost old enough to be mine."

"She doesn't look it."

The point was hard to argue.

"So, is the chair for Juliette?"

Thom shook his head.

"You mind if we end the guessing game and you tell me whom it's for?"

"Orville Crane."

"Orville Crane! Why the hell would you make a chair for that lummox?" Richard's brow knitted. "If he didn't have a wife and house full of kids, I'd worry about you."

"Relax. I'm making it, along with a stool and writing desk, in exchange for the nails I used on my roof and clapboards, and the ones for my floors." Thom waited a moment anticipating some kind of reaction. "What do you think?"

"Sounds fair...uh...I guess."

"What...you have concerns about the deal?"

"Not that, but..."

"But what?"

"Just that I'm surprised Crane gave you the nails on credit. Not like him."

"He didn't."

A puzzled expression showed on Richard's face. "You said you used Crane's nails, and from what I can see, he's yet to receive his furniture."

"Yeah, but he made me deposit one pound, ten shillings, the cash price, as security."

Richard shook his head.

"What's the matter now?"

"I hope you get your money back. Two pence in Orville's pocket is two pence spent...Well, at least you got your nails and hardware."

Thom looked away.

"You got everything, didn't you?"

"Not exactly."

"What does that mean?"

"He has to make the nails for my floor. But I...I trust him."

"Apparently he wouldn't extend you the same courtesy."

"No matter. I have his furniture." Despite the glib response, Thom had second thoughts. Much as he liked to view himself as an adept businessman—his dealings with Captain Brewer a case in point—more often than not, he was an easy touch. With most folks in Tyringham there was no need to deal at arms length. Orville Crane was the rare exception. Hindsight had Thom chastising poor judgment. The furniture would be stained and ready for delivery in several days. He had given Crane his two-week notice six days earlier. In eight more, he would be on Crane's doorstep.

⁓⫘⫘⫘⁓

Thom had finished Crane's furniture two days earlier. More than a week had elapsed since Thom had been to his saltbox. It was the longest such period since he had begun the undertaking in March. Wind-driven snow flurries underscored that the benign weather that had persisted into late November couldn't last. Installation of his oak floor had to await Crane's nails, but that was not a problem. Most of the would-be floorboards still needed half-lap joints carved into the edges where they would be joined. Weeks earlier Thom had seemingly ruled out loose-tongue joints, a fine technique in which a narrow strip was placed between the grooves of adjacent boards, but it was not until he had begun fashioning the floorboards that he had made the final decision. He had convinced himself that the benefit of tedious loose-tongue joints, invisible to those who walked the floors, was outweighed by the ease of half-lap joints. The pragmatic decision, a rebuff of the perfectionism that often ruled his life, drew a silent, albeit ambivalent, celebration.

152

As Thom approached his homesite, he stopped at the edge of the clearing and gazed at his saltbox. The sight was hard to comprehend. He headed inside, where he laid a number of wooden boards across the floor joists. Coupled with others he had previously put down, they created a temporary rectangular work area preferable to both the dirt of the cellar and the elements of the outdoors. He considered fetching some wood and building a fire, but with conditions indoors bearable, he decided his time could be better spent preparing floorboards.

One by one he trimmed the boards. He chiseled grooves along the edges. The alacrity with which he worked stirred memories of Boston. His late mentor would be proud. All morning and into the early afternoon he worked before taking a break. He drank some cider from his canteen. From his haversack he took several carrots, a small cow cumber, an apple and an oversized heel from a loaf of Indian cornbread.

He had finished eating the vegetables and was about to consume the bread when a rustling caught his ear. He stopped chewing and listened. He heard it again. It appeared to emanate from the cellar, the far side of the arch supporting the chimney. He remained still. Again the noise. In all likelihood an animal, perhaps a squirrel or woodchuck or mole, had sought refuge below.

A hammer in hand, stealthily he crawled on hands and knees along the boards that led in front of the parlor fireplace. He peered at the arch below that paralleled the sides of the house. Nothing appeared to be amiss, but the arch, along with the chimney shaft that rose above it, blocked much of his view. For over a minute he waited and listened. Still nothing. He laid the hammer down and negotiated his way back toward the front of the house and got two more floorboards. He carried them back to the area in front of the fireplace and laid them across the joists that extended out over the portion of the arch nearest the rear of the house. With hammer in hand, he crawled toward the rear of the arch. Curled up adjacent to the arch on the cellar floor below, he observed what appeared to be a bearskin. Thom inched further until he was almost directly above the furry mass. At most it appeared to be the torso of a bear. There was no head, only a mound of bearskin. He watched and waited for more than a minute. The mound showed no sign of movement.

He considered climbing down between the joists to the cellar floor, but opted for the safety of his position. For all he knew a wolf or fox might be lurking. Even if it were merely a rabbit or squirrel, rabidity was not out of the question. Admittedly the speculation bordered on the absurd, but discretion could not be faulted. One thing sure, something had invaded his home.

Thom worked his way past the fireplace where he got a thin piece of firing strip about five feet long. He took it back to a spot above the bearskin, intending to reach below and jostle the fur. When he looked down, the skin was there, but it was no longer mounded. He looked around the cellar, as best he could, but saw nothing. He negotiated the floorboards to a point near the front door, trying to check the cellar as he did. He saw nothing. He waited and watched and listened. Nothing. Something lurked within the twenty-three by nineteen foot area of his cellar. Of that he had no doubt. But what?

From his haversack Thom removed his knife, still in its scabbard, and hooked it to his belt. He picked up his hammer, posting himself just inside the front door. He waited. Not a movement. Not a sound. Had he imagined that the bearskin had been raised well above the cellar floor? No way. Regardless, someone or something had put it there.

He opted for a new strategy. He opened the door, but rather than stepping outside, slammed it closed and silently seated himself on the boards that lay just inside the threshold. Again he took up watch. Though the chimney, arch and joists hindered his view, from his vantage he could see the majority of the cellar. Five...ten...fifteen minutes elapsed, and still nothing. Thom remained patient, determined to discover what lay below.

Finally, he heard what he thought was a faint noise. His focus intensified. He heard a creaking off to his left. What appeared to be two hands wrapped themselves around a joist. Thom pulled out his knife. He crouched lower and watched. The head of a youth showed itself between the hands that gripped the joist. The instant the youth's eyes met Thom's, the youth dropped back to the cellar floor. Hammer in one hand, knife in the other, Thom stepped over the boards in the direction of the youth. The lad ducked for cover.

"Come out!" yelled Thom.

No answer.

"I won't hurt you." Thom waited several seconds. "I know you're there. I can wait as long as you."

Thom slipped his knife back into its scabbard and hooked his hammer to his belt. He took several more floorboards and began laying them in a fashion that would enable him to complete a circle around the chimney. He caught a glimpse of the boy's arm. Thom grabbed hold of his hammer.

"I know you're there, under the arch. You might as well come out."

Seconds later, the youth, bearing a knife, stepped forth.

"I told you. I won't hurt you."

The youth gestured at Thom's hammer.

"I'll lay it aside if you put down your knife."

The youth shook his head.

Thom studied the youth. He was thin, several inches short of six feet, a teen. His deerskin shirt and pants suggested he was Indian. "Who are you?"

The youth failed to answer.

"What are you doing here?"

No reply.

"Come up and we'll talk."

The youth shook his head.

Thom needed to win the youth's confidence, but from all appearances that would not be easy. "How long have you been here?"

Clenching the handle of his knife, the youth stared.

"Are you hungry? Would you like some bread?"

The youth shook his head. "I have food."

"Where do you live?"

The youth shrugged.

"You're not from Tyringham, are you?"

The youth remained mute.

Thom wanted to establish a dialogue. Questions seemed the only way. But their constant barrage, an ostensible inquisition, was ensuring the silence of the recalcitrant youth. "Where's your family?"

Nothing more than a stare.

"I'd like to help you." The olive branch drew no reaction. "Do you have somewhere to stay?"

The youth shook his head.

"You can stay here...if you'd like." The desire to win the youth's confidence and establish communication was superseding judgment. "If you put your knife down, I'll lay mine aside." Thom pulled his blade from its sheath and stuck it into a nearby stud. He could grab it in an instant, and he still had his hammer.

The youth, who had held his knife in front of him the entire time, dropped his hand to his side.

"Come up, and we'll talk."

The proposal drew another shake of the head.

"Are you on your way somewhere...just passing through Tyringham?"

The youth shook his head again.

Questions ran through Thom's mind, but they were the same unanswered ones he had asked before. As much as possible, he wanted to avoid repetition. "Can I help you in some way?"

A thoughtful cast appeared on the youth's face. "Doubt it."

Thom gestured toward the outside. "Winter is close. You need some provisions?"

"Nope."

The cavalier response caught Thom by surprise. "Winter gets mighty rough."

A slight smile showed on the youth's face.

"How long have you been on your own?" Thom posed the question, thinking its underlying assumption might prompt the youth to demur.

The youth counted on his fingers. "'Bout nine months. Since early March."

"You couldn't have been staying here all that time. I didn't lay my foundation until June."

"Only been here 'bout three weeks. And that was in the nights."

"Where did you stay before that?"

"In the woods...mostly."

The growing responses suggested progress. "Where are your folks?" Thom waited a moment. "Are they alive?"

Ever so briefly, the youth, who had maintained a steady watch on Thom, broke eye contact.

"You're really—" Thom clipped his tongue. Lecturing the youth that he was too young to be on his own was a bad idea, especially when he had managed to get along for the better part of a year, assuming what he had said was true. And too, Thom was only sixteen when he had left home, and still seventeen when, after spending a year in jail, he had booked on as a boatswain's assistant and sailed across the Atlantic. On the other hand, the youth was perhaps no more than fifteen or sixteen, and being a cabin boy was far less harrowing than living alone in the mountains of western Massachusetts.

"Whatcha gonna do?"

The question took Thom aback. All along he had done the asking. "I don't know, but a boy your age shouldn't be living alone in the woods." The frown that greeted Thom said otherwise. "Suppose I put my hammer down and you put your knife aside and come up and talk?"

"You gonna turn on me?"

"No. I give you my word."

The youth exhibited no reaction.

"Look, the way things stand, I have the upper hand."

"If I come up...promise I can walk out the door?"

The offer, more explicit than Thom's, though hardly his preference, was better than the status quo. "I promise. I won't stop you."

"And I can take my stuff?" He gestured first at the bearskin and then towards a corner of the cellar.

"I promise."

The youth pointed toward the front wall of the house. "You go there."

Thom followed the floorboards to a point halfway between the front window and door.

The youth jabbed his knife into an adjacent floor joist. Thom laid his hammer down. The youth gathered his blanket, bearskin and some other paraphernalia and slipped them into a burlap bag. He flipped it over a joist onto a floorboard. Grabbing hold of the joist, with the agility of a monkey, the youth pulled himself up. He negotiated his way onto the floorboards at the far end of the fireplace. He inched back, so he stood about twelve feet from Thom, but still near his knife.

"Have you eaten?" said Thom. "I have some bread and cider."

"Thanks, but I ate."

"Where do you get food?"

"The Konkapot. Fishin' there is easy. Hunt a little...rabbits and the like. Past summer I grew carrots and squash and picked berries and apples and stuff. And I got more chestnuts than the squirrels got acorns."

"What about winter?"

"Got a good stash. Hidden away...not here."

Thom pointed at the bearskin. "Did you kill that bear?"

The boy chuckled. "Nah, found it dead in the woods. Musta been there for quite a time. The animals had done a job on it. Not a scrap of meat left. But the skin was good. I already had a blanket, but the bearskin will come in handy when the cold sets in."

"Do you—" Discretion curbed Thom's question. "I'm Thomas Webster. Please call me Thom." He hoped the youth would respond in kind. When he didn't, Thom said, "May I ask your name?"

"Picosick. It means red fox."

"Are you by any chance a Stockbridge Indian?"

"You mean Mohican?"

Thom nodded sheepishly. His inaccuracy had him searching his mind. He recalled that before Tyringham had been settled, when the Provincial Legislature had laid out the four Housatonic townships, which later became Becket, New Marlborough, Sandisfield and Tyringham,[99] a mission and town had been established at Stockbridge for the local Indians in exchange for their providing their lands for the townships.[100] Like other white settlers, Thom generally referred to them as Stockbridge Indians. "Sorry, I should know better."

"It's okay. We're used to it. And just to be clear, I'm Mohican (the youth spelled the word), not Mohegan (he spelled that as well). The Mohegans come from Connecticut.[101] Anyway, I'm just part Mohican. My Mom was Mohican. My father was English. He took off when Pico was a baby. Never knew him."

Thom waited, hoping the youth would continue. When he didn't, Thom said, "Did your mother raise you Mohican?"

"She tried, but...it was no use. The missionaries, with their Gospel, had taken over. They pushed our Indian ways aside."

Stories of how many Stockbridge Indians had been driven out for refusing to accept the mission's principles were familiar to Thom. The pattern had become acute following the death of Jonathan Edwards in 1758.[102]

"'Bout the time Pico was ten, my Mom packed up. We moved around, never fitting in. When she died—diphtheria, that's what they said—Pico took what little we had and headed east. Thought about going to Boston. Got this far when I found the school near where the road (he pointed) Beartown meets Brace."

The youth's speech was better than Thom might have expected. The judgmental aspect of the observation registered with Thom, if only for an instant. More intriguing was Pico's occasional use of the third person when referring to himself, but knowing that a prying question would make it harder to earn trust, Thom's curiosity yielded to an innocuous inquiry. "Did you attend our local school?"

"No, but I stayed there a few months...from December until March. Used to leave real early in the morning...before anyone showed up."

The school had burned in early March. The possibility the youth might be connected to the fire was inescapable. It was better left unmentioned, at least for the moment. "Where did you stay after that?"

"In the woods...and an abandoned shed on Brace Road."

"You sure you don't want a piece of bread?"

The youth hesitated.

"Tell you what. We'll split it, not that it's much." Thom reached for his haversack. He sensed the youth was hawkishly eyeing the move. Thom took out the chunk and ripped it apart,

159

extending a hand that held one-half. The youth stayed where he was. "Come on. We'll share a little cider too."

"How does Pico know he can trust you?"

"I gave you my word that I won't stop you from leaving."

The youth took a step forward but stopped. "Suppose I get my stuff first?"

It was not Thom's preference, but with every intention of keeping his promise, he said, "If that's what you want."

The youth took hold of his burlap bag. He pointed to the window on the far wall. "You go over there. Then I'll go by the door."

Thom pushed a board toward the window and grabbed another. He negotiated the first and then laid the second so it ran closer to the window. He moved there."

"I need my knife."

The point was hard to argue, but being disarmed while the youth held a weapon was foolhardy. "Fine. Then I'll need mine."

The youth's face grew taut. "Tell you what. You get yours...and I'll get mine. Then you go back there and slide the board you used to get there away."

"Fair enough," said Thom, realizing that even as he had been silently lauding the youth's independence, he had underestimated his wiliness and maturity.

The youth yanked his knife from the joist. Thom retrieved his blade. As he returned to his position by the window, he contemplated strategy. Sending the boy off to fend for himself was repulsive. Breaking his word was impossible. Offering the unfamiliar youth lodging in Sarah's home without consulting her was out of the question. The best he could do was offer shelter in his saltbox. He slid the board he had used to get to his position toward the front wall. It rotated and fell between the joists to the cellar floor. He looked back at the youth. "Okay, now I'm on an island. You're free to go. But before you do, I've got a proposal. You can stay here. You'll have a fire in the fireplace. Sleep right next to it." The folly of exposing his months of labor to the whims of a young stranger, who, for all Thom knew, may have been responsible for the school fire, had Thom questioning himself. The alternative, turning the youth away, was unacceptable. "It will be a lot better here than in some abandoned shed."

"Why you lookin' to help me?"

"What do you mean?"

Skepticism showed on the youth's face. "My mother used to say, 'Folks got reasons.' What's yours? You know...what's in it for you?"

Seconds before Thom had dismissed the youth's inquiry. It had more substance than he had imagined. It was a challenging question. *Why was he so eager to help the youth?* The answer was complex. The stranger standing by the door conjured images of himself in an earlier day. Thom knew what it was like to have a father who didn't care. Unlike Pico, Thom's father had been there in the household, but it might have been better had he not. No matter how hard Thom tried to please his father, he never could. Constant demeaning drove Thom from home. He said, "You're right. My motives aren't entirely altruistic." A hint of puzzlement on the youth's face prompted Thom to explain. "It may not make sense, but I need to prove, at least to myself, that I'm a better man than my father. You see, like you, I had a father who wasn't there for me." Thom heaved a sigh. "You're right, my offer to help you is not without selfish motivation."

The youth stood motionless for the better part of a minute as he seemingly weighed the proposal. Finally, with gear in hand he headed for the door. He kept an eye on Thom. When he reached the door, he opened it. He looked back at Thom as he stepped across the threshold. He started to close the door but instead moved back inside. He nodded slowly. "That's twice you've kept your word." He lowered his bag to the floor. "If that offer to stay is still open, Pico 'll take it."

"You got it." Gratification, tempered by trepidation, a mind-boggling amalgam, had Thom celebrating and questioning at the same time. He laid his knife down but remained close enough for a quick grab.

The youth removed a sheath from his bag. He put his knife into the sheath and stuffed it into his bag.

"How about that bread and cider?"

161

"I'd like that." The youth picked up a board and, after walking it partway to Thom, placed it where it completed the bridge to the door. He returned to his prior station.

Thom inched in the youth's direction and extended his hand. "I'm Thom."

"I know. You told me." He shook Thom's hand.

The sheepish expression that no doubt painted Thom's face was all but visible to him. "And you are Pico."

"Picosick." The youth spelled it. "But folks call me Pico."

"Then Pico it is."

Thom started to reach for his haversack. Pico pulled back.

"I'm just getting the bread and cider." Thom opened the bag and held it so Pico could see inside. "Here, you take out the bread and tin cup."

Pico hesitated but carried out the request.

Thom picked up his canteen and filled the cup that Pico held. He took the bread, tore it into two pieces and handed Pico the larger. "Let's sit."

They lowered themselves onto a floorboard so their legs hung into the cellar. For the ensuing few minutes they chewed their bread and drank their cider, Pico from the tin cup and Thom, the canteen. Occasionally they exchanged a brief glance, their non-verbal communication indicative that earlier tension was dissipating.

"It's remarkable how you've managed to get along on your own," said Thom.

Pico shrugged. "Mohican boys have learned that for years, least till the missionaries came. That's when book learning became more important than our traditions."

"You seem to know the best of both worlds."

Pico showed a puzzled look.

"You deal well with nature, and based upon our conversation, you apparently got a good education, the kind that comes from books."

"That was my Mom's doing. Made me attend school and work hard, not that she cared for the missionaries' preachin'. She made sure I learned to read and write."

"I assume the missionaries made you read the Bible."

Pico laughed. It was the first time he appeared relaxed. "Yeah, Pico read the Bible, but only as stories. Never took it as gospel. But it served its purpose. Like my Mom used to say, 'Anyone who can read and understand the Bible can read and understand most anything.' Ever since Pico was small, my Mom made me read everything she could get her hands on. Then we'd talk about it."

"Your mother sounds like a wise woman."

"She was. Taught me to learn from everyone. Like she used to say, 'Even the worst person can teach you valuable lessons, if only the mistakes to avoid.'" Pico grew pensive. "You got me usin' my Mom's quotes. That's good. Helps keep her memory alive." He studied Thom. "You got something on your mind. Shows on your face."

Thom did. He was marveling at Pico's worldliness. Exposed to two very different cultures, with the guidance of his mother he had managed to extract the best of each. Thom would have expressed the thought were he not concerned the sophisticated young man might view it as an oily pretense to win him over. "What else did your mother teach you?"

"You really wanna know?"

Thom nodded, aware his question might be viewed like the comment he had judiciously avoided.

"To be fiercely independent. To follow no one blindly...That was one of her most important lessons.

Ever since Thom had left home, independence had been his hallmark. Confidence, trust and other characteristics ebbed and flowed, but independence remained a constant. He gazed at Pico but curtailed what otherwise would have amounted to a stare. The young man reflected more of a youthful Thom than he had previously surmised. On the other hand, the comparison was in some respects as inaccurate as it was vain. Thom wondered again about the young man's parlance, irregularly alluding to himself in the first and third person. Discretion kept a question about the oddity from his lips. He said, "How old are you?"

"Sixteen...but I'll be seventeen in a few months."

"Amazing."

"What's amazing?"

"At your age, to be out on your own and dealing with the world." Thom thought back to the days after he first turned sixteen. He was yet to spend a year in jail and book onto a ship as a boatswain's assistant. Like Pico, he was independent, but put the sixteen-year-old version of himself side by side with Pico, and Thom was no more than a cub. He said, "You sure you have enough food?"

"Yup. Like I told you, I got a good stash. Plus Pico eats lotsa fish."

"You may be doing that now, but another month or so, and the Konkapot, as well as Brewer's Pond, will be frozen."

"And?"

Self-confidence was fine, but it had its limits. One had to be realistic. "Don't tell me you ice fish?"

"Every young boy from my tribe does. In some ways it's easier than summer when you always need fresh catch. Come winter...you dig a hole in the ice, catch all the fish you can, and freeze 'em in a snow pack. You got fish whenever you want." Pico eyed Thom, as if making sure his message had gotten through.

Living in the wilderness, the young boys of Tyringham grew up fast. Their lives were linked to the land, but they had homes and fathers and security, and mothers and sisters who, with division of labor, provided clothes and much of their food. There were exceptions, boys who upon the premature loss of a father were compelled to become the man of the house. But even then, most times they had a home and family to share the responsibilities. Pico, on the other hand, was all alone out in the wilderness fending for himself. How he managed was a mystery to Thom. Doubtless part of the secret came from his Indian culture. An indomitable will was surely another. And necessity, that unique force of uncharted circumstances, had to be playing an omni-present role. Thom said, "Let's get some wood and build a fire."

Pico gestured casually at the floorboards. "Why not these. They're not nailed down."

Thom assumed the quip was sardonic. He would have laughed were it not for the concern it sparked. An Indian boy had been seen around the school prior to the fire. Pico had acknowledged that he had stayed in the school for a time. Folks suspected arson. Pico appeared trustworthy, but Thom could not dismiss the possibility that Pico was linked to the blaze. He was mature, educated, bright, independent and resourceful, but might he harbor resentments owing to fatherly abandonment, missionaries who had tried to strip him of his identity, or tales of how his parents and grandparents had been wheedled off their lands. Hardly sanguine about what he was doing, Thom led the way out the door. Piles of chopped logs and twigs gathered in preparation for winter lay at the edge of the clearing. Pico began carrying them to the house, while Thom chopped another felled tree into kindling logs. Together they transported the remaining wood into the saltbox, lowering all but a few pieces to the cellar floor.

Thom pointed at the parlor fireplace. "It's been virgin long enough. Time for a fire."

"Okay if Pico uses his knife to start it?"

"Be my guest," said Thom with veiled apprehensions.

Pico took a stick and carved back inch-long strips of bark, so they swung out in the shape of a teepee. Thom put four logs into the fireplace, two short ones at either end, atop of which and perpendicular, he laid two longer ones. Underneath he built rising, crisscross squares of twigs with some additional twigs across the top. Pico took a flint from his bag, along with a few small clumps of dried grass that he laid onto the hearth. He repeatedly struck the flint on the hearth, close to the clumps. Sparks caused the grass to smolder. He blew lightly on the grass; harder once it ignited. He grabbed the stick he had carved and held it so the stripped bark touched the flame. The strips ignited, and soon the stick was afire. He held the flaming stick near the crisscrossed squares of twigs. In less than a minute the twigs were blazing.

"Pico generally builds a teepee of twigs under a teepee of thicker wood. But I like your squares, especially indoors where there is no wind."

On occasion Thom had laid sticks in different arrangements but had never thought much about indoor and outdoor distinctions. Unlike Pico, Thom always had a roof over his head. Even on those occasions when he needed an outdoor fire, and those were in milder weather, he tended toward the easy route. A torch ignited from the fire used for cooking was carried outside to awaiting wood.

With the ever-shortening days of late November, daylight would soon yield to darkness. Occasionally on moon-bright nights, Thom made the trip back from his saltbox to Sarah's after dark. With thick clouds prevailing, there would be no moonlight. Negotiating roads in such darkness was problematic. Either he had to leave Pico alone at the saltbox or take him along to Sarah's. Though Thom assumed Sarah would acquiesce, putting her on the spot would be unfair, especially when Thom had no way to vouch for Pico. Regardless, Thom had rejected the idea earlier. He said, "Before it gets dark, I should return to the house where I live."

"Thanks for letting Pico stay."

"Glad to," said Thom, his reservations no less than earlier.

"You won't tell anyone I'm here...will you?" Pico hesitated. "'Cause if you plan to, Pico 'll leave now."

Agreeing was easy because Thom preferred to keep Pico's presence a secret, at least for the moment. "I won't tell anyone. That's a promise." The open-ended commitment echoed in Thom's ears. "If circumstances change and I feel compelled to speak out, I'll warn you in advance. Okay?"

"Fair enough."

Thom picked up his haversack and canteen. He looked around the saltbox. It was a huge accomplishment, a great source of pride. He headed out the door, hoping he had not been foolhardy.

# Chapter 10

NOONTIME, THE 5TH OF DECEMBER, and with the aid of Sarah's wagon, Thom had transported the rocker, stool and writing desk to Orville Crane's place. He had given his two-week notice on the morning of November 21st, and the time had come to get his deposit back. After going to the barn, peeking in and finding no one there, he went to the front of the house and knocked on the door. Moments later Crane's elder son opened it.

"Hello, Elmer. Your father home?"

"Uh...yes, but...let me go see." Without inviting Thom in, he hurried away.

A minute later Orville Crane appeared at the portal. "Afternoon Thom. We just sat down to our midday meal."

"I won't keep you." Thom pointed at the furniture that sat atop the wagon. "I want to deliver your furniture. Turned out well, if I say so myself."

"Okay, bring it in. Over here in the parlor."

Together they carried the items into the house.

"Go ahead. Give the chair a go," said Thom.

"I'll try it later. Thanks for bringing it by." He started to usher Thom out the door.

"Excuse me, but I'd appreciate my one pound, ten shillings."

Crane gestured at the adjacent room where the family sat around the table, a wide board laid across a pair of saw horses. "Can't ya see we're eatin'?"

Under other circumstances Thom would have offered to come back, but miffed that he had been forced to post security and that Crane had unilaterally added the requirement of a fourteen-day notice, Thom stood firm. "Two weeks are up, and it will only take you a minute to get my money."

"Sticks in my craw that you're so pushy."

"Don't mean to be." Thom suppressed resentment. "But I'd appreciate my money."

"Fine." A growl gainsaid the acquiescence. "Gimme a moment."

A minute later Crane returned. He handed Thom one pound, four shillings.

"I gave you a pound, plus ten shillings as a deposit." Thom reached into his pocket for the letter Crane had signed.

"Put the paper away. I know what it was."

"May I have my six shillings?"

"You'll get 'em when I got 'em."

"That wasn't our agreement."

"I said—you'll get 'em when I got 'em." Crane folded his burly arms. "After bargin' in and interruptin' our dinner, ya oughta be grateful for what ya got."

"I'm sorry, but we had—"

"Orville, your stew is getting cold."

"Be right there, Hannah." Crane stepped to the door and opened it.

Instinctively Thom stepped outside. With second thoughts, he glanced back at the furniture. Taking something, perhaps the rocker, as security, giving Crane a taste of his own medicine, seemed apropos. "When can I expect my money, Orville?"

"Like I told ya—when I get it." He shut the door.

Thom stood outside on the threshold, stewing for several seconds. He was angry with Crane, but also, himself. How could he have allowed the intransigent blacksmith to treat him that way? But making a scene in the midst of the family's meal would have been a mistake. The reasoning, an excuse intertwined with logic, did little to alleviate frustration.

*⁓∾∫∬∾⁓*

Pico had been staying at the saltbox for more than a week, and far from a burden, he was proving to be an asset. He had quickly learned to use a chisel and was hewing grooves along the edges of boards. For a novice his work was good. Admittedly he was slow, but that was to be expected. When Thom had first welcomed Pico into his house, he had not anticipated his generosity would be mutually beneficial. Having a helper

168

quickened the installation of the floor, and, equally important, Thom was discovering the joy of being a mentor.

Concerns whether Pico had adequate food stocks had Thom repeatedly raising the issue. Pico shrugged the matter off. Though the calendar still showed two weeks until winter, minor come-and-go snows of November had been followed by the better part of a foot during the first week of December. Past patterns suggested the ground might remain white until April. A stash in May, readily replenished in the warmth of summer, could dissipate in winter. Pico claimed skills as an ice fisherman, but with long, dark December nights leading to the unforgiving months of January and February, many an unprepared dweller of the wilderness could go hungry long before the advent of spring.

Thom was certain if Sarah knew that Pico was staying at the saltbox, she would provide him with food. But disclosure required Pico's permission. Thom never sought it. He told himself that Pico would prefer his privacy. Thom might have taken food for Pico from Sarah's buttery, but his conscience labeled the well-intentioned act, stealing.

Pico and Thom had worked past midday on the saltbox floor. It was half-done. Three weeks had passed since Thom had joined the guys at the Hogshead. Shortly before two, an impulse drove him there. Unlike spring, summer and early autumn when labors ran from morning to night, once the cold, dark days of winter arrived, folks began visiting the tavern in the afternoon.

"Over here," said George Whitaker, who was seated with Ezra Jenkins and Orville Crane. "We've got room."

Thom had hoped that Richard or even Johnny Woodstone or Paul Cooper might be there. They weren't. Thom slid into the booth next to Whitaker, across from the other two. His eyes met Crane's. Thom looked away. Common sense dictated that Crane, not he, should feel uncomfortable, but reasoning and emotions diverged.

Jenkins pointed at the menu board. "You're in luck. Heath is serving his special today: *meat à la Dinsmore*."

The reference to Wendell Dinsmore, the local shoemaker, indicated the fare, as usual, was leather-like. But Heath could get

169

away with it. He ran the only tavern for several miles. His location on the Albany-Boston Post Road guaranteed success. Weary travelers accepted his second-rate food and meager accommodations. Everyone slept in the loft, with the lucky ones getting the three beds. Others got the floor for one pence less.

"What's it supposed to be?" said Thom. "Pork or venison...or beef maybe?"

"Mutton," said Jenkins. "Of course, if you ask me, it's the typical mystery meat." Jenkins scooped a chunk onto his spoon and held it up. "Dried up whatever...mixed with turnips, parsnips and God knows what."

As Mary the barmaid approached, Thom said, "The fare, along with an ale." He reached into his haversack, which he had hung on the corner of the booth, and pulled out his mess kit. "Can you fill this with an extra order?"

Whitaker poked him in the side. "Sarah doesn't feed you anymore?"

"No, nothing like that. She's a great cook."

"So, why in the name of culinary madness do you want an extra helping of Heath's slop?" said Jenkins.

Thom would have ignored the question were he not confident that silence would draw more pointed inquiries. But his response needed to be guarded lest he breach his promise to Pico. "Building a house, a body needs food."

"Food, yes." Jenkins gestured at their trough. "But this?"

"You're eating it, aren't you?" said Thom.

"Touché." Jenkins shoveled a spoonful into his mouth. "So, how's your saltbox coming along?"

"The exterior is done, top to bottom, and soon the floor will be in."

"You'll need some furnishings." Whitaker's coy smile was hardly subtle. "Let me know. I'm sure we can work something out."

Thom recalled the sconces he had seen in the Yankee Trader's barn, but why give the wily businessman the upper hand? "I expect to make most everything myself."

"Suit yourself." Whitaker looked across at Crane. "You're awfully quiet."

"Who...me?"

"No, our fine governor, Thomas Hutchinson."

"Speaking of him," said Jenkins, "all that mess with the tea is getting out of hand. Mobs in Philadelphia and New York forcing East India's ships to sail back to England without unloading their cargo. It's sedition with a capital *S*."

Whitaker, his mouth filled with stew, garbled, "King George must be livid. If what they claim about the treasury is true, they're desperate for revenue. Folks here are begging for trouble."

"You got that right," said Jenkins. "Last month when I was in Boston, tensions were running sky high. The radicals tried to force the tea ships back to England. Governor Hutchinson refused and ordered them unloaded."

"So...they unloaded the tea?" said Thom.

Jenkins shook his head. "Boston, Roxbury and some other towns, spurred by that nut Sam Adams and his Sons of Liberty, passed resolutions to prohibit it. They want the ships, all three of them, sent back without paying the tax.[103] A gent traveling west from Boston to Pittsfield—I talked to him earlier today—told me Hutchinson barred the ships from leaving until the duty is paid."

"Can he do that?" said Whitaker.

"You bet he can." In his inimitable way the lawyer made the point by raising his voice. Bombast and bravado were his stock in trade.[104] As for credentials, like many in the legal profession, his came not from education, but bits of knowledge acquired as an apprentice to the clerk of a Massachusetts Bay Colony court. He said, "I don't blame Hutchinson. As much as we need to make our wishes known to Parliament, mob rule can't be allowed. Hutchinson has to put his foot down."

"Where does the matter stand?" said Whitaker.

"According to the traveler, it's a stalemate. Hutchinson is firm, and the agitators are intractable."

"Well, it won't surprise me," said Thom, "if Hutchinson folds his tent."

"What folly leads you to that conclusion?" said Jenkins.

"Look at Philadelphia and New York. The tea went back to England."

"Maybe so," said Jenkins. "And all it did was make us worse off."

171

The seeming *non sequitur* confused Thom. Perhaps Jenkins, a windbag, admittedly an articulate one, was digging in his heels with rant, rather than reason.

"You don't get it, Webster, do you? I see it on your face."

"Now that you mention it—No." Thom suspected Jenkins was bluffing. Whether at the poker table or that of debate, the lawyer was prone to such tactics. Aggressive bets, aggressive talk, won him many a game. But often he paid the price when his bluff was called.

Jenkins sat back and folded his arms.

Thom grew more convinced the lawyer was ducking the issue. Thom was not about to let him. He said, "So—enlighten me."

Hesitation, enough to slip in a smirk, preceded the lawyer's response. "Now that the tea has been shipped back from New York and Philadelphia, Boston is out on a limb...all alone. Hutchinson won't back down. In the end Massachusetts, our colony, will be left by its lonesome to face England's wrath. The rest of the colonies will turn a blind eye, along with a deaf ear."

Thom swallowed hard. He broke eye contact, but only after he had viewed the lawyer's expression, a smirk broader than its predecessor.

"Damn," said Crane. "Those radicals in Boston are gonna get us nuttin' but trouble. Parliament's gonna kick our asses."

"You got that right," said Jenkins. "Like someone at this table—his name to go unmentioned—the Sons of Liberty, or should I say, sons of bitches, keep going off half-cocked."

The cool silver of his spoon slipping over skin apprised Thom of his fidgeting fingers.

"You see," said Jenkins, "Hutchinson has an ace up his sleeve. Under the law, his customs' officers can seize a ship if the tax on its tea isn't paid within twenty days after docking. Once they do, they can sell the cargo and use the proceeds to pay the wages of the Crown's representatives.[105] That includes Hutchinson himself. According to what this fellow from Boston told me, one of the ships, the Dartmouth, arrived on November 27th. In about a week, on December 17th, the Sons of Liberty will discover that their highhanded tactics are a recipe for disaster."[106]

172

"It'll serve those radicals right." Whitaker shook his head. "Don't know why the damn fools bite the hand that feeds them."

Jenkins directed a challenging stare Thom's way. "You disagree?"

Thom did. Like most in Tyringham, he had vigorous objections to the autocratic dictates of Parliament. But given the trio with whom he was sharing the booth, as well as the wounds he was licking, he needed to sail a tight course. A loose tongue could land him on the rocks. He said, "Refusing to pay the tax and demanding that the ships return home with their cargo is hardly biting the hand that feeds us. We in the colonies should have a voice about the taxes we pay. And for that matter, charging us a tax is a novel way to feed us."

"Jeze!" said Whitaker. "Don't be so literal. You know what I meant. They protect us from the French and the Indians, not to mention the Dutch and the Spanish. It costs a pretty penny. They need our help defraying the costs...or maybe you think we're entitled to a free ride."

Discretion counseled that Thom look for safer waters, but in the face of the hackneyed argument, acquiescence, or more precisely, poltroonery was difficult. He said, "When asked to pay taxes, we should have a voice."

"Mobs of malcontents preventing ships from being unloaded—You call that a voice?" Jenkins shoveled a spoonful of stew into his mouth.

"Well...people have to do something when subjected to rules with no representation."

"Excuse me," said Jenkins, his partially chewed stew on full display. "Did you say...'no representation?'"

Unlike Crane whose face was blank, Thom knew what Jenkins was implying. "If you're referring to virtual representation, the contrived justification of predisposed philosophers, forget it."

"I, for one," said Jenkins, "think the concept has merit. But forget what I think. Men more erudite than I, the likes of Thomas Hobbes, have articulated the view. But be that as it may..." Jenkins held forth both hands, ensuring no one interrupted. "Let us return to the question, the one you, Mr.

Webster, conveniently ignored. Do you believe that mobs, rather than laws, should govern?"

"Yeah," said Whitaker. "You want a bunch of crazies bringing chaos into our lives?"

"You know," said Thom, "if, like you, I was a Yankee Trader, bartering this and that, most everything but tea, the status quo would be fine. I could say, 'the hell with my neighbors.'"

Whitaker leaned back. "Oh—you want to get personal." A stranglehold on his pewter mug, he glared at Thom. "I'll show you personal." He banged the mug on the table. "Maybe if I were a convicted criminal who served time in jail, mobs, rather than laws, would appeal to me too."

Thom swallowed hard. Out of the corner of his eye he caught a glimpse of Crane's smirk. The blacksmith who had welshed on his agreement was quietly watching from the sidelines while the guy he had rooked was taking a beating.

Silence, more than a minute, supplanted what had been a spirited debate. Three gloated while the fourth languished. When conversation finally resumed, Thom assumed the taciturn role that Crane had previously occupied. In contrast, the blacksmith was vivified, especially given the cerebral topic. The upcoming winter, the anticipated bleak weather, dominated the discussion.

~∘∘))⟫⟫∘~

December was more than half over, and the saltbox floor was nearly complete. Seventeen seventy-three had been a year of accomplishment for Thom. Though the interior work remained largely undone, his vision of a home, conjured during his days in Boston, had gone from pie in the sky to reality. Thom had ample reason to feel satisfied. With Sarah and Richard, and the addition of Pico, he had a support structure. Whether that might narrow was a distinct possibility. The fiercely independent lad was a good bet to strike out on his own. More than anything Thom yearned for a family of his own and, most of all, a woman to love...a woman who would love him...a woman together with whom he could make love.

174

Pico was ice fishing in Hop Brook. Sarah had attended the Sunday meeting and had an invitation to spend the remainder of the afternoon with a neighbor. Thom had caught up on some chores at her home. Seated alone in his room in the rear of her house, he felt himself drifting lower. He needed to get out. With two hours of daylight remaining, he donned his good breeches, waistcoat and frock, and headed south, walking a mile or so down Mt. Hunger Road and then east to the south side of Brewer's Pond. As he approached his destination, a debate raged. Should he turn back? Should he venture into the inveigling den? Back and forth he vacillated. Anxiety counseled that he retrace his steps. Recollections of the spring day he had given Juliette Chandler a ride home on Lodestone said otherwise. Memories of her voluptuous body pressed to his back, the captivating lilac fragrance she wore, exhorted him to take the risk.

Thom left the road and headed toward Juliette's house. Rather than using the clearing that fronted the neat log cabin, he chose a path through the adjoining woods, preserving the opportunity, if necessary, to turn around unnoticed. Once astride the structure, he gazed out from the trees. His heart raced. The sun, low in the southern sky, had already begun to drift west. Its rays, glistening on the crystal white flecks of ice that layered the earth, cast a golden glow on the southern-facing front of the cabin. Smoke pluming from the top of the chimney evanesced as it floated upward into the clear, crisp atmosphere. An about-face was possible, but the likelihood the fruitless return would amplify earlier despondence pushed him onward. As he reached the door, Thom hesitated again. He took a deep breath, the cold air causing him to cough. His hand, as if armed with a mind of its own, rapped on the door. There was no turning back. Moments later, Juliette stood at the open portal.

"Why Thom! What an unexpected surprise?"

"I was out for a walk, and as long as I was passing by, I...I thought I'd stop, case you had something that needed fixing, the hand of a man." He took note of her smart gown with quilted petticoat. Luring charms shaped her outfit.

"That was very thoughtful of you."

175

Hopes for an invite appeared realized. She stepped back and motioned him into the doorway. He no sooner poked his head forward than she gestured to her right. "I'm sorry, but I have company. Darby Walters is visiting."

From his seat Walters waved. "Hi Thom."

"Uh...hello Darby." The lump in Thom's throat throttled his voice. He looked back at Juliette. "I...I'll be on my way. Sorry if I interrupted."

"Oh, that's okay."

Thom hurried off. Why, he asked himself, had he come? True, she had given him an invitation, but that was months earlier. He hurried back toward Mt. Hunger Road. His disappointment was not only manifest, but also surprisingly acute. It made no sense. Numerous times he had rejected the idea of visiting Juliette. She was too old. Why then, with the closing of the door, did he feel as if a dagger had been thrust into his heart? Why did he suddenly long for her? As much as the questions defied logic, the answers were eminently clear. Emotions were devoid of reason. A largess, long unwanted, once sought and denied, begot heartache. Head down, dispirited, he shuffled through the snow. Images of Juliette turning him away from her doorstep flashed in Thom's head. The more they reverberated, the more disheartening they became. Discomfort snowballed into humiliation.

༄༅༅

In 1659 the General Court of Massachusetts had imposed a fine of five shillings on those who tried to celebrate Christmas. Nearly a century had passed since the law had been repealed. Still Christmas Day, 1773, was hardly a holiday in Tyringham, Massachusetts.[107] Other colonies, particularly in the South, had begun to commemorate the birth of Jesus with increasing observance and festivity, but not Massachusetts. Among Anglicans, Roman Catholics and Lutherans, the Twelve Days of Christmas, the period from December 25th to January 6th, had seen growing celebration with alcohol-spurred merriment in the streets and occasional fireworks, but in Congregationalist

Massachusetts old taboos died hard. For residents of the Bay Colony, Tyringham included, Christmas was a normal workday, devoid of what traditionalists deemed the shameless degradation of the Lord's birth. However, Sarah Albright viewed it differently. Celebration of the holiday, albeit private, was appropriate, provided the bounds of good taste were maintained. She adorned the interior of her home with holly and ivy and prepared a feast that set the day apart from others. With each passing year the ritual's scope expanded. Seventeen seventy-three was no exception. The dining room table was bedecked with her fine Holland tablecloth, yellow-brown from the dye of the butternut tree, along with polished pewter, rather than daily woodenware. Thom donned his embroidered linen waistcoat, silk cravat with laced edge, and silk stockings bearing clocks.[108] Sarah read aloud the final chapter of the Book of Deuteronomy where God led Moses to the top of Mount Nebo that he might see, but not go thither into the Promised Land.[109] Sarah loved the passage, the symbolism it conveyed, as Moses, on the brink of the land God swore to Abraham, Issac and Jacob, died in Moab in his 120th year. A recitation of the "Lord's Prayer" followed, after which they embarked on the glutinous feast she had prepared. A sumptuous fish chowder began the meal. Roasted goose, pompion casserole,[110] apple fritters and molasses-sweetened cornbread, along with Santa Cruz rum, came next. An apple pie, its heavenly aroma an aphrodisiac of decadence, topped with cinnamon ice cream, along with maple sugar candies and a raspberry tea, completed the repast. Ordinarily a rapid eater, Thom savored each bite as he dined with gentility befitting the sublime spread. With stomach full, he leaned back, occasionally reaching for a sip of rum or a nibble of maple sugar candy.

"Hope we can do it up like this next year," said Sarah.

Thom was more than willing. But if Sarah was hoping he would continue to live there, she would be disappointed. The ambiguity left him at a loss for words.

"Don't worry. I know you'll be moving on. And I don't blame you. If I were twenty-some years younger and your age, no way would I stay longer than necessary in an old lady's back room."

"C'mon, you're not an old lady." Echoes from his feeble attempt at disagreement had Thom cringing.

"In my mind I'm not...but to a young fellow like you, I'm an old woman."

Acquiescence was out of the question, but Thom was not about to stick another foot into his mouth. He shook his head.

Sarah winked before taking a sip of her tea. "Bottom line—you want to live in a home of your own. And speaking of that, how's your saltbox coming?"

"We just finished the floor this week."

"That's great. But who's *we*?"

Thom nearly choked on his Santa Cruz rum as he struggled to keep from breaking his promise to Pico.

"You okay?"

"Uh...yeah." Thom cleared his throat, choreographing steps to dance around his stumble. "My saltbox is a team effort. Yours truly, and, of course, Lodestone. Without him dragging the heavy loads, I couldn't have built the house." To avoid eye contact, Thom sipped his rum. He chided himself for the slip of the tongue.

"Did you—" Sarah turned in the direction of the front hall in reaction to a rap of the brass door knocker. "Who could that be?" She glanced at the English Bracket Clock, a mantel timepiece brought across the Atlantic by her grandfather. "After three o'clock on Christmas Day?"

"I'll see," said Thom, getting up from the table. "Who's there?" he said, as he approached the door.

"Richard...Richard Thorn."

Even before Richard finished repeating his name, the familiar voice had Thom reaching for the door and opening it.

"Sorry to barge in." Tucked under his arm, Richard carried a newspaper. "But I had to tell you what happened in Boston, unless by chance you've heard already?"

Thom shook his head. He looked at Sarah.

"Got me."

Thom ushered Richard in and started to take his frock.

"No...no, I'll only stay a minute."

Sarah, who had risen from the table and moved to the brink of the hallway, said, "You'll do no such thing, especially on Christmas Day. You'll sit down and have some apple pie and cinnamon ice cream, along with some candies and a cup of tea or, if you'd rather...a noggin of mead."

Thom might have pressed Richard, but there was no need. He was inching toward the dining room. He was a sucker for the alcoholic liquor, made from Sarah's special formula of fermented honey, yeast, spices and water.

"Have a seat," she said, as she went to fetch the seductive libation.

"In a second." Richard handed Thom his frock. "First I have to tell you both about Boston."

"You can do that soon enough. For now, sit down and relax." A minute later Sarah returned with Richard's drink. She took her seat at one end, with Thom at the other, and Richard on the side nearer the hearth.

"As everyone knows," said Richard, "it's been a stalemate with those three ships of the East India Company sitting in Boston Harbor for weeks. The Sons of Liberty, along with the gathered throng, prevented the ships from being unloaded, and Governor Hutchinson barred the ships from leaving until the duty on their cargo is paid."

"But according to Jenkins," said Thom, "Hutchinson has the law on his side. After twenty days he can sell the cargo and use the money to pay the salaries of the Crown's employees. If recollection serves me, the twenty days ran out about a week ago."

"You're right. On December 17th, to be precise."

Thom groaned. "You don't have to tell me. The cargo was seized."

Richard shook his head.

"Seriously?" said Sarah.

"Rather than misstating the story, let me read it to you directly from the December 20th edition of the Boston Gazette. Dan Heath was nice enough to save me a copy at the Hogshead when the travelers' wagon came through yesterday morning." Richard unfolded his newspaper. "I'll skip all the stuff you already know and cut right to the chase."

*"The people finding all their efforts to preserve the property of the East India company and return it safely to London, frustrated by the tea consignees, the collector of the customs and the governor of the province, DISSOLVED their meeting.—But, BEHOLD what followed! A number of brave & resolute men, determined to do all in their power to save their country from the ruin which their enemies had plotted, in less than four hours, emptied every chest of tea on board the three ships commanded by captains Hall, Bruce, and Coffin, amounting to 342 chests, into the sea!! without the least damage done to the ships or any other property. The maiters and owners are well pleas'd that their ships are thus clear'd; and the people are almost universally congratulating each other on this happy event."* [111]

"Wow!" said Thom, as he struggled to digest the startling revelation.

"Pretty amazing, isn't it?" said Richard. "According to what Heath heard from the travelers, there were thousands in the crowd down near Faneuil Hall and the Old South Church when about fifty or sixty men, dressed as Mohawk Indians—but apparently none too well disguised—climbed aboard the three ships and tossed the tea overboard. [112] The travelers said the cargo was worth about eighteen thousand pounds. Of course, their information was fifth hand at best."

"Hutchinson must be out of his mind," said Thom.

"I doubt Parliament will be thrilled once they get the news." Sarah raised her cup. "I've only got a little tea left."

Thom rose to get the kettle from the fireplace crane.

"Don't get up. My cup is still half-full. I was referring to the tea stored in the buttery." She heaved a sigh. "Given what's happening, it will be hard to come by."

Richard chuckled.

"Something funny?" said Sarah.

"Sorry, I wasn't laughing because you may have to do without tea. I was thinking that matters have gone well beyond a boycott, what with the events in Boston Harbor."

"Any guesses how the royal government will react?" said Sarah.

The three looked around the table at one another. No one tackled the question. Thom suspected they shared similar views. Retribution in one form or another was inevitable. He said, "Whatever the consequences, I, for one, am glad they dumped the tea, though a different harbor might have been preferable. New York or Philadelphia would have been nice, or, better yet, down south in Charleston. Of all the colonies it seems we're always the one in hot water."

Richard, who was nursing his mead, pulled his noggin away from his lips and stared at Thom. "I hear what you're saying, but circumstances all but excluded those cities. Unlike Boston where the consignees of the tea were Hutchinson's family and friends, the tea agents in the other ports canceled their orders or resigned their commissions in support of the boycott."[113]

"I know," said Thom, familiar with the point. "I was voicing wishful thinking. And don't get me wrong. I support the action one hundred percent."

"Well, I do...and I don't," said Sarah.

"What does that mean?" An edge sneaked into Richard's voice.

"Don't get me wrong. I'm all for resisting tyranny, but destroying private property is another matter."

"C'mon," said Richard. "We're talking about the East India Company, a government-blessed monopoly. And keep in mind that the tea was consigned to Hutchinson's corrupt cronies."

"I understand. But all I'm saying is that wanton destruction of private property gives me pause." Sarah peered in the direction of her prized clock. "But pause only. To be heard, sometimes people need to do what they need to do."

The redundant cliché was hardly the epitome of logical explication. Nevertheless, it reflected Thom's feelings. He looked down the length of the table and said, "Well put."

A puzzled look appeared on Richard's face, but he made no comment.

"How did folks at the Hogshead react to the news?" said Thom.

"Not sure. Few were there, plus I was in a hurry."

"Ought to be interesting grist for the trough," said Thom.

"Even more interesting," said Sarah, "will be the reactions of Governor Hutchinson and Parliament."

◯◯◯◯◯

Bent on enhancing Pico's food supply, Thom had spent the morning hunting deer or whatever meaty game might present itself. For several hours he had staked out opportune spots to bag his prey. Most of the time he had hidden in a small thicket. An occasional rustling would arouse him from growing lethargy, but a few crows and sparrows or an occasional squirrel were all that crossed his path. Though a gray sky helped him blend in, he wondered if the barren vegetation, coupled with the contrast of the pristine snow, rendered him visible to the wary animals. In an effort to improve his luck, he shifted to a new location between two maples. He rolled several balls of snow and piled them in a makeshift fort about three feet high, complete with a one foot square opening through which he could unobtrusively keep a lookout and shoot. Armed with his powder horn and his club butt fowler, named for its hefty convex butt,[114] Thom watched and waited, hoping a potential target might appear among the spindly birches and poplars.

Thom could handle a gun. Following a shot, he could reload his smooth-bored fowler in less than thirty seconds, assuming no hitches. But he was no marksman. Beyond thirty or forty yards, he depended on luck, more than expertise. In part he attributed it to his weapon. A fowler lacked the accuracy of a rifle. But Thom's proficiency or, more precisely, his lack of it played a bigger role. A year earlier Richard had proved the point hitting targets from fifty yards with Thom's fowler. Try as he did, Thom could not duplicate the performance. Thom might have opted for a more accurate rifled weapon, which with grooved barrel imparted spin to a bullet enabling it to maintain a truer path, but he already had his fowler, and, unlike a rifle, his fowler could deliver a variety of smaller-sized shot. It was also quicker to load.[115]

Nearly two hours had elapsed with Thom crouched behind his snow fort waiting to fire his first shot. Amongst the trees, at fifty yards, a deer stepped into view. It meandered from Thom's right to his left. Straight ahead on a line to twelve o'clock, the deer stopped and bowed its head, nibbling at sparse weeds. A pair of birches, midway between Thom and his prey, obscured half the deer. His finger on the trigger, Thom debated whether to fire or hope for a better shot. The deer raised its head. Imminent departure was a distinct possibility. Vacillation, even for a few seconds, could mean opportunity lost, and opportunity lost could mean no opportunity. Thom squeezed the trigger. Cocked hammer struck flint, spark ignited, powder exploded and ball fired, all with virtual simultaneity. The deer scampered away. Thom heaved a sigh as he watched the graceful animal vanish through the woods. He reached for his powder horn but halted. It was past midday. The idea of waiting several more hours for another chance was ludicrous. The hunt needed to be postponed to another day.

Thom packed up his gear and headed to his saltbox. Pico met him at the door.

"You got your gun today. Gonna hunt?"

"I already did."

"And?"

"What you see is what I bagged." Thom shrugged. "I had hoped to shoot a deer."

"Venison is good. Need some?"

Thom shook his head. "I wanted it for you."

"Appreciate that, but I got a deer. Shot it with my bow and arrow, 'bout a month ago. Cut it up, salted and smoked it and packed each piece in ice I made from snow. It's stored in my stash." Pico appeared to study Thom. "Seems you didn't believe I got lotsa food." He shook his head. "Why can't white men understand? We've lived and survived in these woods for centuries."

They had indeed, and done it well. Thom was getting the point. Nevertheless, it was hard to accept that Pico, only sixteen, was self-sufficient. "You amaze me. At your age...it's hard to fathom."

"Fathom?"

"Understand...how you manage."

"Why? It's what we learn...Anyway, from what you told me, you were 'bout my age when you boarded a ship and sailed across the ocean."

The remark stirred images of Thom's rebellious youth. "I was nearly eighteen. A year or so makes a big difference, and, regardless, I was a boatswain's assistant. I merely had to do as I was told."

"Well...we do what we have to. And don't forget, Pico has an advantage."

"Advantage?" From Thom's perspective, circumstances were the opposite. "How do you figure?"

"Pico grew up in two worlds, the Indians' and the white man's. Mom made sure I learned from both...and took the best of each. The Indians taught me to deal with nature. The missionaries taught me history and science and religion, not that Pico cared for theirs." A moment later Pico was out the door. He returned carrying a piece of meat. "Thought you might like a venison steak."

The idea of taking food from Pico was untoward, but refusing, unthinkable. Together they cooked the venison, along with some carrots Pico had brought. They dined on the floor in front of the hearth. A hearty bread with apple butter that Thom had carried in his haversack completed the repast.

A question, one that had lingered in Thom's mind since they had met, bubbled to the surface. Having evolved from strangers to friends, the need to suppress curiosity had faded. "I've been wondering—but feel free to tell me to mind my own business—why you sometimes refer to yourself in the third person?"

About to take a bite, Pico halted, his countenance pensive.

The reaction stirred second thoughts. Voicing the nosy question may have been a mistake.

"Back when I was living in the woods, it got mighty lonely. I needed someone to talk to. The squirrels and birds and trees were good listeners, but when it came to real conversation, one with back and forth, forget it. And so I talked to myself...a whole lot. Often my brain said one thing, while my heart, another. I got in the habit of letting *Pico* speak for my brain, and *I,* for my heart. At first it was a game, a way to ease the loneliness, but gradually it grew into a tool of self-debate."

A thinker himself, familiar with solitude, the unexpected explanation intrigued Thom. "So, depending whether you use *Pico* or *I,* one can tell if you're talking from your mind or your heart."

"Not really. Now when I'm with others, I tend to use *Pico* and *I* interchangeably. Whether a coin is called a shilling or twenty pence, it's the same." Pico chewed his last bites of venison. He said, "Been making lath, just the way you showed me. Come...see." He led the way from the parlor to the dining room. He pointed to a pile in the far corner. "Pico cut them so they stretch across three studs."

Thom picked one up. "Nice work...very nice," he said, as he examined the two-inch wide, hand-riven hickory board. Rough and irregular, with bumps and crags, it was imperfect, but with lath that *was* perfect. Along the grain, as Thom had taught, Pico had hacked splits into the board, increasing its ability to accept and retain the plaster that would seal the home from howling winds. Thom looked at two more. They were equally good. "You're a damn good lath man."

"Not hard to make."

The point had merit, but fashioning the many strips needed to line the interior walls was time consuming. "That may be, but you've saved me many hours."

"Pico's not a leech. Like you, he earns his room and board."

"You do indeed." More and more, Thom was seeing his generosity recompensed.

"Once we've made the lath, you'll teach Pico more house-building skills? Perhaps Pico will build one of his own, someday." He gestured all around. "Kinda late to learn from this. Already built."

"Not on the inside." Thom started to reach for the hatchet that lay next to the pile of lath. Before he could, Pico grabbed it.

"Pico will make more strips while you put them up."

The division of labor, an efficient approach, had definite appeal. Nevertheless, Thom shook his head. "Let's first put some up together. That way you'll learn every step."

Pico smiled.

The reaction rekindled memories of days following Thom's arrival in Boston when his mentor had taken Thom under his wing. He had involved Thom in every phase, educating him in the details. And evenings when the work was done, he had exposed Thom to the architectural, scientific and mathematical principles underlying the procedures. Thom felt the glow he saw on Pico's face. Thom welcomed the opportunity to be a teacher. Unlike his days in Boston where knowledge flowed mainly in one direction, he realized there was much he could learn from Pico. Thom said, "We'll teach one another."

Pico shrugged, as if to suggest they had been doing so all along.

Thom contemplated whether he was reading more into the gesture than it connoted. Knowing Pico, it was possible the subtle message was intended...On second thought, probable.

Together they hacked and hewed and trimmed the strips of hickory lath and nailed them crosswise to the vertical studs, leaving roughly a quarter-inch space between adjacent strips that later would be filled with the plaster overlay. The teamwork enabled the endeavor to move faster than if Thom were doing it alone. There were intangible benefits too. The company and the conversation they shared made the process more satisfying.

# Chapter 11

AS THE DAYS OF JANUARY 1774 waned, the long nights waited until after five o'clock before descending upon the Berkshires. But once their mantle took hold, especially when clouds were thick, apart from a kerosene lantern and a fire at the hearth, the darkness was total. Outside the black of night was pervasive.

Thom and Pico had finished nailing the lath to the interior walls. Months earlier Thom had stored a supply of sand and limestone, the latter nearly as plentiful as the former in the mountain terrain. With a heavy hammer Thom pulverized the limestone and added sand and water to make a mixture of plaster. With temporary vertical lath guides in place, he dragged a wooden board upward between the guides as Pico fed the plaster onto the board. The plaster coated the wall and oozed through the spaces between the permanent horizontal rows of lath, creating a seal while assuring adherence.[116]

The duo switched roles with Pico dragging the board and Thom administering the plaster. The process moved so rapidly that Thom, contrary to his original plan, opted for a second sandy brown coat. A final smooth white coat followed. Thoughts of someday paneling the parlor and/or dining room, complete with chair rails and wainscoting, percolated. For the time being, white walls, perhaps with a coat of red paint, sufficed. Green, made from copper compounds such as verdigris, was too expensive. Even if Thom were wealthier, he would not have opted for the garish display.

Pico and Thom were applying the finish coat of plaster when they heard a knock at the door. Thom put a finger to his lips. He pointed at the cellar. "Be there in a minute," he called out.

Once Pico had hidden, Thom opened the door.

"Seems you've pulled another of your vanishing acts," said Richard. "More than a month, and no one has heard from you."

"I've been working."

"Aren't you going to invite me in?"

"Uh...sure," said Thom, though hints of Pico's presence all about rendered the concession reluctant.

"I'm on my way to the Hogshead, but first I want to see your handiwork." Richard stepped inside. "You seem jumpy. Something wrong?"

"No." The alacrity with which the response leaped from Thom's tongue belied the reply.

Richard gave him a look before gazing around the premises. "Wow, it's really shaping up. I'm impressed." He stepped to his right into the dining room, on through to the kitchen and into the parlor. "It's a real home."

"That was the idea."

"I know, but with a single guy it's generally your basic cabin."

Thom pointed to a spot several feet inside the front door. "I plan to put stairs here leading up to a loft."

"Damn, you're going for the full treatment." Richard gestured toward the hearth. "You never told me you bagged a bear."

Dealing with Pico's bearskin was a delicate issue, and Thom was unprepared. "I didn't...exactly."

"What's that—the remains of the world's largest pussycat?"

Lying to his best friend was unacceptable, but no way could he break his promise to Pico. "It's a bear, but it's a long...long story."

"I've got time, especially for a tale of big game."

"Uh...there's not much to tell." Thom focused on the bearskin, avoiding eye contact with Richard. "And it's...it's not all that interesting."

"On the contrary, it's becoming more interesting by the second. Maybe you killed it with your *bare* hands?" With a gleam in his eye, presumably occasioned by the play on words, Richard leaned around where he could see Thom's face. "There's more to this than you're letting on, isn't there?"

Denial, an outright lie, was problematic. "I...I'd rather not say."

Richard stared at Thom protractedly. "What's going on?"

"It's my bearskin." The voice came from the kitchen. A moment later Pico entered from the rear of the parlor.

"You didn't need to come out," said Thom.

"I know, but that would have left you in a tough spot."

"Well, I would have managed...or at least I would have tried." Thom turned to Richard. "This is Pico. He's been helping me with the house."

"Nice to meet you, Pico. I'm Richard." His expression hinted that his curiosity remained rampant.

"Let me explain," said Pico. "Last autumn Pico began staying here, not that he was invited. One day, Thom caught Pico hiding in the cellar. He coulda thrown me out but didn't. He's been very kind."

"Are you from around here?" said Richard.

Pico shook his head. He went on to detail how his father had abandoned his mother, their experience with the missionaries and his mother's death.

"If I understand, you came to Tyringham more than a year ago. Where did you live before that?"

"At the schoolhouse...till it burned down last spring."

Richard's eyes widened.

"Pico had nothing to do with that," said Thom. He saw doubt in Richard's face. "He had no reason. The fire left him homeless." The logic was excellent. An uncomfortable silence suggested the explanation was ineffective.

"I'm on my way to the Hogshead," said Richard. "Hoped you'd join me."

"Sure." Thom's usual reluctance was absent. He welcomed an opportunity to convince Richard to keep Pico's presence a secret. Not knowing whether Richard might balk, broaching the subject would be difficult in front of Pico. Thom grabbed his frock and, along with Richard, headed for the Hogshead.

They were no more than a few yards from the house when Richard said, "What are you doing?"

"What do you mean?"

"The Indian boy."

"Pico...What about him?"

"What about him! The school...need I remind you it went up in flames?"

189

"You're not suggesting Pico's responsible?"

Richard remained mute.

"C'mon...why would he when—"

"Maybe it was an accident. All the same, it burned down when he was there. If you're not careful, your lovely saltbox could be next."

"You're making something out of nothing."

"Am I?" Richard looked Thom in the eye. "So—you're not worried?"

"Not really." The response, a poor effort to deny misgivings, failed to negate them. They walked a little farther, each with his own thoughts. Thom said, "I appreciate your concerns, but you have to promise you won't tell anyone about Pico."

Richard jerked to a halt. "Just why must I do that?"

"Because I promised Pico if he stayed I wouldn't let anyone know." The screaming illogic of the purported justification, as well as the frown on Richard's face, forced Thom to rethink his approach. "And because I'm asking you...as a friend."

"I don't like it, but...I'll tell you what. For now, I'll keep silent. If and when I change my mind, and I will if there's something more linking your friend to the schoolhouse fire, I'll let you know before I make the disclosure. Fair enough?"

Thom hesitated but, knowing he had no bargaining power, nodded.

Minutes later they arrived at the Hogshead. They joined George Whitaker, Ezra Jenkins and Orville Crane at a table in the center of the tavern.

Thom's gaze met Crane's. The discomfort on Crane's face convinced Thom they had the same thought. Crane was yet to pay Thom the money owed. The lapse of time hinted that the blacksmith might try to dodge the obligation.

"We were discussing what happened several weeks ago in Boston," said Jenkins. "By now, word must have reached Parliament."

"Predictions how they'll react?" said Richard.

"Not the specifics, but one thing sure, they won't take it lying down. One way or another, they'll make us pay. And I for one," said the attorney, "don't blame them."

"Is that so?" said Richard.

"Hey, what do you expect with a shipload of tea, more than three hundred chests, dumped into the sea.[117] You expect them to sit by? Hell, it wouldn't surprise me if they have troops occupy Boston, at least until the tea and the duty on it is fully paid." Jenkins looked around the table as if seeking confirmation. "As a matter of fact, I wouldn't blame them if they did. The damn Sons of Liberty with their do-as-they-please, flout-the-law attitude, have invited it."

"Well...perhaps if we're lucky," said Whitaker, "it'll just be Boston's problem."

"Dream on, McDuff." Jenkins folded his arms against his rotund torso. "If the other colonies have any brains, they'll keep their noses clean and avoid Parliament's wrath. As for Massachusetts, our goose is cooked. And for that matter, rightly so."

"What do you mean, 'rightly so?'" Richard glared at Jenkins.

"Save the nasty puss for the moles that frequent your garden." Disdain oozed from the lawyer's voice. "Massachusetts is a colony, nothing more. We're the child of England, our Mother Country. They protects us from foreign powers and Indians. Like every child, we depend upon such protection. But like every child, from time to time we become impudent, and need to be put in our place. Tantrums, like the Tea Party in the Boston Harbor, demand discipline."

"Excuse me!" said Whitaker.

"Don't tell me you disagree, George?" The lawyer's eyes were wide.

"In fact, I do."

Umbrage from the Yankee Trader, ordinarily an enthusiastic member of the lawyer's choir, surprised Thom. It pleased him as well.

"Why," said Jenkins, "when you accept Parliament's legislative authority, would you have a problem?"

"Legislate...fine. But treat us like children. No way!" Whitaker rapped his tankard on the table.

"Since when did you start agreeing with the rebels?"

"George doesn't agree with us," said Thom. "But like us, he resents being patronized."

191

"Oh my," said Jenkins. "Pour a couple ales down his gullet and look who becomes feisty."

"Good for him," said Whitaker. "Because he happens to be right. Your condescension irks me."

"Of all the..." Jenkins trailed off in audible muttering.

Richard, who was seated between Whitaker and Thom, slapped the two on the back. "Hear, hear. I believe you've accomplished the impossible. You've muzzled the Massachusetts Mouth." He raised his tankard. "A toast to a moment of silence." The others, save Jenkins, joined in the salute.

A bristling Jenkins glared at Crane. "*Et tu*...my smithy friend?"

Puzzlement sculpting his face, Crane lowered his tankard.

Jenkins shifted his focus to the others. "Guffaw, if you must. But like our brethren from the South, your insolence is a poor mask for envy."

"Envy...the South? What are you babbling about?" said Richard.

"The secular philistines in the southern colonies devote their energies to accumulating wealth. Why?—to hide their godless and uneducated inadequacies."

"What does that have to do with our discussion?" said Whitaker.

Nothing, suspected Thom, familiar with the lawyer's technique for wriggling out from the short end of a debate. He had seen the lawyer do it before. Like an illusionist, he utilized a distraction. A *non sequitur* was the perfect device.

"Think about it," said Jenkins. "Folks in the South don't know squash about anything involving matters of substance."

"He's right," said the normally taciturn Crane, his face beaming.

The comment drew a chuckle from Thom. The blacksmith provided Jenkins with the perfect audience.

"Here, I'll prove my point." Jenkins sat up taller. "There are eight colleges in the colonies. Harvard, the oldest, nearly one hundred forty years, and most esteemed, is here in Massachusetts."

192

"Reverend Bidwell might beg to differ. He graduated from Yale," said Whitaker.

"He might," said Jenkins, "but his view would be biased. Anyway, that's not the point. Yale is in Connecticut, a northern colony. New Jersey has Princeton and Rutgers; Pennsylvania has Penn; New York, Columbia; Rhode Island, Brown, though that institution is dubious, what with the radical curriculum and non-sectarian admission standards adopted by its Baptist founders; and then there's the Johnny-come-lately Dartmouth that recently opened its doors in New Hampshire. And before anyone gets excited, I know, Virginia claims William and Mary. But that's the only college south of Philadelphia. The Carolinas, Maryland and Georgia have nothing. Form over substance—that's the southern way. Gentility and manners are pretenses. Education, the kind that produces a learned and accomplished society with good Christian values, takes a back seat to a bourgeois mentality."

"Damn," said Crane, making eye contact with Thom for the first time in nearly an hour. "Ezra knows his stuff. Unlike most who spout manure, he gives ya the facts, straight from A to Z."

Thom glanced at Jenkins. He squeezed his lips, restraining the urge to call the lawyer on the ruse. Any buffoon could memorize the names of the eight colleges that dotted the colonies. Rattling them off while the real issue vanished in their dust was a charlatan trick that could fool only a halfwit. Of course, Orville Crane was exactly that. Well...almost. Thom assumed that Richard saw through the stratagem. As for Whitaker, skilled as the Yankee Trader was at the bait and switch, he was a good bet too.

~᭳᭳᭳~

Like a fox slithering through the bushes of the Beartown Mountain woods, the days of February, a mere four weeks, had come and gone with little fanfare. On average Thom was at his saltbox five days a week, skipping the days when, with howling winds, the thermometer plunged. Occasionally he stayed overnight. Most times he rode there on Lodestone, but now and then he took the long walk from Sarah's place up to Beartown

Mountain. It was a sunny morning, the first week of March, as he wended his way up Mount Hunger Road. A storm the evening before had covered the ground with several inches. Stately bowing evergreens displayed pristine white mantles. Towering oaks and maples, bearing slim powdery coatings, contrasted against the cobalt sky.

Nearly a year had elapsed since Thom had begun building his home. Driven determination, at times bordering on crazed obsession, had literally and figuratively enabled the seemingly insurmountable undertaking to get off the ground. Fixation on the project had helped suppress the torment attributable to the heartbreaking loss of Polly's love. Dogged persistence through summer and fall had kept Thom preoccupied as he prevailed in the race to produce an enclosed structure before winter's return. But winter, the Berkshire's long, harsh night, at least in Thom's eyes, had been remarkably benign. Four walls and a roof had enabled him to labor in relative comfort, notwithstanding what the elements dealt. Dressed in layers, a fire blazing in the fireplace, he and Pico had turned the shell into a livable structure. They had installed a trap door leading from the rear of the kitchen to the cellar. They had added a stairway that began inside the front door and led to a loft over the parlor and one side of the kitchen. Pico, originally a squatter, had played a bigger role in the transformation than Thom had expected. He had enabled Thom to take on new roles. At times Thom was a mentor. Others, he was an older sibling. Occasionally, he was a father figure. Most times, a pal. Sometimes, the pupil. Two winters had slipped by since Polly had wed. On the calendar they had been identical. Both had been cold with abundant snow. But within the confines of Thom's mind, they felt like night and day.

As he turned onto the Albany-Boston Post Road, the sparkle of snow melting beneath the warm glow of the March sun caught Thom's eye. In rapid metamorphosis the foreboding gloom of the prior night's storm had yielded to a fresh white blanket. Thom's step quickened as he neared his saltbox. He had a new outlook. Perhaps he was ready to get on with his life. In some respects he already had.

With a fierce blow Pico drove his tomahawk into the face of the large sugar maple. He drew the razor-sharp hatchet out and with careful aim gashed the tree a second time forming a perfect "V." In late February and early March when daytime temperatures had often sneaked past forty, only to dip below freezing at night, maple sap had begun to flow. Rather than bear the expense of imported cane sugar, many of Thom's Tyringham neighbors, like others in the Northeast, made maple syrup and sugar from the countless maple trees that dotted the Berkshire forests. Long-time locals claimed that European settlers had learned to make maple syrup from the Stockbridge Indians in Tyringham at Camp Brook.[118]

Pico inserted a hollowed-out elderberry stem into the wedge he had hacked, allowing the sap to drain into his birch-bark bucket. Thom watched as Pico gashed another maple.

"Can I try?" said Thom.

Pico handed him the tomahawk.

Thom struck a well-angled blow. He drew the tomahawk from the tree and struck it again. The second gash was equally deep, but the two oblique lines were more than two inches apart at their closest. Thom pulled the tomahawk from the tree and struck it once more. The newest cut was no better than its predecessor. He gave the tomahawk to Pico. "You better make the cuts."

Pico went around to the opposite side of the maple and, with remarkable ease, hacked another perfect "V." "Takes practice," he said. He handed Thom the third and last of his elderberry stems and birch-bark buckets. "You can do this part."

Thom slipped the stem into the tree and set the bucket below. "Good thing you've got me along. I can't imagine how you'd manage otherwise."

Pico laughed. "Our backgrounds taught us different things."

"I suppose, but when I was your age, I knew far less than you do now."

Pico shrugged. "You grew up in an English town, while my childhood was spent living off the land."

What Pico had said was accurate, but candor forced Thom to concede it failed to credit the independence, maturity and remarkable range of skills that Pico had acquired. "When I signed on as a boatswain's assistant, my buttons were bursting because I was on my own. Next to what you've accomplished, it was nothing. All my needs, food, clothing and shelter, were provided. Sure, I labored long at tedious chores, but higher ups told me what to do and when. Next to you, I was greener than the Emerald Isle from which my mother's ancestors came."

As if Thom had been talking to himself, Pico went about his business pouring another bucket of water on a maple tree to facilitate the flow of sap.

Thom made a mental note. Often his silence, a disconcerted display of vanishing poise, left him on the short end of a debate. Without uttering a word, Pico had managed to make light of Thom's point. Many times Thom had observed that one's manner of speech could be more important than what one said. But never had he seen the art of silence better demonstrated. As Pico hung the last of his birch-bark buckets from a maple, Thom watched intently. The day's work had been completed. Drop by drop, the buckets would fill overnight.

The following morning the two were back at the task. From the firewood out behind the saltbox, Pico fetched a log about two feet long. He hewed one side, flattening it into a stable bottom. He hollowed out the upper side creating an elliptical vessel on top. He gathered about twenty stones and placed them into a fire he built in the center of the clearing that fronted the saltbox. He fetched the birch-bark buckets of maple sap and poured them into the hollowed-out log. He put the hot stones into the carved-out log, causing water in the sap to boil off as steam. Patience, the passage of time, turned the sap into a thick, gooey, sugary syrup. From a shaded area out behind the saltbox, Pico gathered snow and rolled it into a large ball. He placed a portion of the syrup onto the snow. Gradually the chilled syrup crystallized into maple sugar.[119] Pico repeated the process again and again.

With each step, even those that seemed obvious, Thom asked questions. They helped him commit the process to memory. But he also had a more subtle purpose. Numerous times he had lauded Pico's skills, but by taking the role of the keenly interested student, Thom validated those skills and communicated respect. It was one of the many lessons Thom had learned from his mentor in Boston; however, it was uniquely ironic in that Thom had learned it on that rare occasion when he was the teacher, and his mentor, the student.

# Chapter 12

THE CALENDAR INDICATED one week until spring's official arrival. While the peak of Beartown Mountain remained white with snow, the area fronting Thom's saltbox, with its southern exposure, revealed ever-growing patches of bare ground. Two hundred yards west of his home where a wall of sheer granite descended vertically over twenty feet, sun-drenched icicles, some taller than Thom, sparkled as water dripped from their dagger-like tips. Winter was certain to breathe some last gasps, but an irrepressible sun, higher in the sky with each passing day, had all but subdued nature's wrath. Soon robins would chirp, crocuses would sprout and trees would bud.

Inside the saltbox, spring was in full bloom. Afternoon sunbeams shining through the front windows, coupled with a blaze at the hearth, warmed the interior close to seventy. With the benefit of Pico's labor, projects once presumed to be distant endeavors had been tackled. Chair rails had been installed in both the dining room and parlor. A pair of cranes capable of swinging pots in and out of the dining-room fireplace had been affixed. Two simple bed frames and a pair of chairs for the dining room had been fashioned. In a few weeks, Thom planned to move in, though he anticipated spending a night or two each week at Sarah Albright's for the foreseeable future. Much as he would have been happy to live exclusively in his own home, knowing that she would appreciate the company motivated the compromise.

While the Tea Party in Boston provided grist for conversation, and most assumed its worst reverberations were yet to be heard, the winter in Tyringham had been quiet. Like the hibernating animals, folks had spent much of their time holed up in their homes. To be sure there was activity, much of it at the Hogshead, as well as Sundays at Reverend Bidwell's, but compared to warmer seasons, activity had been at its ebb.

With several weeks having passed since Thom had been to the Hogshead, he pushed himself to make an appearance. It was busy, and a number of the regulars were there. Peter Blake, Wendell Dinsmore and Deacon Hale were seated near the door. They were good enough fellows, but Thom found conversation with the Deacon difficult, and spending time with Peter, Polly's husband, was a byway to the blues. An inviting gesture from Paul Cooper, who was seated in the corner with George Whitaker and Ezra Jenkins, drew Thom in their direction. He always felt more comfortable when Richard was among the group—evidence that his acclimation to life in Tyringham was still a work in progress—but a trio of Cooper, Whitaker and Jenkins was acceptable.

"Have a seat," said Whitaker, making room for Thom on his side of the booth.

"Haven't seen much of you lately." Jenkins waved his arm, catching Mary's attention. "An ale for our friend."

"I've been busy with my house, a combination of that and winter."

"How's it coming?" said Cooper.

"Better than expected. Details on the interior remain, but otherwise it's built."

"It looks good from the outside," said Whitaker. "Last week while I was out your way, I took a detour to see it. If the inside is anything like the exterior, it's a fine place."

"Appreciate that." Thom took a swig of the ale Mary delivered. "Thought I might find Richard here tonight."

"He's been almost as scarce as you." Jenkins shook his head. "Defies logic. Single fellows like you and Rich, free as birds, oughta be here more than us married guys."

Thom shrugged, not that he disagreed.

"Did you hear what happened to Ben Franklin?" said Whitaker.

Thom shrugged again.

"He was publicly reprimanded in England. It happened back in January. Folks in Boston heard about it last week, and a fellow passing through told Issac Winslow yesterday."

"Why the reprimand?"

"Well, you probably recall that last year there were accusations against those who leaked the Hutchinson letters, the ones in which our Governor urged Parliament to send more troops to suppress any rebellion here. According to Issac, Franklin came forward and admitted he was responsible for the leak. It caused a big to-do. Parliament and King George were livid. And Hutchinson went nuts. They say he was madder than a hog with a hornet up its ass. Anyway, they gave Franklin what for. Word has it, he's as welcome in England as a leper with smallpox."[120]

"Any news how the powers that be across the Atlantic are reacting to December's Tea Party?" said Thom.

"Not yet," said Jenkins, "but pounds to pence, they'll kick our asses."

"I, for one, support the action," said Cooper. "Parliament thinks they can treat us like chattel. Action, not words, is the only language they understand."

"I can't believe you radicals." Whitaker's fingers adroitly manipulated the tips of the long whiskers that formed the lower margin of his beard. "You're no better than pirates and thugs. You destroy other people's property, and you cheer about it as if it were a noble deed."

"George is absolutely right," said Jenkins. "We purport to be civilized, governed by laws, not mobs."

"You make it sound simple."

Jenkins shot Thom a look.

"Parliament shows no regard for us. They make laws without giving us a say. You expect us to sit back and do nothing?"

Jenkins fed Thom another glare before turning his gaze to Cooper. "Like you, apparently Mr. Webster views the Tea Party as a glorious deed."

"Did I say that, *Mr. Jenkins*?" Like the lawyer, Thom could turn the respectful term of address into one of condescension. "As a matter of fact, I asked you a question, and I didn't hear an answer."

"Ooh...the normally reticent one suddenly has a prickly tongue." Jenkins smirked. "But fine, refresh me as to your inquiry."

Thom hesitated, as he carefully reframed his question. "Given that Parliament consistently ignores us, what would you suggest?"

"Voice our objections with determination and, of course...patience."

"We've done that for decades," snapped Cooper. "And what has it gotten us? Nothing!"

"Not true," said Jenkins. "We won the repeal of the Townsend Acts, as well as the Stamp Act."

"Well, Hallelujah." Cooper raised his tankard in a gesture of sardonic salute. "They repealed the Stamp Act. And why?—because the British merchants screamed for it. The truth is that every time Parliament removes one burden, they stick us with another. Worse yet, by asserting absolute power, they've made a mockery of our legislative assemblies. Hell, the way they treat us, we're three steps lower than second class." Cooper rapped his tankard on the oak table. "Relentless abuse demands drastic steps."

"What are you suggesting?" said Whitaker. "Outright rebellion?"

"I don't know...but one thing sure, it's not the status quo."

"Unless I'm mistaken," said Jenkins, "my wise neighbor is proposing widespread civil disobedience to the lawful dictates of our Mother Country." He folded his arms. "Like a petulant child, you think a tantrum will work."

That Jenkins reprised the familiar refrain was no surprise to Thom. How far the lawyer dared push it remained to be seen.

"Unfortunately," said Jenkins, "if such petulance persists, it will be met with a stern rebuke." He focused on Cooper. "Would you seriously risk the possibility of hostilities?"

The barrel maker hesitated as if his alcohol-fueled tongue had suddenly come face to face with reality.

Jenkins raised his eyes to the Heavens. "Lord help us." He looked across the table, but directed himself to Whitaker, rather than Cooper. "Can you imagine our rag-tag militias battling the likes of the British Redcoats? Talk about a mismatch."

"They said the same thing when David fought Goliath." The instinctive utterance, its genesis hardly reasoned analysis, reverberated in Thom's ears as if it had come from someone else.

"Yes...I suppose they did." Jenkins punctuated the slowly delivered comment with several theatrical nods. "But David, strong and smart, was the rare exception that proves the rule. Almost always the strong prevail." He glared at Thom. "You tell me—What chance does an inept bunch of farmers armed with second rate weapons have against the finest trained and equipped fighting force on the face of the earth?"

Thom swallowed hard. The idea that the colonists could defeat the British army was absurd. That many Americans, perhaps even a fifth, would side with England, compounded the improbability.

"I rest my case." Jenkins reached for his brew and drank heartily.

Thom eyed his ale but did not imbibe. He was busy digesting what had been said. Hopes of convincing Parliament to grant the colonies the authority to legislate their own destiny were quixotic. Succumbing to the autocratic will of Parliament was outrageous. Defeating the British army was chimerical. A variety of tactics were open to the colonists. Sober analysis suggested they were all fruitless.

A lull supplanted the usual banter. Whether Cooper and Whitaker, like Thom, were lost in their own thoughts or relaxing with their brews, Thom couldn't tell. As for Jenkins, no doubt he was gloating.

Finally, Cooper said, "I have a question for all of you to consider. Please, think about it, and give the others a chance to independently weigh it, before answering."

Whitaker jabbed Thom in the side. "Sounds like our barrel-making brother is about to hit us with something earthshaking, perhaps an inquiry as to the exact type of cheese the moon is made of."

"Muzzle yourself," said Cooper. "I have a serious question. What would you do if we went to war with England?"

"You call that a serious question?" Whitaker contrived a gnarled expression of disdain. "Snow in July is more likely."

"I for one would—"

"Ezra, do me a favor and hold your answer until everyone has had a chance to think."

The lawyer frowned. "Fine. I'll humor you."

Quiet returned to the table, though the forced lull was different from its predecessor, at least for Thom.

"Long enough," said Jenkins impatiently.

"You all have your views?" Cooper's inquiry was met with a chorus of nods. "Let me start with you, Thom. What would you do?"

Thom took a deep breath. "Well...understand, I believe the scenario is highly unlikely, but, having said that, if England declared war on the colonies, or visa versa, I would stand with the colonies."

"How about you, Ezra?"

"You fellows know my feelings. England is our life blood. It's my Mother Country. No way would I take up arms, treasonous arms, against it."

"Does that mean you'd take up arms against your fellow colonists, individuals like Thom, who take a different view?"

"I don't know. But one thing sure—and it's nothing personal—I wouldn't fight on his side of the battle lines."

Cooper turned to Whitaker. "What about you, George?"

"It's a stupid question, a hypothetical that won't occur, so I have no intention of answering it." He pressed his lips together in a defiant pose.

"Thanks for your kind cooperation, George. Perhaps I can be just as—"

"Don't get on your high horse with me, Paul."

A reluctance to get into the middle kept Thom from pointing out that Whitaker was in no position to take umbrage. With the exception of Jenkins, few in Tyringham were more supercilious than the Yankee peddler.

"Now that we've played your little game," said Whitaker, "what do you—"

"You didn't play *my little game*. You dismissed my inquiry as nonsense."

Whitaker turned to Jenkins. "At least now he understands what type of question he asked." He looked back at Cooper. "Just so you get your chance to speculate in your wild world of fantasy, tell us what you would do if the colonies went to war with England. And better yet, humor me by estimating the likelihood of this farfetched happening."

Cooper grew stoic. Thom made a mental note of the exercise of self-control. He hoped he might follow the lesson in the future, not that he could picture himself doing so after consuming the several pints of alcohol that Cooper had imbibed.

"To answer your second question first," said Cooper. "I don't expect a war."

"Congratulations," said Whitaker. "At least you have retained a trace of sense."

"More than I can say for someone else." Cooper turned away from Whitaker. "If you ask me, the possibility of war is about one in five."

That was the first time Thom had heard anyone suggest the risks were that high. He disagreed but conceded the chances might be greater than he had previously assumed.

"As to what side I would take," said Cooper, "there's no doubt. I would be with the colonists."

Thom looked around the Hogshead. Down the road, might he find himself at war with some of his Tyringham neighbors? The scenario was unlikely, but the possibility made him shudder.

⚬₥₥₥₥⚬

Months had elapsed since Thom had delivered his carefully crafted furniture to Orville Crane. Several times their paths had crossed during the winter. Thom had allowed the issue of the unpaid six shillings to go unmentioned, hoping that Crane would satisfy the obligation without the need for embarrassing reminders. No such luck. Apparently Crane was bent on letting the debt fade into oblivion. What rankled Thom more than the money was that the dumb, but crafty blacksmith might be gloating.

On his way down Beartown Mountain from his saltbox to Sarah Albright's, Thom detoured off the Albany-Boston Post Road to Crane's place, not far from the Konapot River. As he

204

climbed off Lodestone, the pounding of Crane's hammer coming from the barn drew Thom there.

"Afternoon," said Crane, continuing to pound a glowing piece of iron held against his anvil by a large pair of tongs.

"Good afternoon to you," said Thom. He waited for the hammering to cease.

Crane raised his tongs and eyed the piece of iron, its tip still red. He pounded it again before laying it aside. "Still needs more fire," he muttered. He turned to Thom. "So, what can I do for you?"

Confident that small talk would not mitigate the distasteful task, Thom cut directly to the chase. "I was in the neighborhood, so I stopped for my six shillings."

"Six shillings?" Crane displayed a quizzical look.

"Yes, the six shillings you owe me."

"That I owe you?"

"Remember—I deposited the full price for my nails and hardware as security until I delivered the furniture."

"Yeah...and ya brought the stuff, and I gave ya your dough...and so what?"

Either Crane was a damn good actor, or he had forgotten the debt. The latter was impossible. "At the time you returned my deposit, you were six shillings short. You never repaid that."

Crane looked up at the sky and muttered, "Damn, I get second-rate stuff, and the guy duns me for extra dough." He looked back at Thom. "Seems ya got a real bad memory."

"I've got a bad memory." Despite restraint, Thom's voice grew louder.

"Ya heard me! I paid ya the whole shot."

"You did not!"

"The hell I didn't!" Crane folded his muscular arms.

Speechless, Thom glared.

"If I owed ya money, the way ya claim, how come ya didn't say nuttin' when I saw ya at the Hogshead several weeks back or when I saw ya there way back in January?"

"I didn't want to embarrass you in front of everyone."

"Sure...ya come here callin' me a deadbeat and claim to be a nice guy."

Thom stared at Crane in disbelief. For several seconds the two exchanged glowers.

"Damn! I can't believe you'd screw your neighbor for a few crummy shillings!" Crane made a motion as if to bang a fist on his anvil, stopping but a few inches short. He stormed over to the corner of his barn. He returned with a bag of nails. He tossed it at Thom's feet. "Three pounds of six-penny nails. Take 'em, and get the hell outta here!"

Thom did a quick calculation. Three pounds of six-penny nails equaled thirty pence, less than two shillings. "That's a fraction of what you owe me, not that I want a bunch of six-penny nails."

"Have it your way. I wuz gonna be a big man about it. Give ya them nails even though ya ain't got no right to 'em. Unlike some fellows, I don't treat my neighbors like cheats."

Thom gazed at the bag, as well as several nails that were strewn about the ground near his feet. Crane was shortchanging him and adding insults to the rip-off. Blood boiling, Thom started to walk away.

"See—that proves my point."

Thom stopped in his tracks and looked back at Crane. "What point?"

"Ya knew I didn't owe ya nuttin'."

"You no good—" Thom clipped his tongue. Trading nasty epithets with the lying smithy would serve no purpose. He shook his head, untethered Lodestone and walked him out toward the road. He vowed that in the future he would be wiser than to trust Crane's word. Better yet, he wouldn't deal with Crane at all. Before mounting, Thom paused. Could his memory be faulty? No way. But Crane was so emphatic. Was it possible he had made full payment? The explanation was too remote to merit credence. Less remote, and far more galling, was the possibility that Crane might gloat, and, worse yet, badmouth Thom.

<hr/>

"Soil is nice and soft. Easy to work." Thom dragged his hoe through the compliant earth. Together with Pico he was clearing a plot about twenty-feet square out beyond the northeast corner of his saltbox. He had chosen the location, rather than one directly behind the structure, in order that the cultivated area would reap the benefit of a better southern exposure.

"Wish we didn't have to wait another month to plant." Pico tossed a couple of small rocks off to the side.

"Well...it's nice to be out here, instead of cooped up inside."

Pico nodded as he drove a shovel into the moist ground.

Thom mopped his brow. The beads of sweat that draped his forehead were welcome. He estimated the thermometer was pushing sixty-five, and with the sun ever higher in the spring sky, the early April day was a bonus. No doubt there would be colder ones, and April had a penchant for a last-gasp snowfall, but the corner had been turned.

"Afternoon, Thom."

The voice turned Thom's head. Coming around from the front of the house was Johnny Woodstone.

"What brings you up this way?" Thom met the lanky, six-foot mason at the edge of the newly cleared plot.

"Heard you built a fine place. Had to see for myself. Sure enough, it is. I checked it out before circling back here." Woodstone pointed at the foundation. "Where'd you learn to lay fieldstone like that?"

"Boston. Had a great teacher. Taught me all kinds of stuff."

"See you got a helper." Woodstone gestured at Pico.

The unexpected visitor had Thom debating how to handle the situation. The best he could do was stay composed. He called Pico over. "Pico, this is Mr. John Woodstone, the finest mason for miles around."

"Nice to meet you, Mr. Woodstone."

"And you too...Peego...I say that right?"

"Pico." He spelled his name. "It's short for Picosick. It means red fox in Mohican."

"Pico has been living here with me for several months. He helped do the floors and walls and the entire inside."

"What brung you here...to Tyringham?" Woodstone seemed to study Pico.

"My mother died more than a year ago. I was left on my own."

207

"Thom said you've been with him for a few months. Where'd you stay before that?"

"In the schoolhouse."

Thom winced, never expecting that Pico would be so candid.

A glance from Woodstone suggested Thom's reaction had not gone unnoticed. "When you say the schoolhouse, you talkin' about the one near the crossin' of Mt. Hunger and Smith Hill Road...the one that got burnt?"

"Yup, that's the one."

Thom thought better of interjecting an explanation, sensing it would come across as defensive.

"Did Sam Eaton know you—"

"Sam who?"

"Sam Eaton. He took care of the school. Did he know you wuz stayin' there?"

"Doubt it, since I never came till everyone was gone and left in the morning before they returned."

"I see," said Woodstone, as he seemingly mulled over what he had learned.

"Sure was a tough winter." Thom doubted his ploy, an effort to change the subject, fooled anyone. "Good to see the spring finally come."

"Sure is." Woodstone heaved a sigh. "Maybe them folks that settled in Georgia ain't so crazy after all."

"Perhaps, but come July, maybe they'll be saying the same thing about us." Thom voiced the rhetoric if only to convince himself of the advantages of New England life. It was certainly better than what he had experienced during his childhood in England, though he preferred the milder winters of his former homeland. He said, "Would you like to see my house from the inside?"

"I wuz hopin' you'd offer."

"Right this way." Thom glanced at Pico. "You gonna join us?"

"Thanks, but...if memory serves, Pico's had the tour."

The two men laughed before circling to the front of the house. As they approached the door, Woodstone said, "Seems like a decent sort. How'd you come to take him in?"

"He needed a place to stay." Thom hoped the circumspect answer might avoid further inquiry. He opened the front door and, with a grand gesture of his arm, made way for Woodstone to enter first. "My humble abode."

Woodstone stepped into the tiny hallway. He glanced left at the parlor and then right at the dining room. "Not so humble." He looked up the stairs in the direction of the loft. "Nice...very, very nice."

As Thom closed the door behind them, he sensed the smile that was painting his face. Apart from Richard and Pico, Woodstone was the first to view the interior, and while Woodstone may not have been as well educated or articulate as many of Tyringham's residents, when it came to construction, his skills were top drawer.

"Lead the way, and I'll follow."

"With pleasure," said Thom, though the choices, clockwise or counterclockwise or up the stairs, were limited. He headed to the loft and then back down. Next he chose the counterclockwise route around the main floor, going through the dining room, kitchen and buttery, and, lastly, the parlor.

"Ya do good work," said Woodstone. He stepped onto the hearth and ran his hands over the bricks that rose upward to the chimney. "Mind if I see the cellar?"

"Sure, if you want, but don't expect much. It's just a cellar." Thom lit a kerosene lantern and circled back to the trap door where he guided the way to the dirt floor.

Knees bowed just enough to avoid banging his head, the lanky Woodstone moved about the perimeter. Along the way he caressed the stones that formed the foundation. Now and then he reached up and examined the beams and joists supporting the floor above. Once he had gone full circle, he eased toward the middle. He felt the stones that formed the home's center arch, slipping his fingers into the tiny gaps. He ducked low and stepped beneath the arch, pressing his palms against its undersurface. As he came back out from under, he said, "Damn...couldn't do better myself. You, my friend, got the know-how when it comes to house buildin'."

209

"Thanks," said Thom. He looked around. Amidst the dimly lit and dank surroundings, he felt a glow as bright as that which reigned outside.

# Chapter 13

SEATED NEXT TO RICHARD, with Paul Cooper and George Whitaker on the opposite side of the booth, Thom was having a great old time at the Hogshead. Stomach laden with several brews, plus an ample portion of lamb stew from the table's common trench, cares were distant. April had been a decent month, and the first half of May had exceeded expectations. In another week, with the risk of frost eliminated, he could plant his garden. He was living full time in his saltbox with Pico. A day or two each week he stopped by Sarah's for a few hours to help out there. Occasionally he stayed the night. All things considered, life in Tyringham was good, though not so good as when he was courting Polly.

Whitaker banged an empty tankard on the thick wooden table. "This summer, the four of us are going hunting. Gonna bag us a bear."

"A big one," said Thom, not that he expected they would. Deer was the biggest he hunted. A part of him sensed the alcohol talking, but he welcomed freedom from the inhibitions of his usual mantle of modest reserve. A swagger, even if superficial, felt good. Tankard raised, slumped back in his seat, Thom spotted Reverend Bidwell coming through the tavern's door. The normally stoic Reverend—his reserve, however, unlike Thom's, a demeanor of confidence, not diffidence—was animated.

"My friends," called out the Reverend, barely across the threshold, "please give me your attention. I have important news." He held up pleading hands as he sought to quiet the rowdy establishment. His further entreaties, along with those of others, gradually stilled the throng.

"Friends," he said, "just minutes ago a courier from Boston stopped off with disturbing news. Several days ago, on May 12th to be precise, word arrived from across the sea that Parliament, in retaliation for the Tea Party, passed legislation closing the port of Boston."

A collective gasp yielded to an angry din. As Reverend Bidwell sought to quell the raucous gathering, someone called out, "With the harbor closed, how will we get the things we need?"

"I don't know," said Reverend Bidwell. "I don't know."

Ezra Jenkins, who sat two tables from where Thom was seated, yelled, "See, I warned you fools you were begging a backlash. Spit in the eye of Parliament enough, and sooner or later they'll blow it back into your face."

"Go to hell, Ezra," barked a voice from a table behind Thom. Silently, Thom applauded the sentiment, though a fistful of knuckles in the mouth of the pompous lawyer would have been more satisfying.

"Folks, please...please, listen," said Reverend Bidwell. "I know you're upset, but hear me out."

The racket diminished, but quiet sufficient to allow him to continue ensued only after numerous others echoed his call.

"According to the courier," said Reverend Bidwell, "until Massachusetts pays the taxes on the dumped tea and reimburses the East India Company for the loss, the port will remain shut."

"Hell will become Eden before we'll make such payments!" screamed Hogshead owner Daniel Heath.

Thom pounded his tankard on the table, as others shouted support for the rebellious utterance.

"As you already know," said Reverend Bidwell, "Governor Hutchinson has been under fire for months. Most of you probably heard how the Boston Gazette accused him of crimes greater 'than his life can repair or his death satisfy.'"[121] I assume you've also heard that his ailing Lieutenant Governor died in March."

"Good riddance," came a shout from across the room.

Another yelled, "I would have loved to be among the crowd who gave three cheers when his casket was placed into the ground."

Thom anticipated Reverend Bidwell would chide the hecklers' insensitivity. Instead the clergyman said, "I understand

Governor Hutchinson has been recalled to England. General Thomas Gage has replaced him as acting governor."

The name meant little to Thom, and the subdued reaction of his neighbors hinted that they might be in the same boat.

"The courier had little information about General Gage, except that he's apt to be more austere than Hutchinson."

"Any word how folks in Boston are reacting to all this?" said Richard.

"I'm not sure," said Reverend Bidwell, "but according to the courier, Sam Adams convened an immediate town meeting. Knowing him and his Sons of Liberty, they won't take it lying down." The Reverend paused. "I guess that's all I have for now." A buzz hung over the Hogshead as the Reverend joined a group along the far wall.

Thom and his tablemates redirected themselves to one another.

"I'd sooner tie my damn breeches around my neck than kowtow," said Paul Cooper.

"You're damn right!" said Thom. "It's high time we let the turkeys in Parliament know where we stand."

Whitaker groaned.

"You disagree?" snapped Richard.

"I didn't say that." Whitaker's tone was equally sharp. "But I'd be a damn side happier if that crazy tea party had occurred in Philadelphia or Charleston. Let folks there have their port shut."

Thom's gut, rebellious, especially filled with ale, balked. His brain, its sagacious side only partially impeded, reacted otherwise. Whitaker had a point. A colonial challenge to Parliament's authority was wonderful in theory, but did the defiance have to come from Massachusetts? He said, "How do you think the other colonies will react to the closing of Boston Harbor?"

"If you ask me," said Whitaker, "they'll all cheer...from a distance. Sure, they'll encourage us to continue the fight, but when the chips are down, they'll leave us to fend for ourselves."

"No way," said Richard. "They'll be there when we need them."

"I hope so," said Thom, far less certain. Then again, there was a possibility that Richard, a brew or two ahead of his pals,

213

might be less sanguine once his alcoholic bravado wore off. Thom turned to Cooper. "What do you think, Paul?"

The barrel maker leaned back, his eyes narrowed in a thoughtful pose. "I don't know. I'd like to think that all the colonies will stand with us, but..." For an instant he frowned. "You never know. They might turn deaf ears and blind eyes."

"You can bet on that," said Whitaker. "And surer yet, England will make an example of us."

"Let 'em try," said Richard, glaring at the Yankee peddler. "If they do, your namesake, King George, will have his hands full with thirteen seditious colonies. And let me tell you, spread up and down our lengthy coastline, that's one helluva challenge, even for the mighty British military."

⁓↬↬↬⁓

A week had passed since news regarding the closing of the Boston port had arrived. Along with Sarah, Thom was in the back of the Albright homestead tilling her garden. They had nearly finished when Richard approached aboard his dapple gray. Struggling to catch his breath as he tied the steed to a fence post, he said, "You won't believe what's been happening in Boston. They've turned it into a garrison."

"You're kidding," said Thom.

"Don't I wish. Johnny Woodstone came by my place after talking with Dan Heath at the Hogshead. A rider from the east had given him the news."

"You got any details?" said Sarah with uncharacteristic impatience.

"Word is that Gage, our new governor, is occupying Boston with five thousand Redcoats. He's vowed that neither he, nor England will tolerate sedition."[122]

Images of armed Redcoats patrolling the streets filled Thom's head. The pall that likely engulfed the otherwise vibrant city kept him silent.

"On the bright side," said Sarah, "Tyringham isn't Boston. What's happening there should be of little consequence here, not that it's any solace for those folks."

214

"According to what Johnny heard," said Richard, "people predict the situation will grow worse. They're concerned for the safety of our leaders. To protect Sam Adams, they put bars on the doors and windows of his home."[123]

"A lot of good that'll do if a brigade of Redcoats storm the place," said Thom. "I wonder if Adams is having second thoughts about the Tea Party."

"Apparently not. Johnny says he's still organizing the resistance. He's urging the other colonies to suspend trade with Britain. And listen to this: He even took his seven-year-old son out for a walk on the Boston Commons while the Redcoats were practicing their drills there."[124]

"The man has guts," said Sarah.

Thom silently conceded the point. Whether Adams was as wise as he was courageous was less clear.

"And by the way," said Sarah, "did either of you know that Davenport Adams, Sam Adams' third cousin—he's once or twice removed—lives here in Berkshire County."[125]

"Seems I heard that," said Richard. "Oh...before I forget, Johnny delivered another not-so-great tidbit. Contrary to what many folks had assumed, King George is no more sympathetic to our cause than Parliament. While the debate raged whether to close Boston's port, he went before Parliament and exhorted its members to do so."

Thom chuckled.

Richard gave him a look.

"Don't mind me. I'm laughing at myself. I was among the gudgeons who claimed His Majesty would plead our case." Thom recalled his days in Boston. Most believed King George was a steadfast friend of the colonies, Massachusetts included. Events were proving otherwise.

◦◦◦◦◦

As Thom put the final brushstrokes of whitewash to the picket fence fronting Sarah's home, she came out the door.

"Not fair, all the chores you're still doing for me."

"Consider it pay-back for the cut-rate room and board."

Her brow furrowed.

"C'mon, the road ran both ways."

"Maybe so, but it was hardly level, plus I enjoyed the company." Her firm tone suggested the assessment was not open to debate. "You'll come for dinner tomorrow? And before you respond, understand—I won't take *no* for an answer."

"You've twisted my arm."

"And you'll bring your young friend as well."

The invitation caught Thom by surprise, not that it should have. Counting on Richard to keep Pico a secret was one thing; expecting the same from Johnny Woodstone was unreasonable, especially with no request for secrecy. Thom might have made an overture to Woodstone, but Pico nixed the idea, lest it appear he had something to hide. "Who told you I had someone staying at my place?"

"Just to keep the record straight, it was less a matter of being told than being asked. Following Sunday's meeting, June Smith inquired about the Indian boy who was living with you. When I gave her a blank look, she told me not to play dumb. She said that everyone in Tyringham knew about it. When I responded, 'Not everybody,' I guess she believed me." Sarah looked Thom in the eye. "How come you didn't tell me?"

"Well, Pico—that's his name—preferred I not say anything. He made me promise to keep quiet. Otherwise he wouldn't stay."

Seeming dissatisfaction showed on Sarah's face.

"What's the matter?"

"I'm disappointed."

"Disappointed?"

"You couldn't convince him to bring me in on the secret? You know I would have been glad to help."

"I'm sure you would, but really...that wasn't necessary." The horizontal stone lips that carved across the space normally reserved for Sarah's warm smile had Thom swallowing hard. Telling her she wasn't needed was an insult.

"Perhaps you didn't trust me. Maybe you thought I'd break my word and blab."

"C'mon, you know that's not true."

"Do I?"

216

Thom broke eye contact. He could offer explanations, but they would be disingenuous. Once he had gotten to know Pico, his conscience had counseled that he seek permission to tell Sarah. If Pico refused, so be it. But Thom had avoided the issue.

"Don't you think he would have enjoyed my cooking?"

"I'm sure he would." In all the time that Thom had stayed with Sarah, never had she laid guilt at his doorstep. There were moments of differing views and minor friction, but never this. She wouldn't do it lightly. That wasn't her way. If only he could say he had pressed Pico to allow disclosure, but he couldn't. "I'm sorry," was the best he could manage.

The tension in her face eased as she breathed in slowly and gradually exhaled. She said, "So, you'll bring him with you for dinner tomorrow?"

"I'll encourage him to come. That's a promise."

"Fair enough." She smiled. She started to go into the house but stopped. "Oh, I don't know if you're aware, but your friend may have a problem."

"Problem?"

"Some folks think he's responsible for the fire at the school last year."

"I'm sure he isn't." Even as Thom voiced the sentiment, he knew it was grounded on wishful thinking, not evidence.

"Word has it—and mind you, I'm not suggesting it has merit—one of the kids saw an Indian boy hanging around the school a day or so before the fire. There are rumors that he may have been sleeping there."

The source of the latter tidbit was easy for Thom to surmise. When Johnny Woodstone had visited Thom's saltbox, Pico had mentioned staying in the school. To that extent Sarah's information bore a measure of accuracy. On the other hand, the gossip it had apparently spawned regarding the fire was more dubious. Regardless, gossip, often a fountainhead of trouble, was hard to dispel.

*⟋⟋⟋⟋⟍*

It was the second Sunday of June 1774. The balance of the month, plus July, August and September lay ahead. Owing to his distaste for the harsh New England winters, Thom regularly reminded himself of the favorable stretch remaining. He had a lot to be thankful for. His saltbox, long a figment of a fertile imagination, had come to fruition. Thanks to Pico, company, once a rare commodity, was part of labor, meals and down time. Life was good. Recollections of dark days enabled him to appreciate his circumstances all the more. Months had passed since he had last attended a Sunday meeting. Week after week he had contemplated the possibility, but inertia, perhaps a euphemism for procrastination—there was always next week—had prevailed. Chores were an easy excuse, but with Pico's help, a benefit never anticipated when his home was begun, none were pressing. The least Thom could do was take one day to give thanks. He invited Pico to join him. He was certain his young friend would decline. Neither said it, but both knew that Pico's presence at the prayer service would be a source of discomfort. Bothersome questions, as well as looks, both real and imagined, would be inevitable. Even if circumstances were different, Thom would not have pressured Pico to accompany him. As small a role as religion played in Thom's life, he had no need to push it onto anyone, especially one whose childhood had been scarred by proselytizing missionaries.

Reverend Bidwell was at the door greeting the worshippers. After an exchange of pleasantries, Thom entered the parlor, planning to take a seat in the last row. Before he could, Paul Cooper, seated with his family, about halfway back, offered Thom the adjoining seat. With mixed emotions Thom accepted. Much as he wanted the security of the back corner, having a place next to his friend Paul had definite advantages.

"Good to see you here," said Cooper with a hearty handshake.

"Thanks for allowing me to sit with you." Thom's words bore the stiffness of his straight-backed chair. With the many times he had comfortably bantered with Paul at the Hogshead, his lack of ease was illogical. Yet it made perfect sense. This wasn't the Hogshead. Thom didn't have several brews in his belly. Paul was sitting tall with his family beside him. In a nutshell, Thom was an outsider.

A moment later Polly and Peter entered the parlor. Thom lowered his head before Polly could make eye contact. Still the vision of her beautiful face and shapely silhouette danced in his head. Out of the corner of his eye he watched her negotiate her way down the other side of the room past his row. Tantalizing as it would have been to have her seated at his side, having her located several rows back where she remained invisible had its benefits. For the next few minutes Thom remained immersed in his own thoughts, all of Polly: how lovely she was; the marvelous moments they had shared; and the guilt that accompanied such reflections.

Reverend Bidwell commenced the meeting. Thom's eyes directed to the clergyman; his mind was adrift. That changed when the Reverend moved on to his sermon.

"My friends," he said, "rather than speak of faith or virtue or the like, today I wish to relate some information conveyed by a gentleman who, on route from Virginia to Boston, stayed here last night. I believe the matter bears importance to our community and, indeed, the whole of Massachusetts."[126] Reverend Bidwell moved his gaze over the gathering. His deliberate pace drew their full attention. "Rather than sit by in the face of the injustice that England inflicts upon our colony, our friends in Virginia have taken a stand. I have here two recent pronouncements of the Virginia Legislature, the House of Burgesses, which, as some of you know, has been disbanded by Lord Dunmore, the Governor of Virginia, for advocating positions contrary to those of the Mother Country. These pronouncements give reason to believe we do not stand alone."

The Reverend raised the papers aloft. A buzz, albeit subdued, pervaded the parlor. Were the gathering at the Hogshead, doubtless the reaction would have been raucous.

"The first, a resolution adopted on the 24th of May, declared the 1st of June, just past, 'a Day of Fasting, Humiliation and Prayer' owing to the 'great Dangers to be derived to British America, from the hostile invasion of the City of Boston' by virtue of the action of Parliament ordering the closing of said port as of said June 1st."[127]

Traces of conversation, uncommon at Sunday meetings, oozed forth. Reverend Bidwell did nothing to discourage them.

Cooper whispered to Thom, "Perhaps we're not alone in our fight."

"Perhaps so," said Thom, buoyed by the unexpected news.

The Reverend held his papers aloft again. "The second document, entitled 'An Association, Signed by 89 Members of the Late House of Burgesses,' which, along with the first, I will make available following this meeting, provides, among other things, and I quote:

*'We his Majesty's most dutiful and loyal subjects, the late representatives of the good people of this country, having been deprived by the sudden imposition of the executive part of this government from giving our countrymen the advice we wish to convey to them in a legislative capacity...find an act of the British parliament, lately passed, for stopping the harbour and commerce of the town of Boston, in our sister colony of Massachusetts Bay...a most dangerous attempt to destroy the constitutional liberty and rights of all North America.'*

"The Association recites objections to the tax on tea and the attempt of the East India Company to harm America and recommends, and I quote again:

*'...our countrymen, not to purchase or use any kind of East India commodity whatsoever, except saltpetre and spices, until the grievances of America are redressed. We are further clearly of the opinion, that an attack, made on one of our sister colonies, to compel submission to arbitrary taxes, is an attack made on all British America...*"[28]

A voice in the back called out: "Hear, hear."

Reverend Bidwell's approving nod, a departure from usual decorum, drew cheers, admittedly restrained, but remarkable for the staid milieu.

"My friends," he said, pausing long enough to allow the remaining din to subside, "it appears we have an ally. No longer can the powers across the sea treat our cries like the howl of a lone wolf atop an uninhabited mountain. Once one man stands up alongside the oppressed, more will follow. Massachusetts is no longer alone in its confrontation with British authority. The call has gone out for all of the colonies to join in solidarity, and I, for one, anticipate our neighbors will answer that call."

Thom sat taller in his seat. Instead of a sermon laced with sin and guilt, the man at the lectern desk was armed with a fighting spirit. The inattention associated with Thom's attendance at the meetings had evanesced in the face of the rousing message. The endless gaps that separated the hourly chimes of the Brass Lantern clock on the mantle of the Bidwell dining room were absent. Time flew amidst the galvanized atmosphere.[129] Before long the Reverend had voiced the final amen.

Cooper turned to Thom and said, "If the members of Parliament thought the Tea Party was nothing more than the angry voices of a few Boston dissidents, they're in for a rude awakening."

"You got that right. Several million irate colonists stretched over a thousand miles can't be ignored." Fist clenched, Thom underscored his words with a slow, but decisive nod of his head. He and his countrymen would not be treated as slaves. The days of Hobbes' Leviathan, Parliament's all-powerful rule, were numbered. A part of Thom sensed his bravado was grounded upon rhetoric more than facts. Still the Reverend's well-spoken words were superior to the alcohol that had previously buttressed such optimism.

For weeks, reticence, coupled with expedience, had kept Thom from attending the Sabbath meeting. Serendipity had him select an apt day to come. Ordinarily Thom disdained superstitions. They were foolish shackles enslaving the mind. But folks had runs of luck, both good and bad. Perhaps his time for a good run was at hand. Passing up the opportunity would be a shame. Odds were it would not come again soon. He stepped out of the Bidwell home into the comfortable spring air. When next he visited the Hogshead, he might take a seat at the card players' table. He might have gone directly there, but it was Sunday. And there was never a game on Sunday.

Thom and Pico were returning from two hours of fishing in the Konkapot River. Thanks to Pico, who had speared two fine trout, it had been a productive venture. Thom, a novice in the art of spear fishing, had done little more than chase prospective catch away. Nevertheless, the lesson had been fun, especially knowing their efforts would be rewarded with a tasty dinner. Halfway back to the saltbox, Deacon Hale crossed their path.

"Good afternoon, Deacon," said Thom.

"Same to you."

"Have you met my friend, Pico?"

"Don't know that I have."

Pico extended his right hand and exchanged greetings with the Deacon.

"Did you hear that Darby Walters got engaged to Juliette Chandler the day before yesterday?"

"Uh...no," said Thom, nearly gagging.

"You must have known they were courting?" said the Deacon.

"Well...yes, but it...uh...hasn't been all that long."

The Deacon gave Thom a look. "C'mon, you can't blame Darby for snatching her up. A peach like Juliette doesn't come along everyday." The Deacon gazed up at the western sky. "I better get a move on before the sun dips behind the mountains. Lotsa chores waitin' back at the house. You fellas have a nice day." He headed off.

Pico peered at Thom with an odd expression.

"Something the matter?" said Thom.

"Seems I should be askin' that question."

"Come again?"

"You weren't yourself once Mr. Hale...the Deacon told you 'bout that lady, Juliette...that she plans to marry...I forgot his name."

"Walters...Darby Walters."

Pico gave Thom another look.

"What's the matter now?"

"You didn't explain."

222

Thom shrugged. "Unexpected news...caught me by surprise." He knew there was more to it. He was envious. Why—made no sense. Admittedly, Juliette was attractive...for her age, but any interest he had in the older woman was at most temporal. On a day-to-day basis her strong personality was more than he could bear. Still he felt a pang, a subtle gnawing. On second thought, it was not subtle.

Thom dismounted Lodestone and hitched him to a birch that adjoined the home of George Whitaker. Months before, Thom had eyed a pair of pewter sconces, a bit discolored, in a corner of the Yankee peddler's barn. With a little luck they would still be there.

Thom climbed the front stoop of the cape style home. He paused to savor the warm sun of summer's first day. How distant the desolate, gray days of winter seemed. All through late spring and summer he reminded himself to relish each fine day. The Berkshire Mountains afforded too many of a less appealing vintage to allow the good ones to slip by unappreciated. The fall colors were spectacular, but after a few quick weeks, barren trees foreshadowed a lengthy stretch of cold, dark days. Folks lauded the magnificence of snow-covered hills, and while Thom acknowledged the pristine beauty of the trees, especially evergreens draped in white, the price of such splendor was outrageous. Howling winds turned the canvas barren. Bitter temperatures delivered pain. Thom drew a full breath, a celebration of the magnificent late-June Berkshire day. He rapped on the door. Whitaker's younger son, one of five children, answered.

"Good afternoon, Mr. Webster."

"It certainly is." Thom glanced back over his shoulder, eyeing the green foliage that suffused the trees. "Is your father home?"

"He's out in the barn. Would you like me to call him?"

"No, I'll go back there." Thom headed to the barn. The door was open, and inside he found Whitaker puttering with an old wagon wheel.

"Hello, George."

Whitaker looked up. "And hello to you." He gestured all around. "Something you need?"

Thom shook his head. "Not really. I was passing by and decided to pay a visit. But as long as I'm here, I might as well look." As he reached the far corner, he spotted the sconces but quickly moved on. "What do you want for this big copper pot?" The need to be as artful as the peddler, not genuine interest, motivated the inquiry.

"Two shillings...and for a third, I'll throw in the small one next to it."

Thom continued until he had circled to the spot where Whitaker was working.

Whitaker leaned his long-spoked wheel against the adjacent wall. "What do you think of Parliament's newest restrictions?"

"Restrictions?"

"You haven't heard?"

"Not really. What did they pull this time?"

"Give me a second. I've got it written down in the house, and I want to get it right. Ezra Jenkins stopped by earlier and filled me in." Whitaker hurried into his house, returning a minute later. "I knew we were looking for trouble when we threw dirt in England's face. The damn Sons of Liberty couldn't leave well enough alone."

"Fine. I know how you feel, but rather than delivering a lecture, tell me what Parliament did."

Whitaker eyed his paper. "They passed what's called the 'Massachusetts Bay Regulating Act.'"

Just from the title, Thom knew he wouldn't like it.

"According to Jenkins it replaces our elected assembly with a Mandamus Council."

"What the hell is a *man...*"

"Mandamus." Before spelling the word, Whitaker, as he so often did, tugged his bushy beard. "I'm not exactly sure. Ezra could tell you better. But anyway, Governor Gage appoints the members. They're supposed to sit in Salem. Under the law Gage also appoints and fires all our law officers."[130]

"Damn," said Thom. "They'll be running everything. We're worse off than before."

"No fooling." Whitaker bore a smug look. "Now that the pigeons have come home to roost, perhaps you feel their droppings."

The unsavory image, as well as the distasteful news, vividly etched itself in Thom's mind.

"All along we moderates have tried to tell you rebels that defiance would compound our problems. You refused to listen. Now look where we are."

Thom bristled, his reaction dictated more by the manner in which Whitaker had delivered his message than its merit. "You prefer we do nothing while Parliament treats us as chattel?"

"That's not the point."

"Not the point?...Then what is?"

"They have the power, plus we need their protection. We all know it. And more important, they know it. They have us over a barrel."

The undeniable logic reminded Thom of his readings of the radical French philosophers who argued for the rights of the masses. Ordinary folks deserved justice, but if they rose up against the autocratic rule of royalty, they were bound to be crushed. England had been more benign with the American colonies than had the French kings with their subjects, but if pushed, the British, with their highly trained and well-equipped army and navy, could put the upstart colonists in their place. Nevertheless, principle, or perhaps more accurately, indignation found its way to Thom's tongue. "We're entitled to our rights."

The groan that passed from Whitaker's mouth denied even lip service to Thom's declaration. "By the way," said Whitaker, "amidst your grumbling you never gave me the chance to finish telling you the news...or maybe you're not interested?"

Being patronized galled Thom, but being left in the dark was worse. He waited, but when more information was not forthcoming, irritation yielded to curiosity. "Fine. Tell me what else came down the pike."

"Okay, but you needn't be testy."

Thom bit a sarcastic lip.

"Town meetings have been outlawed, except upon royal authorization."

225

Before Thom could react, Whitaker put up a halting hand. "Let me finish." He glanced at his notes. "Freeholders here in Massachusetts can no longer elect juries. Under Parliament's new 'Administration of Justice Act,' should Governor Gage feel that a jury in Massachusetts may be partial, he can move a trial to another colony or, if need be, to Britain. The law is aimed at reviews of actions by British officials or troops, but it can be used whenever."[131]

The blast had Thom gulping, his rifle mouth stripped of powder and ball.

"Rather taciturn...aren't you?" Just above the upper margin of Whitaker's scraggly beard, an unmitigated smirk punctuated his words.

"It...it's not fair."

"Maybe so. But since when was the world fair, especially when nations are involved?" Whitaker folded his arms. "We in the colonies had it pretty good. Up and down the coast it was like a comfortable hammock. But we couldn't leave well enough alone. We had to get ornery. No surprise, Britain flipped our hammock upside down. Now we can sleep in the mud, our backs mashed beneath the tread of British footprints."

Conceding to the Yankee peddler was degrading, but the latest regulations justified the ugly picture he had painted. The canvas of Thom's mind exacerbated the repugnant image. A loathsome Hobbes-like monster, the British Leviathan, was ravaging the colonies.

Whitaker reached for the larger of the copper pots. "So...you wanna buy the pair or just this one?"

"I'll pass," said Thom. He glanced in the direction of the sconces. His appetite for the handsome wall decorations had evaporated. He said, "Enjoy the day, George."

# Chapter 14

"BE THERE IN A MOMENT," called out Thom, responding to a knock at his door. He and Pico were finishing a late dinner. With the calendar not far beyond the summer solstice and the days at their longest, the sun, though low in the sky, was yet to set. Thom stole a peak out the dining room window to see who might be there. Visitors at his Beartown Mountain saltbox were few, especially well into the evening. Apparently the caller was too close to the door for Thom to see. "Who's there," he said, before opening the door.

"Ezra Jenkins."

Thom had spent many an evening with the lawyer at the Hogshead, but neither had ever graced the other's threshold. As he opened the door, Thom found it difficult to imagine that the self-centered Jenkins would take the time to see his handiwork. "To what do I owe this unexpected visit?"

"Did you hear that Pete Dodge's barn burned down yesterday morning?"

"No. That's too bad."

"Folks are saying your Indian friend—what's his name?"

"Pico."

"Yeah...that he might be responsible."

"That's ridiculous," said Thom instinctively.

"Maybe...and then again, maybe not." Jenkins inched into the doorway. "Mind if I come in?"

Thom motioned him into the dining room where Pico was seated. Were the parlor not unfurnished, apart from a rope bed at the rear, Thom would have led the lawyer there. He gestured Jenkins to a chair and pulled a small bench to the table where he seated himself.

"Understand—I'm not accusing the boy. Just telling you what folks are saying." He turned to Pico. "A gentlemen who lives near me lost his barn yesterday. Some think you're responsible."

"I heard you before." Pico put a finger to his chest. "I didn't start any fire."

Jenkins pulled back. "I'm not saying you did." He looked at Thom. "Matter of fact, I'm on the boy's side. Thought he could use a lawyer and—"

"What makes folks think Pico did it?"

"A barn doesn't go up in flames by itself, except maybe from lightning, and there weren't any thunderstorms, not even rain, yesterday."

"But what makes them think Pico's responsible?"

"He was at the school when that fire occurred."

"He was staying there...So what? Needing a roof over his head, no way would he burn it down."

Jenkins reared back. "Hold on. I already told you. I'm not accusing the boy. I'm telling you what folks are saying. And from what I hear, Pete Dodge wants him arrested."

"Arrested?" Out of the corner of his eye Thom observed the agitation on Pico's face. "That's crazy!"

"Calm down," said Jenkins. "Don't take your hostility out on the messenger, especially one here to help."

Insofar as Jenkins purported to be a messenger, Thom conceded the point. Whether the lawyer was there to help or a rabble-rouser looking to make a few shillings was debatable. "You heard Pico. He told you he didn't do it."

"Sure, I heard him, but—" The look on the lawyer's face made it clear he put little stock in the bald denial. "You mind if I ask him a few questions?"

Confident Pico was innocent, and given that he had already said the same, Thom saw no harm. "Do you want to answer his questions? You don't have to if you'd rather not."

A hint of indignation showed on Pico's face. "Let him ask. I'll answer."

"Where were you yesterday morning?" said Jenkins.

"Spear fishing...down in the Konkapot around the bend, about a half-mile from Brewer's Mill."

"Anybody with you?"

"Nope."

"Anybody see you?"

"Doubt it. Least Pico didn't see anyone."

228

Jenkins nodded, but his opaque expression suggested it was the product of ruminations, not agreement. "You catch any fish?"

"A pike."

"We had it for dinner," said Thom. "That proves what Pico says is true. I can vouch for him."

A furrow rippled the lawyer's brow. "He caught a fish. Doesn't prove he didn't start a fire." He turned to Pico. "That look of flames in your eyes won't do you any good if there's a trial."

"Whad'ya expect when you're accusin' me of torchin' somebody's barn?"

Jenkins shook his head. "How many times must I repeat myself? I'm not accusing you. I'm merely trying to get the facts straight."

"That may be, Ezra," said Thom, "but you have a mighty unfriendly way of doing it. At times it sounds like you don't believe Pico."

"Look—sooner or later he's gonna face tough questions, and it might better be now from me than when he's in a courtroom."

"Wait a second. You're talking as if there's going to be a trial. He hasn't even been charged."

"Well..." Jenkins leaned back. "I've seen these things before, and given what I've heard, charges are a safe bet."

Thom glanced at Pico. Though nothing showed, underlying fury was likely.

"About what time did you go fishing?" Narrowed eyes hinted at a predisposed skepticism.

"Can't say exactly. 'Bout an hour past sun-up...I guess."

"And what time did you return?"

"Round noon or so."

"That's an awful long time to fish, wouldn't you say?"

Tension showed on Pico's face. "I swam in the river for a while. Then I took a nap under a big elm. I also picked a few blackberries."

Jenkins turned to Thom. "The boy bring back any berries?"

"His name is Pico," snapped Thom. "And—"

229

"No, I didn't bring them home. I ate what I picked, along with a chunk of bread, spread with apple butter. I brought that with me."

"The Konkapot is still mighty cold for swimming, wouldn't you say?"

"Warm enough...for Pico."

Jenkins muttered, "Wouldn't get me in there before mid-July."

Thom sensed that the lawyer's cross-examining style was irritating Pico more and more. The last thing he wanted was a flare-up. He said, "Seems you've covered the territory. Pico told you what he was doing and that he knows nothing about the fire."

"Yup. That's what he said." Jenkins pawed at his fleshy double chin. "I'd be glad to dig a little deeper...'less you prefer otherwise."

A glimpse of Pico confirmed what Thom knew. Pico had endured too much of the browbeating attorney. Whether the indignity was calculated to prepare Pico for what he would face, as Jenkins claimed, or the sadistic delight of a nasty gadfly, Thom couldn't say. Perhaps both elements were at play. Regardless, the time to halt the inquisition had arrived. Thom said, "You've asked enough, Ezra."

"Fine, one last question, not about the fire." He turned to Pico. "Why when you refer to yourself, do you sometimes use *I* and *me*, and other times, you say *Pico*?"

Thom wondered how Jenkins would react to the anticipated explanation. Talking to oneself, using the first person to reflect one's heart and the third person, one's mind, was arguably as impressive as it was odd.

Pico looked Jenkins in the eye. "How'd you come here?"

A puzzled look came over Jenkins. "On my horse. But what's that got to do with anything?"

"Your horse got a name?"

"Yeah...Falcon."

"You call him Falcon?"

"Of course. What else?"

"A moment ago you referred to him as...*my horse.*"

Jenkins' eyes widened.

Admittedly the analogy was curious, but Thom relished the fact that Pico had not only been discreet but had bested the lawyer at his own game.

"What kind of—"

"Hold on, Ezra," said Thom. "A minute ago you wanted to ask one last question. You did that, and you got more than an answer. So, consider the matter put to bed."

"Fine...if that's how you want it." A scowl on his face, Jenkins got up from his seat.

It crossed Thom's mind to offer his guest a brew. That would be the neighborly way. But Thom preferred to see Jenkins leave, and presumably that was Pico's preference as well. Thom ushered Jenkins out the door. Once the lawyer was clear of the house, Thom returned to the dining room.

"I didn't set any fires." Pico's small brown eyes honed in on Thom. "Do you believe me?"

Thom struggled to maintain eye contact. "Yes, I believe you."

"You're not just saying that, are you?"

"No, I really believe you." Thom was sufficiently sure of Pico's innocence that he was able to express the words with conviction. Still he could not deny a small, nagging hint of doubt. The two gazed at one another for what was little more than a second or two of uncomfortable silence, but time has a curious way of slowing in such disquieting moments.

Finally, Pico said, "They're gonna arrest me. We both know it."

"C'mon, you can't..." Logic slowed an otherwise spontaneous reaction. The likelihood that Pico would be arrested was great.

"They'll say I'm guilty."

The point was more debatable than its predecessor. "You don't know that."

"They need a scapegoat. What better than a half-breed who was stayin' in the school they lost?"

The argument begged debate. Thom found it hard to answer the call. The best he could muster was, "Some folks may be biased, but others will be fair-minded." Tales of the Salem witches reverberated in Thom's head. Tyringham was hardly

231

Salem. On the other hand, what chance did an Indian youth have in conservative western Massachusetts?

⁓൞᪥᪥⁓

The following morning Thom was up at the crack of dawn. He climbed from his bed at the rear of the parlor, dressed and headed into the kitchen for his bever. Some mornings Pico was there already. Others he could be found outside working in the garden or doing other chores about the property. Thom made himself a bowl of porridge which he downed, along with a noggin of metheglin. Owing to a sweet tooth, he had a taste for the spiced honey wine, though he limited the morning indulgence. He went out the back door to the garden. No sign of Pico. He circled the house, and still, no Pico, not that it was a shock. Occasionally Pico slept late. Thom went back inside and climbed the stairs to the loft, Pico's sleeping quarters since the weather had begun to warm. The moment Thom reached the top of the stairs, alarm bells sounded. Pico's bearskin, coat, blanket, bow and arrows, as well as the rest of his things, had vanished. Only one of Pico's spears remained.

Thom stepped from the stairs onto the loft and picked up the spear. Attached to the point was a note:

*Sorry to leave like this. Thanks for everything. Hope you spear lots of fish.*

*Pico*

Thom read the note a second time. He looked around the loft for anything else that Pico might have left. There was nothing. He climbed back down the stairs to the main floor. He checked each room, for what he wasn't sure. He went back outside and searched all around the house. He observed nothing out of the ordinary. He sat down on an oak log where, with an elbow propped on his knee, he rested his chin on an open palm. A sense of melancholy took hold. He should have foreseen the possibility that Pico would run. He should have stepped forward more strongly in Pico's defense and discouraged him from any rash action. Having Pico as a companion had been a joy. Their

232

relationship bore intriguing complexity. At times it was father and son. Others it was teacher and pupil, sometimes with Thom the student. But always they were friends. Thom had lost a son. He had lost a pal. In their place, a familiar companion, loneliness.

⚬⚬⚬⚬⚬

Two days had elapsed since Pico had disappeared, and each provided further confirmation he was not coming back. Thom had tried to immerse himself with chores both inside and outside his home. Work dragged. Besides lacking a second pair of hands, an enervated spirit curtailed efficiency. He was cutting a board that was to become a parlor shelf when a knock at the door drew his attention. His first reaction, that Pico might have returned, had Thom racing to the portal. He opened it. Standing on the stoop were Constable Waterman and Peter Dodge.

"Good afternoon, Thom," said the Constable.

"And to both of you. What brings you this way?" Thom had a strong suspicion.

"I'm here to arrest the young fellow, Picoset, for the fire at Pete's barn."

"He's not here."

"When do you expect him back?"

"I don't," said Thom. "He left two days ago."

Whether the Constable's expression was peevish or skeptical, Thom was unsure. Perhaps it was peevish skepticism.

"You're telling me he left and you don't expect him to return?"

Thom nodded.

"Where did he go?"

"I have no idea."

"You're asking me to believe that this young man who has been living with you for a year suddenly left with no indication where he was going?"

"That's exactly what I'm saying. But he left a note. I'll show it to you." After motioning the pair into the dining room where they seated themselves, Thom retrieved the note. The Constable read it and showed it to Dodge.

"See that," said Dodge. "The creep flew the coop. That proves he's guilty."

"Does not," said Thom. "He left because he knew he wouldn't get a fair shake."

The Constable folded his arms. "Are you sullying the good name of Berkshire County's judicial system?"

An affirmative answer was certain to invoke the Constable's wrath, but no way would Thom concede Pico's guilt. He said, "Pico is an Indian. He's a stranger in Tyringham. Lots of folks have made up their minds."

"You're damn right!" said Dodge. "That's because he's guilty."

Thom gestured at Dodge but focused on the Constable. "You see. That's exactly my point. Pete's made up his mind already."

"Of course, Pete's the complainant. But folks, the ones who'd do the judging, would be fair."

"Sure," muttered Thom, just loud enough for his guests to hear.

"Thomas Webster," said the Constable. "That's no attitude for a citizen of our community. Hell, if everyone felt that way, we'd have no justice system at all."

Judgment counseled the futility of debating the matter. "Look—I have no idea where Pico is."

"Damn," said Dodge. "They should have arrested him months ago for the fire at the school. If they had, my barn would still be standing."

"You've got no call to say that."

"I damn well do."

"Men," said the Constable, "bickering will get us nowhere."

"Well, with the bastard gone, that's where I am—nowhere! And damn it, I've got no barn."

The Constable heaved a sigh as he got up from his seat. "Pete, we might as well go." He turned to Thom. "If your Indian friend shows up, you let me know."

Without responding, Thom got up and ushered the two men out of his house.

In the days immediately following Pico's disappearance, Thom drew inward to escape the constant allegations that he had harbored an arsonist. Regardless whether folks would have confronted him with the accusation, it was a safe bet it was on their minds. And too, his link to Pico was apt to re-ignite slurs regarding his own stint in an English jail.

Before Pico had left, Thom had planned to attend more Sunday meetings, but staring eyes and whispers and halted conversations were too hard to endure. He avoided the Hogshead, afraid its patrons, both sober and inebriated, might live up to the establishment's name and, like wild boars, feast upon him. Whether his fears were legitimate or grounded upon misguided apprehensions made no difference. Thom refused to expose himself to the risks. He withdrew to the safety and solitude of his saltbox and the immutable mountain woods that surrounded it.

With his garden planted and nature supplying adequate rain, apart from occasional weeding, demands for care were minimal, and with but one mouth to feed, the plot provided ample provisions. Some chickens Sarah had given him added eggs to his diet. A couple of rabbits he caught furnished a small source of meat. Occasionally he fished the Konkapot. With a stick and twine and hook and worms, he had modest success. With his spear, none. Mostly, Thom spent his time working around his saltbox. For two days he labored installing a path from his front door around the east side of his house to the garden. First he dug, hacked and lugged limestone. Owing to its naturally flat layers, the rock was ideal for the walkway. Shaping the edges of the stones was unnecessary because he laid them in non-contiguous holes that hopscotched their way from beginning to end. Next he turned his attention to the interior of his home. Furniture he had anticipated making during the upcoming winter jumped to the top of his agenda. For the parlor he made two chairs, identical to the two he had made for the dining room. That way they could double in the event he had company for dinner, not that he anticipated it would happen soon. He

235

made a simple two-seater bench to which he planned to add a back at a later time. The bench and two chairs, while hardly affording the parlor a semblance of formality, enhanced what, apart from a bed in the back corner, had previously been barren space.

On days when the sun shone, he worked under the shade of the great oak that towered about fifteen yards from the southeast corner of his saltbox. When it rained, he labored indoors. The more Thom made, the more his head filled with ideas. The process reminded him of a phrase his Boston mentor had voiced: "The more we learn, the more we learn we don't know." The adage, uncharacteristically hackneyed for the wise teacher, was often accompanied by a sage comment, the kind that made Thom eager to discover what he didn't know. Unfortunately the projects Thom pursued failed to inspire the eye-opening predicate he had experienced in Boston. They became part and parcel of a dispirited existence, reminiscent of the time when he had begun the foundation of his house. Day after day he moiled in an effort to escape himself.

He had just finished installing four wooden peg hooks on the wall adjacent to his bed. He headed into the buttery to prepare dinner when he heard a knock. He went to the door and opened it.

"C'mon, we're going to the Hogshead," said Richard.

"Not even a *hello*?"

Richard shook his head. "With a hermit like you, I've gotta be tough." He looked Thom in the eye. "Everything okay?"

"Pretty good."

"It's been weeks since I've seen you."

"Well...I've been busy."

"What—picking whortleberries?"

"No, just stuff...around the house."

Richard's brow furrowed. "We've been this route before. And in case you've forgotten, I won't take *no* for an answer."

"How about next week?"

"Nope." Richard tugged Thom's arm. "You need to get out, and, anyway, I need you to come. I'm meeting Jenkins and Whitaker there."

"Great. So, you're all set."

"On the contrary, that's why I need you."

The odd rationale left Thom wondering if he had missed something or, perhaps, he had misunderstood what had been said. "You mind feeding me that again?"

"Jenkins and Whitaker—we both know their views. I need someone at the table who isn't deaf...someone who won't constantly sing the praises of King George and Parliament." Richard extended his index finger nearly jabbing it into Thom's chest. "And that someone, my friend, is you."

Thom heaved a reluctant sigh.

"Save your moaning for another day. As I said before, I'm not taking *no* for an answer!" A raised voice dared defiance.

For the first time, Thom seriously considered the overture. A small repast hours earlier left his stomach growling, not that the fare at the Hogshead could delight his appetite. "Okay," he said, "but I expect recompense for this."

"Fair enough." Richard made an imaginary mark in the air with his finger.

"What the hell was that?"

"I deducted one debit from the many you owe me." A broad smile decorated Richard's face.

Thom gave his friend a shove. "C'mon...Let's go."

Minutes later they arrived at the Hogshead. Like every such establishment, it bore a wooden signboard. The one at the Hogshead hung from chains attached to an inverted L-post. Most times when Thom visited the tavern, the sign, perhaps owing to its familiarity, went unnoticed. Even when noticed, it went largely unread. The same might have transpired were it not for the stiff breeze. The sign's uncommon sway caused Thom to stop long enough for a second look. At the top, emblazoned in big, carved, gold letters was: "HOGSHEAD TAVERN," followed by "Good Food, Drink, and Lodging," and the crimson coat of arms of King George III at the bottom.[132] Thom contemplated the sign. Winds of change, indicative of more than the weather, were blowing. A massive storm might be brewing.

The tug of Richard's hand on his sleeve pulled Thom from his musing and through the door of the Hogshead. They joined Jenkins and Whitaker, who were seated in the corner booth nearest the door.

"Mary!" yelled Jenkins, "add some stew to our trough, and two more ales for my friends. And stick in more meat this time!"

With pleasantries exchanged, Whitaker said, "Thought you went among the missing again."

Thom shrugged. "Been busy with stuff around the house. Don't know where the time goes."

"You heard from that Indian kid, the one who was staying with you?"

Thom anticipated the spicy offering might be part of the fare, but did it need to be an appetizer? "Pico—I haven't seen him."

"Dodge is convinced the kid was behind—"

"George, why don't you let it be?" Richard turned to Jenkins. "Any thoughts about where we should build the new meeting house?"

"The land adjoining the cemetery near Deacon John Jackson's property seems perfect."

"I guess there's some support for that," said Richard. "Of course, lots of folks want it near town center, just north of the convergence of Mud Land and Mt. Hunger Road." He looked at Thom. "What do you think?"

"Either one seems okay." Thom preferred the site near town center, but more so he preferred to be non-controversial.

"Personally," said Jenkins, "I like the spot near the cemetery, not that anyone will listen to me. They only want free legal services. The Reverend asked me to check the title once we have a site. He hooked Peter Blake for the surveying." Jenkins gestured at Richard. "The Reverend manage to collar you?"

Richard nodded.

Whitaker laughed. "Leave it to the Reverend. He doesn't leave a stone unturned."

"You comparing me to a stone?" Richard sported a smile.

"Look at it this way," said Jenkins. "The comparison could have been worse."

Richard nodded. "When you put it that way...you have a point."

Thom gulped his ale which, along with additional stew, the usual mystery kind, had just arrived. Amidst the light mood, earlier misgivings diminished.

238

"A few folks object to the meeting house," said Whitaker. "Claim it's mainly for religious purposes, and they shouldn't have to pay."

"Yeah," said Richard. "The same heathens who say they shouldn't be taxed to pay the Reverend's salary."

Thom dug his spoon into the communal trough. He shoveled the food into his mouth. He recognized a piece of carrot. There was meat as well, and though it was impossible to identify, it was softer than the Dinsmore leather the Hogshead normally dished. Thom had opinions regarding the topic of conversation but kept his thoughts to himself. His readings of Montesquieu had convinced him that church and state should be separate. He was not about to voice the view when even his pal Richard disagreed. Tyringham, like all of Massachusetts was predominantly Congregationalist. Most aspects of the religion were tightly intertwined with daily life. Those who were otherwise disposed were welcome to move to places like Rhode Island or Pennsylvania. Such was the prevailing attitude.

"Speaking of religion," said Jenkins, "I assume you fellas heard the news regarding Parliament's most recent action in regard to us."

"You mean the 'Quebec Act?'" said Whitaker. "I heard about it yesterday."

It was unfamiliar to Thom, and judging from Richard's puzzled look, he too was unaware.

"I can't say I like it," said Jenkins, "but as my late father used to say, 'folks who fool with trouble, generally wind up with misery.'"

"Yeah," said Whitaker, "that sums it—"

"Wait a second," said Richard, waiving his spoon at Jenkins. "Not all of us know what that law—whad'ya call it—is about."

"The Quebec Act." Jenkins reached into his pocket and pulled out a piece of paper. "I got the news yesterday. I got the *what-fors* right here. The list is pretty long." He unfolded the paper. "Among other things, it guarantees the French in Canada the freedom to practice their Catholic religion."[133]

"You gotta be kidding!" said Richard. "Why in the name of sorry sanity would Britain bless the practice of Catholicism in one of its colonies, let alone one where most are French Catholics?"[134]

"That's exactly the point," said Jenkins. "Britain has lots of problems on its plate. It can't afford more, especially in a strategic place like Quebec City, the mouth of the St. Lawrence...the northern gateway to North America. If Britain denied the French Catholics the right to practice their religion, they'd rebel, and France would be eager to help them. Allowing those folks their religion and customs is a sage strategy. Appeasement averts insurrection. It enables Britain to maintain a firm hold on its northern-most colony in the hemisphere." Jenkins' eyes moved over his three companions. With his chest as puffed as his portly belly, he made no effort to conceal the hubris associated with the lesson he had just served.

"Damn," said Richard. "I can't believe that you're pleased with the Quebec Act."

"Who said I'm pleased? I merely explained what it did, and, by the way (he waved his paper in the air), there's a lot more. But before I get to that, let me dispel any confusion about my views. First: I dislike the Quebec Act. Second: From Britain's standpoint, it's brilliant. Third: The damn radicals here in our colonies are responsible. It's the trouble I referred to earlier when I mentioned my dear old dad—May he rest in peace."

Much as Thom resented the lawyer's didactic style, he conceded the disturbing information had been conveyed clearly.

"See," said Whitaker. "Ezra and I have been telling you for more than a year that Britain would make us pay. You refused to listen. Maybe now you'll get the message."

Thom squeezed his lips together as he endeavored to hide his feelings. The bad news was hard to stomach, but what irked him more was watching Whitaker ride Jenkins' high horse.

"Something the matter, Webster?"

*Yeah, you, mucker.* Thom wondered if his face hinted at his thought. Actually voicing it was another matter.

Whitaker shook his head. "It burns my ass. We're getting bashed because the damn radicals keep pulling idiotic stunts." He turned to Richard. "And don't give me one of your buddy's mocking looks. If you were in my shoes, trying to run a business, and certain goods got scarce because a bunch of crackpots were shooting off their mouths, you'd be hot too." Whitaker gritted his teeth. "That Quebec Act that Ezra was talking about—you can't deny that it's a slap at us here in Massachusetts. Parliament wanted to stick it up our Massachusetts Bay asses. No doubt they held their ever-loving noses when they allowed those damn Catholics to maintain their customs and religion. It was a direct response to the damned paper, 'The Right of Colonists,' that nut Sam Adams penned for his Committee on Correspondence.[135] He endorsed mutual toleration, except for Roman Catholics."

"Maybe." Though Thom uttered the spontaneous reaction softly, it was loud enough to draw the eyes of his tablemates. He needed to buttress the comment. "Britain's 'Toleration Act' did the same thing."

"Whoa...look who's got a view," said Whitaker.

"Lay off." Fire showed in Richard's eyes.

"Fine," said Whitaker. "But think about it. The Brits dislike the Catholics as much as we do. By sanctioning Papist practices, expanding the rights of the heathens in Quebec while taking ours away, Parliament let us know where we stand."

Though heathens may have been an inapt term, Thom found it hard to deny that the Act slammed Massachusetts. Slammed it hard.

"The Quebec Act," said Jenkins, "did a few other things." He glanced at his notes. "It extended the Quebec boundary along the Ohio River beyond the Alleghenies and repealed the prohibition of westward expansion of Canada. It allowed the people of Quebec to retain their civil and property laws. And one more tidbit, it vested Canadian legislative power in a bi-racial council. Though according to what I heard, action by the council requires royal approval from Britain."[136]

"How do you like them apples?" said Whitaker. "They give the Catholics their own legislature after dissolving ours." He looked Thom in the eye.

Thom turned away.

"You made your point before," said Richard. "You needn't rub it in."

Whitaker smiled before scooping in a mouthful of stew.

Dinsmore, the cordwainer, approached the table. "We're getting up a card game. Any of you interested?"

"Count me in," said Jenkins. He tugged at Whitaker's arm. "C'mon, I need a four-flusher who's as easy to read as the big sign at Brewer's Mill."

"Oh really," said Whitaker. "Just for that, I'm gonna take you for more than a few shillings." He looked across the table. "You boys gonna join us?"

Richard shook his head.

"Not tonight," said Thom. He had taken enough of a beating.

"Suit yourselves," said Dinsmore. "But remember, when you don't play...it's our loss." He smiled and headed off with Jenkins and Whitaker.

Richard slid around to the opposite side of the booth.

"Of all people, why do we hang out with those two?" said Thom.

Richard looked all around as if making sure no one was listening. He leaned forward and whispered, "'Cause no one else 'll have us."

Thom knew his pal was joking, but the comment struck a chord. Unlike Richard, he wasn't gregarious, and there were others, especially the older fellows, with whom he felt uncomfortable.

"On second thought," said Richard, "you have a point."

"I do?" Thom's earlier question, coupled with a moment of rumination, hardly classified as the epitome of brilliance.

"Why *do* we hang out with Whitaker and Jenkins? They're pompous as hell, though I have to admit that next to the lawyer, the peddler is a sweetheart." Richard surveyed the room. "The vast majority of Tyringham, and that includes those who frequent the Hogshead, condemn Britain's conduct—the 'Intolerable Acts,' as most term them—and still we spend our time with the narrow-minded blowhards." He shook his head. "Are we nuts?"

"Probably...though it has its advantages."

"Oh really?" said Richard, his eyes wide.

"Yes, really," said Thom, recalling a sage remark from his Boston mentor. "Despite their ranting, they're both smart, and Jenkins, pain in the ass that he is, has plenty of information. Chatting with those who share your views is nice, but facing those who don't, requires greater objectivity. Unfortunately, with Whitaker and Jenkins, that benefit comes with incessant aggravation."

"You know...that makes sense. Still I'd rather spend my time with guys like Woodstone and Cooper and..." Richard's gaze moved upward toward the ceiling. When he finally looked back, he said, "Fine—then answer me this. Why do we spend our time with Crane?"

"Well..." Logic forced Thom to concede that the blockhead blacksmith was aggravation with no brains. He heaved an extended sigh. "You got me."

# Chapter 15

FEET FIRMLY PLANTED, Thom slipped his index finger into the hand-forged trigger guard of his club butt fowler. He took careful aim and squeezed the trigger. Sixty yards away the one-foot square wooden target remained motionless. "Damn! Four tries and not a single hit." He moved aside as the next in line stepped up to shoot.

"Well, look at it this way," said Richard, struggling to keep a straight face. "At least you managed to complete the march without falling." Richard was referring to the march the militia had taken from town center, up Royal Hemlock Road toward Hop Brook, down Smith Hill Road, along the Konkapot River to the area of Mud Lane. The hike was part of the training exercises for Tyringham's militia which, according to rumor, were about to double from two to four times per year.

There was a time when Thom attributed his poor marksmanship to his lack of a rifled gun. Though slower to use and limited to a single-sized round ball, it was notoriously more accurate than a fowler.[137] Months earlier, Richard, who had a rifled gun, had switched weapons with Thom. As usual, Richard was the better shot. No longer could Thom blame his poor performance on his fowler.

"Jeze, this heat is stifling," said Richard.

Thom took a deep breath and gazed upward. Apart from a few isolated, quilted clouds, the blazing sun, high over head, ruled the blue, July sky. He mopped his sweaty brow. With the temperature hovering close to ninety-five and the humidity oppressive, temptation cajoled him to echo Richard's complaint. He didn't. Despite scant religious conviction, cursing the warmth of a summer's day would be tantamount to blasphemy. He reached for his canteen and took a series of large swallows. The crystal water, drawn from the Konkapot, refreshed. And with the rippling river close by, there was no need to conserve. Refills were readily available.

Thom looked around at his compatriots. They were a congenial group, but far from a fit fighting force. He turned to Richard. "If the time comes when we have to do battle with the British, how do you think we'll fare?" The inquiry, comparing an amateur group of civilians to well-equipped professionals, was inane.

Richard drew an exaggerated frown. "Those Redcoats won't stand a chance. Damn, one look at us, and they'll laugh themselves to death." He looked Thom in the eye. "Why the sudden question?"

"I don't know. Just wondering, I guess, what with relations growing more and more contentious."

"Contentious, yeah...but nothing that will end up on the battlefield. Hell—even the Virginia Resolutions, with all their grumbles, urged the deputies of the Philadelphia Congress to affirm allegiance to King George."[138]

The point, that war was unlikely, was sound. Why then, Thom wondered, did he have misgivings? Perhaps it was his tendency toward pessimism. The propensity had been established early in his harsh childhood and compounded during his confinement in an English jail. Not until he had set out on his own did confidence begin to develop. During his years in Boston it had flourished. It had continued when he had arrived in Tyringham and had begun dating Polly. But with a crashing thud, her father's veto had turned back the hands of time. From the distant recesses of his brain, fountains of negativity and incompetence had bubbled back to the surface. Thom had done much to drive them back into the depths, but echoes still reverberated. Before they could take hold, he endeavored to implement the wisdom of his Boston mentor. "No matter how dark the clouds overhead, somewhere up above the sun reigns. Look for that bright spot." With the precept in mind, Thom silently revisited the issue of war. Suppose it did occur? The Minutemen, generally the best quarter of any Massachusetts local militia, were better trained and equipped than their brethren. Might they fare respectably against the Redcoats? The question begged an affirmative answer. The facts demanded otherwise. The Minutemen, though a step up from the militia, were a bunch of farmers. Thom gazed up at the sky again. The sun shone brightly. Amidst its largely blue canvas, fluffy white clouds, anything but dark, offered cottony beds. Were any fool to lie there, his crash through the ephemeral vapor was inevitable.

⌒∿🙰🙰∿⌒

The sight of Reverend Bidwell coming up the path drew Thom from a seat on his favorite granite boulder. "Hello Reverend." Thom laid aside a dowel he had been filing.

"Good afternoon, Thom." The Reverend peered alongside the house. "Looks like you grew yourself a mighty fine garden."

Thom would have shared the credit with Pico, but reluctant to divert the conversation to his departed Indian friend, he opted for a more apropos benefactor. "Credit goes to the Lord, his ample balance of sunshine and showers."

The Reverend looked to the Heavens. "Indeed God has blessed us. And speaking of him, I thought we might see more of you on Sundays when we sing his praises."

Thom gulped. Prudence had guided his tongue to steer clear of a problematic path. The alternative he chose turned out worse. "Well, I've been meaning to come more often, but..." The lack of a good excuse left him dangling mid-sentence.

Patient or, maybe more precisely, cleverly astute, the Reverend waited.

Thom gestured, first at his saltbox and then his garden and surrounding land. "It's amazing how much there is to be done around one's house. One can work day after day, never leaving home, and still have much to do."

Reverend Bidwell nodded. "And no doubt hard work deserves praise. Besides being necessary to provide food and clothing and shelter, it's good for the body, as well as the spirit."

Thom smiled, assuming the Reverend had let him off the hook.

"But work by itself doesn't complete a man. The soul requires nourishment too. Giving thanks to God, prayers and devotion, along with self-examination and kinship with one's community, are imperative."

Thom felt a lump in his throat. "Uh...yes...they are."

246

The Reverend patted Thom on the shoulder. "Don't worry. I didn't come here to lecture you."

Maybe, but I got your message. Thom simply nodded.

"Have you stayed abreast of the restrictions Parliament has imposed upon us?"

"Uh...I think so, unless more news arrived in the past week."

"Well...two days ago we got word that Parliament enacted distressing amendments to the '1765 Quartering and Mutiny Act.'"

"What now?"

"With Boston's Castle William inadequate to house the four regiments of British troops that are stationed there, Parliament has legislated that British soldiers be quartered in empty houses, inns and barns and, if necessary, private homes, here in the colonies. If that weren't enough, we have to furnish the soldiers with candles, bedding, cooking utensils, beer and rum, and a few other things that, at the moment, slip my mind."[139]

"Do those put upon at least get compensation, not that it would recompense the injustice?"

"Believe it or not, they must bear the expense."

The response, the opposite of what Thom had anticipated, left him speechless.

"It's intolerable...I know." Dismay showed on the Reverend's face. "Not that I wish the other colonies ill, but I'm glad Parliament applied the quartering provisions to them too. That should make them sympathetic to our plight here in Massachusetts. And speaking of solidarity, it appears to be growing."

"You referring to the call by the dissolved Virginia House of Burgesses for a Continental Congress and a boycott of East India Company products other than saltpeter and spices?"

"Yes, but more than that. Recently Virginia demanded that we enjoy the same rights afforded British citizens. They want the colonies to cease trading with Britain. Exports are slated to stop on August 1st, and imports, three months later."[140]

Thom shook his head.

"You disapprove?"

"On the contrary—just surprised. I wonder how the other colonies will react."

"Seems we're getting the answer already. Leaders in Providence, New York and Philadelphia have joined the call for a Congress."

All along Thom had feared that if the crisis deepened, Massachusetts would be left to fend for itself. The newest information suggested otherwise. He said, "What do you think of Virginia's call to halt trade with Britain?"

"Courageous...very, very courageous. But it's a double-edged sword, and Britain may wield the sharper edge."

That thought, though not in the same prose, had crossed Thom's mind. The colonies depended upon Great Britain for many of their goods, and many pounds flowed into the colonies as a consequence of what they exported. Terminating commerce with their primary trading partner would be tough medicine. Very tough. Regardless, Thom viewed the news as positive. He said, "I appreciate your stopping by and filling me in." He took a deep breath. "I...I'll try to improve my attendance at the Sunday meetings."

"Good, because we'd love to see more of you...And that brings me to the primary purpose of my visit."

Thom struggled to hide concerns, unable to imagine what surprise the Reverend had saved for last.

"Most of our meetings are held at my house, and that's fine. I have the room, and with forty-eight chairs,[141] not that I mean to boast, my home fits the bill. But a growing community like Tyringham should have a real meeting house. Support for the idea is growing. But if it's to become a reality, we'll need the skills and labor of many." The Reverend looked Thom in the eye. "Any idea where I'm headed?"

The upcoming pitch wasn't subtle, but wanting a moment to weigh his response, Thom said, "Not really."

Reverend Bidwell smiled.

Whether it was the affable mien of a friendly clergyman or a polite message of disbelief, Thom was uncertain.

"Well...let me spell it out for you." The Reverend patted Thom on the shoulder with one hand as he gestured at Thom's saltbox with the other. "You're one of the most talented builders in Tyringham."

"Thank you," said Thom, sensing the ulterior motive. "My home can't hold a candle to yours."

An abashed look, rare for the clergyman, painted the Reverend's face. "Mine may be a bit fancier, but—"

"A bit?" Were Thom speaking with someone other than Reverend Bidwell, he would have uttered a sarcastic *sure.*

"Well, the difference between our homes is a matter of cost, not skill. My home may be larger with more ornamentation, but your workmanship is as good."

The flattery, though exaggerated, was seductive. But concern for the Reverend's motives, along with modesty, compelled Thom to downplay his talents. "I've seen your home, both inside and out, including the masterful arch from which the chimney and several fireplaces rise. Doubtless, there is much I could learn from you."

The Reverend eyed Thom's saltbox. "Your exterior work is exemplary. Others have told me the interior, the stone work included, is equally good. Clearly, there is much I could learn from you."

Thom soaked in the praise.

"Your design and building skills would be a huge asset in the construction of a new meeting house. And with you being single, you must have more time than the family men of our community."

Seconds before, Thom was on the verge of assent, albeit reluctant. The possibility he might be asked to do more than his share sparked second thoughts.

"I see your hesitancy." Reverend Bidwell stole a peek at the Heavens and muttered, "Sometimes your guidance turns me into my own worst enemy." He looked back at Thom. "Relax. It's not as bad as it sounds. Whatever we build will be small and simple. Down the road, perhaps we'll enlarge and add embellishments...maybe someday a steeple. But the initial structure will be functional. We should have close to forty workers, so no one will be asked to shoulder an undue load. A day each week from spring till early fall ought to do it. And those who volunteer will be relieved of their usual congregational contributions."[142]

The dispensation was little consolation to Thom. Though his taxes included money for the congregation, owing to rare appearances at Sunday meetings, his contributions to the collection plate amounted to a pittance.

"From what I've heard, apart from raising the frame, you built your house yourself. Unlike many folks who are morally indebted to their neighbors, you're not. That said, I'll understand if you turn me down."

All along Thom had felt the four walls of the spiritual leader's pressure closing in on him. Refusing the clergyman would be difficult. But just when it had appeared Thom had no way out, the Reverend had provided an open door. The opportunity was tantalizing. But would his conscience balk? In recent weeks he had begun drifting back into a solitary world of despondency, a barren place in which he fruitlessly endeavored to escape himself. Giving in to the overture had its cost, but passing up a chance to become a valued member of the community might spawn regrets. He said, "You can count me in."

Reverend Bidwell smiled.

Thom wondered if he had been manipulated. If so, the manipulation had been masterful. Even so, there was ample reason to believe the result was in his best interests.

"Before we get ahead of ourselves," said Reverend Bidwell, "understand that at this point a new meeting house is nothing more than an idea in the making. Many are yet to endorse the concept. The plan could evaporate. If and when it becomes a reality, countless details, not the least of which are location and design, will have to be worked out. I'll be happy if come next spring we break ground."

Not to wish the Reverend bad luck, but as far as Thom was concerned, the longer the wait the better. He said, "As I indicated, I'll be glad to help."

Along with his friends Richard Thorn and Paul Cooper, Thom squeezed his way into the back corner of the courtroom at the Great Barrington Courthouse. Knowing the crowd would be large, the trio had arrived early. With an hour remaining until court was scheduled to convene, the hall was packed. Richard, Paul and Thom were forced to stand. Before long, others would have to wait outside.

It was the first meeting of the Berkshire County Court of Common Pleas since Governor Gage, in accordance with his powers under the Massachusetts Bay Regulating Act, had begun appointing the colony's judges. Residents throughout Berkshire County had come to Great Barrington concerned how and who would dispense justice in the area they called home. While most cases involved nonpayment of debts, the court's jurisdiction covered all types of litigation, including those involving foreclosure proceedings and title to real estate. To colonists like Richard, Paul and Thom, little, if anything, was more important than their land. Having such matters controlled by outsiders was anathema.[143]

"Damn," said Paul, "there must be six or seven hundred men in this courtroom."

"And more coming every minute." Thom stood on his tiptoes to better survey the scene. "Ought to be some very interesting proceedings today."

"If any transpire."

Thom found it hard to deny Richard's point. Unless many there were removed, the conduct of business would be all but impossible.

"I'm glad you guys insisted I come," said Paul. "When you suggested it, I was less than enthusiastic. But you were absolutely right. This is not to be missed."

"It's bound to rattle Gage's cage," said Richard, adding a self-satisfied grin.

"He deserves it." Cooper ignored the histrionics. "And from what I hear, it's gonna be like this all across the colony."

Thom pushed up onto his tiptoes again. Even at six feet it was hard to see. More men were trying to squeeze their way in. He mopped his brow. The courtroom was stifling, but he didn't mind. The event justified the inconvenience. Hundreds of men trying to speak over the noise created chaos. Still the chaos bore an anomalous beauty. Militiamen were there, but they had left their guns at home. That ordinary farmers were unarmed made their resistance to an autocratic governor backed by the strongest military in the world more compelling. An intangible, perhaps a unity of spirit, seemed stronger than a force of superbly skilled and sartorially splendid Redcoats. For a change Thom felt a part of something much larger than himself.

Increasing numbers attempted to cram into the courtroom. They filled the area behind the bench where the judges were supposed to sit. Every nook and cranny of the courthouse had been taken by the ever-growing throng. Thom tuned his ears to the conversations around him. Reactions paralleled those of Thom and his two friends. Occasionally he blocked out the noise and marveled at the assembled mass. A stranger to his left smacked his back much the way one might after a few brews at the Hogshead. To be sure many had imbibed, but Thom suspected the smack was the product of zeal's inebriation, not alcohol. Thom returned the friendly stroke.

"You betcha," said the fellow. "We're gonna be heard."

Thom nodded, conscious that the smile he flashed resounded as loudly as a shout.

The appointed hour for the court to convene arrived.

"Look—right over there," yelled a man in a blue, tri-cornered hat. "It's that damn Tory, David Ingersoll."

As several shoved Ingersoll, Thom joined those who hissed and booed. Thom knew Ingersoll only by reputation, but that was enough. The pompous lawyer and magistrate, who in the past had represented the towns of Great Barrington, Sheffield and Egremont in the General Court of Massachusetts, had exercised his authority with little sympathy for the grievances of the Massachusetts' colonists. He was among those who, to the ire of his Great Barrington neighbors, had delivered a speech lauding Governor Hutchinson just before he had returned to England. A cheer rang out when Ingersoll, attempting to enter the courthouse, was dragged away by the mob.[144]

More judges arrived. The sheriff endeavored to clear the way for them to take their places on the bench. The effort was in vain. No way would the crowd yield.[145] Another half-hour went

252

by, and it became apparent no judicial proceedings would take place. Nevertheless, few left. Most waited the better part of an hour after court had been scheduled before ceding the territory.[146]

"Shall we go?" said Paul.

"Okay by me," said Thom.

The trio worked their way out the front entrance of the courthouse. Thom stepped into the fresh Great Barrington air. Off to his left he heard a man say, "A rough count showed our numbers at fifteen hundred."

"Did you hear that?" said Thom. "Fifteen hundred of us. Can you believe that? Out here in Berkshire County."[147]

"Amazing," said a stranger. "This oughta show Gage what we think of his scheme." The stranger pumped a fist into the air. "You from Great Barrington?"

"Tyringham," said Thom.

"I'm from New Hampshire. I was in Sheffield visiting family and decided to come to the courthouse for a look-see. Damn, if you folks from Massachusetts aren't turning tyranny on its head. 'Course, up New Hampshire way, we're doin' pretty good too. I suspect you heard how we came to the aid of Boston."

"Uh...sorry," said Thom. "Can't say that I did."

"Well, let me tell you." The stranger puffed out his chest. "Our Committee of Correspondence is supportin' Boston. Governor Wentworth, damn fool that he is, thought he could run roughshod over us. First he garrisoned Fort William and Mary, Portsmouth's only fort. Then, with the backing of the Rockingham Sheriff, he prohibited our Provincial Assembly from meeting. He forced the members out of their chamber." The stranger shook a fist.

The man's animation, the verve with which he spoke, inspired Thom as much as the information. If it reflected attitudes throughout the colonies, Massachusetts was not on its own.

"We folks in New Hampshire won't be intimidated. If Wentworth, and for that matter King George and Parliament think otherwise, they're in for a rude awakening." He looked Thom in the eye. "You know what our Assembly did after Wentworth shut 'em down?"

253

Thom shook his head.

"They moved to a tavern where they made plans for a Provincial Congress. I've yet to hear the result, but you can be sure, they won't give in to Wentworth."[148]

"Good for them," said Thom.

"And good for us." The stranger put an arm over Thom's shoulder. "You boys have a good ride back to Tyringham.

"You too...that is to New Hampshire."

"Well, for now it's just Sheffield. Another week till I head home."

As the man went on his way, Thom turned to his friends. "The spirit of resistance is spreading. Let Parliament chew on that."

Cooper put a hand to his stomach. "Speaking of chewing, I'm starved. Suppose we grab a bite at Josiah Smith's place.[149] Word has it, the food there is a helluva lot better than the Hogshead."

"That doesn't say much," said Thom. "Even Rich's slop is better than what Heath dishes out."

"That's debatable."

Richard pretended to bristle, but a smile sabotaged the act. He gestured at the crowd. "Any place around here is bound to be mobbed."

Cooper threw up his arms. "So, you suggesting we starve?"

"Nah, just you fellows," said Richard. "I've got plenty to eat in my haversack. I'd share it, but no doubt my gastronomical shortcomings would be too much for you boys to bear."

Thom glanced at Cooper. They were over a barrel. He refocused on Richard. "Under the circumstances, we'll suffer with whatever you brought."

Richard folded his arms. "Fine, but that suffering better be in silence."

Neither Paul, nor Thom uttered a word.

*⁓ᴓᴓᴓ⁓*

Just beyond Twelve-Mile Pond, aboard Lodestone, Thom turned off Smith Hill Road to Brewer's mills. During the preceding winter he had continued to house his faithful steed in Sarah's barn. Any inconvenience, having to walk to Sarah's to fetch Lodestone, paled in comparison to the need to protect his horse from the harsh elements. In the back of his mind Thom harbored plans to build a barn behind his saltbox, but not for several years. Thanks to Pico, work on his home had progressed faster than expected, enabling Thom to embark on projects that otherwise would have been distant. While ideas for the interior ran rampant, he generally reserved them for the winter season. In the meantime he was determined to enjoy the beautiful summer sunshine. He decided to build a small, log shed to shelter Lodestone. The simple structure would allow for storage of a few tools and other odds and ends. Unlike his saltbox, where plans were carefully committed to paper, Thom envisioned the shed in his mind. Small pine logs, his property had an ample supply, were perfect for the job. For the roof he preferred flat planks, and so, he went to Brewer's Mill.

Negotiations for the boards, twelve planks, each ten feet long and a foot wide, enough to allow the roof a tiny slope, proved easy. He was about to board Sarah's wagon and leave, when Issac Winslow approached. If Thom had been a minute quicker, a passing wave would have sufficed, but standing face to face, he had to extend a more neighborly greeting. "Good afternoon, Mr. Winslow." Thom never felt comfortable calling Polly's father by his first name.

"Hello, Thom." Winslow extended his hand and shook Thom's. "Nice to see you."

"And you too." The pleasantry hardly conformed to Thom's thoughts.

"I've heard nice things about your saltbox. About a week ago I was up your way on Beartown Mountain, so I decided to see for myself. Gotta tell you—that's a mighty fine house you built. Walked all around it. The more I looked, the more impressed I was."

"Appreciate the kind words," said Thom, taken back by the unexpected flattery. "If I knew you were there, I would have invited you in."

"Matter of fact, I knocked, but I guess you were out." Winslow hesitated. "Don't take this wrong, but I...didn't think you had it in you."

The comment erased the satisfaction Thom felt a moment earlier.

"I didn't mean that the way it sounded."

*Sure,* thought Thom, reluctant to buy into the apparent white lie.

"No, you really surprised me. You're a better man than I realized." Winslow's nod punctuated the compliment with a seemingly heartfelt stamp.

Thom could only wonder: What if Winslow had felt that way when he had asked for Polly's hand, before Peter Blake had come into the picture. Might Winslow have given his blessing? The thought was as painful as tantalizing.

"I understand you've volunteered to help in building the new meeting house, assuming there is one. I look forward to working with you. I'm sure you'll be a great asset."

"I appreciate that. And I look forward to working with you." Common courtesy dictated the response. Thom climbed onto the wagon and headed on his way, pondering what had just transpired. He glanced over his shoulder in the direction where Issac Winslow had been standing. Hard as it was to imagine, working with him might be okay.

⟳⟳⟳⟳

Having laid the last log, Thom stepped back and surveyed the four sides of his shed. Set upon a base of crushed limestone, which allowed for drainage and protected the four base logs from rotting, it was a simple, imperfect structure. Far from his customary standards, it had two parallel rows of logs running east and west, with notches near the ends that interlocked with notches in each succeeding course running north and south. The ten-by-ten makeshift frame, unimpressive as it was, was ideal for the purpose. Across the breadth of Massachusetts, such structures, their dimensions somewhat larger, were home to people, rather than horses.

Hoof beats coming from out front caught his ear. Around the side of his house, he spotted Richard approaching on his dapple gray.

"What's up?" said Thom, as Richard dismounted.

"Been fishing in Twelve-Mile Pond." He unhooked a sack from the horn of his saddle and held it open. "Take a gander. Three trout, two pike and I'm not sure what the spotted one is. Anyway, six, a record for me, is more than I can use. Take a couple. Anything but the spotted one. I have to try that myself."

"I'll take a trout. Come on inside. We'll clean them together."

They walked to the house.

"You'll never guess what I saw coming up here, not far from Royal Hemlock Road." Richard paused, as if allowing Thom a moment to conjecture. "Lyman Brown's barn is burned to a crisp."

Thom winced. He tried to conceal his reaction, though he suspected Richard could read it. Whenever there was a fire, folks were apt to think of Pico. Perhaps he was still in the area. "That's really unfortunate. I feel sorry for Lyman."

"Yeah...losing a barn really hurts."

"Any idea how the fire started?" As Thom posed the question, he debated its wisdom.

Richard nodded.

"Arson?"

"No, definitely not. Brown did it himself."

As much as the disclosure provided relief, it prompted confusion. "Why would Lyman burn down his barn?"

"Oh, it wasn't intentional. Just a silly accident. Seems Lyman left a canister of milk out in the barn yesterday afternoon. By the time he remembered, it was after dark. He went out there with a kerosine lantern. He tripped over a pitchfork he had left near the stall where he keeps his cow. He went head over heels and banged his head. The lantern landed in a pile of hay. The thing flamed up faster than a linen shirt soaks in a cloudburst."

"Lyman's okay, isn't he?"

"Yeah, a little bruise on his forehead, though maybe a bigger one to his pride. On the bright side, he managed to get himself, his cow and two horses out okay." Richard pointed. "That's a neat little cabin you're building."

"That thing?"

"Yeah, that thing." Richard walked toward the shed, stopping a few steps away. "You planning to build your own little town here?"

Thom forced a smile but suspected a looking glass might prove it a simper.

"Quarters for slaves, maybe?"

Were others present, discretion would have guided Thom's response to the facetious question. "I hadn't thought of that, but if you're offering to be the first, you're on."

Well aware of the structure's purpose, Richard jerked back. "Uh...I...wouldn't think of stealing Lodestone's new home."

Thom smiled. He had no doubt a mirror would have revealed something very different from moments earlier.

"By the way," said Richard, "did you hear what the people of Cambridge and those from Exeter did in response to the Intolerable Acts?"

"Don't think so."

"On July 28th, in Cambridge, they held a town meeting, itself a no-no. They voted to help their neighbors across the Charles River in Boston. They're sending all kinds of donations. It's a huge show of support."[150]

"Any word of Parliament's reaction?"

"No, but c'mon..."

Thom recognized the absurdity of his inquiry. In response to the Tea Party the preceding December, Parliament had closed the port of Boston. The squeeze put on the city demonstrated that rebellious conduct would not be tolerated. Cambridge's show of solidarity was bound to make Parliament livid. "I see your point," said Thom. "So, what about Exeter?"

"Much the same. Remember that fellow from New Hampshire, the one who was visiting family in Sheffield?"

"You mean the guy at the Great Barrington Courthouse who told us how their Assembly adjourned to a tavern after Governor Wentworth banned them from meeting?"

"That's the one. Anyway, folks up his way in Exeter held a provincial congress this past month. Like Cambridge, they urged the people of New Hampshire to aid Boston. Word is they're sending goods and supplies, along with letters promising support.[151] Can you imagine Gage's reaction, not to mention that of Parliament? No doubt the bastards assumed their tactics would strike fear and force compliance. They must be seething."

"Serves them right." Thom thought for a moment. "Looks like Exeter's provincial congress may have another effect. Apparently folks in New Hampshire have had their fill of Governor Wentworth. As far as they're concerned, he and his dictates can go to Hell."

"That sums it up fairly accurately." Richard looked Thom in the eye. "You've got something on your mind."

"Oh, I was just thinking...all along Jenkins has insisted that the other colonies would walk away holding their collective noses once England's horses began dumping their loads on Massachusetts."

"I don't think he put it in quite those words."

"Maybe not, but that was his message."

Richard's expression turned pensive...noncommittal. "So, you're convinced Jenkins had it all wrong."

"Don't tell me you disagree?"

"Well...yes and no."

Thom stared at his friend.

"First off," said Richard, "we're a long way from getting support from all the colonies."

"I suppose, but you have to admit what Jenkins claimed is little more than Swiss cheese."

"Yes...but—" Richard thrust out a halting hand before Thom could voice his self-satisfied comeback. "That doesn't mean he's all wet."

"You gotta be kidding!"

"Not in the least." Staccato rendered Richard's response even more emphatic. "In case you've forgotten, Jenkins' main contention was that one way or another, Britain will kick our colonial asses. Just because we get support from other colonies, doesn't imply we'll ultimately get our way."

Thom would have acknowledged the logic had annoyance not superseded. "You suggesting we should give into the swine

259

from across the sea; that we should not have gone to the Great Barrington Courthouse and protested; and that—"

"No, that's not at all what I'm saying!" Richard folded his arms defiantly. "I'm merely trying to view the situation objectively. Like it or not, we face a tough road ahead. Whether Jenkins is ultimately proved wrong is anything but a closed question."

Thom disliked the message. His silence, however, conceded its merit.

# Chapter 16

THE SETTING SUN, skimming the tree line, its westerly rays nearly tangent to the front of the house, angled through the windows. Thom had finished his evening meal and, as was his custom in the summer months, he would turn in shortly after dark. That way he was well rested and ready to rise at dawn. Like nails and tea and tools, daylight was a valuable commodity, not to be wasted. Lumber and limestone, ever abundant, demanded less frugality. But even with those resources he had grown more provident. Thom knew the reason. Pico may have been gone, but his influence remained. Though rarely discussed, visible differences in the way they had consumed plentiful resources had impacted Thom. Without fanfare Pico had endeavored to take from nature only that which he needed. In a pattern of half-conscious change, Thom's respect for his environment had grown, and as it did, so too, his kinship to both the land and the young man. It was part of the ongoing process in which each had learned from the other. Shaped by different worlds, contrasting cultures, they had shared knowledge and drawn insights, more by example than instruction.

Thom was storing jam in the buttery when he heard a rap at the door. Ordinarily he would have opened it without hesitation, but visitors at such a late hour were atypical. He went to the parlor window and peered out as best he could. Whoever was there was standing too close to the door for Thom to see with his angled view. He stepped into the hallway and said, "Who's there?"

"British officers." The voice was resolute.

Thom opened the door. Standing before him, impeccably dressed in long, red waistcoats, with tails trimmed in black and white, were two Redcoats. Rarely since his days in Boston had Thom seen British army men at such close quarters. "Can I help you?"

"We're on our way from Boston to Albany and require housing for the night. The Hogshead was packed, and we were informed that your house was nearby and you live alone."

Thom would never refuse a passerby, but before he could react, the second officer said, "Lest you're unaware and before you make a decision you may regret, know that under Parliament's Quartering Act, should you fail to afford us billets, you will be subject to punishment." The officer stood tall, his boring eyes, two beads of intimidation.[152]

"Come in," said Thom. Tension and resentment supplanted what a moment earlier had been willingness to be a gracious host.

The officers, their tri-corner hats still on their heads, stepped through the doorway. As the duo surveyed the premises, Thom scrutinized them. Silver buttons, roughly a dozen, up and down the turned-back lapels of their waistcoats, were complemented by stripes sewn around each buttonhole. White braided insets overhung the black cuffs of their coats.[153]

The taller of the two nodded. "Quite adequate. This will do."

"You can sleep in the loft." Thom pointed up the stairs. He was not about to give up his bed, not when he felt put upon.

"We have our bedrolls," said the second officer. "We haven't eaten. You'll feed us, please."

The word *please* tempered the brazen imposition, but the firm tone left no doubt that the request was, in reality, a demand.

"Take your things up to the loft, and I'll prepare something." Thom gestured to his left. "I'll meet you in the dining room." He went into the kitchen. His culinary skills were limited, but on those rare occasions when he had guests, he endeavored to serve as tasty a meal as he could. In his buttery he had an excellent bean porridge, a cornmeal brown bread and half an apple pie that Sarah had given him. He threw together a suppawn porridge, adding extra water that all but turned it into gruel. He brought it out with some cheate bread, slightly stale, and two tankards of beer.[154]

"Enjoy," said Thom, as he set the paltry repast before the officers.

The one sipped his brew. "You got some rum?"

Thom nodded.

"I'll have some too," said the other.

Thom went back and poured two mugs. He spurned the urge to top them off with water and brought them to the officers.

Rather than join them at the table, Thom returned to the kitchen. Having to serve them was enough of an affront. He had no desire to watch them dine.

When they finished, the one who had said *please* earlier, the less imperious of the two, called out, "Appreciate the vittles." They headed up to the loft.

The following morning Thom was up before the sun. He enjoyed a hearty bever of tasty bean porridge, sweetened with maple syrup. On the dining room table he left more gruel-like porridge and cheate, along with the same two tankards of beer the officers had passed up the night before. When they came down from the loft, he invited them to partake. While they ate, he ground some corn meal in the kitchen. Once they finished, they went up to the loft. Minutes later, Thom heard their footsteps as they came back down. The sound of the door opening was followed by the reverberation of its closing. Thom went to the dining room window. He watched the Redcoats disappear down the path into the woods.

"Good riddance," he said. His jaw tightened before he repeated, "Good riddance, you lousy lobsterbacks."

It was early morning. Thom wondered if it might be the eve of war. He stepped outside. The peaceful trill of a robin caught his ear. The possibility that thunderous echoes of cannons might drown out the dulcet notes of the feathered friend was inescapable. He breathed in the fresh Berkshire air. How different a battle-scarred countryside would be. Landscapes favored with the beauty of wildflowers might be awash with bodies ripped apart by bayonets. Decaying flesh might drown the sweet scent of fragrant petals. He strolled around the corner of his house to his garden. He gazed up toward the peak that rose beyond the plateau bearing his saltbox. The steep slope paled in comparison to the mountain the colonists would face if and when war with the Mother Country transpired.

Seated with Sarah atop her wagon, Thom tugged the reins on Lodestone drawing the wagon to a halt alongside his saltbox. Common sense told him there was no reason to be nervous, but even before he had ridden Lodestone to Sarah's place and hitched the stallion to her wagon and driven her back to his house, the tension had been undeniable. Hundreds of times they had eaten together at her home, but this was the first time he was making dinner for her. It was not as if she had high expectations, a meal such as she would make for a special occasion. Thom had told her his menu, a turkey ragout, along with sallats and cornbread. At Sarah's insistence, not that Thom resisted, she had made a peach cobbler and a syllabub.[155] The jitters were undeniable as he seated himself across from her at his dining room table board. He had covered it with a piece of linen. He would have used a tablecloth, if he had one. A pair of pewter platters replaced the usual wooden trencher.

"Very tasty," said Sarah, following her first sampling of the stew.

Whether the comment was sincere or the gracious words of a diplomatic guest was hard for Thom to discern. Regardless, the praise helped alleviate his uneasiness. He took a bite. It wasn't half-bad. An ample supply of parsnips, squash, onions and tomatoes, heavily seasoned with salt and garlic, had produced a tasty mixture.

"You know..." Sarah trailed off into several pensive seconds. "You've never told me much about your English childhood."

Abating discomfort was back on the rise. "There's not a lot to tell."

Spoon halfway to her mouth, Sarah stopped midstream. "Sounds as though it may be very interesting. But if you'd rather not discuss it, I understand." She waited a moment. "I know you spent time in jail. As far as I'm concerned, that's no big deal. Anyhow, I meant the years before that."

"Well..." Thom gazed into space. Perhaps the time to share what lay buried in the tombs of his past had arrived. If so, what better ear than Sarah's to hear it? He took a deep breath. "Where should I start?...My Mom...she died while I was in jail. She was a fine person. But my father (Repugnant images of the burly tyrant filled Thom's head.)...ruled our house with an iron fist. He was downright mean, especially when he was drunk, which was most of the time. No matter what I did, it was wrong. If I painted a hundred feet of fence and every spot but one was flawless, he would dwell upon the lone miscue as if it were the only area on which my brush had left its mark. And never, ever did he spare the rod. His hand, a switch, a belt...I tasted their sting more times than I could count."

"Were you an only child?"

"No. I had two younger sisters. One died of pneumonia when she was only seven."

"Did your father treat your sisters any better?"

"Yes and no." Images of the dingy, stark house where he had spent his formative years emerged from the recesses of Thom's mind. "He didn't hit them, but he was anything but loving. They were girls, and girls didn't count. Basically he ignored them. They were my Mom's concern. Much as I longed for my father's approval, if he had ignored me, it would have been better than what he dished me." Thom shoveled some stew into his mouth. His words, the visions of his past, echoed. "Funny...it's hard to say which was worse, my time in jail or living in the same house as my father. I never thought about it that way, though one thing sure, when I got out of jail, no way was I about to return home, especially with my Mom having died."

"As the eldest, indeed only son, you must be entitled to inherit your father's estate."

Thom laughed. "He can keep his damn money, not that he had much. I want nothing from him." Thom no sooner spoke the words than he realized they were not altogether accurate. Way down in the depths of his soul remained a yearning for the approval he had been denied. In Boston his mentor had given him the approbation for which he had long been starved. It lifted him, motivated him and made him a better person. It was beneficial, but his mentor was not his father. The hole in his heart remained. It always would. His childhood void was cast in stone, and that void left him vulnerable to circumstances of rejection. Issac Winslow's refusal to approve his marriage to Polly was the incomparable example. Thom took another bite of his stew. He chewed it thoughtfully. He was a decent man, far better than his father. His measure as a human being should be judged by his conduct, not the often capricious estimation of others. The insight, though hardly a panacea for ingrained tendencies toward self-flagellation, had liberating possibilities. He gazed across the table. "I'm glad you asked me about my childhood."

A skeptical cast showed on Sarah.

"I'm serious." Thom lifted his tankard of cider. "Here's to you." He took a drink. *Here's to you, Mom...both of you.* The unspoken words brought a conscious smile to Thom's lips.

⁓⁓⁓

Excitement from the Berkshire County Courthouse persisted. With Governor Gage prepared to seat his handpicked judges in Worcester on September 6, 1774, Richard cajoled Thom to relive their early August exploit. Thom was willing, but only if they went on to Boston. That would add forty miles to the seventy-mile trip to Worcester. Neither needed to twist the other's arm. The two bachelors, their responsibilities far less than most colonial men, were eager for the adventure. They decided to travel to Boston first. They would time their return west to Tyringham so they passed through Worcester on the sixth of September.

Bedrolls in tow, aboard Lodestone and Gray Mist, they departed on the last day of August. The sturdy horses, in top condition following an active summer, could comfortably make the trip in three days. The evening of the second night, they stopped at a tavern along the Albany-Boston Post Road about ten miles east of Worcester. The instant they opened the door, a din, no less than the Hogshead at its most frenetic, had Thom doing a double take.

"Wild place," said Richard.

"That's an understatement." A hand on Thom's shoulder turned his head.

"You got any news?" said a burly fellow with no hair.

"News?"

"About the powder, Cambridge...war...anything."

Thom shook his head.

The burly man eyed Thom curiously. "You ain't a Tory, are ya?"

"God forbid...What's going on?"

"Ain't you heard? The damn Redcoats grabbed the colony's powder stash near Boston. Somebody said their ships are shelling the city."

"You sure about that?" said Richard.

"I ain't sure 'bout nuttin'. Thought you fellas might shine a light on the rumors. They're comin' faster than a hare with a dozen hounds on its ass."

"What else have you heard?" said Thom.

"This...that. All sorts of crap. A guy over there (the stranger pointed) claims the Redcoats are marching through the countryside. Thinks dozens wuz killed. Claims the colony is under siege.[156]

"You think it's true?" said Thom.

"What?" said the fellow.

"All of it...Any of it?" Thom wanted something definitive.

"Ain't got no idea." He waved his arms wildly. "Can't tell nuttin'. One minute ya hear one thing. The next, it's another. 'Nough to drive a sane man crazy. All this on top of Gage sticking us with that Man...Man something council..."[157]

"Mandamus?" said Richard.

"Yeah, that's it. Manday...whatever."

"Any idea what folks plan to do?" said Thom.

"Come mornin', lots are headin' to Cambridge."

"Why they doing that?"

"Cause that's what others are doing."

The logic, or lack thereof, struck Thom. Not wanting to offend the stranger, he chose his words carefully. "Do they know why the others are doing it?"

"Got me." The stranger gestured at a tankard he was holding. "Gotta get a refill." He headed to the bar.

Thom looked around the tavern. Animation, mostly chaos, reigned. He turned to Richard. "Whad'ya think?"

Richard shrugged.

"That's my typical response, not yours."

Richard heaved a sigh. "Damn, just as I feared. You're contagious."

Knowing he had invited the jab, rather than retort, Thom refocused on the issue. "What should we do?"

"Maybe if we talk to others, we can get something more definitive. No offense to that fellow (Richard gestured toward the bald stranger), but..." He heaved an exasperated sigh.

"You've got a point," said Thom. "But first, let's get something to eat. I'm famished, not to mention parched."

They ordered the fare, a facsimile of Hogshead swill, along with dark ales. Once their stomachs were replenished, they circulated among the patrons, garnering as much information as possible. Folks came and went. New arrivals added to the rumors. Circumstances appeared increasingly ominous. Many feared the colony of Massachusetts was under siege.[158]

"What's true?...What's false?" said Richard.

"God knows." Thom surveyed the crowded tavern. "It's like the game we played when we were kids, passing a secret from ear to ear. By the time we finished, the story had changed completely."

"I know what you mean, except in this case we've got a dozen stories." Richard scratched his head. "What should we do?"

Not wanting to arm Richard's prickly tongue, Thom repressed an instinctive shrug. "We could go to Cambridge. It seems to be the thing to do." Thom recognized the absurdity of his response. It mirrored what the burly stranger had said. Compounding the folly, it invoked the same fatuous justification. He tried to convince himself there was a distinction. Cambridge was near Boston, their destination. The logic drew a silent chuckle. The purported distinction was a rationalization. He would have chosen Cambridge irrespective whether it was near Boston. He wanted to go where folks were going—to the action.

"I agree," said Richard. "Tomorrow morning we head to Cambridge."

After a night sleeping in a crowded room of the tavern, on the morning of September 2, 1774, Richard and Thom were up with the sun. A hasty bever and they were off to Cambridge. It was early afternoon when they arrived at the Cambridge commons. Several thousand, mostly militiamen, were gathered there. Rumors of battles and colonists killed and British troop movements abounded. Most were unsubstantiated, but one gained credence. Two or three hundred British soldiers had rowed up the Mystic from Boston to the powder house at Winter Hill where they had seized the colony's biggest gunpowder supply. The soldiers had taken the powder, along with some cannons, to Fort William and Mary. Governor Gage was, indeed, confiscating the colony's munitions.

"Unbelievable!" said Thom, as he gazed across the sea of men.

"It's even wilder than the scene at the Berkshire County Courthouse when we blocked the seating of Gage's stooges."

Thom silently debated the point. What had transpired in their home county was hard to top. But Richard was right. Tensions had heightened to another level. War, so long an implausible hypothetical, was in the air. It could break out at any time. Perhaps it already had in Boston. Perhaps the British warships had shelled the port. And perhaps the blood of colonists had been spilled.

A man standing not far from Thom pointed off to his left and called out, "Over there, beyond the crowd, on that horse, that's City Commissioner Hallowell."

The accuracy of the identification was beyond Thom. Not only was the man far away, but even face to face, Thom would not have known him. Regardless, Thom joined the others, hissing and yelling at the man. A shot, or what sounded like a shot, rang out. Whether it was fired at Hallowell or in some harmless direction, Thom had no idea. At most he could attest to having heard a loud noise.

Someone yelled, "The revolution has begun!" Shouts, most hard to decipher, grew louder and more pervasive.

"Do you think we're at war?" said Richard.

"Could be." Thom considered loading his fowler, but surrounded in all directions by friendly militiamen, there was no need, at least for the moment. He noticed a tall, stately man about forty standing a few feet away. The man, quieter than most, seemed to be assessing the situation. "What do you think?" said Thom.

Countenance thoughtful, the man leaned on his rifle. "If we're not at war already, I suspect it's close at hand."

The comment echoed Thom's thoughts. Awestruck, he watched the amazing array. Like the Berkshire County Courthouse, most were farmers, but farmers ready to do battle with the mighty British army.

A chant spread through the crowd demanding the resignations of the Mandamus Council members, Judges Danforth and Lee. Thom joined in the cry.

Two men were escorted onto the steps of the courthouse. They were no more familiar to Thom than City Commissioner Hallowell. Word had it they were Judges Danforth and Lee, and that they had submitted their resignations. Cheers accompanied the circulating news.[159] The crowd began to move. Along with Richard, Thom followed.

"Where do you think we're going?" said Richard.

"Got me."

A stranger close by said, "I suspect we're headed down Tory Row, perhaps to the home of Lieutenant Governor Oliver."

Before long, the four thousand militiamen had surrounded the Lieutenant Governor's house. Stationed a considerable distance from the rear of the structure, Thom joined the newest round of angry chants. Word, racing through the mass with the celerity of wind-driven flames in a drought-stricken hay field, fueled more cheers. Oliver appeared and resigned, though only after protesting the intimidation-induced action.[160]

Richard slapped Thom on the back. "We got those British bastards on the run!"

"Yeah, that'll teach 'em to mess with us." Behind Thom's words, just above a semi-conscious level, lurked a sagacious suspicion that the success of Cambridge was an isolated incident in what was bound to be a formidable progression of events.

Resignations forced by a mob were scant proof how the saga would ultimately play out. The dose of reality gave Thom pause, but only pause. He refused to permit such cautionary logic to interfere with celebration. Bravado felt too good.

⁕

After spending a night in their bedrolls on the Cambridge Commons, Richard and Thom spent two days in Boston. Physically the environs conformed to what Thom recalled from his days living there. But it had a different feel. A visit to the home of his late Boston mentor highlighted the point. The building looked the same, but with his mentor gone, it was nothing more than lumber and bricks and mortar. Thom thought of knocking on the door, but why? The occupants were strangers. He had no desire to see what changes they had made to the interior. Thom wanted to remember the premises the way his mentor had decorated it. Modifications, even beautiful ones, would disrupt cherished memories.

A stop at the Boston Commons was an exclamation point. Thousands of British soldiers draped the landscape, transforming the city's centerpiece, the people's haven, into an indecorous field of intimidation. The Boston that Thom saw was a Boston he didn't know. It justified the colonists' cause. The gulf dividing the American colonies and their Mother Country widened.

On the 5th of September, Richard and Thom rode west toward Worcester. Militias from all around had descended upon the area, determined to thwart Governor Gage's plan to seat his yes-men in the Worcester County Court of Pleas. That the people of Massachusetts would no longer have justice dispensed by their own peers was unacceptable; having it in the hands of Governor Gage's flunkies was an outrage. As determined as Governor Gage may have been to manifest his authority,[161] the people were equally determined. Just as they had blocked the way at the Berkshire County Courthouse in August, they could do so in Worcester.

Together with more than twenty others, Richard and Thom had laid out their bedrolls on the planked floor of the loft of the Creekside, an inn about a mile from Worcester center. A man about Thom's age preparing to bed down next to him said, "You fellows goin' to the courthouse tomorrow?"

"You bet," said Thom.

"Oughta be somethin'."

"You got that right." Thom motioned toward Richard, who was organizing his personal belongings in his haversack. "My friend and I rode a fair piece to be here."

"Ya here with your local militia?"

Thom shook his head. "Just the two of us."

"Don't tell me folks out your way don't support the cause?"

"Not that," said Thom. "It's a matter of distance. We're from Tyringham. It's seventy miles west of here, in Berkshire County."

"Oh—you folks are ahead of us." The man's face bore a gleam.

"Excuse me," said Thom.

"Yeah, I heard how ya blocked Gage's judges from sittin' in your court."

"We sure did." Thom was bursting his buttons. "My friend and I were in the courthouse when it happened."

"Damn, so unlike me...ya ain't virgins."

For an instant the comment confused Thom. "Oh, you mean we've done this courthouse-blocking routine before."

The fellow gave Thom a look. "Yeah, that's what I meant. But in case you thought I meant somethin' else, just to set the record straight, I've got a wife and four kids." He winked. "So, tell me—what was it like?"

"Well...the first time I bedded a woman..." Thom shook his head. "Only teasing. This time, I know you're referring to Great Barrington."

"Yeah, though afterwards I'd love to hear 'bout the other."

Images of the Great Barrington Courthouse intertwined with recollections of Thom's first sexual encounter. As different as the birds and the trees, they bore remarkable similarities. Thom briefly relished the odd musing, but forced himself to focus on the former. "It was remarkable. There we were, a bunch of ordinary citizens, mainly farmers, defying the most powerful country in the world. Their hand picked judges, empowered to determine our rights, resigning and promising not to enforce Parliament's law."

"Did you put guns to their heads?"

"Matter of fact, we were all unarmed."

"Unarmed?" The fellow shook his head. "Not gonna be that way tomorrow. All our militiamen—that includes yours truly—got our guns."

The weaponless success at Great Barrington tempted Thom to suggest a similar approach, but as an outsider, who was he to make such a suggestion? Regardless, telling this fellow would have no impact.

The man chuckled.

"What's so funny?"

"Oh—I was picturing Gage's reaction after we take over the court tomorrow. Word has it he calls Boston a lone pocket of rabble-rousing radicals. Fool that he is, he thinks folks like us in the countryside will roll over and play dead. Seems he's in for a rude awakening." The man reached for his Moller Musket and stood it, butt to the ground, at his side. "If Gage and his thugs are lookin' for a fight, we'll give 'em one."

Thom pointed at his Club Butt Fowler that lay next to his bedroll. He had anticipated leaving it with Lodestone when he went into the courthouse. With that plan revised, he said, "If Gage's bootlickers want a fight, they'll get it." To what extent the words constituted bluster occasioned by contagious enthusiasm, not to mention brews consumed on the main floor, was hard to judge. Thom didn't care. He was caught up in the moment. "By the way," he said, extending his right hand, "my name is Thom...Thom Webster."

"Ben Stone." He shook Thom's hand. "Assuming you and your friend don't prefer to march alone, you're welcome to go with our militia tomorrow."

"Appreciate the invitation." Thom drew Richard's attention and introduced him to Stone. The trio bonded amidst tales of youthful exploits. Soon enough they called it a night. Thom's rest was far from uninterrupted. Perhaps the strange

273

environment, a crowded loft far from his solitary saltbox, was responsible. More likely, the culprit, anticipation.

∼∽∭∿∼

Marching alongside Ben Stone at the rear of the Sturbridge militia, Richard and Thom arrived at the packed Worcester Courthouse. The crowd, much larger than that which occupied the Berkshire County Courthouse, exceeded anything Thom had imagined. Estimates ran in the neighborhood of five thousand, including a thousand or more armed militiamen.[162] Apart from gatherings to hear sermons of the era's most renowned clergy, such an assembly was foreign to Thom. That all these common folk had come together to resist the dictates of Parliament and the King's handpicked governor was hard to fathom. Under the Massachusetts Bay Regulating Act, Parliament had empowered Governor Gage to appoint all judges, sheriffs and marshals. The people of Massachusetts had no power to remove them. The law was clear. Everyone knew it. But there in Worcester, with numbers amazing, their zeal manifest, the people were defying the law.

Thom turned to Richard. "Can you believe this?"

"It's...it's..." Richard shook his head. "Words don't do it justice."

Soon the twenty-five judges, sheriffs and marshals arrived to a chorus of intimidating shouts and jeers. Militiamen barred the officials from the courthouse and marched them off to Daniel Heywood's nearby tavern where they were forced to sign documents promising not to hold court under the new law. They were marched back through the ranks of the intimidating throng and compelled to repeatedly reiterate the renunciations of their offices.[163]

All the while the crowd roared.

With goose bumps palpable, Thom shouted as loud as anyone.

274

# Chapter 17

ACCOMPANIED BY RICHARD on his dapple gray, reluctantly Thom guided Lodestone along the Albany-Boston Post Road toward the home of Peter and Polly Blake. Members of the community were gathering there to raise a barn. It wasn't that Thom objected to helping Peter and Polly; simply that he felt uncomfortable. Several days earlier Deacon William Hale had asked Thom to join the crew. Saying *no* was too hard, and once Thom had acquiesced, he had to show up.

Thom and Richard cut over onto Mount Hunger Road, following it until they reached the Blakes' home, a full cape, so termed because it had two windows on each side of the front entrance. With a base comparable to Thom's saltbox, the one and one-half story home had a low pitched, gabled roof, but unlike Thom's, the length of the slope in back was the same as the front. It had a large center chimney, low eaves and eight-foot corner posts.

By the time Thom and Richard arrived, roughly twenty men, along with numerous teenage boys, were out behind the house where the barn was waiting to be raised. They were gathered around Peter Blake who, together with his father-in-law Issac Winslow, was arranging assignments. Despite his experience, Thom remained in the background, preferring that others with expertise act as crew chiefs. A call for two more men to handle the ropes that would pull one side of the frame from its position on the ground to vertical had Thom volunteering. He had found an unobtrusive role in the initial phase.

Well-organized teamwork abounding, the throng raised the four sides of the frame. Work progressed efficiently, and before long, trusses to support the roof were in place. Deacon Hale enlisted Thom to join seven or eight others installing rafters. Comfortable with heights, he was happy to work in the relative solitude of elevated space.

The midday was the better part of a half-hour away, and much of the frame was complete. The clang of a cowbell drew Thom's attention. Polly was vigorously shaking the copper device, calling the men to an area where the females, young and old, had spread a huge picnic lunch. It was the first time since arriving that Thom had caught a glimpse of Polly. Indeed it was the first time in months that he had seen her. From his lofty perch he stared. Even at forty yards, with cowbell in hand, she was beautiful. With Thom's imagination supplementing that which his eyes could barely see, the distance, if anything, magnified her radiance. With a white frilly cap, decorated with corresponding lace, white trim on her two-thirds' length sleeves and a rose petticoat, she put the other women to shame. Of that Thom was certain, though his transfixed gaze saw only Polly. He closed his eyes, contemplating what might have been. This could have been his home, his barn and his life. More important, Polly could have been his wife.

"Hey, you plan to sleep up there, Webster?"

The call of his name halted Thom's ruminations. He opened his eyes.

"It's time to eat," shouted Wendell Dinsmore.

Thom started down. He stole another glimpse of Polly. He made certain to stamp the lovely lines of her curvy silhouette into his memory bank, not that it was necessary. The image had been indelibly recorded long before.

He stepped onto the ground and went to the edge of the adjacent woods where Lodestone was tied in the shade of a spindly poplar. He got his meskit and tin cup from his saddlebag and, after fetching a drink for Lodestone, got himself an array of pork and chicken and turnips and sallats, along with a cup of dark ale. He joined Richard, who was sitting on a bolder with Johnny Woodstone, out back under the shade of a giant elm.

"Take a load off," said Woodstone.

Thom tried to join them, half-sitting and half-leaning against the side of the rock. The limited space made it impractical. He parked himself, legs crossed, on the ground.

"C'mon," said Woodstone. "We can make room."

Knowing all three would be uncomfortable, Thom said, "Thanks, but I'm fine down here."

"Suit yourself," said Richard. He gestured at the barn frame. "Coming along pretty good."

"We'll have it done well before the sun sets." Woodstone held up a chicken leg. "Damn good eats."

"You got that right," said Richard. "You see the pies...three kinds...and that flummery? Couldn't be better."

Woodstone shook his head.

Richard did a double take. "I can't believe you're gonna give me an argument."

"Not that I got somethin' against those desserts. Just that they're second rate next to what you boys enjoyed."

Thom kept his head down, afraid that Woodstone had caught him ogling Polly.

"C'mon, I'm talkin' about your trip to Worcester and Cambridge. That musta been a hoot—seein' Gages' goons resign in front of thousands. And to hear them denounce those stinkin' Intolerable Laws, even if they done it outta fear." Woodstone heaved a sigh. "Damn, I wish I coulda been part of that."

"Chances are, you still can," said Richard.

"Very funny. Not enough that I was laid up sick when you all packed the courthouse in Great Barrington. Ya gotta rub salt in my wounds." Woodstone turned to Thom. "Now I know why your pal's last name is *Thorn*."

"Johnny, if you'd listen, rather than insult me, you'd realize that I'm serious."

Woodstone laid his spoon down. "Okay, I'm all ears. So, tell me, how I can turn back the clock and be part of Worcester and Cambridge?"

"Not them, *per se*," said Richard, "but their equivalent. Think about it. In just a matter of days, courts of common pleas in other neighboring counties are scheduled to convene. No doubt Governor Gages' flunkies will be eager to dispense his version of justice. No reason why some good citizens from Berkshire County, Tyringham included—and that means you Johnny boy—can't be there soliciting resignations."

A broad smile appeared on Woodstone's face.

"I accept your apology, John." Like Woodstone, Richard smiled, though his was more of a smirk.

277

Thom enjoyed the banter of his pals. His comfortable position on the sidelines enabled him to be an analytic observer. Over several years he had seen Woodstone's attitude toward the Mother Country evolve. When Thom had first come to Tyringham, Woodstone had voiced mixed feelings about England's rule. With the passage of time he, like many others, had grown more militant. Grievances met with deaf ears and, worse yet, intolerable legislation had exhausted patience. Simmering frustrations had boiled.

"How come you fellows are eating back here?"

The sound of Peter Blake's voice as he approached interrupted Thom's ruminations.

"They told us vassals that the riffraff has to know its place." Richard gestured up at the elm. "Actually, it's a great spot."

"As long as you're comfortable." Blake glanced at the partially completed shell. "Mighty kind of everyone to pitch in."

"You did the same for me when I built my saltbox," said Thom.

"Be that as it may," said Blake, "I appreciate you lending a hand. And by the way, I was watching you work. You've got the speed of two. As for quality, there's no doubt—evidence your saltbox." Blake pretended to doff a non-existent cap. "Webster, you're a good man."

"What about me?" said Woodstone, feigning hurt.

"Hey, what can I say?" Blake focused on Thom and whispered, but loud enough for all to hear, "Hard to believe the good Lord could create something like him."

Thom laughed. He knew that Blake and Woodstone were dear friends and that the jibe underscored their mutual affection. On the other hand, the plaudits Blake had sent Thom's way were less predictable. They were also appreciated. Jealous though Thom was of the man married to Polly, there was no denying that Peter Blake had class.

⁓᷿᷿᷿᷼⁓

Days had passed since the glorious moments at Worcester and Cambridge; the sublimity, however, endured. With unremitting passion, Tyringham's militiamen who had earlier marched to the Great Barrington Courthouse were still reiterating their tales of triumph, complete with embellishments. But Richard and Thom, the only locals who had gone to Cambridge and Worcester, garnered the most attention at the busy Hogshead. Folks who rarely noticed Thom were seeking him out. Those who had missed all of the courthouse antics bore receptive ears as they sought to share in the escapades, if only vicariously. An abundance of ale and beer and rum helped sustain the ebullience.

With tables packed, Thom, like numerous others, roamed the establishment with mug in hand. Old man Garwood, seated at the large table in the center, latched onto Thom's wrist as he passed by. "I'd give twenty shillings to have seen Oliver's puss when he was forced to resign. Did he really look like a scared rat?"

"Nah, he was homelier." Though Thom, who had been around the rear of the Lieutenant Governor's house, had never seen Oliver, he had heard descriptions, mostly fourth or fifth hand. "Anyway, if I compared Oliver to a rat, the nasty rodents would take offense...and rightly so. But let me tell you, I'd lay ten-to-one Oliver browned his breeches."

"Serves the lout right." The raspy-voiced Garwood cleared his throat. "Is it true that several of Gage's judges were tarred and feathered in Worcester?"[164]

For an instant Thom yielded to the alcohol. He had consumed more than usual, nearly a half-dozen brews. "Worse than that. Why they—" The lack of a story contained the urge to allow hyperbole, indeed fabrication, to rewrite the truth. Recollection of the confusion occasioned by the countless rumors at Worcester and Cambridge pressed him to stick to the facts. He said, "Nobody was tarred and feathered, not that the bastards didn't deserve it."

A frown on his face, Garwood's arm dipped, his tankard rapping the table. "So, let me guess, the judges in Cambridge weren't chased from town by dung-throwing militiamen."

Garwood's vivid version was too appealing to negate. Thom said, "Personally speaking, I didn't see the judges shelled with manure, but..." Thom faded into pensive reckoning.

"So, it mighta happened?"

279

"Hey, if that's what folks say, who are we to suggest otherwise?"

The verve in Garwood's face re-appeared. He said, "Tell the Brits that Massachusetts is gonna give 'em hell."

"Not just Massachusetts," said Thom. "The other colonies will be with us."

Garwood raised his tankard. "To Lord North and Parliament...May they rot in hell." He took a swig. "And they thought they could isolate Massachusetts. Turn it into an island."

Orville Crane, who was standing nearby, piped in. "Garwood, what the hell are ya jabberin' about? Massachusetts ain't no island."

Garwood shook his head. "Crane, you numskull. It's a figure of speech!"

"Well, your speech ain't none too good. And don't ya shout at me!"

"I will if I want!"

"Don't waste your breath," said Thom. "Crane won't get it."

With fist clenched, the blacksmith glared at Thom. "Maybe you'd like one of these, right in your ugly kisser."

"Pathetic," said Thom, and he turned to Garwood. "Did you know that Orville does his smithing atop his head? It's even harder than his anvil." Out of the corner of his eye, Thom caught a glimpse of the fire in Crane's eyes.

The blacksmith banged the adjacent table. "Ya think you're real smart 'cause of what happened in Cambridge. Ya won't be laughin' when all hell breaks loose."

"What's that supposed to mean?" said Garwood.

"That the Redcoats 'll kick our ever lovin' asses."

"That so?" said Thom. "Just how do you figure that?"

"Well...according to Ezra—and if anyone knows, he does–the more we piss off England, the harder they'll bash us. Ezra sez—"

"Ezra says this...Ezra says that." Garwood scowled. "Damn it, Crane. When was the last time you had an original thought?"

"C'mon," said Thom. "That's not a fair question. You know a lead block can't think."

"Oh yeah," barked Crane. "At least I don't house Indians who burn down other people's places." He pointed a finger at

Thom's face. "'Course it ain't no surprise, what with ya bein' an ex-jailbird and all."

Garwood's eyes widened. "You served time in jail, Thom?"

"He sure did." Crane, whose voice had grown louder, paused long enough to sneer at Thom. "Mr. Big Shot here done a year, didn't ya?"

Thom froze, conscious that the question had drawn the attention of others near Garwood's table. He suspected that most had heard about his past.

"Hey, everyone," shouted Crane, drawing the ears of many more. "Get this. Thomas Webster is a two-bit thug. He did time in jail." Crane glanced at Thom. The look communicated whose ass was about to get kicked. "C'mon, Thommie boy, tell all of Tyringham about yourself."

Thom stood motionless as more and more of his neighbors eyeballed him.

The din in the Hogshead lessened.

"Pipe down," hollered Crane. "Give Thommie the floor. He wants to tell ya about his criminal past, how he done time in prison."

The Hogshead grew quieter and gradually silent. All eyes were trained on Thom. Expectant faces waited.

Thom hesitated, debating what to say. Explanations, extenuating circumstances, would ring hollow. His conviction and time served were the bottom line. He said, "Back in England, before I came to Massachusetts, I served a year for hitting a man."

"Beatin' 'im is more like it," barked Crane.

Unable to dispute the characterization, Thom stood mute.

A buzz, rapidly amplifying, pervaded the Hogshead.

Crane leaned Thom's way and whispered, "Mess with me, will ya."

Thom lowered his head. He remained the center of attention, but the exhilaration associated with recent events in Cambridge and Worcester had evaporated. Those exploits had grown distant...more distant than what had transpired on the other side of the Atlantic over a decade earlier.

"It's inevitable, isn't it?" said Richard.

"Yup." A brew in hand, Thom sat on the bench behind his friend's house. His visits there were infrequent. More times Richard would stop by Thom's saltbox, often to lure Thom to the Hogshead, a town meeting or some other gathering.

"It's coming, as sure as the winter."

Thom studied the crescent moon already visible in the twilight. The warm, early September evening felt more like July. It was the kind that could delude one into thinking that autumn might never come. But like the sun which vanished nightly beneath the horizon only to magically re-appear in the opposite sky, the change of seasons was a certainty. It was in the air. And so too, was war. Both were just a matter of time.

"I think we can beat them," said Richard.

Thom shifted his gaze from the Heavens, demonstrably eyeing his friend. "Oh really?"

"I don't know. Maybe it's wishful thinking. But the way I see it, we've got a huge advantage."

"Please...share with me the wonderful rationale behind this so-called advantage."

"We're here."

"No fooling."

"No, give me a chance." Richard leaned back, seemingly collecting his thoughts. "Britain has to send its army across the Atlantic. Our colonies stretch across more than a thousand miles of wilderness, an expanse far bigger than England. How can an army, even a well-trained one, control such a vast area?"

The point had merit. Britain faced a formidable challenge. But history reminded Thom it was not insurmountable. "The Romans did it. Caesar conquered all of Gaul and more."

"Aha," said Richard, "but owing to Rome's inability to reign in the hinterlands, the empire crumbled."

"Yeah...after how many centuries?"

"Details...details." Richard frowned. "Whose side are you on?"

"C'mon, that's not fair. You know I'm playing devil's advocate."

"Devil...yes. As for advocate...that's another matter." Before Thom could protest, Richard continued. "But you see my point? Throughout the colonies we have militia, not to mention more and more Minutemen. We can fight the British army here, there and everywhere. And not just in open fields, but in the woods and hills."

The scenario for a colonial victory was tantalizing, but not enough to wheedle Thom into ignoring the strategic realities of war. "The British army won't fight us in skirmishes here and there in the woods. They'll march in concert sweeping through our cities and towns, taking control of our supplies and key strongholds. And lest you forget, they also have the most powerful navy in the world. So much of what we need, not the least of which are weapons and ammunition, comes by sea. They can blockade our ports and cut off our supplies."

"Damn, you're such a pessimist."

There remark bore truth, but its failure to address the substance of the underlying issue did not fool Thom. "If we were standing on a cliff and you recommended we jump off because we might be able to fly like birds, and I voiced doubts, you'd dismiss them. You'd tell me I'm a pessimist."

"Well—you are. And as for your cliff-jumping analogy, it makes Crane's typical logic seem brilliant."

"Thanks a heap."

"Your welcome." Richard smiled.

Thom stemmed the urge to compound the sarcasm. "Do you have any other reasons to believe we have an advantage over Britain?"

"I'll give you three: France and Holland and Spain."

Thom's effort at self-restraint crumbled in the face of the convoluted exegesis. "Now who's making Crane look smart? A trio of countries that would love to do us in hardly constitutes an advantage."

"In case you haven't noticed, those three countries despise England, not to mention its growing empire and mercantile policies. They would love to see England get its comeuppance. What better opportunity than war on our soil? They have fine navies, lots of supplies and, who knows, they might even lend their soldiers."

The possibility, though far from convincing, intrigued Thom enough to mull it over aloud. "Soldiers from France or Spain could give us a boost. If one of them decided to attack England, the British would have to fight on both sides of the Atlantic." Thom observed a non-receptive expression on Richard's face. "What's the matter now?"

"The pessimist is suddenly doing a one-eighty, becoming a hope-springs-eternal optimist."

Thom wanted to protest, but how could he? How likely was it that France or Spain, or for total absurdity, Holland, would attack England? It could only be done by sea. Three hundred years earlier, England had established its undisputed naval superiority by defeating the Spanish Armada. An attack on England would be tantamount to suicide. Thom said, "All right. I got carried away. But damn, as long as I was buying into your pipe dreams, you could have gone along."

Brow furrowed, Richard shook his head.

Thom got the message. He could babble on as long as he liked, but it would only tighten the noose he had slipped around his own neck. He said, "If war breaks out—"

"*When*, not *if*, is more accurate."

"Fine—*when*." Eager to get to the issue, Thom conceded the point. He said, "There are loads of people throughout the colonies—that includes Tyringham—who disagree with our cause. When push comes to shove, they'll fight with the Redcoats. How in God's name will we deal with that?"

"Got me, and it's not like I haven't thought about it." Richard heaved a sigh. "Having our neighbors shoot at us and visa-versa is hard to imagine."

"Wait a second. When you put it that way, it's not so bad. Maybe I could give Crane a taste of my Fowler."

"You're making jokes, but it's a serious problem. It wouldn't surprise me if ten, maybe even twenty percent of the colonists will remain loyal to England. Put another way, many of our enemies will be living among us."

"How the hell will we know which side people are on?"

"Easy...If they support England, they're on the other side." Richard smirked.

"Now, who's making ridiculous jokes?" The unrepentant expression that met Thom's eyes convinced him to move on. "At least with jerks like Jenkins, we won't have to think twice. As sure as pigs like mud, he'll back England. But others aren't so outspoken. And others yet are on the fence."

"Well...they'll have to get off."

"I wish it were that simple." Thom sensed that Richard was missing his point. "Some of the silent ones will pretend to support our cause while remaining loyal to our Mother Country. Britain will have built-in spies in every town."

"Damn." Richard gazed at the treetops as he seemingly digested the knotty concern. "Keeping information from the enemy will be virtually impossible."

"Virtually?"

"I stand corrected. Impossible."

Having been wrong several times during their discussion, the concession should have lifted Thom. It didn't. Tyringham was a neighborly place. But war would put a new twist on matters. Misgivings and suspicions would run rampant. Opposing loyalties would eradicate friendships. Rancor, even violence, was bound to follow. It was no way to live. Regardless, it was certain to come with the territory.

⁀ఎఎ⫘ఎ⁀

"I don't mean to pry," said Richard, as he and Thom, their path lit by a nearly full moon, wended their way from the Hogshead along the Albany-Boston Post Road. "But as a friend, I have to tell you that you're handling Crane all wrong."

"Oh really?"

"If you prefer I keep my trap closed, say the word, and I'll shut up."

A tempting offer, but obviously not what Richard wanted. Give him his say, and if it's too aggravating, tell him to mind his own business. "Okay, I'll listen, but how long, remains to be seen."

"I don't know the details of what happened in England...why you spent time in jail. And frankly, I don't give a two-penny damn. But that's not the point."

Thom squeezed his lips together. It was the only way he could keep from lashing out.

"You need to bring the facts behind whatever happened across the sea out into the open."

The advice, which required more than sharing a confidence with a close friend, exhausted Thom's patience. "Give me a reason why."

"As I said, I don't care what happened, but it's for your own good. If you don't expose your unseemly utter, Crane will milk it for all it's worth. He'll get the best of you."

"God...talk about an insult. You think I can't outfox Crane."

An unreceptive look painted Richard's face.

Thom couldn't blame him. Obviously Richard was not suggesting that Thom was too slow to stay a jump ahead of the dimwitted blacksmith. "Okay—so what's your point?"

"Dull as Crane is, he lacks the brains to win a debate with logic. But if he's got something untoward or embarrassing on someone, he uses it. I've seen him do it to others. The moment he's in a tight spot, he resorts to his nasty tidbits. If you keep the details of your jail time hidden, Crane will use it against you...again and again. You'll come out looking like the god-awful cesspool out behind Parker's stable. Crane, on the other hand, will sparkle like the rapids of the Konkapot on a bright spring day."

The analysis had more validity than Thom wanted to admit. Ever since he had gotten out of jail, he had tried to bury the ugly phase of his life. At times the method had worked. No one knew. No one asked. It was as if it didn't exist. In Boston one of Thom's shipmates from England informed Thom's mentor that Thom had served time across the sea. His mentor respected Thom's preference to leave the details unexplored. As far as his mentor was concerned, Thom was capable, conscientious and trustworthy. Whatever the prior misadventures, they were Thom's business. That was how Thom wanted it, and that's how it was. Silence had proved a tried and true way of dealing with the issue. Why should he abandon the method? The answer to the rhetorical question was easier than outwitting Crane. With Crane it wouldn't work. It had failed already. It would continue to fail. Thom inhaled, as he swallowed his pride. "I see your point."

"So, the next time Crane throws up your past, you'll let your dirty laundry hang out where fresh air and sunshine can quench the stench?"

Thom ignored the feeble jocularity. He had more important matters on his mind. "I didn't say that."

A puzzled expression painted Richard's face. "I thought you said you agreed with me."

"I said: 'I see your point.' And now that I do...I'll think about it."

The Sunday meeting had drawn a large turnout. With Thom's encouragement, Richard, who had stopped attending services following his wife's death, had joined him for the event. Whereas town meetings were men only, since this was a Sunday church meeting, the women attended despite knowing the focus was on the mounting tensions with Britain and the growing prospects for war. The women filled the seats in Reverend Bidwell's parlor, while the men stood on both sides and to the rear extending back into the adjacent room.

"My friends," said Reverend Bidwell, "such a turnout would do my heart well were it not for the fact that matters of war, rather than Godly concerns of peace and faith and fellowship, bring forth such a throng. At the outset I wish to acknowledge Giles Jackson and Benjamin Warner (Reverend Bidwell gestured to his left at the two men), both of whom ably represented Tyringham in this year's County Congress when it declared our loyalty to King George, but rebellion to Parliament.[165] Recent events raise doubts whether we can maintain loyalty to our King. Even as we gather here, our fellow colonists began meeting on the fifth of September in Philadelphia at the Continental Congress. Of our thirteen colonies, twelve have chosen to partake in that mission. Georgia

287

did not see fit to send delegates. Among those representing our great colony is Samuel Adams, the leader of tyranny's resistance and the author of so many erudite expressions of the principles we hold dear. John Hancock, who just happens to be a cousin, albeit slightly removed, of the Sprague family of Berkshire County, will also be representing us.[166] But lest I digress too far, suffice it to say that Massachusetts will be well represented. With God's guidance, hopefully the other colonies will select men of such wisdom and competence. For if we are on the road to war, it is imperative that our colonies travel that road united. So much of what brings us to the current state of affairs has occurred here in Massachusetts. Sadly, though not unexpectedly, Parliament has retaliated, enacting legislation closing the Port of Boston, taking away our right to assemble, and depriving us of our courts and our provincial council. Fortunately, our brothers and sisters throughout the other colonies are standing with us in solidarity. The direction that next we travel lies in the hands of the Continental Congress. With God as their guide, we trust they will map a just framework, halting the tyranny that deprives us of the fundamental and inalienable rights to which every man is entitled."

As the Reverend continued, Thom's mind drifted. Whatever else was said would be window dressing. The point had been made. The course the colonies would take depended upon what happened in Philadelphia. Until that was enunciated, discussion of the issues was nothing more than talk. Adopting and implementing a strategy had to await the outcome of the Continental Congress.

Thom gazed around the room. If and when push came to shove, who could be trusted? Richard went without saying. There was no doubt about Reverend Bidwell. And Johnny Woodstone and Paul Cooper were sure bets. Dinsmore, the shoemaker, would support the cause. Or would he? He wanted the rights of British citizens, but following the Boston Tea Party, he took issue with the destruction of private property. He declined to join the entourage who helped block Gage's judges from being seated at the Great Barrington Courthouse. And what about Willard Brown and Arvin Miller? Thom knew them to say hello, but not well enough to be sure which way they would go. Thom's eyes raced over the crowd. Most everyone wanted more rights. That did not mean, however, that if war broke out, all of them would side with the colonies. Some like Ezra Jenkins were sure to remain loyal to England. And his parrot, Orville Crane, who, like any parrot had a vocabulary limited to a potpourri of birdbrained utterances, was likely to follow Jenkins. Or would Crane? He was a blacksmith, not a farmer. His bread was buttered by the citizens of Tyringham. Could he risk becoming an outcast? And the same could be said for George Whitaker. He had a small garden, but he had gotten rich and fed his family as a Yankee peddler. Whitaker, well off, was happy with the status quo, but in all likelihood, out of self-interest, he would join in the fight against England.

Thom continued to study his neighbors. About two-thirds were predictable, but that left a third that were not. Each of them presented a danger. Seeming friends could turn out to be spies. And too, a few that Thom thought easy to predict would turn out otherwise. Tyringham, like every town throughout the colonies, would not be fully united. This would not be a war against a hated enemy. It would be war with their Mother Country. Many in the colonies had relatives across the ocean. Allegiances would be tested. And unfortunately, moles, seeming friends of the cause, were certain to lurk everywhere.

⁕

As Thom replaced a worn board on the door of Sarah's barn, his mind wandered. Back at his saltbox, he had finished building his shed, a satisfying addition to the property. His garden, already harvested, had been readied, as much as possible, for the following spring. The English grass he had planted around his home had withstood the onslaught of weeds and summer's heat. Even a pessimist could not deny that his house and land were in good shape.

With September waning and the advent of the Berkshire winter arguably closer than the calendar indicated, despite the cloud of war's unsettling threat, in many respects Thom was in a good place. Unlike the preceding winter, when, with just the shell of a home, he had faced the challenge of making the interior habitable, his chores for the snowy season were not imperative. Practical and decorative additions, such as shelves, moldings and furniture, were on the list. He was free to take his time, embellish his work and let patience and determination produce the extraordinary workmanship of which he was capable. All along his efforts had quality, but quantity had held the upper hand. Circumstances had changed. Quantity's reign had ceased. No longer could the inhibiting yoke of compelled efficiency squelch the appetite for utmost craftsmanship. If labor's finer fruits demanded time, so be it.

Musings of how his life in Tyringham had metamorphosed filled Thom's head as he sanded Sarah's barn door. The irony of what the colonies faced intertwined with personal thoughts. The undertaking that had occupied him during the preceding eighteen months paled in the face of the challenge confronting Massachusetts and its American neighbors. Each involved a huge dream. But the latter, grounded in concepts of life and liberty and property, a lifting of Parliament's onerous burdens, unlike a saltbox, was abstract. The forces the colonists would face were anything but. The vaunted British army and navy, the most powerful fighting forces on the face of the earth, were real.

To build his saltbox, Thom had to confront nature, a pristine mountain forest, often enveloped by rain and wind and snow. But as much as nature was his enemy, it was also his friend. It provided land for his home, stone for the foundation and lumber of many kinds for the walls, floors and roof. If war broke out, England, unlike nature, would be purely foe. Its legendary military had more weapons and bite than the harshest winter.

"Enough with the door!"

The sound of Sarah's voice jolted Thom from his reflections.

"You've done too much already. Come in and have some pompion pie and tea."

"Tea?"

"Only teasing." With the tea boycott in full force, few colonists were consuming what, save alcohol, had long been their beverage of choice. Raspberry and bayberry leaves, and sage and dittany, and even hardhack, a shrub of the rose family with hairy leaves and colorful flowers, were but a few of the mediocre and wanting substitutes that folks tried in an effort to replace their taste for tea. "But as for pompion pie, I'm serious. It's hot from the oven, and a tankard of cider to wash it down awaits."

No further invitation was required to pull Thom from his work. A minute later he was seated at Sarah's dining room table, taking the first bite of the delectable pie. "Fabulous sweet flavor wrapped in a flaky crust. You outdid yourself."

"It's the least I can do with all the chores you still do for me. And by the way, I packed you a dozen jars of jam, pickled beets, apple butter—"

"You talk about what I do. Thanks to you I enjoy frequent respites from my own culinary ineptitude."

"C'mon," said Sarah, "we both know that your coming here means more to me than it does to you. As a widow, and hardly a young one, I don't get out and about the way you do."

"Well—the truth be known, I don't get out much either, and in case you've forgotten, like you, I live alone. Having a place to enjoy a good meal, along with good company, sure is nice." A thought, one that had rarely crossed Thom's mind, emerged. Sarah Albright had become the surrogate for the mother he had lost as a teen. He gazed up at Sarah, standing with ever-impeccable posture at the opposite end of the table.

"What kind of look is that?"

Without a mirror he couldn't say. It was not the yearning, come-hither smile that he had often directed at Polly, but, unable to bring his sentiments to his lips, he hoped his expression hinted at the affection he felt for the kind and charming woman. "How come you're standing there? Sit down and indulge. I guarantee it's scrumptious."

She shook her head as she gestured at her checkered linen gown, its yellow-brown lines the product of butternut roots and bark. "I have to watch my figure."

Another time Thom might have balked, but at that moment he had no reason. A mother had little need to partake of her savory creation. Watching her son sufficed. He said, "Will you at least sit down?"

She poured herself some dittany tea and took a seat. "Yesterday, while I was down at the gristmill, I was speaking with Captain Brewer. He talked with someone from Philadelphia regarding the happenings at the Continental Congress."

"What did the Captain say?"

"Not a whole lot. Apparently the delegates are keeping mum. They meet privately and refuse to share their discussions. Seems they plan to wait until they're finished before they open up."

"That's a bad sign," said Thom.

"Why do you say that?"

To what extent his conclusion had been dictated by frustrated curiosity rather than logic, Thom wasn't sure. "Seems to me they'd be forthcoming if they were in agreement." His words, almost as if they had come from another, had him questioning the reasoning. "Getting a dozen diverse colonies to agree is a tough assignment. Take Virginia, for example. It was founded by single men who have maintained the ways of English society. Do you think they'll see eye-to-eye with the family-oriented Congregationalist way of life we have here in Massachusetts?[167] And there's radical Rhode Island, not to mention Pennsylvania, with its diverse population and acceptance of wide-ranging religious practices, and—" The look on Sarah's face clipped Thom's tongue. "I kinda got carried away, didn't I?"

"A little...but your underlying point has merit."

"Did Brewer convey any other tidbits about the Congress?"

"Nothing specific, except that the delegates are socializing a lot. Word has it they bring in a huge supply of good drink. Supposedly it's to foster strong bonds. That way shared resentment against England's tyranny will outweigh the issues that divide them. If you ask me, it's an excuse to carouse."

"Did Brewer say if they've done anything concrete, even if he didn't know the specifics?"

She shook her head.

"Well...it could be worse. With most everything Parliament has done aimed at Massachusetts, the other colonies could have given us lip service while turning a blind eye. Their willingness to have a Congress is a step in the right direction."

"Too bad Georgia isn't attending, but what can you expect? Why should they start paying their dues now?"

"Huh?" said Thom, unable to make sense of the remark.

"Don't waste your energy. It was a bad joke. I was alluding to the fact that it's a debtors' colony."

"When you put it that way, you've got a point. Double-dealers who ignore their obligations aren't likely to be concerned with others."

Sarah displayed a scolding look. "Not a very charitable thing to say."

"Unless I'm hearing voices, you led me down that unchristian path."

"Well, you didn't need to follow." Her sheepish expression negated whatever sting her words conveyed. "Not to change the subject—" She shook her head. "Why do I use that god-awful phrase?"

"So you can change the subject while pretending not to."

Sarah acted as if she hadn't heard the jab. "Do you think we're on the brink of war?"

Thom nodded. He had rehashed the question with his pals enough times that the reaction was instinctive. "Don't you?"

"Yes, but..."

He waited. When nothing was forthcoming, he said, "But what?"

She heaved a sigh. "War...the killing...Isn't that supposed to be a last resort? Something between despised enemies?" She shook her head. "Our ties with England remain strong. It's our Mother Country. We're talking family."

"Sometimes it happens in the best of them. They call it patricide. And fratricide. And—"

"Yes, Mr. Sophocles. I've read 'Oedipus.'"

Thom hadn't. Rather than show his ignorance, he kept quiet.

"You make my point."

Whether she was referencing his silence or what she had said before, Thom had no clue. Regardless, he was in no position to counter.

"Family members killing one another is insane. Are we headed for an insane war?"

"Life, liberty...rights to fair treatment are hardly insane concepts."

"No need to get excited."

"I didn't—" Thom clipped a defensive tongue. The rancor he had exhibited seconds before echoed in his ears. Why was he growling, especially at Sarah? The answer was easy. He was fed up with Britain's autocratic arrogance and where it was leading. For years attempts by the colonies at rational discourse had been met with harsh laws. Frustration spawned of futility had turned patient ears feral. Guns and bloodshed were fast becoming the only way to communicate. Good sense urged a better alternative, but there was none, not when Parliament, King George, Lord North and their agents in the colonies were deaf.

"Assuming fighting does break out, do you think we might demand independence?"

*Independence.* The word struck with the force of a blunderbuss. Thom shook his head. "We simply want the God given rights of our British brethren."

"So, one way or another, we'll remain British colonies. Right?"

Thom nodded, slowly at first and, after further consideration, more decisively.[168]

# Chapter 18

ALONG WITH ALL ABLE-BODIED Tyringham men between the ages of sixteen and thirty, Thom had come to the grassy area of town center. Though farmers and workmen dressed in the clothes they wore for daily life, their increasingly frequent training exercises bore greater purpose.

Back from a meeting on September 21ˢ at Worcester,[169] David Wharton addressed the group. "Last week I attended a gathering of our colony's patriot leaders to improve the preparedness of our local militias. For more than a century many towns in our colony have organized a portion of their militia into a special force of Minutemen who are ready to march on a moment's notice.[170] Recently Worcester County directed each of its towns to organize a third of their militia in that manner, and we in Berkshire County are following Worcester's lead. Here in Tyringham we are expanding the ranks of our Minutemen. They will increase their training to two or three times per week. After consultation among ourselves and with potential candidates, based upon political reliability, enthusiasm, and strength,[171] the following individuals, all under the age of thirty, have been selected as Minutemen."

As Wharton prepared to read the names, Thom had mixed emotions. The time commitment was a negative. Perhaps membership in the militia was enough. That's how he saw it before the names were called. His thinking changed once the list was read. His closest friends, Richard Thorn, Paul Cooper and Johnny Woodstone were all chosen. Being left out was a slap in the face. He certainly had the strength. His involvement at Great Barrington, Cambridge and Worcester had proved his enthusiasm. Apparently he was deemed politically unreliable. Did people distrust him because of his youthful English criminal record? Were there fears he was a Loyalist in Patriots' clothing? Or was something more sinister at work?

Those chosen as Minutemen were invited to step forward as a unit. Thom's jealousy was undeniable. He surveyed those, like him, who were not selected. His eyes focused on Woodrow Moody. That the odd little fellow was excluded was no consolation. Had he been picked, Thom's slight would have been worse.

As David Wharton once again addressed the group, Thom listened to little. Details regarding an improved system of riders who would be ready to spread alarms held little interest. Such matters were the concern of the Minutemen. Nevertheless, Thom longed to be among their ranks.

⁓⟳⟳⟳⁓

Seated on a log near the north end of Twelve-Mile Pond with fishing pole in hand, Thom soaked in the sun's bountiful rays. Remaining autumn days when the outdoors could be enjoyed without at least donning a doublet were few.[172] Thom's chances of success would have been greater were his line in the Konkapot River, but relaxation, more than a large catch, was his goal. The concession had been underscored when he had chosen the spot rather than a shaded rock around the bend where the fish were known to bite. It was rare that Thom set aside an afternoon to ease back and relish the tranquil elegance of his Berkshire environs.

A hook baited with an earthworm drooped from the line of his pedestrian pole, a thin four-foot maple branch. A real fisherman would have spurned the inferior accouterment, but Thom was hardly a real fisherman, especially that clement day in early October. He gazed across the placid waters at the blazing palate of commingled hues painting the opposite shore. Peak color was but a few days away. He closed his eyes, allowing the after-image of the scene to fill his head. He breathed deeply and savored the obliging zephyr that caressed his cheeks. Even momentary thoughts of possible war evanesced amidst nature's peaceful cornucopia.

Thom began to nod off, his mind drifting from reverie toward dreams.

"Mind if I join you?"

The voice plucked Thom from the vast, but distinct universe of his mind. He struggled to get his bearings.

"You're not likely to catch many fish that way."

Thom looked up and saw Issac Winslow. "I suspect you're right, but I doubt I'd catch a whole lot more with my eyes open."

"So...why you fishing?"

"I'm not really." The look that greeted Thom's words caused him to rethink his reply. "Well, I am, sorta, but mainly I'm just taking in Tyringham at its best."

Winslow nodded.

Thom was unsure whether the gesture communicated concurrence or camouflaged a judgmental reaction. Regardless, the arrival of Polly's father had cast a dark cloud over Thom's serenity.

"I understand what you're saying. Matter of fact, I was kinda doing the same, enjoying a solitary stroll around the pond." Winslow's arm extended toward the pastoral expanse. "God blesses us with a magnificent mountain sanctuary. Most times we neglect to savor it."

"My sentiments exactly, though you expressed them better." Flattery, more than accuracy, motivated the unctuous response.

Winslow gestured at the log where Thom sat. "Mind if I join you?"

Voicing his preference was out of the question. "Please, feel free."

"Free...Out here, that's exactly how I feel." Winslow plunked himself down onto the fallen timber. "Of course, these days, what with Parliament taking away our rights, it's not easy." He shook his head. "Damn. I apologize."

"For what?"

"You're here trying to enjoy peace and quiet, unhindered by chaos, political and otherwise, and I show up, park myself on your log and launch into a diatribe."

"I'd hardly term your comment a diatribe."

"Maybe, but it trespassed on your solace."

"Not really, and, anyway, company is always nice." Bathed in golden sunshine, the diplomatic lie rolled off Thom's tongue as easily as trout slipped passed his line. Though the affability of

Polly's father the last time their paths had crossed ameliorated tension, Thom was anything but comfortable. "Back in August, were you at the Great Barrington Courthouse when we blocked the judges?" Thom knew the answer, but small talk, a device to conceal self-consciousness, not information, was his aim.

"I sure was. It was amazing. I wish I coulda seen Governor Gage's reaction. All along he's claimed rebellious voices were confined to Boston. Bet he was shocked...not to mention furious, having citizens way out in the Berkshires defying him. Probably kicked and yelped worse than a wild stallion getting its first taste of a saddle." Winslow hesitated, as he seemingly reveled in the imagery that had streamed from his tongue. "The list of counties blocking his judges and other toadies keeps growing. Word has it, the tally is up to seven. Wouldn't be surprised if the last two follow suit."[173]

"And we, here in Berkshire County, were first."[174]

Winslow patted Thom on the back. "When I was young, older folks fretted about my generation. Claimed we were lily-livered lambs, waiting to be slaughtered. It damn well made me mad. But I gotta tell you. Folks don't talk that way now. Or any that do, oughta have their lips sown shut, and that's with chunks of soap in their mouths." He gave Thom another pat. "Yup, you boys have got spunk. No doubt about it. Us men that fathered your generation got a reason—namely you boys—to be proud."

Too bad you didn't feel that way when I wanted to marry your daughter. Or was it that you were only proud enough to have me as a neighbor, not a son-in-law? Thom tightened his grip on his fishing pole as he digested the sarcastic thoughts.

Winslow leaned around and looked Thom in the eye. "Speaking of proud fathers, does yours live in Massachusetts?"

Thom shook his head. "England."

"Oh...that's right. You came here from across the sea."

Perhaps the lapse explained Winslow's earlier expression of pride. It was possible he had not heard about Thom's background, particularly his time in jail. Or maybe it had slipped Winslow's mind. That was not beyond the realm of possibility. Unlike Thom, who had endlessly dwelled on his rejection, to Winslow it was another tidbit of insignificant information. There was also the possibility that Winslow's words of pride were generic to the many young patriots. Had he been thinking specifically about Thom, he might not have uttered them. Explanations raced through Thom's head, and if he had to place a bet, the correct one was none of the foregoing. Odds were, Winslow was well aware of Thom's stay behind bars; he had merely played dumb.

"Don't mean to pry, and stop me if you want, but you hear from your father often?"

Thom shook his head. "We didn't—" He clipped his tongue. The unpleasant family history was none of Winslow's business. "You might say we're out of touch."

"Yeah...I guess oceans have a way of doing that." Winslow gazed off into space. "I probably have some distant cousins in England. Not really sure. Our family has been here for a century. Over the years we lost track of the descendants of our grandparents' grandparents." For a moment he grew pensive. "That's kinda sad, but with times like this...maybe it's not all bad. Makes it easier...I mean if war comes."

The idea that he could be fighting against his father or other relatives was not particularly troubling for Thom. And understandably so. After his mother had died and he had left home, for all intents and purposes he had no family. He said, "If there are battles fought, they'll be with the British army and Parliament. As far as I'm concerned, the people of England are fine."

Winslow nodded. "When you put it that way, I have to agree. War or no war, the people of England aren't our enemies. We only want the same rights that they enjoy." He chuckled.

Thom waited a moment on the chance Winslow might clarify the peculiar reaction. "You mind explaining the humor?"

"I was laughing at myself. When it comes to war, we forget to separate the people from their government and leaders. Uh...let me rephrase that. *I* forget. Thanks for reminding me."

A jerk on Thom's fishing line drew his attention. He raised his pole. A fish was leaping about at the end of the twine.

"You hooked one!" said Winslow.

Thom had. A skinny little sunfish, all of six inches.

"Success."

That was debatable. Baiting hooks, handling and cleaning fish were hardly Thom's favorites. Unlike hunting where he enjoyed the sport, as well as the catch, he fished for food, not pleasure. Yes, he had caught a fish. But what did it mean? He had to handle the squirmy thing before throwing it back, and the experience of being hooked was no pleasure for his puny catch. Both Thom and the sunfish were losers.

"Better than nothing," said Winslow.

"I suppose," said Thom, rather than argue the point. He freed the slippery fish and tossed it back into Brewer's Pond. Rather than re-baiting his hook, he laid his pole on the ground behind the log.

"Lucky fish," said Winslow.

Thom nodded. "Not so lucky fisherman."

"Oh, by the way, that's really nice what you do for Sarah Albright."

"I don't do that much. And whenever I do, she's ready with a tasty meal. A lot better than my cooking. Plus she's constantly giving me pies and preserves and whatnot."

"Maybe so, but she gets the long end of the stick."

"How do you figure?"

"C'mon...she's a widow. Living alone in that house has to be lonely. Having you come by brightens her life. She views you like a son."

Despite welcoming the characterization, Thom groaned.

"Voice all the skepticism you please, but you're wrong. She used that very phrase when I spoke with her about a month ago. She speaks very highly of you." As Winslow got up from the log, he paused long enough to add, "Excellent judge of character that she is, I'm sure she's right."

Thom watched Winslow disappear up the bank. His visit had been unexpected, but more surprising was that it had brightened Thom's day. That Sarah spoke highly of him was gratifying. That Winslow did, the real shocker, was a huge bonus.

A knock halted Thom as he was about to ladle some Indian corn meal into a kettle of water. "Be there in a second." He went to the front door and opened it.

"Seems I have to keep tabs on you," said Richard.

"What does that mean?"

"That you've disappeared again."

Thom shook his head. "I've been around. You, on the other hand, have been busy with your Minuteman training."

"Aha...so that's it."

The look accompanying the words had Thom regretting his jealous utterance.

"Look—I know you're disappointed, but the constant training is no picnic."

"Maybe, but..." Judgment counseled he not voice more envy. "You hungry?"

"Ever know me not to be?"

They headed into the kitchen where Thom grabbed a small loaf from which he dug out a pair of trenchers.

"I'm sorry you weren't chosen for the Minutemen."

"Hey, it's not your fault." Thom tossed corn meal, along with some cabbage and carrots and potatoes and beets into his kettle. He threw in a couple of Sarah's pork sausages, preserved with heavy salt.

"Damn, if I knew you ate like this, I'd come around more often."

Thom chuckled. Little did Richard realize that but for the company the beets and sausages would not have found their way into the hodgepodge. He stirred the mixture and, after hanging it from the crane that adjoined the fireplace, swung the kettle around so it hung over the flames.

"Did you hear about the fire yesterday at Amos Mansfield's place?"

"No. Was it bad?"

"Not really. Just several bales of hay out in his field."

Thom put another log into the fireplace. "They know how it started?"

"Not exactly...but one thing sure, someone set it."

Tongs in hand, ready to adjust the log, Thom stopped. "How can you be certain?"

301

"On a cool, gray day in autumn, four hay bales, each fifty yards from the next, don't suddenly catch fire." Richard plopped down in one of the dining-room chairs. "Hay bales aren't a huge deal, but one never knows what might be next. A barn, the mills or someone's house. Folks are concerned."

Thom eyed the blaze that burned a few feet away. Flames of red, yellow, green and blue danced. Crackling wood snapped an erratic beat. A couple of harmless sparks flashed. The sight was seductive. Thom turned and gazed around the interior of his saltbox. Several thousand hours he had toiled and sweated to build the home. How quickly an arsonist could turn it into ashes and rubble; mere minutes with the help of kerosene. The thought chilled him, even as proximity to the roaring blaze provided warmth. He went into the kitchen and poured two tankards of beer splashed with rum, one of which he gave to Richard.

"I assume you heard that Gage barred the General Court from convening in Salem."

"I did." A tankard in one hand, Thom stirred the kettle with a ladle he held in the other.

"If Gage assumed the members of the court would bow to his will, he better think again. Just this afternoon Cooper told me that ninety of the elected delegates defied the bastard. They met in Concord on October 5th as a Provincial Congress. They plan to meet again in Cambridge to establish a regular meeting schedule, along with standing committees and a budget."[175]

Thom continued stirring.

"Damn," barked Richard. "The people of Massachusetts institute their own legislature after telling Gage to go to Hell, and you don't find that exciting?"

"Oh...sorry."

"Sorry...What kind of reaction is that?" Richard studied Thom for a second. "Don't tell me it's still that Minuteman thing."

Thom nodded. "Do you know why I wasn't chosen?"

"Hold it...Let's back up." Richard rocked his chair onto its hind legs. "Unless I'm losing my mind, before the selections you were half-hoping you wouldn't be picked."

"Yeah...but that's not the point." The absurdity echoed in Thom's ears. "Just tell me. Do you know why I was left out?"

"Well...they couldn't pick everyone."

"Damn it. That's no answer, not when they took Homer Blakely." Thom placed a hodgepodge-filled bread trencher in front of Richard.

"What's wrong with Blakely?"

"C'mon, we both know I'm a helluva lot stronger and smarter—and God, you name it—than the broomstick maker."

Richard sighed. "Someone...or ones—I'm not sure which—blackballed you. Exactly who, I don't know."

"You know why?"

He hemmed and hawed. "Well...rumor was there were concerns about your politics."

"My politics! You gotta be kidding!" Thom jabbed his spoon into his trencher. "How could they doubt my support for the cause?"

"I don't know. It's possible someone had it in for you. Or maybe (Richard broke eye contact), it had something to do with your background and the jail time, the fact that you're from England and...I really don't know."

The unsatisfactory explanation left Thom frustrated, but taking it out on Richard served no purpose. He ripped off a crusted rim of his trencher and shoved it into his mouth. "If you find out who or what is behind my blackball, you'll tell me. Right?"

Following a moment of seeming recalcitrance, Richard nodded.

Thom eyeballed his friend. "Is that a promise?"

"Promise."

<br>

⁓⁓

<br>

October 29, 1774. By the time Thom arrived at the Hogshead, close to seventy had gathered, and with more arriving by the minute, the throng had moved outside where all could hear. Two days earlier the Massachusetts Committee of Safety had issued its plans for the protection of the colony. Deacon Hale who had traveled to Boston to follow the events had just returned. Folks had been told to congregate at the Hogshead at three o'clock for his report.

Johnny Woodstone, who was standing next to Thom, said, "Amos Walters claims that someone from Springfield told him the Committee might opt for a surprise attack on the British army."

Thom was skeptical. Persistent rumors and wild speculations, reminiscent of the frenzy that surrounded the events in Cambridge, justified cynicism. "You think the Committee would do that?"

"Hard to know," said Woodstone. "It's hard to know anything. The other day when I was down at the mill, a guy said that fightin' had broken out in Boston. Supposedly he got it from a reliable source. Turned out his reliable source was a fellow from Hop Brook who claimed he'd been misquoted. Claims he said: 'It wouldn't surprise him if fightin' broke out in Boston.'"

"Damn, these days, facts, the kind you can trust, are rarer than daffodils in December." Thom looked around. The crowd had grown well past a hundred. Deacon Hale appeared atop the Hogshead's front stoop, a mere two steps high.

"My friends, may I have your attention." He waited several seconds for the din to subside. "My friends...please."

Others called for silence until quiet prevailed.

"Good folks of Tyringham, as you all presumably know, I was in Boston for several days learning about the Committee of Safety that was recently established by another committee of our Provincial Congress. In a minute I'll share that information, but first let me tell you what I observed." Hale cleared his throat. "In Boston Harbor, English warships, their sides lined with guns, sit poised. On the Boston Commons, what is supposed to be the people's commons, the white tents of the British army dot the landscape. And in an intimidating show of force, the Redcoats march regularly.[176] As of now the gulf that splits Boston from the rest of our rural colony resembles the divide between our Congregationalist traditions and the beliefs of the soulless atheists. Admittedly the tentacles of the Intolerable Acts invade our hinterlands, but towns like Tyringham all along the Post Road remain cloaked in the mantle of freedom. On my travels east and back west from Boston, over and over I saw local citizens, not Gage's judges and sheriffs, controlling their affairs. For all intents and purposes, Gage has begrudgingly ceded such power to us and our town meetings."

Someone handed Hale a tankard. He drank several swallows before continuing. "Let me now turn to the Committee of Safety, what it is and what it can do. It has nine members. Three are from Boston. The remaining six come from the outlying counties. The Committee is empowered to call out the militia. To do so requires a majority vote, including four not from Boston. Officers and soldiers must obey the Committee, which, if need be, can establish another committee to purchase weapons, ammunitions and supplies."[177]

A voice from the rear, one that Thom recognized as Ezra Jenkins, bellowed: "The very creation of this Committee of Safety all but begs for war with England."

The remark drew cheers, catcalls and shouts of all sorts.

"Hear me out," said Hale. His call for attention did little to still the uproar. He waited and tried again. "Please, tone down." Others joined in his request. Gradually order returned. He said, "The accusation that the Committee of Safety seeks war against England is preposterous. Their purpose is to put Massachusetts in a state of readiness; to let Governor Gage and Parliament and Lord North know that we demand our rights as citizens; and to make it plain that we will not be intimidated. Make no mistake, if England persists in its tyrannical ways, the citizens of Massachusetts are ready."

A raucous cheer, one lasting a full minute, rang out. When it subsided, Hale continued. "The Committee of Safety has expanded the system of riders and alarms who, in the event of British troop movements or armed conflict, can spread the word enabling our Minutemen, as well as our militias, to spring into action.[178] The Committee urges us to hone our skills in the use of arms.

Off to Thom's right someone shouted, "If the Redcoats want a fight, bring it on."

"We'll give 'em hell," yelled another.

As Hale stepped down from the stoop, spirited shouts resounded.

Woodstone turned to Thom. "We're on the brink."

Thom looked around. Tyringham was hardly the center of the colonial universe, but given what had transpired throughout the colonies in recent months, it was a legitimate gauge of the mood. "Whad'ya think?"

"About what?"

Thom was uncertain exactly what his question had intended. He said, "Can we defeat the British?"

"We damn well can!"

Thom nodded, not that he felt sanguine about the assessment.

"Gentlemen...gentlemen." Ezra Jenkins had climbed the stoop and was begging for attention.

His appeal was met with boos and shouts of *windbag, bootlicker* and other derogatory cries.

"Get yourself a Redcoat, ya hoary Tory!" yelled Woodstone. He turned to Thom. "Hoary Tory—you like that?"

"Yup. And I assume that's *whorey* Tory." Thom spelled the homonym he had substituted.

"Good one!" Woodstone smacked Thom on the back.

"Give the man a chance to speak," said Issac Winslow, who had joined Jenkins on the stoop.

"He's gotta be kidding," said Woodstone. "Why is Winslow standing up for Jenkins?"

"Got me," said Thom.

Winslow repeated his call to let Jenkins be heard. The clamor lessened, as many in the crowd encouraged others to heed the request of the respected elder.

"Why should we listen to Jenkins?" came a shout from the rear.

"Because..." Winslow held up his arms. "Because," he repeated louder than before, "...in Tyringham every man, none excluded, has the right to speak."

His words drew calls for the unruly to be silent.

Winslow waited until he had the attention of all. He said, "How...when we decry Parliament's refusal to give us a voice in the laws that govern us, can we deprive any of our citizens the right to speak? Is it not the rule of our town meetings that every man be heard? That one may disagree with Ezra is no reason to silence him. Lest we not be guilty of the tyranny we abhor, let us hear him out." Winslow stepped off the stoop, leaving Jenkins there alone.

"Citizens of Tyringham..." Jenkins moved haughty eyes over the throng.

Amazing, thought Thom. With a single, patronizing look the squirrelly lawyer had squandered most of the capital that Winslow had mustered.

"Do you really believe that you, untrained men of the land, can defeat the strongest military force on earth? Imagine thousands of Redcoats sweeping through our cities and across the countryside. Picture hundreds of warships, each armed with scores of cannons, bombarding ports crucial to our economy. Boston, New York, Philadelphia, Baltimore, Charleston and Savannah will be ravaged. The army will march through our colonies, while the ships will sail up and down our rivers...the St. Lawrence, the Connecticut, the Hudson, the Delaware, to name a few. British soldiers will lay waste to this land we call home. What lunacy leads you to believe—"

"How dare you call us lunatics?" bellowed someone.

The shout drew more yells. Winslow jumped back onto the stoop and, with the support of many, halted the disruption.

Jenkins stuffed his thumbs into the pockets on either side of his brass-buttoned vest. "Challenge the British on the battlefield, and the outcome is inevitable. Absolutely inevitable. Pretend if you wish. But you know it. I know it. We all know it. Fathers and sons, your blood will be spilled. Cities and towns will be pillaged. Homes will be rubble. And adding insult to injury, England will come down on us harder than ever. Already they have proved that. The Tea Party brought us laws you term 'intolerable.' Push England to war, and Parliament will impose burdens worse than intolerable. They will punish your sedition."

Jenkins ran a stern gaze over the gathering. "The canvas is before you. The choice is yours. Accept that we are a colony of England ruled by Parliament, or allow absurd dreams to guide you into a quixotic joust with windmills. You decide...But should you opt for treason...should war, foolhardy war, be your choice, I, for one, will remain loyal to my Mother Country. I will remain loyal to England."

Jenkins stepped off the stoop, accompanied by a brief hush. Thom weighed the irksome message. Even more irksome was his inability to refute it. Objectivity dictated an English victory. The costs, the consequences of that victory would be huge. Thom kicked the ground with the heel of his shoe. The alternative, yielding to British tyranny, was outrageous.

"Whad'ya think?" said Woodstone. The cockiness he had exhibited minutes earlier had vanished.

The inquiry drew Thom from his ruminations. "I damn well don't like it."

"But...ya think we can defeat the British?"

The silence that had followed Jenkins' departure from the stoop had answered the question already. But hubris refused to succumb to reasoned judgment. Intransigence suppressed perpetual pessimism. Still Thom could do no better than, "I don't know...I just don't know."

"I hear ya." Woodstone stared into empty space. He heaved a sigh. "You're not suggestin' we oughta give in to England, are ya?"

"No way!" Thom folded his arms in grim defiance. "War, whatever the risks, is better than tyranny. We're entitled to the rights and freedoms of British citizens. Anything less...forget it!"

Woodstone banged a fist into the palm of his other hand. "Couldn't have said it better myself."

※

"C'mon," said Richard. "We're on our way to the Hogshead."

Thom, who had answered the door without his shoes, was about to relax after a day of chores. "Not me. Not this evening."

"You want to know what occurred in Philadelphia, don't you?"

"Of course...So tell me."

"Don't know. But according to Cooper, Deacon Hale got the scoop from a rider this afternoon. To avoid a bunch of misstated versions, the Deacon plans to share the details with everyone at the Hogshead." Richard pointed at Thom's feet. "Get your shoes on, and let's go."

Thom grabbed his shoes. "Did Cooper tell you anything about what the Congress did?"

"Don't think he knew. Anyway, he was in a hurry to round folks up."

Thom could not recall having been to the Hogshead on consecutive days. He said, "Things are happening fast."

"Yeah, and this one could be big."

About that there was no doubt. With the threat of war looming, the Congress was a major test. The other colonies seemed to be lending support, but with push coming to shove, their posture could grow more temperate, leaving Massachusetts to deal with its unique problems. If so, Massachusetts, hardly capable of facing England on its own, would be in dire straits. Then again, there were some in rural Massachusetts who advocated an analogous tactic. With a little discretion, the problem could fall on Boston, rather than the whole of Massachusetts. "Let's go," said Thom, his shoes buckled.

By the time they arrived at the Hogshead, a crowd, one approximating that of the day before, had gathered. With darkness fast descending, they had somehow packed themselves into the tavern. Richard and Thom squeezed in along the wall, as Deacon Hale climbed up onto a chair. Once the throng had been quieted, he said, "It seems these get-togethers are becoming a daily habit. As you all, no doubt, know, we've called you here to share the outcome of the Philadelphia Continental Congress. It was convened from September 5th until its adjournment on October 26th. During that time the members kept their proceedings secret lest erroneous conclusions be drawn about matters being discussed. It was—"

"C'mon, tell us what happened," came a shout from the far corner.

Not one to be intimidated, Hale gave the heckler a look, the kind that bore little subtlety. The eager crowd, sensing that unruliness would only prolong their wait, silenced the heckler and quieted themselves.

After waiting longer than necessary, Hale continued. "Foremost among the actions of the Congress was the adoption of a Continental Association, an agreement providing that each of the colonies will cease to import any British or Irish goods by

December 1ˢᵗ of this year. The—" Hale's halting voice, coupled with stern eyes, checked a burgeoning cheer. "The Continental Association requires all colonies to terminate participation in the slave trade as of that same date. It provides that the colonies stop exporting any goods to Britain, Ireland or the West Indies as of September 1, 1775.[179] In deference to South Carolina whose economy is so dependent upon the rice trade, rice is exempt from the restriction on exports. The exception became necessary in order that the Association be unanimous. Without it South Carolina would have seceded."[180]

After briefly checking some notes, Hale continued. "Those, my friends, are the key results of the Continental Congress." He grabbed some papers from the bar and held them up. "I have here copies of their formal declarations. They will be posted on the rear wall, enabling you to read the precise details. Before concluding, I want to share some additional information that was passed on to me by word of mouth. While I assume it to be accurate, I can't be sure." He glanced at his notes again. "From what I was told, delegate Joseph Galloway of Pennsylvania pressed a plan for a Continental Union whose American legislature would be subservient to Parliament."[181]

Calls of *nay* and *no*, as well as hisses, rang out.

Hale held up his hands. "Galloway's plan, whatever it may have involved, went down to defeat." There was a brief cheer before Hale added, "The conservative delegates did, however, prevail upon the Congress to send a deferential petition to King George."

Nays and hisses, decidedly more demonstrative than a moment earlier, resounded.

Rather than take action to quell them, Hale waited until they subsided. Once he continued, his voice turned somber. "I am told that almost to a man the members of the Congress agreed that war with our Mother Country...England...has become inevitable." He stood stoically, perhaps anticipating a reaction. There was little more than a buzz. Men, many of whom had consumed their fill of alcoholic beverages, appeared frozen in the face of the sobering message. "My friends, there is one last bit of news I wish to share. Let me read to you the words of a resolution that was adopted by the Congress on October 8th, more than two weeks before adjournment." Hale went to his notes and read:

*"Resolved: That this Congress approve the opposition of the inhabitants of Massachusetts Bay to the execution of the late acts of Parliament; and if the same shall be attempted to be carried into execution by force, in such case all America ought to support them in their opposition."*[82]

A cheer, far more raucous than any that had preceded, broke out. Hale pumped a fist into the air, drawing even louder shouts.

Richard threw an arm over Thom's shoulder. "See that! The rest of the colonies are with us."

"They damn well are!" Thom looked around hoping to spot Jenkins among the crowd. Too bad the bombastic lawyer was a no show. Having repeatedly insisted that the other colonies would leave Massachusetts to face the British alone, he deserved an earful. For an instant Thom contemplated giving Jenkins that earful the next time their paths crossed, but he dismissed the idea. The lawyer's response was easy to anticipate. Massachusetts had won a battle. So what. England would win the war. The logic was sound. Its reality was depressing, but only for a moment. Massachusetts had gained the support of the other colonies. Whatever the future held, it was a time for celebration. Along with the others, Thom hooted and hollered.

# Chapter 19

THOM BREATHED A TIRED SIGH as he eased down into the rocker he had made for Sarah. He had spent the entire day cutting and piling firewood so she would be well supplied for the winter. The cool, early November weather was perfect for the task.

"It's a flip," said Sarah, as she handed Thom the mug filled with the beer, rum and sugar mixture.

He started to vacate her seat.

"Stay there. You've earned it."

Ordinarily he would have ignored her urging and gotten up, but bushed as he was, he sank back down. "Thanks," he said, before downing ample swallows of the tasty beverage. He closed his eyes as he rocked back and forth several times.

Sarah seated herself in the maple hardback along the parlor's far wall. "You oughta find yourself a nice woman."

Thom's eyes popped open. "Excuse me." An acerbic tone negated his otherwise apologetic words.

"I said: 'You oughta find yourself a nice woman.'"

"I heard you the first time." Thom sat up straight, stilling the rocker's motion. "Whether I court...whom I court...is my business."

"The only problem—you're not taking care of it."

Thom shot her a look.

"You know I'm right. So don't give me a hard time."

She was, but that wasn't the problem. He had found a woman. He had been ready to marry her. But Polly's father had vetoed the idea, and she had wed another man.

"How about Penelope Chambers? She's a sweet thing."

*Mousey was more precise.* Thom suppressed the sentiment. "I'd prefer you leave my love life to me."

"I would if you'd do a better job of handling it. And about the Chambers girl, I have it on good advice that she would be very pleased if you called upon her."

312

The information was flattering. Flattery was nice, but the thought of having Penelope Chambers for a wife, a lifelong commitment, was a bad deal. Even the barters at Whitaker's barn were never that unfair.

"What's wrong with Penelope?"

"I didn't say anything was."

"Maybe not in words...but your expression did."

Thom groaned.

"Sure—dismiss what I say without giving *one* solitary reason."

"Look, I can decide for myself whether a particular woman is right for me."

Sarah shook her head.

"Just what does that mean?"

"That you still have Polly Blake on the brain. And don't frown because I saw you peeking longingly in her direction at the Reverend's place."

"Just when do you claim that occurred?"

"Oh...about six months ago."

"Six months ago!" Thom rapped the heels of his hands on the rocker's arms. "Even if it did, and I don't admit it, that's ancient history!"

"Would be...if you weren't still stuck on her." Sarah looked him in the eye. "Truth is: you've put Polly on a pedestal so high that no other woman could come close."

"Well, you have to admit—" Pointing out how extraordinary Polly was, would prove Sarah's point. Thom resumed rocking.

Sarah eyed him. A hint of smugness crept into what had been an impassive face. "Twenty-five years from now, you want to be alone like me?"

Twenty-five years, a few less than the total since Thom's birth, was a long time. "I should live that long."

"You certainly should...and a lot more. And let me tell you, lest you have any doubts, my years before my Edgar died—may he rest in peace—put those without him to shame."

The painful nostalgia in Sarah's words silenced Thom. He waited several seconds anticipating she would continue to press the subject.

313

"I know. You want me to drop the matter, and if that's what you want, so be it...for today." She leaned back. "Of course tomorrow...might be a different story."

Thom sipped his flip, long enough to find a way to change the subject. "You think there's any chance Parliament might offer a conciliatory response to the Continental Congress?"

Sarah laughed.

"What's so funny?" he said, though the reason for her guffaw, his poorly disguised effort to curtail her interrogation, was obvious.

"Your question reminded me of an incident when I was ten. I was digging out behind our home when my father asked what I was doing. I told him I was searching for gold. I asked if he thought I was crazy. After trying to change the subject, he wished me good luck."

Thom chuckled. Sarah had seen through his ploy. She had also assessed the likelihood Parliament would be conciliatory. He said, "Well, the bad news shouldn't come until next year."

Sarah muttered under her breath, loud enough for Thom to hear. "A month for the news to cross the Atlantic, time for Parliament to react, plus another month for that reaction to get here." She nodded. "That sounds about right."

∽᷅᷅ᴽᴽᴽᴽᴽᴽ∾

On those rarest of days when all chores were brushed aside to simply bask in the beauty of his Berkshire environs, Thom strolled along the serpentine, northwest shore of Brewer's Pond. With numerous promontories, each unique, the strip of water, the better part of two miles, was more interesting than most lakes that dotted the western reaches of the colony. Around each bend a different tableau revealed itself. Although the variegated blaze of autumn had faded, with little more than the verdant shades of evergreens and the remaining rusty foliage of oaks testifying to the erstwhile palette, still the graying landscape invigorated Thom. His lungs tasted the clean, cool fall air, enhanced with the sweet scent of balsam fir. The crackle of crisp leaves under foot filled his ears. He paused, looking skyward, where isolated patches of gossamer cloak adorned an otherwise

314

bright canvas. He inhaled deeply before lowering his gaze. The firmament's virtual image, its details nearly as sharp as the actual heavens, loomed fathoms beneath the surface of the glassy waters. Across the way, mountains, cloaked in the robe of countless trees, divided reality and reflection. Thom picked up a small, flat stone and hurled it sidearm. It skipped gracefully four times before retreating to the depths. He closed his eyes, savoring the ubiquitous solitude. A tiny rustling drew his attention. He turned from the shore in the direction of the sound. Fifteen yards away a squirrel was dashing about gathering acorns. The urgency with which it darted underscored how soon the canvas would don a veil of white.

An enormous eastern white pine bearing the three hatchet slashes of the King's Broad Arrow caught Thom's eye. The marvel of nature, towering in excess of two hundred feet, fomented discordant thoughts.[183] The image of the evergreen, which for nearly one hundred years had been emblazoned on flags of the New England colonies,[184] had become a major source of friction, one rivaling the tax on tea.[185] Unlike England, where sources of lumber were scant, eastern white pines were plentiful in North America. Their tall, strong, straight, light trunks were perfect for ship masts, as well as frames and planking. Their pitch and tar worked well for seams and paint and varnish. England needed the trees to maintain the world's greatest navy, and since all New England was Crown Land, the trees belonged to the King.[186] Such was England's view. Most colonists, Thom included, saw it differently. Appropriating the best of New England's trees was a thorn, a costly one, in their sides. The sight of the three hatchet slashes shattered Thom's serenity. The threat of war, which for a change had been absent from his thoughts, blared its discordant notes.

Thom picked up another stone, this one even thinner, flatter and smoother than the one he had earlier skipped. Armed with disquiet's agitation, he fired it harder than its predecessor. Rather than adroitly skimming the surface, the stone listed and plunged into the depths. Thom looked back over his shoulder at the hatcheted pine. He kicked the ground. A second futile kick, and he headed off along the shoreline trail in the direction of Smith Hill Road. He was halfway there when what sounded like a moan coming from among the nearby trees and bushes caught his ear. Uncertain whether it was man or animal or even the wind playing tricks, he cautiously treaded in the direction of the noise. Off to his left he heard the sound again. He pushed past two bushes. He no sooner cleared the second than he saw a man lying face down on the ground. A split-willow fishing pole lay alongside.

"Are you all right?" said Thom.

The man moaned again.

Thom bent down and gently rolled the man over. It was Peter Blake. "Are you okay?"

Blake continued to moan. His face was flushed. He was sweating profusely.

Thom felt Blake's forehead. It was inordinately warm. "Can you hear me?"

Blake briefly opened glazed eyes. He looked through and beyond Thom before closing his eyes again.

"Peter...Peter, can you hear me?"

Blake failed to respond.

Thom raised Blake's head and upper body. He tried again to elicit a response. There was none. He kneeled and lifted Blake, all one hundred sixty pounds, onto his shoulder. Thom stood up from a crouch and slowly carried Blake to the trail. Once there, he called out, "Can anyone hear me? I need help." He waited and yelled louder than before. "Help!...If you can hear me, help!" The silence that had dominated earlier at the water's edge prevailed. He eyed the trail. There was no other way. Step by step, Thom carried Blake toward Smith Hill Road. He had gone about two hundred yards, somewhat more than half the necessary distance, when he stopped to rest. He lowered Blake, holding him up in a standing position against a large sycamore. Once again, Thom tried to rouse him. Another minute's rest and he hoisted Blake back onto his shoulder and began lugging him. Thom's steps grew smaller and harder as he negotiated the portion of the trail that led uphill, away from the water to the road. A steep section had him staggering. The path curved to a more level portion. His steps grew more resolute, but only until he caught a toe on a tree root. Stumbling groundward, he managed to twist his body allowing Blake to land on top. Exhausted, Thom lay there. Finally, he edged to his knees. Once again, he hoisted Blake over his shoulder. He drew in several deep breaths before, with full exertion, he stood up. He inched his way the remaining forty yards to Smith Hill Road.

Totally spent, Thom lowered Blake onto the ground. He tried one more time to elicit a response. Blake moaned, but the sound was one of delirium, not communication. The nearest home was several hundred yards away. Leaving Blake alone while seeking help was ill-advised, but carrying him all that way was impossible. Thom was debating what to do when he spotted a wagon coming up the road. A minute later Daniel Gearfield approached.

"I need help!" yelled Thom, stepping out into the road. "It's Peter...Peter Blake." Thom gestured to the side of the road where Peter lay on a bed of pine straw. "Appears he has a fever...a bad one."

Gearfield climbed down.

"I found him in the woods, near the edge of the pond." Thom gestured in the direction where he had located Blake. "Apart from occasional groans, he has said nothing."

"Probably best we take him to his house."

The two men lifted Blake and laid him on the flat bed at the rear of Gearfield's buckboard. Once they had climbed up onto the seat, with Gearfield at the reins, they took Smith Hill Road to its intersection with Mt. Hunger Road, where, after turning right, they wended their way to the Blake's Cape Cod. The moment they pulled up, Thom jumped down, raced to the door and rapped repeatedly. Seconds later, Polly opened it.

"We've got Peter...in the wagon." Thom pointed. "He's sick. Fever, I think. Found him in the woods near Brewer's Pond."

Along with Polly, Thom hurried to the wagon.

"Is he conscious?"

"Not really."

The men carried the ailing Blake into the house up to a second-floor bedroom and laid him on a bed. They removed his waistcoat and unhooked the two buttons at the top of his shirt. A rash on his upper chest, coupled with his fever, reinforced what

Thom had suspected from the outset. Peter Blake might be suffering from smallpox.[187] If so, he was in dire straits. Throughout New England the devilish affliction had been paying too many visits. When Thom had lived in Boston, there were rampant tales of bygone days when thousands in the city had succumbed to the dreaded disease. Save maybe prayer, and even that had shown little success, there was no known treatment. Among the God-fearing, many believed that smallpox represented the vengeance of an angry God.

"Any idea what it might be?" said Polly, as she ran a moist cloth over Peter's forehead.

Unable to voice the appalling word, Thom shook his head.

"Do you think it might be..." Polly's voice trailed off into nothing.

Thom imagined that she, like him, suspected smallpox. But the word, its knell, as if a self-fulfilling prophecy, was too terrible for her to utter. Regardless, silence would not dispel the scourge. The ensuing days would manifest the nature of the illness. If it were smallpox, the areas of rash would become raised and littered with ugly, opaque pustules. Polly could invoke a variety of household remedies such as herbs and bathing or others passed on from her mother or neighbors, but they would be futile devices to gainsay impotence.[188] Peter Blake would be left to the hands of God.

Thom found it hard to maintain eye contact, fearing his face might be delivering the terrible news his tongue was withholding.

Polly turned to Gearfield.

The bearded man appeared as ruffled as his long, tangled whiskers. "Uh...maybe just a bout of...something he ate...or some such thing."

The rosy, but disingenuous diagnosis had Thom wincing. He said, "Is there anything we can do to help?"

Polly shook her head. "At this point it's in my hands...and that of God."

Driven by the inexorable flow of the Konkapot, the waterwheel at Brewer's gristmill turned round and round. The remarkable hydro-powered concept, though far from new,[189] fascinated Thom. Numerous times he had stopped to watch the relentless rotation of the big wheel. Staring at the drive shaft that extended out through the near wall of the mill, he pictured the large vertical gear that rotated on the opposite side. He visualized it interfacing with the smaller, horizontal gear that turned the spindle, causing a flat, circular granite millstone to grind the grain that lay between it and the millstone above.[190] Thom estimated that each of the millstones weighed a ton.

Armed with a burlap bag containing corn kernels from ears he had grown in his garden, Thom entered the mill. He gave the bag to Brewer's helper and watched as the man began pouring the kernels into the hole in the upper millstone. In his mind's eye, Thom saw them come to rest on the lower millstone, where, squeezed between the huge rotating stones, they were pulverized into flour. The operation intrigued him even more than the sawmill, which was also powered by the Konkapot. Captain Brewer, the owner of both, was a hustler.

Once Thom's corn had been ground and his burlap bag refilled with a supply of flour befitting the upcoming winter, he headed to Lodestone. He was preparing to mount when Issac Winslow approached.

"Good afternoon, Mr. Winslow."

"And to you too." Winslow climbed down from his horse.

"How's Peter doing? Better...I hope."

Winslow sighed. "On the bright side, he's regained consciousness, though he still lapses into periods of delirium. Unfortunately, the pustules have increased in size and number. There's no doubt. It's smallpox."

The disclosure, no surprise to Thom, provoked the obvious question: What were the chances of recovery? Thom avoided the indelicate inquiry.

"Speaking for Polly, as well as myself, we appreciate what you did for Peter, carrying him out of the woods and bringing him home. If you hadn't, he would have died out there."

"Anyone would have done the same."

"Maybe so...and maybe not," said Winslow. "What matters, you did."

Though outwardly impassive, Thom appreciated the approbation. "I hope Peter recovers quickly."

"We all do." Winslow's plaintive tone hinted he was not sanguine about the likelihood. Seemingly hesitant, even self-conscious, his gaze lowered. "I...I owe you an apology."

The utterance left Thom as disconcerted as Winslow appeared. "An apology? What do you mean?"

Winslow raised his head, but any eye contact was at best momentary. "I misjudged you. That saltbox you built—you're far more industrious than I had ever imagined. You helped raise the barn for Polly and Peter, and recently when he was sick in the woods, you rescued him."

"That's what good neighbors do."

"Yes, I suppose that's true. But having said that, I'd say that makes you a good neighbor...a very good neighbor."

In the face of the unexpected kudos, Thom managed an awkward shrug.

"Several years ago, when you were relatively new to our community, I judged you based upon your plebeian background. With limited formal education and living in the back room of a widow's house, I presumed you had little potential. I judged you unfairly. I'm sorry." Winslow put a hand over Thom's shoulder and patted him.

The warm words, the kindly gesture, delved distant reaches of Thom's brain. Such affection and validation had been absent from his childhood. He flashed back to images of the tiny cottage in the English countryside where he had spent his formative years. Life there had been as cold as the hard rocks from which it had been fashioned. Winters, with damp winds whistling through a multitude of crevices, had born a nasty chill. Owing to his father's heavy hand, even on warm summer days, within the cottage the chill had been omni-present. His years in Boston with his nurturing mentor had coated his childhood with a veneer of confidence. But like most veneers, the layer was thin and far from impenetrable. Too often condescending antagonists broke through, exposing deeply stowed and haunting boyhood vulnerabilities. Insecurities seeped to the surface, stifling self-confidence and muzzling a keen intellect. Other times positive moments thickened and polished the veneer. The kind words of Winslow, a father figure, provided such a burnishing moment.

Winslow patted Thom one more time. "You have a good day," he said, just before he headed into the gristmill.

Thom picked up his sack of flour. Thanks to Winslow, it was a good day. Indeed, an exceptional one.

~∞⁀∞~

Thom effervesced as he eyed the walnut and cherry boards that lay on the floor along the parlor wall opposite the fireplace. With quill pen in hand he drew sketches and jotted notes for the armoire he planned to build over the winter. Visions of the finely crafted cabinet, his most ambitious furniture building project to date, excited him.

Its design was clear, at least in his head. Five feet high and four feet wide, it would bear the simple lines and style of Louis XIV French provincial. Tempted though he was to build it from solid cherry, he conceded that carving the front façade would be too dicey. A single mistake could turn prime wood into kindling, eviscerate countless painstaking hours. Instead he designed the piece with rectangular walnut veneer overlays on the doors. That way, a miscue when chiseling the decorative front would only damage a piece of overlay, not the entire front. For the top he planned a flat cornice with chamfered edges, and for the bottom, a serpentine apron, along with short, cabriole legs, bowed outward at their upper reach and inward at their base.

Using a straight edge and a French curve, he sketched his design. He was nearly finished when, out of the corner of his eye, he thought he saw something move outside the parlor's front window. He went to take a better look. As best he could see in the fading light of evening's onset, all appeared quiet. He returned to his seat and resumed drawing. He was jotting several notes when he heard a knock. He went to the door and opened it. No one was there. He was about to close the door when a clicking sound off to his left drew his attention. He spotted Pico squatting low by the corner of the house lightly tapping two

321

stones together. Pico put a finger to his lips and motioned Thom to come his way.

After following the odd instruction, Thom whispered, "It's great to see you."

"Anyone around?" said Pico.

"No."

His voice no longer subdued, Pico said, "I had to be sure before I came in."

Thom pointed at the window. "Was it you I saw several minutes earlier outside the parlor?"

Pico nodded.

"How have you been?"

"Good...You?"

"I can't complain...On second thought, I could, but I won't." Thom led the way into the house and motioned Pico to a seat in the dining room. "You hungry?"

"Nope. Pico ate already."

Thom might have challenged the glib reply had he not gotten to know Pico so well. "Where have you been?"

"Near Sheffield mainly." Pico looked around. "The place looks great."

"Sure...because it's about the same as you helped make it." Thom studied Pico for a moment. "I'm glad you came back. You're gonna stay, aren't you?"

"I guess...if it's okay with you, and so long as folks don't know I'm here. I assume they still blame me for the fire at the school, along with the one that took the barn."

Thom shrugged. "Some do, and some don't."

Pico chuckled.

"What's so funny?"

"It's the ones that do who worry Pico. They'll make my life miserable if they know I'm here."

"It'll be our secret."

Pico shook his head. "Easier said than done."

Thom found it hard to disagree. Pico was not the type to stay cooped up in the house. If Thom were in Pico's shoes, constantly hiding within the four walls of a saltbox would have been out of the question. "But you're gonna stay, at least for the time being."

Pico breathed a sigh. "For the time being."

_~oooboo~_

More than a hundred Tyringham residents stood in a chilly December drizzle at the grave of Peter Blake. Members of the family and close friends had carried his pine-box coffin from Blake's home all the way to the cemetery that lay to the north, across from the home of Captain John Chadwick. From his position behind several others at the foot of the grave, Thom watched Polly, dressed in her black cape and hood, as Reverend Bidwell delivered his funereal sermon. Throughout the preaching, Thom's mind wandered. Much of the time he contemplated the dank chill associated with the misty rain. His focus was often drawn to his feet and the ache that pervaded his toes. Occasionally he became philosophical, pondering why another Tyringham citizen had succumbed to the dreaded smallpox. Was it, as many believed, the wrath of God? If so, why, of all people, Peter Blake? He was a decent man, hard working and a good husband. Why not someone like Willard Stolkham, the lazy, double-dealing liar, for whom deceit was a middle name? Thom gazed over the throng, wondering how many more of his Tyringham neighbors would meet the same fate. Might smallpox, as it had done in other times and places, reach epidemic proportions?

At long last Reverend Bidwell began to eulogize the decedent. Few could deny the praise was deserved. Certainly not Thom. Whatever his envy, no way could he disparage Peter, not in life, and not in death. Reverend Bidwell's praise for Peter generated wails among the gathering. Contagious emotions caused a tear to drip from Thom's eye. Unlike the cold mist that dampened his face, the droplet was warm. The anomaly drew Thom into himself again. Thoughts of his difficult childhood, unfulfilled love for Polly and his own mortality intermingled in illogical juxtaposition. Before he knew it, the funeral had ended.

Thom remained in the background, reluctant to step forward and offer condolences to the grieving widow. Another time, another place, when others were less anxious to approach her, would be more suitable. Thom knew his hesitancy was an excuse. Facing her, particularly at that moment, was too difficult. He was about to leave when Issac Winslow came his way.

"I'm glad I caught you."

"My condolences on the loss of your son-in-law. Peter was a fine man."

"That he was," said Winslow.

Though Winslow's recent geniality mitigated Thom's discomfort, unease was undeniable.

"As I've told you before, we owe you a great debt. Carrying Peter from Brewer's Pond to his home was extraordinary."

"It was only to the place where the woods adjoin the road. Daniel Gearfield brought us the rest of the way in his wagon."

"Yes...I know. But it was you who found and lugged Peter up the hill through the woods. That meant a lot." Winslow looked Thom in the eye. "You're too modest."

Knowing that his diffidence showed, embarrassed Thom more. His efforts hadn't produced a joyous outcome. A glance at the nearby grave furnished confirmation, not that it was necessary. "I'm sorry I wasn't able to save Peter's life."

"No one could. And don't apologize. You rendered a great service to him and to Polly as well."

"A...a great service?"

"Absolutely. Thanks to you he didn't die alone in the woods. He had the chance to say goodbye to Polly, and she, to him. Before he died, he told me how much that meant. And Polly has repeatedly said the same. The opportunity to express their undying love is aiding her in the grieving process. As she put it, were it not for you, she would feel compelled to endlessly reach out for Peter on the other side. Your good deed has freed her of that fruitless burden. For that I thank you." For a moment Winslow became silently pensive. "You're a good man, Thomas Webster. You are indeed." Winslow headed to the grave where his widowed daughter stood.

Thom looked around the gathering. Death was an all too frequent visitor in Tyringham. Sooner or later, each man and woman would succumb to its inevitability. It was one thing when it struck those who had lived sixty, seventy or more years. But often it snatched those far younger, even children, those newly born. Was it not enough that death trespassed on each and every life? Did it need to compound its burden with the loss of loved ones too? Thom gazed at Reverend Bidwell who stood not far from the grave. The devoted man of the cloth, having buried two wives, knew the plight as well as any. He understood the ache that Polly bore, and not merely by virtue of the many graveside benedictions he had delivered.

Thom trudged from the cemetery out to the road. He wended his way up the hill that led to his saltbox. His spirits mirrored the day. According to the calendar, autumn still had a couple of weeks, but winter came early in the Berkshires. A funeral had accelerated its advent. Thom lifted his eyes to the Heavens. Through the overhang of a barren hickory, he could see nothing more than the gray of the misting drizzle. He felt chillingly close to that forbidding world beyond. He glanced back down the road in the direction of the cemetery. Peter Blake, a strapping man in his late twenties, in the prime of life, had been deposited into the earth. The casket could have held anyone, Thom included. An all-consuming consternation gripped him. Thom stood face to face with his own mortality.

⁓⁓⁓

Like bacon frying, Thom's tankard of flip, a mixture of Santa Cruz rum, beer and ample sugar, frizzled the moment he dipped the hot flip-iron into the delightful drink. His feet on a stool, comfortably slouched in a chair a few feet from his parlor's hearth, he luxuriated. Outside the clear, crisp December air was well below freezing, but Thom was toasty warm, thanks not only to a roaring blaze in the fireplace, but also the southern sun shining through the front window. From time to time he closed his eyes, savoring the capricious rhythm of crackling flames.

It was one of those rare moments when Thom, a peerless censor of the bitterly austere season, could find a minuscule oasis in nature's relentless onslaught. The night before he had bedded down early, while outside huge flakes, a wind-driven blizzard, streamed from the Heavens. By morning, the storm, its foreboding countenance as distant as summer, had left an enchanted forest in its wake. High above, an azure canopy

325

crowned the still air of Beartown Mountain. Trees and rocks, the entire landscape, flaunted a cottony mantle. Harsh had evanesced into benign. Wild had turned halcyon. Sinister had grown safe. And bleak, magnificent. Thom gazed out the window trying to grasp the anomaly. Nature had assaulted a bleak landscape, only to leave a fairyland. A sledgehammer's maniacal blows transforming a marred table into a carved and polished masterpiece would have made as much sense.

Thom turned his gaze to the fireplace. The radiant flames were mesmerizing, but they were capable of painting a palette of horror and beauty, both at the same time. Back in Boston Thom had seen the home of a friend go up in a blaze. The appalling sight drew a crowd of gawkers, many of whom marveled at the magnificent, variegated canvas that climbed toward the Heavens.

That nature's wrath could beget beauty and serenity was hard to fathom. The process in reverse, nature's peace siring fury, was equally bizarre. Such was Thom's experience when he had sailed to colonial America from England. Halfway across the Atlantic, their ship sat becalmed as less than a zephyr caressed its sails. Seasoned crewmen warned of what awaited. A skeptical Thom harbored doubts, but just as the old timers predicted, the placidity was the calm before the storm. Nature wreaked havoc, furor and fear.

Thom got up from his seat and walked over to the parlor window. Outside, the pristine landscape was peaceful. All across Tyringham...all across Massachusetts...all across the colonies, peace prevailed. But perhaps it too was the calm before the storm. Might the colonists wake up to violence and bloodshed? Might the drums of war beat? And ironically the death and destruction would only commence after winter's fury had begotten the beauty and joy of spring, when the British army could more effectively march across the countryside.

Thom closed his eyes. For the moment there was peace. A tranquil winter's day prevailed in the Berkshire Mountains of Massachusetts. Ruminations of potential war would not destroy it. He returned to his seat before the hearth. He nodded off, awakening to thoughts of Polly. She was a widow, and the time would come for her to court, perhaps as soon as spring. Might a doorway open, enabling him to resurrect their relationship? Issac Winslow, her father, in recent weeks had been cordial, even laudatory. The possibility that romance with Polly, the love of his life, might be rekindled, warmed Thom's heart with a glow rivaling the nearby flames and sunbeams.

Great as the potential rewards were, Thom harbored doubts. Would he take the plunge? Could he risk a return to the emotional abyss? His musings linked to earlier anomalous thoughts. Like a storm, the ravage of smallpox, its predicate, death, had begotten Peter's peaceful rest in eternity. The illogic was undeniable, but also, undeniably consistent. Affliction had sired serenity. An unwelcome rumination triggered guilt. Peter Blake's body had barely been laid to rest in the earth, and already a vulture was laying designs on his grieving widow. Thom opened his eyes. Logic, carefully reasoned analysis—or perhaps rationalization—came to the rescue. He had done nothing to pursue Polly—yet. His yearnings were nothing more than private thoughts. For the time being he would leave them as such. Come spring, however, like the British, might he march?

Standing on the dirt floor of his cellar, mallet in hand, Thom pounded the iron wedge of his splitting froe into the end of a three-foot log.[191] Using the leverage of the froe's handle, he pried a wider fissure enabling him to pound the froe deeper until the log split. Pico stacked the pieces in the corner of the cellar and set the next log in front of Thom. Back in May, Thom had chopped an ample supply of hardwoods, mostly elm, oak, cherry and ash for the upcoming winter. He had cut the logs into three-foot pieces and allowed them to dry in the summer sun. By autumn, with moisture absent, their weight reduced, they had been seasoned.[192]

All morning Thom split logs. Pico separated them into two piles, one split, and the other, not. The latter, including some a foot in diameter, so-called *all-dayers*, would take their seats in the rear of the fireplace. By noon Thom had split enough for the harshest winter.

"I think we're set," said Thom, eager for the mutton repast that awaited them.

"We need more kindling, sticks and twigs, from the shed."

Pico had a point. Thom's stomach, begging attention, made a more compelling argument. "Let's first grab a bite. The sticks can wait."

A half-hour later, mutton and brew in their bellies, they traipsed through the snow, lugging armfuls of sticks and twigs. They were carrying the final load when George Whitaker approached on his horse. Urging Pico to hide was fruitless. Whitaker had seen them both. "Good afternoon, George. What brings you this way?"

"The fellows are getting together at the Hogshead today. I thought you might join us."

That Whitaker would go out of his way to make the invite pleased Thom. The likelihood that Pico's presence would become public knowledge dwarfed satisfaction. "I'd like to, were it not for chores." Thom gestured with one hand at Pico and the other towards Whitaker. "You two know one another, don't you?"

Pico nodded.

"Yup...we met last year." Whitaker's tone was friendly; whether his thoughts were less amiable was another matter.

Thom tried to appear nonchalant.

Whitaker turned to Pico. "You been back in Tyringham long?"

"A while."

"Hmm..." Whitaker pawed at his beard.

Thom wondered if Whitaker was contemplating possible links to the hay-bale fire at Amos Mansfield's.

"You sure you won't join us? Your friend could come too."

"Appreciate the offer, but with duty calling, I'll pass."

"Well...maybe next time." Whitaker gave Pico another glance before climbing onto his horse and riding off.

Pico stared in Whitaker's direction.

"Whatcha thinking?" Thom had an inkling.

"Now that someone knows I'm here, maybe it's time for me to go."

Thom thought of the hay bales. Averse to adding another reason for Pico to leave, Thom declined to mention them.

"Any suggestions?"

"Uh, it's...it's probably best you use your own judgment."

A stoic Pico looked skyward. "Well, I guess I'll stay...at least for now."

# Chapter 20

THE KNOCK AT THE DOOR caught Thom by surprise. Knocks were uncommon, but one shortly after sunrise was unheard of. He stuck the porridge paddle he was holding into the hasty pudding he had left simmering the night before. He went to the front door and opened it. Ezra Jenkins and a man he didn't recognize stood on the threshold. "Good morning," he said. "What brings you gents here so early on a December morning?"

Jenkins gestured at his cohort. "This is Berkshire County Sheriff Walter Wilcox. We'd like to see the young Indian, Pico. We understand he's staying with you."

Pico, who was nearby in the parlor, stepped forward. "You wish to speak with me?"

"I'm placing you under arrest," said the Sheriff.

"What for?" said Thom, though the answer was predictable.

"Arson. The fire at the school and the ones at Pete Dodge's barn and Amos Mansfield's place."

"That's crazy." Pico's eyes were wide.

"Think about it," said Thom. "Pico used the school as a shelter. He'd be the last person to set it on fire, especially in a cold month like March."

"He can tell that to a judge." The Sheriff snapped a pair of handcuffs onto Pico's wrists.

"Ezra, you don't believe Pico's responsible, do you?"

"Matter of fact, Thom, when it came to the school, I suspected him all along. There wasn't enough evidence to arrest him. Things are different now, what with the blaze at Mansfield's."

"What's all this about a fire at Mansfield's?"

Jenkins flashed Pico a scowl. "Save your confused routine for some dimwitted gudgeon. Hay bales don't go up in flames on a gray December day unless someone sets them afire. The facts say you're that someone. You were at the school when it burned, and now that you're back, so are the fires. Too much of a coincidence."

"You've got no evidence," said Thom.

The Sheriff shook his head. "Fact is—we have a witness. The young Flanders girl, Louise, happened to be passing by the Mansfield property about a half-hour before the hay bales went up in flames. She saw a fellow, about Pico's size, duck behind one of the bales. At the time she didn't think anything of it."

The Sheriff tugged at Pico's arm. "Young man, you come with me." Accompanied by Jenkins, the Sheriff led Pico away to the Berkshire County Jail in Great Barrington.

Thom watched the trio disappear onto the wooded path that led to the Albany-Boston Post Road. Pangs of guilt, at first small, amplified. When Pico had returned, arrest was a risk. But the day before, when Whitaker had discovered Pico staying at the saltbox, the risk had grown. Thom could have urged Pico to run. But he didn't. Worse yet, he had failed to mention Mansfield's hay bales. Unless Pico was guilty of the arson, he would not have known of that recent fire. If innocent, he had no idea that the likelihood of arrest had magnified. Thom's failure to warn Pico was inexcusable. It was selfish. Thom relished Pico's company, not to mention the fruits of Pico's labors. The knowledge that he had yielded to his own wants, ignoring Pico's welfare, played heavily on Thom's conscience.

He went over to the fireplace where he eyed his pot of hasty pudding. Minutes before it had looked delicious. His appetite was gone. He turned and stared out the window. He told himself that Pico had to be innocent. Convincing himself was harder. Regardless, guilt or innocence was secondary. Pico and he were friends. Friends, real ones, didn't benefit themselves at the expense of one another.

<br>

⌇⌇⌇

<br>

The 31ˢᵗ of December, 1774—New Year's Eve. The start of another calendar year was not a big deal, but after sinking into the shortened days of December, and with three months of winter ahead, under other conditions Thom might have partaken in the merriment at the Hogshead. But not as 1774 came to an end. With Pico behind bars, Thom was in no mood for celebration, especially when he felt responsible. The week before he had declined Sarah's invitation for Christmas dinner. In turning her down, he had agreed to come on New Year's Eve, provided she kept it simple. She had largely kept her word, though her apple pie with fresh-churned cinnamon ice cream, topped with a dollop of whip, stretched that word to the limit.

"Any tasks that could use a man's hand?" said Thom.

"Everything's shipshape."

Her response was a foregone conclusion. Thom would need to nose around and see what needed to be done.

"How's Pico doing?"

"Not sure, but knowing him...his adaptability, I suspect he's managing. I plan to visit him...if not tomorrow, the next day." The conversation rekindled memories of Thom's own ordeal back in England. The jail where he had done his time was more crowded and squalid than the Great Barrington lockup. Regardless, being behind bars, deprived of one's freedom, was no bargain.

Thom observed a curious expression on Sarah's face. "You've got something on your mind."

"Well...I was wondering, and you needn't answer if you'd rather not. Do you think Pico is responsible for the fires?"

"I...I don't think so." Thom wished he were certain. He had repeatedly told himself that Pico would never commit such wanton acts. The facts, not the least of which was the addition of a witness, made it hard to exclude the possibility. Pico had the opportunity. Possible motives, his difficult childhood or resentment owing to wrongs the white man had done to the Indians, were undeniable. A broader resentment, a half-blood's rejection in both worlds, could have been at work.

"You sound as though you have doubts."

"Why would I? Pico's a good person." Thom's words echoed in his ears. If he were sure of Pico's innocence, his denial would have been categorical.

Sarah eyed him before sipping her cider. She glowered at her vessel. "I'll take my tea over this any day. I know...I shouldn't complain. The boycott is critical, and folks throughout the colonies have all forsworn tea."

Her change of subject was no surprise to Thom. Sarah didn't feed curious cravings at others' expense.

"At the meeting Sunday, folks suggested that we're at war already."

"Because of the recent Portsmouth incident?"

"Exactly." She took another sip. "Of course, given the way they argued, you can't help but wonder if they had their facts straight."

"I got mine from Deacon Hale. He said he got it from a fellow who spoke directly with one of the men involved in the raid on Fort William and Mary."

Sarah muttered just loud enough to be audible. "Let's see, if you pass it to me...it'll be fourth hand." She chuckled. "Ah...next to mine, probably tenth-hand or worse, it's like straight from the horse's mouth. So, what did the Deacon tell you?"

"Well...as you probably know, for months the colonial governors have been securing powder, arms and shot. They claim it belongs to the King, not our militias. In the meantime, Patriots have seized the caches from the royal garrisons in Providence and New London, among others, and distributed them to our militias."[193]

"I heard all that, but surely the Deacon knew something more."

"He did." Rather than yielding to Sarah's impatience, Thom savored a bite of his dessert. "According to the Deacon, intelligence revealed that the British planned to take control of colonial arms' storehouses, including the one near Portsmouth at Fort William and Mary.[194] Before the Redcoats could move, forty Patriots headed to the fort. Along the way more joined, and by the time they arrived, their numbers were roughly four hundred. They easily overcame the lone British officer who, with just five men, was on guard."[195]

"Did they actually attack the fort?"

"The British fired a volley that was returned by the Patriots. But it could hardly be called a battle."

Sarah shook her head.

"What's the matter?"

"Nothing...I guess...except..." She heaved a sigh. "Shots, the first shots. Does that mean we're at war?"

"C'mon, it was a little nothing."

"Maybe so, but it was more than words." For a moment Sarah studied Thom. "I can tell by your expression. You're not convinced."

"Can you blame me?"

"Maybe...but it seems to me that like Caesar, we've crossed the Rubicon."

"Come again," said Thom.

"Once Caesar crossed that river and marched south toward Rome, the die of war with Pompeii had been cast. The shots at Fort William and Mary, however few, even with no casualties, may well be our Rubicon."

A moment earlier Thom had dismissed her point, but second thoughts left him unsure. The attack on the British garrison was certain to evoke a retaliatory response from King George and Parliament. With four thousand British troops stationed in Boston and more arriving, Sarah's logic could not be ignored. Even naysayers, already in the minority, would have to concede the likelihood of armed conflict.

With several inches of snow coating the Great Road, Lodestone trudged the eight-mile stretch to Great Barrington. The westerly headwind was benign, but supplemented by Lodestone's pace, it dealt a nasty bite. An hour had elapsed before Thom arrived at the Berkshire County Jail. While less than a month of winter had passed, according to Thom's calculation, he had reached the midpoint of the cruel season. He was halfway through the tough five-month stretch that ran from the first of November to the first of April. The mental trick, beginning his calculation on the hibernal months in November, did nothing to shorten the winter, but psychologically it mitigated Thom's blues. By the first of December, three weeks before winter's official onset, twenty percent of his annual sentence was behind him, at least in his mind.

Thom stared at the curious wooden structure. When first he had come to western Massachusetts, the two-story jail of hand-hewn timbers, which served as the residence of its keepers William and Ebenezer Bement, had been renowned for escapes.[196] But in 1773 a stronger door had been added, and surrounding the jail, roughly twelve feet away, a ten-foot high fence with five-inch iron spikes only inches apart, one from the next, had been erected. While it was no Tower of London, from what Thom observed, any escape would be formidable.[197]

Thom approached the fence's large gate. A man with a rifle at his side, stepped out of the jail's door and said, "Can I help ya?"

"I'm Thomas Webster. I'd like to see Pico, the young Indian lad."

The man peered at Thom through the spaces in the fence. "You his lawyer?"

"No."

"Don't look like family neither."

"I'm not," said Thom. "But Pico lived with me before he was carted off to jail."

"You from Tyringham?"

"Yup. I've got a place on the south side of Beartown Mountain, not far from the Post Road."

The man pointed at Thom's side. "Pass your haversack through the space, so I can check it."

Thom did as instructed, and the man examined the contents before placing the haversack over his shoulder. "Yeah, I guess you can see him." He opened the gate and, with gun raised, allowed Thom to enter. He stepped around behind Thom, checking for weapons. He motioned Thom to the jail's door and, after unlocking it, let Thom in.

"How's Pico doing?"

"No problem. He keeps to himself."

"You think he needs a lawyer?" If anyone was likely to know, the keeper was the one.

The keeper pawed at his bristly chin. "He needs someone, but if ya ask me, most of them rabble-rousing loudmouths round these parts ain't worth two pence. Places like Boston got some good ones, so I heard, but the local woodchucks mainly do more harm than good." He studied Thom for a moment. "Ya seem pretty interested in the boy. Maybe you could represent him."

Thom shook his head. An image of the panic that had left him tongue-tied at the town meeting proved he was not up to the job. "How about Ezra Jenkins?"

The keeper burst out laughing.

The reaction was not surprising. If Thom had troubles with the law, no way would he place his fate in Jenkins' hands. Regardless, Jenkins had recently claimed that Pico was guilty.

"Here, I'll let ya in to see the lad." The keeper led the way to the door behind which the prisoners were housed. He allowed Thom to enter, locking the door behind him. Thom spotted Pico curled up alone on the floor in the far right corner.

"What you in for?" said a burly fellow, one of about six other prisoners, all off to Thom's left.

"Just visiting," said Thom.

"Ya sure ya ain't here for murder or maybe kidnapping?" said another, adding a cackling laugh.

Thom pretended not to hear the remark. Disquieting memories of confinement, long buried, bubbled forth. "How you doing?" said Thom, as he drifted in Pico's direction.

"It's not Heaven...but it could be worse."

"He's here to see the Indian," said the man who had cackled.

"Careful he don't set ya on fire," said another. "He's in for arson, ya know."

"You okay?" said Thom in a soft voice.

Pico shrugged. "Yeah...I guess."

Thom worried that the other prisoners were treating Pico as an outcast, perhaps bullying him. His own experience in England had taught him that jails invited mistreatment. The Great Barrington lockup, with multiple prisoners in a common room, was arguably more intimidating than the smaller cells of the jail where he had been housed over a decade earlier. "They giving you a hard time?" whispered Thom, his back to the others. He felt a half-dozen pairs of eyes, like double-barreled rifles, trained on his back.

Pico shook his head. He shifted his position alongside Thom so he too faced toward the corner, away from the other prisoners. He whispered, "The big guy threatened me the first two days. Each day it got worse. One morning I got up early, and, using an old Indian trick, I started a small fire here in the corner. I woke them all up and told them if they didn't lay off, I'd burn the place down, them included, during the night. Since then, nobody bothers me."

The ingenious approach to a difficult situation impressed Thom, but it also generated concerns. Pico's threat of arson, the very crime with which he was charged, lent credence to the accusation. "Is there anything I can do?"

"Yeah...get me outta here."

The candid answer to the rhetorical question discombobulated Thom.

"Only kiddin'." Pico patted Thom on the shoulder. "Nothin' you can do."

The words, as well as the gesture, helped ease a troubled conscience, but only a little. Part of the responsibility for Pico's predicament lay with Thom. Supposedly he had come to help lessen Pico's burden. Why then was his Indian friend playing the role of consoler? "Maybe I could make some furniture or something to satisfy Dodge and Mansfield and—"

"You too?"

"Me too...what?"

"You don't believe me. You think I torched the barn and the hay and the school?"

"No, but..."

"Then why would you pay damages?"

Even before Pico had asked the question, Thom suspected what his friend was thinking. "I...I just thought it might get you out sooner." The look that greeted Thom told him he was on ice thinner than that coating Brewer's Pond.

"I know. You're just trying to help."

"Yeah...but I'm doing a lousy job of it."

"Not your fault."

The kind words were welcome, but they failed to erase the history that led to Pico's confinement. If Thom had been more forthcoming, Pico would likely have left the area before he was arrested. The concession was a knife in Thom's gut. That self-interest, the satisfaction of Pico's company, had occasioned Thom's silence, drove the blade deeper.

"'Bout time you leave," came the voice of the keeper.

Thom glanced over his shoulder at the locked door and turned back to Pico. "Gotta go...I guess. I'll see what I can do." The hollow words echoed in Thom's head. Who was he fooling? He had no plan to free Pico. None whatsoever.

"Appreciate that," said Pico, lending apparent credence to the fatuous utterance.

Thom started for the door.

"Ya gonna take me with ya?" said the burly man who had taunted Thom on his arrival.

Once again, Thom pretended not to hear.

"Ya ain't too sociable."

Thom hurried to the door where the keeper returned his haversack and let him out. He continued out of the building and beyond the iron-spiked fence. Once he reached Lodestone, he looked back at the jail. He closed his eyes. A wealth of thoughts and emotions raced through his head. Images, long repressed, of the dirty, dingy cell that he had called home far across the Atlantic spewed forth. The foul flavor of the disgusting gruel he had consumed day after day coated his palate. The ever-present stench of excrement and urine filled his nose. A breath of wind against his face stirred sensations of the indecorous caress of rats crawling across his cheek in the night. The omni-present screams of the madman who occupied the adjacent cell reverberated in Thom's ears. He opened his eyes and stared off into the woods. Immaculate, white powdery snow, fresh from a light fall the night before, draped a stately pine. Silence, halcyon serenity, prevailed. Thom drew in a deep breath, his lungs filling with pure Berkshire mountain air. He looked back at the jail where, behind the wall and the bars beyond, he imagined Pico seated in the corner.

He untethered Lodestone and climbed aboard. The stalwart stallion was carrying a heavy load, not just Thom, but also the onus of guilt. He rode slowly along the snow-covered road. The light, westerly breeze, now at his back, was negated by the pace of the ride. The road through the woods was deserted; wagon and hoof tracks the only evidence that others had passed that way. The King's arrow carved into a maple caught Thom's eye. Where Pico would have gashed the tree with his hatchet, allowing sweet maple syrup to flow, the British would fell it to feed their insatiable appetite for lumber. A single chevron in a peaceful forest, eons old, offered an unwelcome reminder of the land's violent past and likely similar future. Not long before, the colonists had fought side by side with British troops against the French and Indians. Now the colonists and their British brethren appeared poised to take up arms against one another. People had come to the New World searching for a better life. Somehow, inevitably, animosities dictated otherwise. Such was history since time immemorial. Dating back to Persia and Egypt and Rome and all across Europe, armed conflicts had defined the future. Friends became enemies. War created strange bedfellows, as past enemies became friends, only to again become enemies down the road. Thom pondered the illogic. Unable to make sense of the bellicose world, his mind drifted back to Pico. Amidst his philosophical meandering, thoughts of his friend's tribulation faded into the background, but the weight of blame never lifted. At every turn, over each hill, a unique palette, as sublime as its predecessor greeted him. Still his heart remained heavy and his mind, riddled.

꩜

Nearly home from Great Barrington, as Thom passed the Hogshead, he slowed Lodestone's gait to a walk. He eyed the road ahead. Alone in his saltbox, his mood, already somber, would grow darker. A few brews with friends could be medicinal. Off to his left the sight of Richard's dapple gray convinced him to visit the tavern. He tethered his equine companion next to Gray Mist. He stared at the sign that hung from two chains on the post out front. The neatly carved and painted crimson coat of arms of King George held prominent sway. Though nothing more than handiwork on a signpost, it said a lot, not necessarily what patrons inside were espousing.

Thom opened the imposing oak door. He spotted Richard, along with Orville Crane, Paul Cooper and Ezra Jenkins, seated in the front right corner. Their booth which held four was full.

"Come on...join us," said Richard.

Thom hesitated.

Cooper, who was seated on the outside of the booth, grabbed a nearby chair. "There's plenty of room." He stationed the chair at the end of the table.

"You've twisted my arm." Thom took the seat.

"You can't be coming from home," said Richard. "I stopped by your place."

"I was on my way back from Great Barrington. I went..." Thom debated whether to share the reason for his trip, but with little reason for secrecy and someone likely to inquire, he continued. "I was visiting Pico at the jail." Expressions on the faces of Crane and Jenkins hinted they had no sympathy for the imprisoned youth.

"How's he doing?" said Cooper.

"As well as one could expect...I guess." The response, more automatic than analytical, reflected a desire to remain circumspect.

"It's a damn shame," said Jenkins. "You took the lad in, gave him a place to stay, and how does he repay you?"

"You've got no call to say that!" Thom glared at Jenkins.

Bewilderment appeared on the lawyer's face. He turned to the others. "I laud our neighbor's kindness, and he jumps down my throat."

"Thanks," said Thom, "but I can do without your praise."

"Think what you like," said Jenkins, "but you oughta be thankful the kid's locked up."

"What does that mean?"

"That your saltbox might have been next on his arson list."

"Damn it, Jenkins, you—" A hand on Thom's shoulder turned his head.

"Sorry to interrupt," said Mary. "What can I get you?"

"Just an ale."

"Bring him a spoon as well," said Cooper, gesturing at the table's common trough of stew.

A pang in Thom's stomach made him glad Cooper had expanded his order.

"Just before you arrived," said Cooper, "Ezra was about to pass on some news from England."

"I can just imagine." Lingering irritation prevented Thom from harnessing the sarcasm.

Jenkins gave him a look before shifting his gaze to the others. "According to a rider who was passing through, the actions of the Continental Congress enraged King George. He went before Parliament and condemned them. Both the House of Commons and the House of Lords joined in the condemnation. They resolved to do whatever it takes to stem our rebellious ways."[198]

"Big surprise," said Richard.

"Perhaps you expected a bouquet of roses, along with a note of thanks." Jenkins sneered.

"Well, if they're lookin' for a fight," said Cooper, "we'll give 'em one."

The lawyer laughed, his fat jowls rumbling up and down.

"You find that funny?"

"To tell the truth, Paul, I do." Jenkins folded his arms. "Last summer when I was in Boston, I watched the British army's training maneuvers on the Commons. Talk about a formidable fighting force." He leaned back, his voice shifting into a higher-pitched drone. "And then you have the colonial militias. Tyringham's own, maybe better than average, a perfect example. A bunch of hillbillies carrying muskets designed to shoot deer and rabbits. A joke...a damn joke."

Thom longed to put the smug lawyer in his place, but given the merits of the issue and the skills of the would-be debaters, he directed his mouth elsewhere. He gulped the ale that Mary slipped in front of him.

"Ezra," said Richard, his finger pointed, "you and your Tory friends are in for a rude awakening."

Jenkins laughed scornfully.

"Make fun...all you want. You'll see." Richard glared at the cocky lawyer. "I can't believe you're actually one of them...that when the chips are down, you'll help the bloody lobsterbacks kill your neighbors."

341

"You make it sound like I'm the bad guy. You're the ones advocating treason. I'm following the law, staying loyal to my Mother Country."

"Yeah, loyal to oppressors who steal our freedoms and tax the hell out of us." Richard rapped his tankard on the table as he turned to the others. "And we know why. The status quo suits Ezra's pocketbook just fine." He looked back at Jenkins with an expression that said: *So there.*

The lawyer remained as cool as the snowy landscape that lay outside. "My, my...We do delude ourselves, don't we?" He scratched his head theatrically. "Hmm...so according to the *au fait* Richard Thorn, loyalty to the country that has supported and defended us is an unpardonable sin...while anarchy, tossing tea into the sea, ignoring the rule of law, a noble quest." Jenkins furrowed his brow. "Sorry, my friend, but your perverse excuse for logic doesn't wash."

"You don't think we deserve more rights?" said Cooper.

"That's not the point." Sarcasm dripped from the attorney's tongue.

"Not the point!" Richard glared. "Then enlighten us, Mr. Know-it-all Lawyer, why?"

Jenkins moved his eyes over the others, almost as if he were assessing their worthiness for an explanation. "Much as I hate to be redundant, no matter how many times I repeat myself, somehow you manage to forget. Our colonies here in the New World have survived only because England expended huge sums protecting us. France and Spain, not to mention the Indians, would have pillaged our homes and families and taken our lands were it not for the British army. You all know it. And deep down you also know that England is entitled to recompense. Nevertheless, you demand a free ride—all the benefits, with none of the costs."

"Not so," said Cooper. "We're willing to pay our share, but we want our rights, the same ones afforded English citizens."

Thom nodded emphatically. Cooper had unmasked the flaw in the lawyer's rhetoric.

Jenkins calmly shook his head. "This isn't England. We're not English citizens. Lest you hadn't noticed, we're a colony." His muzzling hand extended in Cooper's direction forestalled interruption. "Don't get me wrong. Additional rights would be nice, but life is never perfect. Diplomacy, not war, is the means to redress perceived inequities. A rational voice draws a receptive ear. Rebellion begets intransigence. And what you gentlemen unfortunately forget—We, here in the colonies, have it damn good!"

"Lovely speech," said Cooper. He turned away from Jenkins, addressing Richard and Thom. "Our friend with the right connections extols the status quo. As a part-time tax collector for our dear Governor—may he rot in hell—Ezra has no intention of biting the hand that feeds him."

"And I suppose you fellows aren't motivated by self-interest?"

Richard pointed a finger at Jenkins. "Wanting basic human rights is hardly the same as looking out for one's pocketbook."

Thom did a double take. Instead of responding, Jenkins dug his spoon into the trough.

"Ezra...you are truly a man of *principal*," said Cooper.

His spoon approaching his mouth, Jenkins halted.

"Don't misunderstand," said Cooper. "That's *principal* spelled with an *al*, not an *le*." As best he could in the confines of a booth, Cooper stood up part way and bowed to his applauding compatriots.

Jenkins bristled but said nothing.

The silencing of the grandiloquent blabbermouth pleased Thom. His objective side confronted the merits of the underlying issue. The vast majority of citizens, albeit in varying degrees, weighed self-interests when deciding whether to support a split with England. The self-evident observation, easy to overlook, reminded Thom to maintain a healthy measure of cynicism. He looked around the table where his four companions sat taciturn. "Do we really want war?" he said. The inquiry, as if involuntarily delivered from Thom's subconscious, drew wide eyes from the others.

"What kind of question is that?" said Richard.

"I...I'm not sure." A genuine effort to analyze his words, rather than defensiveness, triggered the reply.

"Should we let King George and the blustering buffoons of Parliament trample our rights and treat us like toads?" Cooper shot Thom a look.

"Give the fellow a break," said Jenkins, reaching around to pat Thom on the back. "Perhaps he's beginning to see the light."

The lawyer's support was as unwelcome as unexpected.

"You switching sides on us, Webster?" Cooper studied Thom with a penetrating stare. "Maybe the fellows were right to bar you from the Minutemen."

Thom's need to explain himself, already patent, magnified. "I didn't mean that we should cave in to England's pressure, but..." As he searched for the proper explanation, he noted the pique on Richard's face. "I was merely thinking out loud, wondering if communications with our Mother Country should be more conciliatory."

"More conciliatory? You must be kidding!" Cooper jerked back nearly spilling his tankard. "The Continental Congress held out an olive branch. Their Declaration urged restoration, and I quote, 'to that state in which both countries found happiness and prosperity.'[199] What more could you expect when we're being treated like slaves?"

"Slaves?" Jenkins shook his head. "The man who protestith too loudly is the man who exaggerates. Admittedly England's treatment is not ideal—even I will concede that—but we are hardly slaves." Jenkins panned the group, defying them to disagree. "The truth be known, our lot is closer to perfection than slavery."

"Horseshit," barked Cooper. "We're being denied our fundamental rights. That's intolerable. That's a reason to fight. And I, for one, am ready."

"Hear, hear." Richard raised his mug aloft.

"You with us, Thom?" said Cooper.

"Yes...but..." Thom fettered his tongue as faces to his left fired bullets the instant he began to quibble.

"But what?" growled Cooper.

"Well...much as I agree that England's tyranny is outrageous, the issues have two sides."

"All along I thought you were with our cause." Fire showed in Richard's eyes. "Webster, what's gotten into you?"

"A little common sense," said Jenkins.

"Understand," said Thom, "I support the cause. No way should we lie down and let Britain oppress us."

"Fine," said Cooper, "but you can't be on both sides of the fence."

"I'm not." Thom felt the need to explain himself. "Miscalculations could precipitate a war over issues that could be peacefully resolved. Keep in mind that England has many colonies. Caving in to us would be a dangerous precedent. England needs to save face." The regrettable argument reverberated in Thom's head. His views had fallen victim to his own effort to save face.

"Well put," said Jenkins.

"Well put...my foot!" Cooper, his belly loaded with brew, turned to Richard. "It seems your friend spouts the kind of double talk we've been hearing from Governor Gage." He looked back at Thom. "If King George and Parliament wanted peace, they could have rescinded the burdens they imposed over the last decade. Instead they hit us with the Intolerable Acts. Their methods prove the futility of conciliation. To get our rights, we have to fight for them."

Thom sat mute. How, he wondered, had he taken a contrary posture? The answer dated back to a lesson from his mentor. Every dispute, verbal or otherwise, had two sides. Thom had taken the concept to heart. Good intentions led him to play devil's advocate. He became a gadfly. Rather than dispassionately exploring and weighing issues, he tossed oil onto a fire. He knew the recipe well. Start with a hot topic, add alcohol—and plenty had been consumed—and a devil's advocate was likely to get burned. Thom reached for his mug and took a slow drink.

Jenkins rose from his seat. "Much as I hate to leave you boys, I promised my wife I wouldn't be late, and next to God, that's the one wrath with which I dare not fool." He laid a hand on Thom's shoulder. "You and I could get on a whole lot better than I had previously imagined."

The ingratiating words resonated with Thom no better than one of Parliament's repressive pronouncements. He rose from his chair at the end of the booth, slipping into the spot Jenkins had vacated. For several minutes he drifted between the conversation and his own ruminations.

"Another round," said Richard, as Mary passed their table. Once she was out of earshot, he said, "So, how's our community supply of gunpowder?"

Crane, who had hardly said a word, put a finger to his lips before gesturing in Thom's direction.

"He's okay," said Richard.

Crane displayed visible skepticism.

"You mean because of what happened earlier?"

"Yeah and..."

"I assure you. He's with us." Richard turned to Thom. "Tell them you're ready to take up arms against England if we don't get our rights."

"Absolutely." After the earlier fiasco, Thom was not about to equivocate.

"Then how come ya didn't disagree with Jenkins?" Crane looked Thom in the eye.

"I merely meant..." A moment before Thom had concluded that a hedge was out of the question. "I'm with you guys one hundred percent. Either we get our rights, or we fight for them."

"See," said Richard. "I told you Thom is one of us."

Crane frowned.

"C'mon...Thom was at the Courthouse in Great Barrington when we kept Gage's hacks from the bench. And he was at Cambridge and Worcester too."

"Maybe, but it don't mean he ain't a spy."

"Orville, since when do you question a friend's loyalty?" said Cooper. "And to answer Rich's question, out in the corner of my barn, piled beneath a bunch of stuff, we've got six full barrels of gunpowder. It's not the biggest stock in the colonies, but it's not bad either."

Crane pointed at Thom. "If word of this gets out, folks 'll look your way."

The tidbit was hardly worth the responsibility. With many knowing of the stash, word was apt to get out. Thom glanced at the blacksmith. There was a time when Thom had surmised that Issac Winslow had blackballed him from the Minutemen. Perhaps Crane had done the nasty deed.

346

# Chapter 21

ROUGHLY THREE TIMES per month, Thom rode to the Great Barrington jail to visit Pico. Efforts to have the charges against his young friend withdrawn fell on deaf ears. Arraignment moved forward to indictment. A trial in the spring loomed. Thom sought counsel for Pico in Great Barrington. All the while speculations proliferated, mostly as to when, not if, war with England would break out. In western Massachusetts the odds-on bet was that the British army, poised in Boston, would march once the snow melted. Tyringham's Minutemen, like those throughout the colonies, were conducting increased drills, but Thom, having been blackballed, was barred from those exercises. Hibernating in his saltbox, furniture making was his refuge from the cold and lonely winter. It was a sunny day, the 10$^{th}$ of March, when, with the hint of spring abounding, he responded to a knock at his door.

"You're alive?" said Sarah, her tone sardonic.

"What's that mean?"

"You going to ask me in?"

"Pardon my lack of manners." Thom bowed histrionically, gesturing her through the doorway and into the parlor.

She breathed deeply, pulling back the hood on her scarlet cape. "Ah...warm southern sun bursting through the windows and a fire blazing in the fireplace."

Thom took her cape and hung it on one of several wooden pegs adjoining the front door. He motioned her to the rocking chair in the front corner of the room.

"It's like the one you made for me." Sarah sank down into the seat.

"I finished it about a week ago."

"Almost as nice as mine." She rocked back and forth. "Been three weeks, and I haven't heard a peep from you. I began to wonder."

Thom, who settled into the chair opposite the fireplace, shrugged.

"You becoming a hermit...again?"

"Well, winter can..." The unconvincing ring of the utterance, coupled with Sarah's furrowing brow, forced him to rethink his reply. "I've been visiting Pico almost every week."

"How's he doing?"

"As well as can be expected...under the circumstances."

Sarah eyed Thom pointedly. "You don't blame yourself for his predicament, do you?"

"Actually, I do. If it weren't for me, good chance he would have taken off before they arrested him."

"So what." Sarah jerked the rocker to a halt. "Pico's predicament results from the fires, not because he stayed in Tyringham."

"You're presuming he's guilty."

"No...but the fires are the issue."

Thom disliked the logic, but let it pass knowing Sarah was trying to ease his conscience.

"Did you hear the latest from England?"

"You mean about King George imploring Parliament to tighten the restrictions on us?"

She shook her head. "You are a hermit."

This time her logic was better. "Would you like some tea? Uh...goldenrod, not the real stuff."

"Aren't you anxious to hear the news?"

"I'm trying to be a gracious host."

Sarah rolled her eyes. "I'll skip the tea."

"So, what's the news?"

"Word has it that Lord Chatham of the House of Lords introduced a so-called Provisional Act that might avert war."[200]

"Really?" Thom sat up straighter. "On terms we can accept?"

"Some folks think so, and if you give me a second to get my thoughts straight, I'll let you be the judge."

She gazed at the fireplace whose flames had grown smaller. Thom grabbed the opportunity to throw on another log.

"According to what Reverend Bidwell told us at Sunday's meeting, the Provincial Act would allow England to retain its sovereignty over us, but—" She shook her head. "You're frowning, even before I've completed one sentence."

"What do you expect when you tell me we'll be subjugated?"

"I didn't say that."

"No, but you said 'sovereignty.' That's tantamount—" Thom stopped himself. They weren't the same, and provided the colonies enjoyed the rights of English citizens, the condition of sovereignty was acceptable. "Sorry, I'll save my reactions until you're done."

Sarah, as if ignoring his *mea culpas*, rocked back and forth several times before continuing. "Under the proposed Act, England would recognize our Continental Congress, and Parliament would no longer levy taxes on us without the consent of our assemblies."

Thom felt his eyes widen. Perhaps he had gone off half-cocked. "What else would we get if the Act were passed?"

"A few thorns to go with the roses." Sarah took hold of the rocker's arms as she brought the chair to a halt. "We'd have to recognize Parliament as our supreme legislative authority. In addition, we'd have to levy and collect certain revenues for the Crown."[201]

"I should have known there'd be a kick in our backside."

"You act like it's terrible."

"Well..." Thom forced himself to weigh the package. Might it mirror what British citizens across the Atlantic enjoyed? Wasn't that what the colonists had been demanding? Nevertheless, something stuck in his craw.

"You recall the plan that Joseph Galloway presented to our Continental Congress last fall?"

Thom nodded halfheartedly. "You mean an American legislative body whose authority would be subject to Parliament's consent on so-called imperial matters...whatever the hell that means?"[202]

"Exactly."

"Minor detail," said Thom, his reaction dictated by intransigence more than conviction. "Galloway was a conservative. His plan was rejected by the liberal majority."

"You mean radicals?"

349

The distinction had enough merit that Thom could not dismiss it as semantic. Lord Chatham's proposal, though far from a full loaf, was arguably half. "Would we be represented in Parliament, and I don't mean virtually?"

"Uh...I'm not sure."

Thom gave Sarah a look. "So, this wonderful plan may give us the part of a ring where one's finger goes."

Sarah displayed a puzzled expression.

"Think about it. Lord Chatham's plan may leave us unrepresented, and if Parliament, exerting its ultimate legislative authority pays lip service to our American legislature, we'll end up right where we are now."

"I suppose that's possible, but—"

"Has Parliament accepted Lord Chatham's arrangement?"

"No. As I said, it's only a proposal. But it could open the door to a sensible middle ground, one that would avert war while allowing both England and the colonies to save face."

The logic warranted serious consideration, but Thom's emotions, charged over a long chain of events, were not in a mood for patience. "Strikes me that it's a ploy to keep us in bondage." The dissatisfied look his words evoked forced him to weigh the possibility that he was being stubborn. Representatives, one from England and one from the colonies, had offered similar plans to avert war, but as long as both sides refused to give ground, a stalemate would persist. If so, the issues would likely be decided with guns, rather than compromise. Thom wondered whether the barrier thwarting a solution was fashioned from principle or pig-headedness. While the question oversimplified complex issues, there was no denying that pig-headedness, as well as his propensity to play devil's advocate, had shaped his reactions.

The calendar testified that spring was only a day away. Despite heavy drifts on the far side of Beartown Mountain, areas on the southern face devoid of snow confirmed the vernal equinox was at hand. Thom was seated at Reverend Bidwell's home for the Sunday meeting. He was hardly there by choice.

The preceding afternoon the Reverend had unexpectedly paid Thom a visit and asked him to attend. While Thom had avoided an out-and-out promise, he had all but committed himself. He was unsure how many months had passed since he had last attended. The number was far from few.

Thom arrived early. Just as the Reverend was greeting a couple in the hallway, he slipped past, choosing his familiar spot on the end of the last row. Minutes later, Polly, along with her father and mother, entered the parlor. Thom bowed his head to avoid eye contact. His thoughts, however, transfixed on her. He wondered how she was faring as a widow.

As the room filled, Thom remained low in his seat, trying to remain invisible. He sank deeper yet when Juliette Chandler, or make that Juliette Walters, filed in with her husband Darby. If Thom had wanted, he probably could have had Juliette for his own. Her company, with ample charms, bore advantages solitude could not provide. Regardless, discretion confirmed that theirs was not a suitable match. Darby, roughly twenty years Thom's senior, was a far better candidate. Yet pangs of jealousy stirred. And too, irony could not be denied. No where more than at Sunday meetings, the place where reflections should be most pure, did envy creep into Thom's psyche. With surprising ease he dismissed the censurable thought. But knowing God could be watching, he did not escape a dose of fear. If not on earth, then in the eternity might he be called to account, especially given his meager attendance at God's house of worship.

With all but the last row nearly full, Dinsmore, the cordwainer, along with his wife and two boys, took the seats next to Thom.

"Good day, Wendell," said Thom, the first words he had uttered since entering the parlor.

"And good Sabbath to you. Been a while since I've seen you here."

Thom nodded, suspecting discomfort revealed itself.

A moment later Reverend Bidwell stepped to his lectern. "Before proceeding with today's readings and sermon, let me update you on the most recent rumors that have rumbled across the ocean in response to our demands for life and liberty. I suspect you're all aware of the proposed Provincial Act, Lord Chatham's plan to resolve the differences we have with our Mother Country. It seems another such proposal has been introduced by Lord North."

"Lord North—you can't be serious?"

The rare interruption, a voice off to Thom's left, drew everyone's attention.

"Yes, Lord North, the obdurate British conservative. Word has it that he called upon Parliament to avoid levies on any American colony that fairly taxes itself with the cost of the British army stationed there. I understand the House of Commons supports this plan."[203]

A buzz pervaded the room. Reverend Bidwell waited for the disruption to die of its own accord.

"Lest you think that our brethren across the sea have softened their stance, think twice. Some weeks ago Parliament took up a new law entitled the "New England Trade and Fisheries Act." Whether it has been enacted, I'm unsure. Its terms prohibit the New England colonies from trading with any nation other than Great Britain."[204]

An angry outcry, the likes of which Thom had never observed during his infrequent attendance at Sunday meetings, greeted the message. Rather than quelling the disruption, Reverend Bidwell waited until it waned.

"Apparently our neighbors across the sea are bound and determined to keep us in servitude. They fail to comprehend the..."

Thom's thoughts, as they often did at services, drifted. Why had the Reverend visited his saltbox the night before and requested his attendance at the Sunday meeting? It was not as if Thom, blackballed from the Minutemen, was among the local leaders in the struggle for rights. As the Reverend moved on to his sermon, Thom kept his eyes directed at the lectern. His mind, however, engaged in a familiar pastime. It looked beyond his gaze, penetrating the walls and beams, imagining perfect mortises and tenons and critically analyzing the structure's workmanship, both visible and invisible. Compared to most homes in Tyringham, many of which were mere cabins, the Reverend's was like a museum. For Thom, a skilled craftsman, the handiwork was more interesting than a homily. A glance to his left at the paneling that adjoined the fireplace evidenced Reverend Bidwell's appreciation for the elegance of finished wood. A peek at the floor had Thom imagining that the planks were connected, not by common half-lap joints, but expensive loose-tongue joints. A man of means like the Reverend could afford such luxury. With his eyes again squarely on the Reverend, Thom's brain conjured a mental image of the masterfully laid stones of the arch that lay hidden in the cellar below. Just as the splendid stained-glass windows of Westminster Abbey drowned out many a homily, the architectural excellence of the Reverend's home silenced the clergyman's sermon, at least for Thom. Of course, those who frequented Westminster Abbey, unlike Thom, did not require pressure from their spiritual leader, the Archbishop of Canterbury, before they visited the magnificent cathedral.

Once Reverend Bidwell concluded his remarks, instead of moving on to a concluding prayer or hymn, he announced that Elmer Crane wished to address the gathering.

As the gawky teen rose from his seat and came forward, Thom tried to imagine why of all people, Orville Crane's benighted, eldest son would be addressing the congregation. A buzz hinted that others entertained a similar curiosity.

Reverend Bidwell stepped aside allowing Elmer to take his place at the lectern. The lad's hands strangled the edges of the podium. With shoulders slumped, he gazed blankly at his waiting neighbors, all of whom offered their undivided attention. The room drew to an eerie silence.

"Elmer," said Reverend Bidwell, "proceed."

"I...uh..." Beads of perspiration formed on the youth's forehead.

As one who quailed at public speaking, Thom felt a pang of sympathy. Hard as it was for an adult to address the community, forcing a reluctant fourteen-year-old to do so bordered on torture.

"Elmer..." Reverend Bidwell's voice had grown more demanding. "Tell the people of Tyringham the reason you are standing before them."

"I...I set the fires to Mr. Dodge's barn and Mr. Mansfield's hay."

Again the congregation buzzed. Thom's brain raced. Sympathy for Elmer melted in the face of ire's flame. On the positive side, at least the brat had come forward and admitted his transgressions. He had all but exonerated Pico. But Pico remained in jail, and no one could undo the numerous weeks he had languished there. And there was still the fire at the school. Perhaps Elmer was about to take responsibility for that.

The youth started to leave the lectern.

"Isn't there something else you wish to say to the community?" said Reverend Bidwell.

The nervous youth halted.

"Are there regrets you wish to express?"

"Uh...yeah. I...I'm sorry for what I did." He hurried back to his seat next to his father.

You're sorry, all right, thought Thom. Sorry you got caught.

With the congregation still abuzz, Reverend Bidwell gave a final benediction and brought the meeting to a close. He went directly to Thom.

"Elmer's disclosure is the reason I asked you to come today."

"I'm surprised he owned up to it."

"I wish that was what happened," said the Reverend. "He bragged to Wilbur Locke's boy about the fires. Apparently he thought it one big joke, including the fact that your friend Pico was sitting in jail. Anyway, the Locke boy told his father, and one thing led to another."

"What about the fire at the school? Did Elmer admit to setting that?"

"Not to Locke's kid. Of course, that doesn't mean he isn't responsible. We asked him about it, but with no evidence we couldn't get him to admit. For all I know, Orville may have told him to keep his mouth shut, lest the town make him pay for a new school."

"What about Pico?"

"Last night I spoke with the powers that be. I'm confident he'll be released. Dodge and Mansfield naturally want the charges dropped, and as far as the school, nobody knows if it was arson, let alone who did it. At this point there's no basis to blame Pico."[205]

A modicum of relief stepped to the forefront of Thom's rapidly changing emotions. He was not guilt free. At various times he had struggled to suppress misgivings whether Pico was responsible. He said, "What's likely to happen to Elmer?"

An abashed look showed on the Reverend's face. "I suspect he'll get a few raps on the knuckles and behind, along with some extra chores."

"No charges?...No jail?"

Reverend Bidwell shrugged. "I know. It doesn't seem fair, especially after your friend Pico spent time locked up. But Orville has agreed to pay for Mansfield's hay, a few bales. So Mansfield isn't going to press charges."

"What about Dodge's barn?"

"Elmer's only fourteen. And Orville is going to make up for some of the loss by supplying Pete with nails, along with a metal frame and wheels for a buckboard. And seeing as how Orville and Pete are friends, and Pete is a really nice guy, he plans to let bygones be bygones."

Thom heaved a sigh, restraining the urge to curse. Folks had been quick to make harsh judgments when the suspect was an outsider and, more important, half-Indian. They were far more forgiving when the guilty party turned out to be a neighbor's boy. Like other institutions, justice lacked an even hand. Thom squeezed his lips tightly, suppressing the urge to vent.

"I have an inkling as to your thoughts, and I won't try to argue." Reverend Bidwell displayed a thoughtful mien. "Outcomes can be unfair. Injustice prevails. We see it every day. The kindest, most generous and forgiving person is struck dead, while the worst sinner lives to eighty. Who can explain it?" He shook his head. "Not I."

The concession, though hardly a magic elixir, was soothing. Where others might have delivered an explanation replete with double talk, the kind that leavens dissatisfaction into exasperation, Reverend Bidwell had acknowledged the inequity. Thom took a deep breath as he digested the pragmatic message. "Yes...I suppose that's so."

Pico slipped the final board into place. The split-rail fence surrounding the four sides of the twenty-by-thirty foot garden adjoining the saltbox was complete. The fence had taken a week to fashion, longer than Thom had anticipated. Each of its regularly-spaced vertical posts bore a trio of oval-shaped openings through which horizontal wood slats had been inserted. Thom hoped the barricade, over three feet in height, would protect his vegetables from the animals who had dined on them the preceding summer. A white picket fence would have been more attractive, but an effective barrier, not aesthetics, was the primary goal.

A bench, along with a bushel each of turnips and squash, all to be delivered by the end of September, had covered the cost of trimming the wooden boards at Captain Brewer's sawmill. Brewer preferred the barter, rather than a cash payment. Most times Thom shunned the purchase of goods or services on credit. Being in debt was anathema. An outstanding obligation bore the earmarks of indenture. But after a brief self debate, common sense prevailed. Without the wide planks from Brewer's mill, many, many hours would be needed to hand-hew timbers, and the resulting fence would be bulky. The other alternative, no fence, was out of the question. In the preceding summer, much of what would have been an ample crop had been feed for the deer and rabbits and groundhogs and foxes and other wildlife of Beartown Mountain. Judgment dictated that the fence be erected as soon as possible. Payment, the bench and turnips and squash, could be delivered later.

With lengthening, ever-warmer days of spring at hand, and Pico free from the Great Barrington jail, Thom's spirits were high. With necessities provided for, there was time to luxuriate, a pastime not shared by many. He could build more furniture, perhaps add flowers to his garden, or put a stone wall or picket fence in front of his house. A trip east by stagecoach to the Connecticut River, followed by a sail south eighty miles to the waters that linked to the ocean, was not beyond the realm of possibility. More than a decade had passed since the lowly boatswain's assistant had ventured across the Atlantic in search of a new life. Where weeks on a ship in an endless watery expanse would have been confining to some, Thom had found it liberating. Coming on the heels of a year behind bars, it had been freedom personified. And compared to the misery of an abusive childhood, it had been a summertime swim in a warm pond.

"That oughta do it," said Thom, as he stepped back and surveyed their handiwork. "Those damn varmints will need more smarts if they want to steal our vegetables."

"Maybe," said Pico, his tone rife with skepticism.

Thom, his comment notwithstanding, shared the doubt. Others with fences better than what he and Pico had constructed, awakened to find crops chewed from the vine. How the creatures got in and out often remained a mystery, but one way or another, Thom suspected their garden would suffer a similar fate. At best, the fence would mitigate the damage.

Pico headed for the house.

"Where you going?"

"To fetch a couple of brews and some of last night's ragout."

The mention of the meat and vegetable mixture triggered awareness that labor on the fence had left Thom starved. The sound of hoof beats turned his head. He spotted Richard approaching aboard Gray Mist. "Bring enough for three," yelled Thom, as Pico climbed the front stoop. Thom met Richard at a birch where he was tethering his horse. "What's up?"

"Nothin' special. Just thought I'd stop by."

"Good timing. Pico's fetching some eats." Thom gestured toward his outdoor table, the large granite rock that sat near the woods twenty yards southeast of his saltbox. "You'll join us, I assume."

"With pleasure."

Though the temperature was no higher than upper fifties, the sweat of labor, coupled with a strong sun and still air, made it feel comfortable. Pico approached carrying a triangle of three mugs, atop of which a circular wooden trencher was balanced.

"Dan Heath could use your skills at the Hogshead," said Richard, as Pico laid the items on the rock and pulled three spoons from his pocket. Richard patted Pico on the back.

"Good to see you back out in the open air. Sorry you had to endure those many weeks locked up."

Pico appeared blasé.

Despite the noncommittal reaction, Thom suspected that Pico appreciated Richard's words. Thom did. He said, "How often are the Minutemen practicing?"

"Three...sometimes even four times a week." The reticence in Richard's voice was apparent. "At times it gets awfully tedious."

*You're not fooling me.* If Thom had been alone with Richard, he might have called his friend on the point. The effort to salve the wound occasioned by Thom's exclusion from the ranks of Tyringham's elite had been poorly disguised.

"Folks are saying war is a certainty. Can't imagine either side backing down. Were it not for winter, the fighting would have begun already. Now that spring is here, bullets are bound to replace words."

"I hope you Minutemen are a helluva lot better than the general militia."

Richard heaved a sigh. "We've made considerable progress, and our enthusiasm runs high, but between you, me and the trees (Richard gestured at the woods), it's hard to picture us taking on the British army. Jenkins has been saying that forever, and while most of his yap is manure, on this one the facts bear him out. Spinning gold from burlap is a tough assignment. Like it or not, we're a bunch of farmers."

"Do the rest of the Minutemen feel the same way?"

Richard glanced at the sky. "I don't know. As I said, there's lots of enthusiasm when we practice. You don't hear many comments how we'd fare against the Redcoats, but I suspect that doubts, lotsa big ones, have to be stirring."

Perhaps the disclosure was another attempt to assuage Thom's sensibilities; if so, it was another failure. "You never know," said Thom, his thoughts guided by emotions rather than logic. "We still may avoid war. England might give us the same rights as its own citizens."

Richard rolled his eyes.

"Hey...don't be a pessimist. It's enough that one of us has negative propensities. No call for you to get the disease."

The remark drew a smile from Richard.

"War is not a certainty. Even Lord North, tough bastard that he is, apparently hopes to avert it." Thom sensed his message was falling on deaf ears. "Don't forget, he proposed that any colony supporting the government and contributing to the common defense be relieved of taxes other than those needed to regulate commerce."[206]

"Well, hip, hip, hooray for Lord North." Richard raised his arms in a show of feigned exuberance. "The great English nobleman is willing to offer us the leftover rind of a rotted watermelon."

"What do you mean?"

"Just what I said. North, snake that he is, wants to destroy the unity reflected in the Declaration issued by our Continental Congress. His so-called conciliatory resolution is a ploy to divide us.[207] Its benefits are conditioned upon support of the Crown. That means opposing any colony that refuses to knuckle under."

"I wasn't suggesting that we should accept it, just..."

"Just what?"

Thom might have taken on Richard's question, but skepticism that appeared on Pico's face forced him to reassess his argument. It was naïve to believe that the hawkish Lord North would make meaningful concessions to the colonies. "I also heard that Benjamin Franklin is in England working behind the scenes to win our demands."

"Big deal. Franklin is there pressing our demands. He might better get back to flying kites in thunderstorms because no one in England will listen to him, not after the Hutchinson affair.[208]

"Well..." Judgment urged Thom to check his propensity to play devil's advocate, but the urge, an inherent facet of his personality, was hard to quell. It was not long before that he had given Sarah a hard time when she had voiced views diametric to Richard's. "What makes you so sure England won't bend?"

Richard gnashed his teeth. "Damn—given their recent actions, only a fool would listen to their rhetoric. Amidst their lousy overtures they passed the New England Trade and Fisheries Act, what folks are calling the New England Restraining Act, preventing us from trading other than with

England. And in February they officially declared our colony in rebellion.[209] A month later they sent troops to Salem for the purpose of seizing our military supplies. If you ask me, Lord North has laid a Trojan Horse at our doorstep." Richard hesitated, appearing to study Thom. "You disagree. I see it on your face."

"I wasn't disagreeing. I...I was merely thinking."

Richard's brow furrowed.

The reaction triggered a recollection of the day when Pico, while showing Thom the art of making maple syrup, had silently deflected discord. Thom remembered the lesson well. Implementing it was another matter.

"Well?"

"Well what?" said Thom, uncertain how to react.

"You said you were thinking. Aren't you going to say something?" An edge crept into Richard's voice.

Thom forced a smile, one that he hoped might mask discomfort. He glanced at Pico. His young friend was taking it all in.

"I'm not sure I understand you, Thom." Richard's eyes narrowed, displaying a scrutiny similar to his words.

"Whad'ya mean?"

"At Cambridge and the courthouses in Great Barrington and Worcester you were gung ho. In recent weeks you've seemingly changed."

"You're just..." Thom slowed himself. His resolve in regard to England was as strong as ever. Yet there was merit to Richard's comment. Were the observations inconsistent? Maybe...but maybe not. Regardless, Thom needed to tread a fine line if he wanted to avoid a familiar box. Were he not careful, skepticism, the kind that had kept him out of the Minutemen, would mount. "Don't get me wrong. I'm not suggesting we should allow King George or Parliament to treat us like second-class citizens. But I can't help wondering whether, deep down, England wants to work with us, but needs to save face."

Richard shook his head. "If you ask me, you're searching for rainbows."

"What's wrong with that?"

"A whole lot when there's a blue sky and no clouds."

Judgment told Thom a concession was the best way to extricate himself. "You're right. It was nothing more than wishful thinking."

Pico breathed an exasperated sigh.

The overt reaction caught Thom by surprise; Pico's follow up, even more so.

"Why," said Pico, "are folks so quick to fight?"

Richard glared. "When someone steals your freedom, you have to stand up!"

"Yeah...so?" said Pico.

"So?" Richard's gaze remained trained on Pico.

"I'm not suggesting you give up your liberties, but damn...you gotta try everything before you start shootin'. War, war...and more war—what does it get? Lotsa dead bodies and often no winners. My people, the Mohicans, have fought many battles. Many fruitless battles. Too often because sober voices failed to speak up."

Thom dared not say a word. Pico's sentiments reflected what Thom had been thinking. But he had backed off when challenged. He fit the mold that Pico had cast.

"For years," said Richard, "we've tried to maintain peace with England. You give a shilling, and they take a pound, not to mention your soul."

"From what I hear," said Pico, "some in England want peace."

Richard folded his arms, making no effort to camouflage indignation that the young half-breed was questioning him. "Sure...on their terms."

Pico remained mute, though his expression hardly reflected acquiescence.

Richard pointed at Pico. "If and when war breaks out, whose side will the Indians be on?"

Pico chuckled.

"You find that funny?"

"Yeah...guess so." His countenance was thoughtful. "You lump Indians like we're all the same."

Richard shrugged.

"Suppose Pico put all white men—the British, the colonists, and throw in the French and Spanish and Dutch—in the same barrel? How would those apples taste? Well...it's no different with the Indians. There are many different tribes."

Pico's feistiness may have been unfamiliar, and though initially unexpected, with just the briefest reflection, it made sense to Thom. At a young age Pico had taken on the world and survived. A chipmunk, quick to run for cover, he wasn't.

"Any predictions whether more tribes will side with the British or the colonists?"

Though Richard's tone bore a hint of sarcasm, it gave credence to Pico's challenge. The anomaly intrigued Thom.

"Hard to say, 'cept for those that already got close ties. Most will check the wind...see which way it's blowin'. Tribes 'll do what's best for them." Pico looked Richard in the eye. "Like the white man, Indians look out for themselves."

Thom felt a lump in his throat. In part it was attributable to the substance of Pico's views, but more so owing to a troublesome realization they triggered. Thom's respect for Pico, copious though it was, bore the taint of underlying prejudice. Unwittingly, Thom had viewed Pico with a haughty assumption that white men were superior to Indians. It was as if Pico's wisdom and skills had been acquired in spite of his Indian heritage. The distasteful perspective was embarrassing. What made it worse was the possibility that Pico had recognized it.

# Chapter 22

ONCE SARAH HAD RESHUFFLED the cards, Thom, the pone, cut the deck. Sarah dealt them six cards apiece, two of which they each deposited into Sarah's crib. She turned up the starter card, and sure enough it was a Jack.

"His nobs," she said, scoring two points, entitling her to peg forward two places on the Cribbage Board.[210]

Thom played a card from his hand, laying it in front of him and announcing "seven."

"Fourteen," said Sarah, the total of the cards, as she played a *seven* of her own. "Pair," she added, scoring two more points. "Guess what. That puts me in the stink hole." With her points accumulated from earlier hands, she had reached one hundred twenty, just one shy of the amount required to win.

"You better not get that last point, or else I'll tell Reverend Bidwell you've been playing cards."

"The idea that card playing isn't ladylike is hogwash." Sarah reached across the table and snatched Thom's frothy mug of whipped syllabub.[211]

"What are you doing?"

"Getting myself some bargaining power." Sarah winked. "You want your syllabub back, then promise you won't tell the Reverend."

Thom pretended to pout. "Okay...I promise."

Sarah returned his drink.

Thom took a swig. "Damn, that's good." He tossed a *ten* onto the table. "Twenty-four."

Sarah laid down a *six*. "Thirty."

Thom stared at his hand. "Go," he said, unable to play any card that would keep the total within the limit of thirty-one. "And don't you dare add insult to injury by playing an Ace."

Sarah smiled as she reached for a card. "Relax," she said, "I can't play either. Not that it matters since I get a point as the last

363

to play." She adjusted the pegs. "Game hole." She leaned back. "You want to go another?"

"What? So you can beat my brains out again. No thanks." He pushed the cards together into a deck.

"Did you hear about that speech Patrick Henry gave a few weeks back in the Virginia House of Burgesses?"

"I did," said Thom. "Everyone is talking about it. Matter of fact, I looked for it in Heath's copy of the Boston Gazette over at the Hogshead. I wanted to read the whole thing. Surprising that they didn't print it."

"Maybe he gave it off the cuff...so even he doesn't have a copy."

"I doubt that."

Sarah displayed an unreceptive cast. "You never know. Folks say he's the finest orator since Cotton Mather. Maybe better."

"According to what I've heard, Henry told the gathering that war is inevitable. He said England has forged our chains, and they can already be heard clanking in Boston. And word has it that when he ended his speech with a cry of 'Give me liberty or give me death,' the crowd jumped up and chanted, 'To Arms! To Arms!'"[212] The possibility the story may have been embellished as it passed from mouth to mouth crossed Thom's mind, but appealing as it was, absent evidence to the contrary, he preferred to accept it.

"How come Pico didn't come with you this evening?"

"This and that, I guess," said Thom, uncertain of the precise reason.

"He knows he's welcome here, doesn't he?"

Thom nodded. He observed a curious expression on Sarah's face. "What's the matter?"

"Well..." She hemmed and hawed.

"C'mon, out with it."

"There are some in Tyringham—and mind you, I'm not among them—who still have doubts about him. He's an Indian who doesn't quite fit in anywhere, not with his own people and not here. The fact that you're associated with him prompts some to wonder about you."

Thom studied Sarah's face. "What are you saying?"

"Fair or not, Pico may have played a role in your being blackballed from the Minutemen."

The disclosure, not really a shock, generated mixed emotions. There was anger that many who had accused Pico of the fires refused to judge him fairly. But it softened the blow of the blackball. Exclusion by association was less painful than personal animosity. "You're not suggesting I should tell him to leave?"

"Of course not. I simply want you to know the situation."

"I appreciate your telling me." Thom had no doubts about Sarah's sincerity. He was even more certain he would not ask Pico to leave.

✺

Responding to a knock, Thom opened his front door. Richard stood on the stoop. "Good to see you. C'mon in."

Richard shook his head and motioned Thom to join him outside.

"You must be kidding." Thom pointed at a stand of pines whose branches swayed in the howling wind. "It may be April, but apparently Mother Nature failed to get the message."

Richard tugged at Thom's arm pulling him out onto the stoop. He whispered, "I need to talk to you in private. Get your coat, and I'll meet you out back in your shed."

Much as he disliked the idea, since Richard was on his way, Thom acquiesced. He grabbed his coat and tri-corner hat from a peg. He hurried out back, wondering what was behind Richard's odd behavior.

"Why all the mystery?" Thom closed the shed door.

"I want privacy."

Thom gestured in all directions. "What could be more private than a house in the Beartown Mountain woods?"

"I didn't want to talk in front of Pico. It's—"

"Pico is fine. I trust him implicitly."

"I'm glad you do, but..." Richard broke eye contact, as he pushed his lips together.

"But what?"

"Nothing."

365

"Nothing...Then why'd you drag me out here into the cold?"

"I want to talk in private. Is that okay?"

"I guess...if that's the reason." Thom was far from convinced. "So, what do you want to discuss?"

"Remember I promised to let you know who blackballed you from the Minutemen, if and when I found out."

"You know?"

"Not for sure. But I have a hunch, an educated one based on facts, not mere speculation."

"So, who's my saboteur?" Thom's curiosity was far greater than he showed.

"Issac Winslow."

"Issac?...Polly's father?"

"You seem shocked?"

"Well...in recent months he's been very friendly, especially after I carried Peter up from the pond."

"I understand," said Richard, "but a fox, soft and cuddly when curled up, can turn out mighty nasty."

Issac Winslow had never seemed the foxy type, but then again, that was the very nature of the sly animal. "So, what makes you think Winslow blackballed me?"

"A conversation I had with Johnny Woodstone the other day. Some months ago Winslow told him he was checking into your background, something dating back to your days in England. He didn't tell Johnny what or why, but it was clear he had concerns. I immediately thought of the blackball, but rather than say anything, I let Johnny do the talking. Sure enough, he said it was odds-on that Winslow dropped the black ball into the hat excluding you."

"But he wasn't sure, was he?"

"No, but Johnny is a straight shooter."

Thom thought back to the days before Winslow had dashed his hopes of marrying Polly. A cordial façade gave no hint of the impending veto. The scenario squared with Richard's assessment.

"Johnny mentioned that Winslow expressed concerns about Pico. That's the reason I wanted to speak to you alone."

Thom bristled. Recently Sarah had delivered a similar

message. He didn't like it then, and the repetition irked him more. He said, "Fine, but I'm telling you: Pico is okay."

Richard frowned. "I'm only the messenger. I'm not badmouthing your Indian friend. But you need to know that as long as he's here, some will use it against you."

"Let them," snapped Thom. The dissatisfied look that greeted his eyes caused him to add, "My frustration isn't personal. I appreciate your thoughts."

"I understand. And speaking of personal, perhaps you shouldn't take the blackball personally. With war seemingly inevitable, folks are careful to whom they tell what."

Thom pointed at himself. "You telling me I shouldn't take offense when folks suggest I'm gonna side with England? You gotta be kidding."

"That's not what I'm saying."

"Fine. What are you saying?"

"I'm merely reciting the facts. Pico lives with you. You trust him. Others don't. That said, they're reluctant to treat you as a confidant."

"That's ridiculous."

"I'm not about to debate the point. I'm telling you what some are saying."

"Jeze—" Thom slowed himself, if only to curb a sarcastic tongue. "Are you suggesting I shouldn't let Pico live here?"

"I didn't say that."

Reluctantly Thom conceded the point. "If you were me, what would you do?"

"I'm not you, and I have no intention of sticking my nose into that hornets' nest. What you do about Pico is your decision."

Thom struggled to relax a clenching jaw. He hated being an outsider in the community, but no way would he send Pico away. Not only was it unthinkable, as well as unfair, but life would grow lonelier, and chores would no longer be shared. He said, "I appreciate the information. In the meantime, let's go into the house. It's a whole lot warmer...and we could both do with a brew."

"Thanks for the offer, but I told Brewer I'd stop by the mill before two. He's cutting me some planks." Richard opened the door and stepped outside. "See you later."

"You too...and thanks for the information."

"Don't mention it." Richard climbed onto his horse and rode off.

As Thom watched his friend disappear into the woods, he grappled with what he had just learned. He doubted Pico was the reason he had been blackballed. More likely someone had it in for him. Apparently that someone was Issac Winslow.

Thom leaned against the shed with sunken shoulders. All winter he had entertained the possibility of courting Polly in the spring. Spring had arrived, but *hope that had sprung eternal* had been dashed. If Winslow had dropped the black ball into the hat, no way would he approve a relationship with his daughter. And Polly would never defy her father. Thom picked up a small rock and fired it at his favorite granite boulder. The rock flew wildly wide of its mark.

⁂

"Gosh, the atmosphere in there was as tense as a fishing line with a big pike on the hook," said Paul Cooper, as he, along with Richard and Thom, left the newly built schoolhouse, one of four that had been approved for construction following the fire two years earlier.[213]

"Been a while since folks were so testy at a Town Meeting," said Richard.

"Is it surprising?" said Thom, as the trio stopped beneath a large beech tree. "With war so close and not everybody on our side, issues are bigger than repairing ruts in Mt. Hunger Road or the amount of the Reverend's salary."

Cooper, who had taken a step in the direction of his horse, stopped. "As long as you mentioned it, here's what I think. The Reverend oughta waive the past due moneys. Hell, he's one of the richest men in town."

"Yeah, but that's because he got a big inheritance. You can't hold that against him. And don't forget, when he came here

368

twenty-five years ago to help get our settlement off the ground, he gave up a thriving ministry in Kinderhook, New York."[214] Richard reached for his canteen and took a drink. He held the canteen out toward his companions. "Anyone want a swig? It's apple cider, slightly fermented."

"No thanks," said Cooper. He turned to Thom. "Whad'ya think?"

"Well...as one who rarely attends Sunday meetings, I'm in no position to judge. Still it seems we've shortchanged the Reverend. He shouldn't have to beg for what's due him. As far as his being well off, that's neither here nor there."

"So, you'd take food from the hungry to feed the Reverend's taste for English pewter and green walls."

"That's not fair. You make it sound like the Reverend is cheating people. He's an honest man and works hard." Thom looked Cooper in the eye. "You know, Paul, you're doing pretty well. Maybe it's time you give poorer folks their barrels for free?"

"No way is that the same."

"Oh really?" said Richard. "Why not?"

"Well...uh...the Reverend's a man of the cloth."

Thom threw up his hands. "What's that got to do with it?"

"You think Jesus would have lined his pockets at the expense of the poor?"

Thom didn't buy the argument, but in a perverse way it made sense. He glanced at Richard, hoping his pal had an effective rebuttal.

Richard frowned. "Enough already about the Reverend's salary. We've got more important concerns." He took another gulp of cider. "That was good news...what Deacon Hale told us (Richard gestured back toward the schoolhouse) that the Stockbridge Indians signed an alliance with our colony. Be a damn side tougher if they sided with the British."[215]

"Fellows like Jonathan Edwards and George Whitefield probably deserve the credit," said Thom.

"You think so?" said Cooper, his tone suggesting he was primed for another argument.

Though hardly eager for a battle, Thom was determined to defend his comment. "Hey, thanks to them, many of the

Stockbridge Indians are Christians. They share our values." Thom paused long enough to separate his views about the New Light preachers of the Great Awakening and the issue at hand. "Don't get me wrong. Like a lot of others, I have mixed feelings about Edwards and Whitefield and men like them. But without them, there's a good chance the Stockbridge Indians, looking to gain land and influence, would be supporting the British."

"You know," said Cooper, "I hadn't thought about it that way, but you have a point...a good one at that."

The unexpected assent was like sunshine on a day for which Thom's Almanack had predicted rain.

"What role the Indians decide to play is bound to be important. The French and Indian War proved that." Cooper's face grew pensive. "From what I've heard, efforts are being made so tribes that refuse to join our cause will at least remain neutral. Convincing them that our battle with England is a family quarrel, one they should avoid, is like a victory. That's what the British Superintendent for Indian Affairs, Sir...what's his name..."

"Sir Guy Johnson."

Cooper gestured at Thom. "Yeah, Sir Guy Johnson. Anyway, back in January at an Iroquois conference, he told the Indians that the to-do was over the Tea Party in Boston, and there was no reason for the Iroquois to get involved."[216]

"But maybe the Iroquois would help us," said Richard.

"Well...Crane said—"

"Crane!" growled Richard. "Who cares what that idiot said?"

Cooper shrugged. "I hear you...So, you think we should seek support from the Iroquois?"

"You never know," said Richard. "Last winter George Washington recruited fighters from the Passamaquoddys, St. Johns, and Penobscots...as well as the Stockbridge Indians."[217]

"We can use all the help we can get." Cooper rubbed the gnarly growth that decorated his normally clean-shaven chin. "Did anyone catch Dave Wharton's lowdown about the Indians in North Carolina and the territory to the west...something about a treaty being signed last month?"

"I heard him," said Richard, "but damn if I can remember."

"He referred to the Treaty of Sycamore Shoals," said Thom. "I believe he said it was signed on March 17th. As for the details, they're like a Boston fog on a September morn. Something about Daniel Boone and some others buying up land west of North Carolina—maybe in North Carolina too—from the Cherokees, I think. If I understood correctly, they wanted to keep the land out of British control, but whether the Cherokees or any other tribes down there would side with us or the British or whatever, you got me."[218]

"Impressive," said Cooper. He glanced at Richard. "Webster got a whole lot more than I."

"Whether I got it right is another story." Thom chuckled. He felt more a part of the group than he had in a while.

"I told you he's all right," said Richard.

"It's not me who needs convincing," said Cooper. "If it were otherwise, I never would have let Thom know about the gunpowder stored in my barn." He turned to Thom. "Don't mind us—talking about you as if you weren't here." He gave Thom a pat on the back.

The stroke felt good. Knowing others in Tyringham were less kindly disposed was troublesome.

~∞∭∞~

Thom bit into his cornbread. It was passable, considering he had made it himself. Cooking and baking were not his forte. His kitchen was stocked with an adequate supply of herbs and spices—parsley, rosemary, nutmeg, sage, cinnamon, thyme, among others—but he had few clues when to use which or how much. The lamb-based ragout he made for the afternoon meal was a perfect example. A tasty ragout demanded plenty of spices. No one could deny that Thom's was amply spiced. But spiced in a manner that made it tasty was a different story. As Richard had once put it, next to Thom's ragouts, Hogshead's hotchpots were Epicurean. Thom's cornbread had improved, not that he deserved the credit. In the past he had relied on dried pompions to sweeten what he made. Not only did they fail to do the job, but they left his cornbread, as well as other foods he prepared, with an off taste. Thanks to Pico's lessons, maple syrup, a more pleasing sweetener, was in ample supply. Sugar would have done the trick, but limited availability kept its use to a minimum.

Thom placed a poplar wood trencher filled with his ragout on the table-board that Pico had laid across the two dining-room trestles. Thom handed Pico a silver spoon, one of three, all matching, he had purchased in Boston. The spoons, old English style and among his more valuable chattels, were from the early part of the century. Their elliptical bowls, a contrast to the egg shape that was becoming increasingly popular throughout the colonies, connected to a handle with a ridge down the center and a rounded, turned up end.[219] Thom had several wooden spoons, one of which he carried in his haversack. The practice, adopted because of his long-standing habit for misplacing things, obviated the risk of losing one of his silver spoons in the woods.

Thom placed two noggins of metheglin on the table-board and seated himself across from Pico.

Pico sunk his teeth into his chunk of cornbread. "Not bad...Not bad at all." He gazed off into space. "Can't imagine what it's gonna be like, once war breaks out."

"Whad'ya mean?"

"Not a pretty picture—folks supportin' England being neighbors to those fightin' for liberty."

The anomalous situation had crossed Thom's mind loads of times. He had never seriously addressed the issue.

"Take Tyringham. You and your friends gonna visit Jenkins and shoot him and his family?"

With his spoon dug into the trencher, Thom hesitated. "Can't imagine someone shooting him." Thom shoveled a chunk of lamb into his mouth.

"What if he gives information to the British or houses their soldiers or, worse yet, joins 'em in the fighting?"

"Jenkins isn't the fighting kind, at least with a gun. He battles with his mouth."

Pico frowned.

It underscored what Thom knew. He had skirted the issue. There would be those in Tyringham who would remain loyal to King George. Whether it might be five or ten or even twenty percent, the consequences were inevitable. Neighbors would turn into foes. Friends would become enemies. Families would be cleaved. Hard as it was to comprehend, dismissing it as if it didn't exist was folly. "You're right," he said. "Folks like Jenkins, and there'll be quite a few, present a real problem. But your people surely faced the same difficulty when some chose to sign treaties with the white man while others opted to fight."

"Pico knows the history. Knows it well. War carves deep wounds. Some never heal."

"Yeah...I suppose so." Thom drifted into a shell, not the defensive posture of a tortoise, but the cloistered introspection of a philosopher. At times he and his friends, like many throughout the colonies, had viewed hostilities with a mentality of perverse exuberance. Tea parties, most notably Boston's, were celebrated as jubilant fetes of noble achievement. The packing of the courthouses in Great Barrington and Worcester, which barred the judges from their seats, as well as the march on Cambridge, were cheered like games of sport. That Britain's conduct, repressive of rights and liberty, merited a spirited response was a given, but denying that elements of mob anarchy had supplanted reason was self-serving. A gaze into the mirror revealed fault on both sides. Still, when repeatedly ignored, how else could the colonists shout loudly enough to be heard across the vast expanse of the Atlantic? There was no other way. War, as most claimed, was not only inevitable; it was imminent.

Had either side truly weighed the consequences? History was replete with wars. No nation embarked on war planning to lose. Invariably there was at least one loser. Sometimes two. The Hundred Years War, which Thom had studied as a youngster in school, popped into his head. What better example? England and France battling, mainly on French soil, capturing and losing the same territory. Back and forth, gaining and losing the upper hand, they fought on and on. In the end thousands of lives were lost, along with widespread destruction and huge financial costs on both sides. The hostilities, one hundred sixteen years, beginning in the first half of the fourteenth century and ending in the second half of the fifteenth, had been in vain. Though Thom's musing had traveled well beyond Pico's message, there was no denying that the young man across the table-board was

373

the wellspring of the observations. Pico's provocative comments had pressed Thom to examine issues he had avoided in the past. Though the ruminations spawned nothing more than a maze of unanswerable questions, such fruitless routes were better explored than ignored. Blindly embarking on war was madness. Unbridled exuberance frenetically feeding upon itself in a galvanized crowd was seductive, but sage and objective examination of potential consequences was imperative. Thom raised his noggin in Pico's direction. "Is dispassionate prudence inherent to Indian ways...or are you unique?"

Pico furrowed his brow before engaging in a moment of quiescent deliberation. "Your metheglin ferment too long, maybe?"

"Perhaps," said Thom, suspecting the admiration he had communicated had not been lost on his Indian friend.

# Chapter 23

"WE'RE AT WAR!" yelled Cooper, as he rode into the yard that fronted Thom's saltbox.

Thom, who had been clearing some twigs and small branches that had fallen during the winter months, stopped in his tracks.

"We're at war!" Cooper jumped down from his horse. "The British army has marched."

"Where?...When?"

"Not quite two days ago." Cooper grabbed a breath. "Lexington and Concord and all the way to Boston." He tied his horse to a birch.

"They still fighting?"

"Not sure. It may have ceased. But anyway, the militia drove the British army back toward Boston."

"They did what?"

"They drove the British army back toward Boston."

The image of several thousand Redcoats engaging in drills on the Boston Commons rendered the news incomprehensible. The idea that farmers, militia like those of Tyringham, could push back such a formidable force bordered on inconceivable. "Our militia repelled more than four thousand British regulars?"

"Hardly," said Cooper, shaking his head. "More like a column, somewhere between five hundred and a thousand."

"That's still amazing. And you say it was less than two days ago. That's mighty fast for us to get the word."[220]

"Apparently word is spreading like wildfire. As soon as it reaches one town, new riders are carrying it to the next. David Wharton—he's the one who told a bunch of us down at Brewer's Mill—heard it from a rider who was on his way west to Great Barrington. According to the rider the news oughta reach Baltimore within the week."

"Did Wharton tell you anything else?"

"You bet. He had it all written down. Went through it twice." Cooper took another breath. "Give me a second, so I can get it straight, and I'll tell you what I know."

"C'mon, we'll go inside." Thom led the way, and once there, poured two tankards of ale, one of which he gave to Cooper. "Okay, fill me in," he said, as they sat down in the parlor.

"Well...it seems the British—musta been on General Gage's orders—like I said, five hundred or even a thousand troops—marched on the night of the eighteenth from Boston, seventeen miles up through Menotomy and Lexington toward Concord. They planned to seize the gunpowder there and capture John Adams and John Hancock, along with a few others.[221] The gunpowder had been moved from Concord to other storehouses. After the events at Portsmouth and Salem, our leaders anticipated the British would move on caches like Concord."

"So, the fighting took place in Concord?"

"Yes and no."

Thom waited for an explanation while Cooper gulped a swig of ale.

"Somehow our leaders got wind of the British plans in advance, and riders, one circling north and one south, warned folks all across the countryside. Wharton said that the rider who went north rowed out of the city right past the British warship Somerset before making his ride.[222] Then he—"

"Slow down." Thom gestured with his mug. "You're going too fast. I'm getting lost. Go back a step to the 'yes and no', about where the fighting took place."

"It began in Lexington, and then it moved to Concord, and—"

"Wait a second. I thought you said the British were pushed back to Boston."

"Yes, toward Boston."

"But Concord is west of Lexington, while Boston is east...or maybe southeast of both. You said the fighting moved from Lexington to Concord. That's the other way."

Cooper frowned. "Patience, and I'll explain."

Familiar with the area, a map in his mind's eye, Thom stilled the urge to press his friend.

"As I told you, our riders warned the people in the countryside about the march of the British troops. On the road west to Concord, somewhere after five in the morning on the 19th, as the sun was coming up, the British troops encountered a group of Lexington Minutemen led by Colonel John Parker on the Lexington Commons.[223] According to Wharton there were about seventy-five Minutemen, with roughly that many more watching alongside the road. In any event, a shot rang out and—"

"Who fired the first shot?"

Cooper shrugged. "Parker had instructed his men to hold fire until..." Cooper pulled a paper out of his pocket. "Wharton had Parker's exact instructions written down, and I copied them. Parker told his men: 'Stand your ground; don't fire unless fired upon. But if they mean to have a war, let it begin here.'"[224]

"So—the British fired first."

Cooper shrugged again. "Wharton said the rider who gave him the information didn't know. From what he heard, nobody was sure. It could have been one of the spectators on the side of the road or someone from behind a building. Anyway, the Minutemen had begun to withdraw before the first shot, but once it rang out, the British troops charged with bayonets.[225] The Minutemen scrambled into the woods. By the time the carnage was over, eight Minutemen were dead and lots of others wounded."[226]

"Were any of the damn Redcoats killed?"

"Just one...I guess."

Thom felt his blood boil. "So, let's hear the good news—how the Redcoats got driven back to Boston."

"You're getting impatient again."

"I am not." Even as Thom spoke the words, he knew he was. He drank some ale.

"Well...the British continued west, toward Concord, dispersing detachments to search farm houses for weapons and for Adams and Hancock. All the while, more and more militiamen began gathering. They started marching toward Lexington from Concord."

"All right. This is where we drove the bastards back!"

Cooper shook his head. "The militia, which numbered about two hundred fifty, knew they were no match for the larger force of British regulars. They retreated to Concord, to a hill north of town overlooking the North Bridge."[227]

"They surrendered the town of Concord?"

"It was better than being annihilated...And relax."

Thom threw up his hands before forcing himself to calm down. "Okay...so, then what happened?"

"More Minutemen from Acton, Bedford and Lincoln joined those on the hill. Some of the British, about one hundred...or something like that, moved forward to the North Bridge and beyond. From up on the hill the militia began to advance, and so the British retreated to the bridge. Before retreating further, one of the British regulars started tearing up the bridge's planks to hinder the militia's advance.[228] A shot, one fired by a British regular, rang out."

"The bastards." Thom clenched a fist. "And I'll bet they fired the first shot at Lexington."

"Maybe...but at any rate, once the shot was fired, the battle was on. There were casualties on both sides. How many, I couldn't say. Anyway, the British, outnumbered and out-positioned and apparently lacking effective leadership, began to run back to the center of town to the safety of the rest of their troops. They left their dead and wounded behind."[229]

Thom hoisted his tankard. "So, you give the vaunted British army a fight, and they run like scared jackrabbits."

"It's not over." Cooper punctuated the comment with a snicker.

"But the British are heading east...back toward Boston."

"Well, first they searched more farms, albeit futilely, before re-assembling in Concord."

"And then they were driven back to Boston."

"Maybe. I'm not sure." Exasperation registered on Cooper's face. "But if you stop interrupting, I'll tell you all I know."

The message clear, Thom sealed his lips.

"All along the road back to Lexington more militia assembled. Their numbers grew to roughly two thousand. They had positions on the flanks of the British and everywhere. At times from behind trees and walls, at others from ambush on either side, and still others in ordered formations, they attacked the British regulars, repeatedly routing them."[230]

Thom checked an urge to interrupt again.

"From what Wharton heard, the British may have been on the verge of surrendering when a thousand reinforcements sent by General Gage arrived. The last word was that the original British companies and their reinforcements were in retreat to Boston and were taking constant fire from the ever-growing number of militiamen. I'm sure there will be more riders coming our way, but for now that's as much as we know." He turned to the east and looked off into space, as if he were trying to ascertain the events near Boston, not that the human eye could span even a tiny fraction of the more than one hundred miles of forested territory. "For all I know, the fighting could still be going on. And if so, there are no guarantees of the outcome."

"I assume our local Minutemen are readying themselves for what comes next."

"Believe it or not, they've left for Boston."

"Already?" The reaction had barely crossed Thom's lips before disappointment stirred. The information was a painful reminder of his exclusion from the elite group's ranks.

"Forty-five men, twenty-eight from Great Barrington and seventeen from here in Tyringham, marched under the command of Captain William King. How well equipped they were is another matter. One of them, Josiah Dewey from Great Barrington, had no gun."[231]

Thom glanced over his shoulder. In the back corner his smooth-bored, club butt fowler and powder horn hung on the wall. He was hardly among the best shots in Tyringham, but he had a gun. Unfortunately, he was unwelcome. He turned back to Cooper, who, for the first time, bore an expression that invited a response. Thom, who earlier had been a paradigm of impatience, stood mute. A hodgepodge of thoughts, mixed feelings, stilled his tongue. Personal disappointment abounded. Yet optimism percolated. The remarkable events around Boston could not be disregarded. The farmers had met the well-equipped, highly trained and powerful British army on the battlefield, and the men in the fancy red uniforms were on the run. Goliath was scrambling to escape David. Were one to have bet such an outcome in advance, a single shilling might have been sufficient to win several pounds. But like every shilling, the coin had another side. The war had just begun. The colonists remained underdogs. The time to celebrate lay far beyond the horizon. For the moment there was an entirely different and much less uplifting reality. For months there had been talk of war, even of its inevitability, but amidst it all, deep down many thought the differences would be resolved without guns. At isolated moments Thom was among them, though, like many others, separating hope from belief was difficult. Regardless, peaceful resolution had apparently become a wish from the past. The British army had marched out of Boston. They had crossed the Charles River. They had marched onto the North Bridge across the Concord River. And more important, they had crossed the Rubicon. War, replete with guns and bayonets, violence and death, had commenced.

⁓ᴑᴑᴐᴑᴐᴑᴑ⁓

After delivering a quart of maple syrup to Sarah, Thom boarded Lodestone and headed northwest on Mt. Hunger Road, past town center and thence north on Royal Hemlock Road to the farm of George Whitaker. Nearly two days had passed since he had heard the news of the fighting at Lexington and Concord and the retreat of the British soldiers toward Boston. He was eager for an update. Though the Hogshead and Brewer's Mill were better sites for scuttlebutt, the home of the Yankee Trader, a short distance from the Post Road and brisk with activity, was nearly as good. And Whitaker's place offered the opportunity to bag another bird with the same shot. The sconces that had caught Thom's eye many moons before were still in Whitaker's barn, at least they were a few weeks earlier. Armed with the right item to offer in trade, the time to bargain had arrived. Whitaker had an insatiable sweet tooth, and thanks to Pico, Thom had an ample supply of maple syrup. A bottle filled with fifty ounces of the saporous liquid, more precisely dark amber, lay in Thom's saddlebag.

380

"Morning," said Thom, as he climbed down from Lodestone. He tied the big stallion to the weather-grayed, split-rail fence adjoining the barn.

"Same to you," said Whitaker, who was leaning, along with Ezra Jenkins, against the zig-zagging boards of the barrier. "Need something special today?"

"Nope...just passing by, and thought I'd kill a few minutes." No way would Thom manifest designs on the sconces. He was familiar with Whitaker's methods. A customer's interest was Whitaker's cue to raise his price. Need would jack it higher yet. Thom eased his way into the barn and slowly circled the outer perimeter, confirming the sconces remained available. Sure enough, the pewter pair, in need of polish and laced with cobwebs, sat in the same spot they had occupied for countless months. Once burnished with fine sand, they would be an excellent addition over his parlor fireplace.

Thom stepped from the barn close to where Whitaker and Jenkins were standing.

"Tell me what you want, and I'll make you a fine deal." Whitaker rubbed his hands together.

"I'm sure you would. Unfortunately, or maybe fortunately, I'm overloaded with stuff."

Whitaker tugged his beard. "Not a man in town, the Reverend included, who's got everything he wants." His gaze moved to Jenkins. "Ain't that right, Ezra?"

"Yeah, I suppose...Of course, I doubt I'd find a broach laced with sapphires and rubies, the kind my Emma wants, amidst the dust-laden gimcrack in your barn."

"If that's how you feel, the next time you come lookin' for tools, don't be surprised if I send you to Crane who'll charge you top price for new."

Jenkins turned to Thom. "Our Yankee Trader oughta get himself a sense of humor. He doesn't—" Jenkins cut himself off midstream, looking in the direction where Wendell Dinsmore was approaching on the path. "Maybe this time you got a live one, George."

"Dinsmore? You gotta be kidding. Thanks to him, I've got three pairs of shoes. And most every week he gives me the same pitch when he wants something. Tells me—you can't ever have too many shoes." Whitaker turned as Dinsmore drew near. "Wendell, before you ask, the answer is *no*." Whitaker pointed at his feet. "I don't need another pair."

"I understand...but some nice boots, perhaps?"

Whitaker threw up his hands. "You see!"

Seemingly unfazed, Dinsmore headed into the barn.

A frown on his face, Whitaker shook his head. "Give him a few minutes, and he'll be out, trying to get me to make a trade."

"George..." The shrill voice of Whitaker's wife calling from the house turned his head in her direction.

"I believe someone is calling you," said Jenkins, his high-pitched, sugary tone followed by a mocking smile.

"George! I need you right away."

"Coming, Dear." Whitaker heaved a sigh. "And don't either of you say another word." He hurried into the house.

"You see what you're missing," said Jenkins.

Much as Thom often wished he had a wife, at that moment his bachelor status had advantages, especially if one were wearing Whitaker's shoes. Even a new pair from Dinsmore couldn't alleviate the discomfort occasioned by Tyringham's version of the untamed shrew.

"So, what are you looking to buy today?"

"Me?...uh...nothing."

"Sure." Jenkins dragged out the word. "You're here purely on a social call."

The lawyer with loyalist views was not Thom's first choice when it came to getting information about the recent outbreak of hostilities, but satisfying his curiosity, whatever the source, was preferable to acknowledging his interest in the sconces. "It's been nearly two days since I've heard anything about the events in Boston, and as long as I was passing by, what with George sure to be as up to date as anyone, I decided to stop." Thom anticipated Jenkins, ever talkative, would indicate what he had heard. The expected response was not forthcoming. "Don't tell me you have nothing to say?"

"Now that we're at war, one needs to be careful with whom he speaks." Jenkins put a hand to his heart. "My loyalties to England have been repeated many times. Everyone knows where I stand. As for you, that's less clear."

"C'mon, you know I'm with the colonies."

"No need to convince me...Some of your neighbors think otherwise."

The remark rankled Thom, but no way could he blame the lawyer for the aspersions of others. He said, "Even though we're on opposite sides, doesn't mean we can't talk."

Jenkins, as he was prone to do, pulled back in a display of histrionic surprise. "Am I refusing to talk?"

"No, but I thought you might give me an update on the events near Boston. It's not like I'm asking you to disclose monumental military secrets."

A hint of a scowl materialized between the lawyer's lumpy jowls. "I know...you want to rub it in. Brief success has you rebels wallowing in ephemeral glory. Well, be my guest. Go ahead and enjoy, because your foolishness is certain to increase King George's resolve. And that will mean more troops and more ships crossing the sea to suppress insurrection. No way will he or Parliament allow upstart seditionist farmers to call the shots. Papa Bear doesn't take orders from his little cubs."

"True...but little cubs grow into big bears."

Jenkins bristled. "Keep it up, and I won't update you about the fighting."

While Thom sensed that apologetic words would smooth ruffled feathers, knowing others could provide the news, the temptation to gibe the bombastic lawyer was seductive. But uncertain how matters had turned out in Boston, he was loath to flirt with a serving of humble pie. He said, "The last I heard the British troops were near Lexington retreating to Boston."

"Then perhaps you didn't hear that another thousand British troops under the command of Lieutenant-General Hugh Percy came to the aid of those that had marched to Concord and back to Lexington." Jenkins paused, a satisfied smile on his face.[232]

"I heard that but understood the British were in retreat." With a change of fortunes possible, Thom commended the restraint he had exercised moments before. "Did the British regain the upper hand?"

"Well—not exactly."

"What does that mean?"

"Apparently more and more militiamen arrived from all across the countryside, and, rather than fighting fairly, they took advantage of the surrounding woods and hills, harassing the British forces the entire way back to Boston. From what I heard, the fighting grew more intense as the British crossed from Lexington into Menotomy and across the Menotomy River into Cambridge and on into Charleston.[233]

Knowing that Jenkins was reluctant to ever concede anything, Thom suspected he might be getting a massaged version of the conflict. He doubted the Redcoats would have kept retreating if they weren't taking a beating. "So, the British were pushed all the way back to Boston?"

"Who said pushed?"

Thom looked Jenkins in the eye. If the lawyer wished to parse words, let him. The point was made.

"Anyway...the rebels' unseemly tactics angered the British troops to the point where they fired artillery pieces into an oncoming mass of militiamen. That dispersed the scoundrels."

"Did the fighting continue all the way to Boston?"

Jenkins bore an incredulous look. "If it had, the militia would have been annihilated. Shooting from behind trees and from hilltops, they got in their potshots, but a face-to-face battle between a mass of bumpkins and a powerful fighting force...you must be kidding."

"Were there many casualties?"

"According to the grapevine, about seventy-five British troops and fifty colonists killed over the thirty-plus hours of fighting. Of course, there were a lot more wounded on both sides.[234]

With a nod more thoughtful than acquiescent, Thom digested the unfortunate carnage. To get a fuller and more balanced description of the events, he would need to speak with others.

Dinsmore came from the barn. Thom was about to inquire if he had found anything of interest, but before he could, Jenkins blurted out, "You folks may get the chance to use that gunpowder you stored in Cooper's barrels."

The remark startled Thom. Those in the know had presumably been careful to keep such information from a Loyalist such as Jenkins.

Dinsmore glared at Thom.

A lump in his throat, Thom could only imagine the discomfiture on his face.

"Seems you fellows are having a *very* interesting conversation." Dinsmore's fiery eyes trained squarely on Thom.

"You might say that." Jenkins stuffed his thumbs into the pockets of his stylish waistcoat. "What with fighting breaking out in Lexington and Concord, there's lots to talk about."

"So I see," said Dinsmore. His gaze, which had briefly shifted to Jenkins, redirected to Thom, and by the time it did, it was laden with daggers.

"Before you...uh...came out, Ezra was telling me what he had heard about the fighting."

"That so?" The remark slid across Dinsmore's lips as smoothly as Santa Cruz rum on a hot summer day.

"It's not like—" Thom clipped his tongue. The cordwainer's ears were deaf to explanations.

"Well, like the old adage says: 'Two's a couple, and three's a crowd.' So, far be it from me to be the third man up on a two-seated buckboard. You gents have a real fine day." Dinsmore turned and headed down the path that led to Royal Hemlock Road.

Once Dinsmore was out of earshot, Thom said, "What was that about?"

Jenkins displayed a blank look.

"Don't give me that! You know exactly what I mean—the talk about gunpowder out of the blue."

In signature mode, the self-styled lawyer adopted a deeply shrugged pose, one that all but negated his short, corpulent neck.

"Where did you hear about the gunpowder?"

Jenkins bore a pensive cast, but one that was unabashedly feigned. "Excellent question." He scratched his head. "Did you by any chance mention it to me last week or—"

"I did no such thing. And you know it!"

"C'mon...no need to get excited. I was merely trying to recall where I got my information. Anyway, what's the big deal?"

"What's the big deal?" Thom's instincts forewarned him of the futility of debating with the supercilious shyster; exasperation superseded judgment. "We all know about the powder alarms in Portsmouth and Salem. Now that fighting, apparently war, has broken out, any type of arms are a big deal." Thom pointed a finger at Jenkins. "You and I may be neighbors, but the way things are, we're turning into enemies."

"It doesn't have to be that way." Jenkins tacked on an ingratiating smile.

The unctuous expression infuriated Thom more. "A stone-deaf mule is more—"

"Not to change the subject, but you'll never guess whom I saw walking along the Konkapot near Brewer's Mill a few weeks back."

"King George's great-grandmother!"

"Fine...If you're not interested, I won't tell you."

Thom was curious, but not so much that he would give Jenkins the satisfaction of showing it.

"One was male...and the other, female. The latter happened to be Polly Blake." Jenkins studied Thom for an instant. "I knew it would grab your interest."

Thom struggled to appear impassive.

"Her escort was none other than your buddy...Richard Thorn."

"Big deal. So they both happened to be down at the mill."

"I said they were *near* the mill, walking along the river. And if you ask me, they had more than walking in mind."

"I didn't ask you!"

"Whoa—somebody is irascible, not to mention jealous." Jenkins displayed a smirk as pronounced as his portly torso.

"You two going at one another?"

The sound of Whitaker's voice, as he returned from the house, drew Thom's attention.

Whitaker drew closer. "I leave you fellows alone for ten minutes, and right away you're arguing."

"Not me."

"Ezra, you belong on stage."

"That's uncalled for...Thomas."

Thom contrived a look of surprise.

"Your remark was no compliment," said Jenkins.

"Perhaps you took it wrong. Why down South, say in North Carolina, folks get praised for acting skills."

"That's the point. Unlike southern secularists, here in Massachusetts, decent folks, good Congregationalists, know that playacting is immoral frivolity. Reverend Bidwell would tell you that, and he'd also tell you that ridiculing folks, dressing spiteful words in warm, homespun costumes, isn't Godlike."

Though far from a panacea, the lawyer's unmistakable indignation had palliative effects. Thom had managed to get under the windbag's skin.

Jenkins turned to Whitaker. "George, perhaps you can curtail your friend's rude propensities."

Whitaker rolled his eyes, more likely owing to the pomposity with which the request had been uttered, rather than what had been asked. "No way you gonna saddle me with your dirty work." He pointed at the barn. "Is Dinsmore in there?"

"Nah, he left a few minutes ago," said Thom.

"Without hocking me to give him a prized possession for another pair of shoes? What's the world coming to?" Whitaker raised his hands to the Heavens. "So, Thom, what great item of need brought you here today?"

"Nothing. Just a social call."

"Yeah...sure."

"Really, I was passing by on my way back from bringing Sarah Albright a bottle of maple syrup—Gosh, we had a helluva flow this year—and I—"

"You got lots of maple syrup?"

"Yup, mostly dark amber...but as I was saying, I stopped here to get an update on the fighting. You might say Ezra filled me in on it, and I—"

"I could use some syrup, especially dark amber." Whitaker gestured at his barn. "I'm sure there are lotsa treasures in there you'd love to have."

"As I told you earlier, I looked around, not that I was in a looking mood, and I didn't see a thing. Course, it's not surprising. Why just the other day I was telling Pico that we've accumulated far too much stuff."

"You can't ever have too much stuff. Isn't that right, Ezra?"

"George, you're talking to the wrong guy. You want someone to push your wares, you'd be better asking my Emma. She'll give the answer you're looking for."

"You're no help." A scowl transformed into a smile as Whitaker laid an arm over Thom's shoulder. "If you take another look, I'm sure you'll find something of interest."

"Doubt it. Anyway, I'm gonna pass. Too bad, because I got a bottle with fifty sweet ounces sitting in my saddlebag right now."

Whitaker's eyes widened. "Let's take a gander."

"Seems you two might wanna do some business. No need for me to hang around." Jenkins headed off, as Whitaker pushed Thom in the direction of Lodestone, where Thom removed the dark brown bottle. He shook it before pulling the cork from the top. He rubbed the moistened cork on Whitaker's finger.

Whitaker licked the digit. "Not bad. Not bad at all...Let's go into the barn."

Thom stuffed the cork back into the bottle.

Whitaker tugged Thom's arm.

"Okay, I'll look...but don't expect me to trade." As he entered, Thom put the bottle on a table that adjoined the barn door. He circled the interior. "Didn't see a thing."

"You ran around as if you were in a race. You call that looking?"

"I don't need anything."

"How 'bout a froe?"

"Got one."

"What about..." Whitaker looked around as he seemingly searched for the right suggestion.

"Well...not that I need them, but just to make you happy, I'd part with a pint of maple syrup for those dusty, cob-webbed sconces back in the corner."

"A pint! You must be joking. They're worth at least a gallon. Maybe more."

"Hold it. You're the one looking to trade. I was trying to be neighborly. If you don't like my offer, we can forget the whole thing." Thom started toward the barn door.

"Relax. Let's talk...negotiate."

Thom glanced back but took two more steps toward the door.

"A half gallon...dark amber...and you got a deal."

"I'll tell you what—and it's only because I have that bottle with me—I'll give it to you for the sconces."

"A mere fifty ounces for a pewter pair. You can't be serious?"

"Hey, you don't have to do it. And by the way, those sconces haven't moved in two years. Chances are they won't in the next two either."

Whitaker stared at the dark bottle that sat on the table near the barn door. "Damn it, Webster. You've twisted my arm. You've got a deal."

⌒⁀⁀⁀⌒

Prepared to join the rest of the militia, Thom arrived at town center, a short distance south of Reverend Bidwell's property. As the local Minutemen had done a few days earlier, the militia was marching to Boston. Word had it that thousands of militiamen from all across Massachusetts and nearby New Hampshire, Rhode Island and Connecticut had begun converging within a day after the British troops had returned from their ill-fated excursion to Lexington and Concord. According to the reports, conditions in Boston had deteriorated. Militiamen had surrounded the peninsula from Charleston southward to Roxbury.[235]

David Wharton pushed his way toward Thom. "What do you think you're doing here?"

"Pardon me," said Thom, unsure if he had heard the inquiry correctly.

"You're not marching with this militia."

"Why not?"

Wharton looked Thom in the eye. "I think you know."

Thom shook his head, though for the first time he had a notion.

"Dinsmore told us about your conversation with Jenkins at Whitaker's place. Everyone knows that Jenkins is loyal to Britain. Anyone who would tell that Tory about our stash of powder is no friend of ours. To put it bluntly, enemy spies aren't welcome in our ranks."

The explanation was exactly what Thom had feared. "It's...it's all a misunderstanding."

"A misunderstanding?" Wharton glowered. "Tell me another."

"Really. I didn't tell Jenkins about the powder. I swear. He brought—"

"You calling Dinsmore a liar?" Wharton's bark underscored that the allegation would provoke outrage.

"I...uh...know what Dinsmore heard, but it's—"

"So, you admit it's true."

"No, it's not like it seemed."

Wharton folded his arms. "Fine. Let's hear your side."

Thom swallowed hard. His explanation, the truth, would come across like a convenient fabrication. "Just when Dinsmore was coming out of Whitaker's barn, Jenkins told me that he knew about the powder in Cooper's barrels. I didn't tell him about it. I...I have no idea how he knew."

"You expect me to believe that Jenkins, an astute lawyer, chose an inopportune moment to mention the powder for no reason." Wharton pointed a menacing finger Thom's way. "But just for the sake of argument, assuming, as you claim, that Jenkins already knew about the powder—not that I buy the assumption—he would have mentioned it to you only if he were sure you were also a Loyalist."

The argument caught Thom off guard.

"Your silence says it all." Wharton shook his head and muttered under his breath, "Crane was right a few months back when he warned us about you. Too bad we didn't listen." Wharton stormed off.

Thom watched as the other militiamen began forming lines. There was no purpose in trying to join their ranks. Evidence said he was loyal to the enemy. No one was willing to march side by side with a spy.

∼∽∩∩∩∩∽∼

"How come you're back already?" said Pico, who, with hoe in hand, stood at the edge of the garden.

"I wasn't welcome." Thom shuffled over to the plot.

"Not welcome? How come?"

"They think I'm a Loyalist...a damn Tory."

"You—of all people. Why?"

"Remember I told you what happened at Whitaker's barn...how Dinsmore overheard Jenkins commenting about the stash of powder in Cooper's barrels?"

"Just 'cause of that, they're cuttin' you out?"

"What can I say?"

"Don't need to." Pico jammed his hoe into the soft earth. "Your so-called neighbors are creeps. Indians, white men—they're all the same."

"What's that mean?"

"Ah, don't mind me. Just comparin' your pot to mine, not that now's the time to be goin' on about myself. Last thing you wanna hear."

"Oh yeah?" said Thom, his curiosity piqued. "You know what they say, 'Misery loves company.' So, be my guest."

"Well..." Pico leaned on his hoe. "Bein' half-Indian and half-white, folks in the tribe, especially the kids, treated me like the varmints that ate their maze. That's why my Mom tried the white man's world. It turned out worse. Once she died, knowin' I wasn't this or that, I took off on my own. Wasn't 'cause I wanted to. Just that the other choices were worse."

"I understand, but..." Thom's own situation remained foremost in his mind. "Unlike you, I'm not half and half. I'm all Patriot." The pained look that greeted his eyes prompted second thoughts. The distinction he had drawn purported to justify the prejudice that Pico had endured. "Sorry. You're right. We've both been ostracized for no good reason."

Thom went to the shed to fetch a spade. His mind remained focused on the conversation. How Pico was born was

391

totally beyond his control. That people excluded him was bigotry. The discrimination Thom experienced was political. With war begun and sides chosen, the colonists had to be wary of spies. Suspecting Thom of duplicity, though erroneous, was not irrational. Moments earlier, Thom had reacted as if his exclusion were the more egregious. He had gotten it backwards. Pico, not he, had the greater right to complain. It was possible that Pico had drawn that very conclusion. Rather than making the point, he had exercised discretion and, as he was wont to do, chosen silence.

# Chapter 24

DURING THE REMAINING DAYS of April and early May 1775, information about the state of affairs in and around Boston circulated throughout Massachusetts and all of the colonies. The network of riders, one that had developed well before the hostilities at Lexington and Concord, had grown more efficient. Over those weeks following the initial shots, though the threat of armed conflict constantly loomed, for all intents and purposes the status quo persisted. But word that the Patriots had driven the powerful British army back to Boston, routing the Redcoats along the way, had buoyed the colonists. Reports that the militiamen had the British army bottled up in Boston, with the sea their lone source of supplies or route of escape, emboldened the Patriots. Support for their cause swelled. Still some, not merely Loyalists, disputed the wisdom of war. Demand rights, indeed, but compromise. That was their mantra.

From across the sea, amidst the rattling of sabers, came signals suggesting the door to a peaceful resolution remained ajar. Word had come that some in Parliament had proposed ample concessions to the colonies in order to avert armed conflict. In March, Edmund Burke had implored Parliament to exercise sovereignty over the colonies if they consented.[236] Rumors circulated that Benjamin Franklin, who was in London, was working behind the scenes with Admiral Viscount Lord Richard Howe to reach a settlement. Franklin sought annulment of all legislation governing the American colonies that had been passed without their representation. His sole concession was payment, which at one point he offered from his own pocket, for the tea destroyed during the Boston Tea Party.[237] And there was the possibility that the hawkish Lord North's Conciliatory Resolution (providing that any colony that contributed to the common defense and supported the existing government would be relieved of any taxes, except those involving commerce) might gain support in Parliament.[238] Radicals on the western side of the Atlantic shunned the Resolution as a ploy, a stratagem to split the colonies;[239] and the fact it had been sent separately to each colony, bypassing the Continental Congress, supported their argument.

Other actions across the sea suggested that those seeking reconciliation were chasing pie in the sky. The enactment of the New England Trade and Fisheries Act, prohibiting New England from trading with any nation other than England, was a prime example. Extension of the Act to New Jersey, Pennsylvania, Maryland, Virginia and South Carolina added to the evidence,[240] as did revelations that General Gage had been directed to use force to impose the terms of the Coercive Acts.

With each passing month it grew more likely that the colonists would have to battle for the freedom their ancestors had sought when they had sailed from England to the New World a century and a-half before. Echoes of the shots fired at Lexington and Concord drowned out assertions that war might be avoided.

As spring entrenched itself, for the most part Thom remained cloistered at his homesite with Pico. Now and then the two fished the Konkapot River and Twelve-Mile Pond. On a couple of occasions Thom visited Brewer's mills, but not once did he attend a town meeting or Sunday service at Reverend Bidwell's, and he never visited the Hogshead. Among the Tyringham Patriots he was *persona non grata*. The Tyringham Loyalists, likely less than ten percent of the population, had no desire to associate with him either, not that Thom desired their company. The last thing he needed was to lend credence to the notion he was a Tory. And so, Thom spent his days largely within the boundaries of his own land. Ordinarily that might have been fine, but doing it because he was unwelcome left a nasty taste in his mouth. With most of his neighbors zealously united, Thom felt like an outsider. Emotional fetters, not physical barriers, imprisoned him.

Doubtless Richard would have been there for Thom, but like so many others he had gone to Boston joining the Minutemen and the militia who had surrounded the city.

394

Fortunately, Thom had one neighbor upon whom he could rely—Sarah Albright. At least once each week he went to her home. She appreciated his visits, as well as the chores he did, but unlike the past, Thom deemed himself the greater beneficiary. He was happy to have a friend outside the confines of his property. And too, Sarah enabled him to keep abreast of ongoing events. Such were his circumstances one rainy, mid-May day when he arrived at her house.

"Quick—come in before you drown," said Sarah, the moment she opened the door.

"Once I reset a loose stone in your walkway."

"You'll do no such thing." She grabbed his sleeve and tugged before he could return to the walkway. "Get in here this instant! You can adjust that ridiculous rock some other time."

Thom stepped inside and wiped his shoes and allowed any dripping from his clothes to subside. He hung his tri-cornered hat on a peg adjacent to the door. Sarah brought him a cloth with which he wiped his face and hands. He followed her into the kitchen, seating himself on the bench that lined the wall opposite the window. Sarah poured two mugs of cider.

"Let's go into the dining room. It's more comfortable."

Damp as he was, Thom might have resisted, but knowing Sarah preferred a seat with a back, rather than the kitchen bench, he followed her into the more formal space. As he entered, the English Bracket Clock that adorned the mantle opposite the fireplace, one of Sarah's most prized possessions, chimed noon. The twelve melodious rings, coupled with Thom's indecorous state, made him all the more conscious of the room's grace. He seated himself at the Hepplewhite style table, taking note of its fine workmanship. He had plans to make something similar to replace the trestles and board in his saltbox. It wasn't that the existing arrangement was impractical or embarrassingly pedestrian—indeed a board and trestles was the benchmark in Tyringham—but Thom appreciated finer things, and more so when they were self-made. With his cabinet-making skills growing, he was developing the wherewithal to decorate his home with his own finely crafted handiwork.

"A lot's been happening in recent days," said Sarah, as she placed a tray of scones in the center of the table and seated herself.

"You talking about Lexington and Concord...or perhaps the siege of Boston?"

"I know you're aware of those. I'm referring to news that just arrived. For one: The Second Continental Congress convened in Philadelphia about a week ago, and one of our own, John Hancock, was elected president.[241] Can you imagine that?"

The disclosure reminded Thom of the numerous times he and his friends had debated whether the other colonies would leave radical Massachusetts to fend for itself once push came to shove. Subsequent events had proved otherwise. Still the outbreak of hostilities had the potential to spark a new reluctance. If so, the penchant was yet to take hold. The election of John Hancock, a citizen of Massachusetts, suggested the colonies remained united. Lord North's conciliatory wedge had failed to divide them.

"At Sunday's meeting Reverend Bidwell told us about a major coup in New York. He heard about it from a rider who stayed at his home. According to the rider, on the same day that the Continental Congress reconvened, a band led by Benedict Arnold and Ethan Allen captured Fort Ticonderoga. They did it without firing a shot. All the British soldiers were asleep. Even the one sentry was dozing."[242] Sarah paused, as she appeared to study Thom. "You don't seem impressed."

He shrugged. "Strikes me that any fort that can be taken so easily can't be all that valuable."

"You know where it's located?"

"Over the New York border, a hundred fifty or so miles north and a little west of here...I think."

"That's about right," said Sarah. "It's in a narrow stretch near the southern end of Lake Champlain, not far from the northern tip of Lake George. That's what makes it strategically important. It blocks the northern access of ships coming down from Canada along the New York-Vermont border."

"Not all that effectively, given that it was taken without a shot." Thom suppressed a smug laugh.

"So you think." Sarah's inflection bore a hint of sarcasm. "Of course, you were just a youngster in England back in the 1750s during the French and Indian War when sixteen thousand British troops tried unsuccessfully to take it, then called Fort Carillon, from a French force one-quarter the size."[243]

Thom, who was sipping his cider, choked.

"A year or so later the British managed to capture it, and that's when they renamed it Fort Ticonderoga. The name—Pico could tell you—comes from the Iroquois word *Cheonderoga*, which means 'place between two waters.'[244] Besides its strategic location, its recent capture has a more important aspect. Care to guess?"

Thom would have loved to, if only to gain a measure of redemption, but he had no clue. He shrugged, this time from embarrassment.

"Until now, our militias throughout the colonies had almost no cannons. All that has changed. The walls of Fort Ticonderoga were lined with them, close to one hundred from what I've heard. Battlefields are apt to become more level, now that the British aren't the only ones armed with heavy artillery. Of course, there's still the challenge of getting them from the fort to...wherever. You still don't seem impressed."

"Just the opposite. But I had to wipe the egg from my face before reacting." Thom thought for a moment. "Hard to believe...First we drove the British back to Boston. Next we surrounded the City. Now Fort Ticonderoga has been captured without a shot." He leaned back. "Seems the peerless reputation of the Redcoats may be tarnishing. Perhaps turning yellow."

"Folks at Sunday's meeting had the same feeling. Well—not that the Redcoats are cowards, but that they're not invincible."

Thom breathed a sigh.

"Why the moan?"

He lowered his gaze. "Can't you guess?"

"When you put it that way, I think I can."

Thom suspected she had surmised that his status as an outcast had occasioned the reaction. Rehashing that disheartening subject was not his preference. He said, "Any word about the current situation in Boston?"

"From what I've heard, roughly fifteen thousand militiamen have poured in, not just from Massachusetts, but Connecticut, Rhode Island and New Hampshire as well. Pretty much *ad hoc*. In the meantime the Committee on Safety, using the powers granted by the Provincial Congress, has attempted to organize an army, rather than militias that act independently. According to Reverend Bidwell, the Committee on Safety is in the process of raising an organized and disciplined army of eight thousand."

*Eight thousand.* Thom contemplated the number. "Before Lexington and Concord, seems I heard that General Gage had forty-five hundred Redcoats under his command."

Sarah nodded. "That's my recollection too. Of course, it won't be any surprise if King George sends more once he gets word of the fighting and the retreat to Boston."

"Hmm..." said Thom, thinking out loud. "Assuming a ship left Boston within a day or two after the British army returned there, and depending upon the Atlantic winds, King George ought to be receiving the bad news within a few days."

"I'd love to be there for his reaction," said Sarah. "And better yet, when he hears that Ticonderoga fell because his soldiers were asleep."

Thom ran the edge of his hand across his throat. "I have a feeling the heads of several British officers may roll."

"Literally?"

That the inquiry was presumably facetious did not deter Thom from responding. "No. Though in General Gage's case, I wouldn't shed any tears."

∽∾∿∾∽

The second half of May drifted by, and so too did the first two weeks of June. Apart from Sarah, Thom had little contact with the outside world. Were it not for Pico, his circumstances might have provoked gloom. But having one loyal friend with whom he worked, ate and laughed each and every day made a huge difference. Any blues paled when compared to the misery that had ensued three years earlier when he had been denied Polly's hand in marriage.

With their broad array of combined skills, Pico and Thom lived an easier life than most in Tyringham. Though their diet was hardly Epicurean, their table was rich with meat and fish, thanks mainly to Pico's hunting and fishing talents. From the cellar came an ample supply of vegetables from the preceding year's crop, and soon their enlarged and improved garden would yield more of the fresh variety. From the skins of two deer that Pico had killed, Sarah had sewn them each a new deerskin vest and pants. Thom had added more shelves to the walls of his saltbox, made shutters for the windows and laid a limestone walkway leading to the garden. His home with enhancements exceeded the vision that had predated its construction. When winter arrived, not that he was wishing away the upcoming summer, he would build more furniture, including a dining room table. Earlier plans were yielding to a more versatile option. He was leaning toward a popular New England style, a chair whose tall back had a large round tabletop attached. When folded down, it became a table.[245] Besides eating there, he and Pico would use it for leisurely pastimes, among them cribbage. First Thom would need to teach Pico the game. A mental image of a hutch for the parlor had also taken shape.

Within the confines of his plot, Thom's life was good. When he ventured further, whether in actuality or via his imagination, misgivings, lurking below the surface, bubbled forth. Further yet from the confines of his land, a far more violent prospect, war, was brewing. Were it not for Sarah, Thom might have closed himself off from the outside world, opting for the predictable security, comfort and serenity of his acreage. Looking over the trees that lay beyond the clearing fronting his home, his eyes could move laterally from the southeast to the southwest. Off to his left, in the morning he could watch the sun climb above the treetops. In the evening, to his right, pastel palettes of pink and lapis floated over towering oaks and pines, soon yielding to the chimerical twinkle of a celestial panorama. Unwelcome as he was in the countryside that lay beyond his saltbox and the surrounding woods, coupled with the Heavens above, the vista largely defined his universe.

It was the twenty-first of June, but inordinately chilly for the first day of summer. Three-weeks had passed since he had been to Sarah's. She had been away, twenty miles to the north in Pittsfield, visiting a cousin. Before she had left, she had arranged in advance for Thom and Pico to join her for dinner that late June day. It was shortly after midday when she answered their knock at her door.

"Don't you two look smart?" Sarah gestured at their deerskin pants and vests.

"Our favorite seamstress used her extraordinary talents to fashion them."

"And fashion them splendidly, she did," said Pico.

"Flattery will get you everywhere."

Thom pulled back melodramatically. "Does not your Bible chasten you to spurn such compliments, lest vanity prevail?"

"It does indeed, but gracious host that I am, rather than denigrate the honeyed words of my guests, I painfully swallow them." With theatrics no less than Thom's, she exhibited a tortured look.

Bouquets excessive, Thom suppressed the urge, albeit sincere, to pay tribute to her endearing sense of humor. Not all in Tyringham enjoyed her knack for intermingling lighthearted propensities with austere Congregationalist values.

Sarah led the way into the dining room. Three place settings with polished pewter chargers atop her glazed Holland board-cloth indicated they were in for one of her special meals. Thom could all but see the Hepplewhite style table that lay beneath.[246] "Exquisite, as always," he said.

She motioned them to sit before heading into the kitchen.

"At least let us help bring in the food," said Thom.

"Well...if you insist."

Minutes later they were all seated, their respective platters bearing a Cornish hen, buttered waxed beans, pompion casserole and pickled purple cabbage. Sarah poured them each a noggin of Santa Cruz rum.

Pico took a sip and then turned to Thom. "Is this ever a step up from that carrot beer you whipped up last week."

"Have you ever tasted his goldenrod brew?" said Sarah.[247]

"Have I ever." Pico displayed a pallid expression. "'Course, it's a far side better than the dandelion cider he makes each spring."

400

Thom curbed the temptation to defend himself, silently conceding that several of his alcoholic brews, particularly those from squash and beets, as well as those Pico had mentioned, left much to be desired. Stacking them up to Sarah's Santa Cruz rum, was like comparing Hogshead slop to the victuals they were about to consume. Utensils in hand, Thom *spoiled the hen* on his platter. One taste confirmed the wisdom of avoiding a defense of his homemade beverages. His tongue could better be used to savor the scrumptious meal. They dined quietly, their occasional conversation given to praise the repast.

With platters cleared, and each replaced by a dish of Indian pudding, symmetrically dotted with dried plums, and topped with a sauce of molasses, butter and milk,[248] Sarah said, "What do you think about the latest fighting near Boston?"

"New fighting?" said Thom.

"You haven't heard?"

Thom shrugged. "Need I remind you that I'm not the most popular person in Tyringham?"

"Well, seeing as how it's the talk everywhere, I just thought...but anyway...The colonial troops somehow got word that the British army, in an effort to break the Patriot stronghold around Boston, planned to occupy the Dorchester Heights, and—"

"Where are the Dorchester Heights?" said Pico.

"Charlestown...to the north of the city." Sarah held up her hands as if invoking an imaginary map. "When the Patriots observed a buildup of British troops off the coast, they dug in on an overlooking hill. Just before I left Pittsfield, someone told me it was Bunker Hill, but others here in Tyringham claim it was Breed's Hill.[249] I guess they're next to one another. Anyway, whichever it was, about three thousand British troops tried to march up the slope. About twelve hundred colonists were at the top, waiting behind an earthen fortification they had made the night before."

"Sounds like the British had the numbers, but the colonists had the location," said Thom.

"You're right about the location. As for numbers, from what I understand, the colonists had another twelve hundred behind the fortifications protecting their flanks. So the troops on each side were fairly even."

A vivid image of the scene appeared in Thom's mind. "The colonists must have given them hell. Mowed the Redcoats down as they marched up the hill."

"Not exactly," said Sarah. "Keep in mind—the Redcoats' guns have bayonets, and they could get close before they were in range of the colonists' muskets. The way it was told to me, the colonists' commander, General Prescott, ordered his men to hold their fire until they saw the whites of the British eyes."[250]

"Don't tell me the colonists waited so long they were overrun," said Thom.

"No, but..."

"Sarah, I don't like the sound of that hesitation." Thom shoveled a spoonful of Indian pudding into his mouth.

Sarah glanced at Pico. "Is he this irascible when he's at home with you?"

"Even worse." A smile showed on Pico's face, as he struggled not to laugh.

"Now that you two have had your fun, tell me what happened."

Sarah, as if she hadn't heard Thom, sipped from a teacup. "Loosestrife—it's no better than blackberry, hardhack, dittany, goldenrod or you name it. What I wouldn't give for a *real* cup of tea."[251]

"Are you going to tell us what happened?" said Thom, despite sensing impatience would only prolong his wait.

"Well...the colonists repelled the first advance of the British...and the second too." Sarah took another sip. She gave the cup an acerbic stare. "But on the third advance the British broke through the colonists' lines and captured the hill."

"Jesus." Thom caught the dip of Sarah's eyebrows. "Excuse my ill-chosen table language, but I take it the Redcoats prevailed."

"Not exactly."

Though better than an out-and-out *yes*, the answer, far from an unequivocal *no*, left Thom unsatisfied. "What is that supposed to mean?" he said, his pique poorly disguised.

"That you, my friend, are cranky."

Coming from Pico, the jab caught Thom off guard. Though doubtless in jest, it forced him to confront himself. Barking at Sarah, especially after she had gone to great lengths to serve them a delicious dinner, was inappropriate. "I'm sorry. I—"

"No need to apologize. I asked for it. Dragging my story out wasn't cricket, especially when folks around these parts are giving you..."

"...a hard time?" Thom completed her comment once it appeared she might leave it unfinished.

An abashed look on her face, she nodded.

In his most indulgent moments Thom managed to make allowances for the attitude of his Tyringham neighbors. If he were in their shoes and concerned that someone might be an enemy spy, would he not spurn the individual? Most times he was less forgiving. People had no right to treat him like a leper. He had done nothing wrong. The familiar ruminations percolated, but knowing he was not alone, he forced himself to curtail the silent debate. "So, what was the outcome at the Dorchester Heights?"

"I'm not altogether sure...at least when it comes to picking the winner and loser. From what I was told, both sides declared victory. The British pointed to the fact they captured the hill. The colonists countered with numbers. Over two hundred Redcoats were killed, more than twice what the colonists lost. The Redcoats had far more wounded. But arguably the most significant upshot was less concrete. British claims that their highly trained lines would rout the farmers have been deflated again."[252]

Thom turned to Pico. "Seems you were right." He looked back at Sarah. "Pico predicted that the British would be in for a rude awakening once real fighting broke out."

"What made you think that?" said Sarah.

"Folks defending their homes and freedom have more at stake than paid soldiers. They may lack training, weapons and uniforms, but they've got a cause."

*Might the same have been said about the Indians when defending their lands against the newly arriving colonists?* The unseemly history inherent in the question kept Thom from voicing it. Quick analysis reinforced the decision. Pico had

403

pointed out the advantage of greater motivation. He had not suggested that it guaranteed victory. The colonists needed to keep that in mind as they embarked upon war.

"Breed's...or Bunker Hill...may change the conflict," said Pico.

"You think so?" said Sarah.

"Yeah, war's expensive, especially if you gotta send troops across an ocean."

"Yes...but...so what?" said Thom.

"Well, England may have assumed their first shows of force would end rebellion. Appears they were wrong. They could be in for a long war. Folks back home may not wanna pay for it."

"Excellent point." Sarah turned to Thom. "You agree, don't you?"

"Uh...yes," he said, momentarily distracted by another notion. The echo of his halfhearted concurrence prompted him to add, "Absolutely." He refocused on his other thought. Pico's logic had outpaced his own. All along Thom had known his Indian friend was bright. There was no doubt about that. Still Thom had been selling him short. In Thom's mind Pico was bright—for an Indian. The haughty realization, one he had entertained before, had Thom swallowing hard. Egalitarianism was one of his hallmarks, at least so he thought. A hard look in the mirror was overdue. He glanced at Pico, thankful his friend was unable to read his mind.

"There have been some other goings on of late," said Sarah.

"More fighting?" said Pico.

"No, but preludes perhaps. Our provincial Committee on Safety had been in command of our militias. The Second Continental Congress has assumed control of the army, and about the same time that the battle was taking place at Bunker Hill, they named George Washington the Continental Army's Commander-in-Chief."[253]

"Do they have the power to do that?" said Thom, his focus midway between the conversation and his thoughts.

"Funny you should ask. Deacon Hale posed the same question."

"And...what did he think?"

"He wasn't sure. As I said, he asked the question, but...kinda like he was thinking out loud.

The lack of an answer had Thom drawing upon his readings of political philosophy, applying them to the facts. "Well, the way I see it...the various colonies each elected delegates to the Continental Congress. So, they're our elected representatives. But there's no underlying document...call it articles of authority, a constitution or what you will, defining their powers." For a moment he analyzed his own comments. "Impossible to say what they're authorized to do."

"If they weren't given powers, might they be purely advisory?" said Sarah.

"Makes sense," said Thom, "except...except that seems inconsistent with the reasons behind their appointments."

Sarah frowned.

"You disagree?" said Thom

"I don't know, but it seems like outsiders are suddenly running the show. Two months ago Tyringham had its own militia. Just last month the Massachusetts Committee on Safety took charge of the province's troops,[254] and already another body, not even in our colony, has taken control."

"But if we're going to fight England, we need all the colonies on one page. Someone or some entity has to take charge. Right?"

"Maybe..." said Sarah, her inflection hinting her ambiguous answer carried more negativity than her choice of words. "By the way, I understand the Continental Congress also created a Merchant Marine and banned trade with Canada."[255]

"Banned trade with Canada? Under what—" Thom clipped his tongue. A moment earlier he had endorsed the need for centralized leadership. But all too quickly leaders could assume power, and power had its dangers. He liked the concept of the Continental Congress, but without checks it might wield authority, absolute power, exactly like Parliament. Well, not quite. In the Continental Congress, unlike Parliament, each of the colonies had delegates representing them.

Pico laughed.

"What's so funny?" said Sarah.

"It's all so familiar."

405

The puzzled look on Sarah's face mirrored Thom's confusion.

"For years Indian tribes have tried to unite...often against a common enemy, another tribe or the white man. But most times the alliances have failed. Squabbles over power and the like. A few have been successful, the Six Nation Confederation of the Iroquois, a good example."[256]

"I thought there were five," said Thom.

"There were...for about two centuries, but the Tuscarora were added, more than fifty years ago."

The disclosure underscored for Thom how little he, like the vast majority of the colonists, knew about the ways of their Indian neighbors. He said, "How are the nations of the Iroquois connected?"

"You really wanna know?"

The question was embarrassing. Pico, who had been living with him for about two years, gave his full attention whenever Thom spoke about political theory, philosophy, history or other intellectual subjects. On the other hand, when Pico talked about Indian culture, Thom lent no more than half an ear. Despite esteeming Pico's skills, Thom conceded that his behavior inhibited his friend from opening up about his cultural past.

"Even if he doesn't care," said Sarah, "I'd love to hear about the Iroquois."

"I would too," said Thom, the seeming insincerity of his belated enthusiasm reverberating in his ears.

Pico swirled his noggin of Santa Cruz rum. "Within an Iroquois tribe you have clans made up of families with common maternal roots. The clans are led by chiefs. The chiefs are organized into councils. They exercise the executive, legislative and judicial functions of the tribe. When the Iroquois tribes formed a confederation, the tribes gave their authority to the Confederation government, much like the individual clans had given their power to the tribes' councils. It's kinda what you'd have if the colonies, with their thirteen provincial assemblies, opted to give their power to a common government."[257]

"Interesting," said Sarah. "You have a remarkable understanding of the subject. How'd you manage to learn so much?"

"Thanks to my mother. She made me read every night. Talked to Pico about everything. After she died, I still tried to learn. While staying at the school here, I read everything in sight, usually more than once."

Sarah turned to Thom. "He's quite the young man."

"He is indeed," said Thom, who, following the lesson on the Iroquois, realized that he had again underestimated Pico's knowledge and intellect. When first they had met, Pico had mentioned how his mother had made him read, but Thom had failed to explore the subject further. He had no idea what Pico had read. His oversights caused chagrin, and compounding that chagrin were the underlying assumptions he had made. All too often, with just the two of them alone in the saltbox, Thom had dominated conversations, and when addressing matters involving book learning—and he often did—unwittingly Thom became didactic. Thom could only wonder how often Pico may have silently endured self-indulgent lectures. Likely many of the subjects were new to Pico, but with Thom's tendency to harp back to common themes, uncharted territory became familiar. Worthwhile lessons grew into repeated sermons, which in time morphed into monotonous harangues. Thom gazed at Pico. Early on he had realized that they shared a number of similarities, most strikingly their fierce independence. Thom had also observed that around others both were listeners. What had escaped him, however, were the possible reasons. Reticence, a lack of self-confidence, dictated Thom's behavior, whereas polite, but self-assured discretion motivated Pico. Thom wondered why the distinction had not come to him sooner. It was not subtle. In social situations when addressed with potentially discomposing circumstances, if and when they responded, he and Pico reacted differently. Defensiveness, accompanied by faltering speech, typified Thom, while Pico, however terse, remained resolute.

"Thomas Webster!"

His name, sharply uttered, drew Thom's attention. He realized he had drifted into the distant chasm of his own mind.

"Would you kindly answer me?"

He looked at Sarah, but with his private thoughts still fresh, managed to calm what otherwise might have been a discombobulated tongue. "You were speaking to me?"

"She offered you another helping of Indian pudding."

"By all means, yes." From the mantle behind him, the Brackett clock chimed melodiously. The sound, like Sarah's syrup-draped pudding, was sweet. Sweeter yet were the two people with whom he was seated. Thom looked at one and then, the other. "Thank you both for being such good friends." That his comment, coming out of the blue, drew puzzled looks was no surprise. He focused on Pico. "Many thanks." He turned to Sarah. "And many thanks to you."

❧

Pico and Thom turned off the Albany-Boston Post Road and headed onto the wooded path that led to the saltbox. "You haven't said a word since we left Mrs. Albright's," said Pico.

Thom shrugged.

"Now there's a lively response."

"Don't mind me. I've been thinking."

"That's a new experience."

Thom welcomed the jibe. The identical comment spoken by Jenkins or Crane might have been caustic, but between the two friends it communicated affection.

"So, whatcha been thinkin' about?"

His private nature induced Thom to address the inquiry with a question of his own. "How do you feel about your father abandoning you?"

"It's his problem." The response shot from Pico's tongue like a bullet from a musket.

"It makes you angry, doesn't it?"

"I suppose...but like I said: 'It's his problem.'"

"Does it bother you?"

"Bother me?" Pico shook his head. "Makes me mad, but that's about it."

"So, other than that, it's ancient history?"

Pico stopped at the saltbox threshold and studied Thom. "This about me...or maybe you?"

408

Thom hesitated, well aware the pause conceded the point.

Pico climbed the stoop and opened the door for Thom. "That my father took off on my Mom and me says nothin' about Pico...what kind of person he is. Mom told me that over and over. As Pico said: 'It's his problem.'"

Pico's anger was apparent, but equally apparent, he did not define himself by his father's conduct. Could Thom say the same about himself? No way. All his life he had been searching for the approval he had never received from his father. In Boston he had found it, and he had thrived. It had fueled a voracious appetite to learn, initially perhaps for the wrong reason, a craving for approbation, not thirst for knowledge. When he left Boston for the hinterlands, the need remained, and childhood vulnerabilities, just below the surface, were primed to rear their odious head. Thom gazed at his saltbox. Since his days as a lowly boatswain's assistant, he had accomplished a lot. He had learned a lot. Admittedly recollections of his untoward childhood irked him. But he was not his alcoholic, abusive father. He no longer needed the man's approval. He did not even want it. As he stepped through the doorway, he breathed a sigh. A taxing yoke, an emotional fetter, one that stretched across a vast ocean, had slackened. Was he totally free of it such that he would face the world with devil-may-care confidence, insulated from the reactions of others? Definitely not. On the other hand, their opinions would hold less sway.

# Chapter 25

THOM HAD ARRIVED HOME a couple of hours earlier after spending a week in Westfield helping an old friend from Boston frame a structure. It was the longest Thom had been away from Tyringham in several years. Pico, who had not accompanied Thom on the trip, was out, perhaps fishing the Konkapot or hunting in the woods near Brewer's Pond. Outside a misting rain, a brume so fine it was hardly more than an overhanging cloud, draped the slopes of Beartown Mountain. With habit his helmsman, Thom took his twenty-two year old, 1753 copy of Poor Richard's Almanack down from the shelf and opened to July. The early part of the month was to be "followed by rain and thunder" on the 9th, 10th and 11th.[258] Whenever Thom used the publication to forecast the weather, he silently laughed at himself, well aware that a look out the window provided more accurate information. A cursory glance at the gray day, though slightly damp, gainsaid any threat of thunder and lightning. But logic wasn't the point. He enjoyed using his Almanack, and, more important, it provided an excuse for a day indoors woodworking. A productive May and June had outdoor chores around the saltbox in excellent shape.

Thom fetched a two-foot board of ash, soon to be a kitchen shelf, and began beveling the edges. A knock at the door drew his attention. The best part of two months had passed since anyone had come calling. He got up from his parlor bench and opened the portal. On the stoop stood Issac Winslow, David Wharton and Wendell Dinsmore.

The sight of the unexpected triumvirate ruffled Thom. Chances were he would dislike whatever had brought them. Might a death be the reason for their visit? They would come only if the victim were a friend, not a mere acquaintance. The thought spawned panic. Could it be? Was Richard, off with the Minutemen in Cambridge, killed?

410

"You mind if we come in?" said Wharton. He gestured behind him at the dank veil of limited visibility.

"Oh, sorry," said Thom. "You...uh...caught me by surprise." With the aplomb of Orville Crane on a bad day, he started to lead them into the parlor. Wood shavings spread across the floor changed his mind. He turned back, bumping into Dinsmore. "Oops...sorry. Uh...let's go into the dining room." He led the visitors there. Heart in his throat and shaking, he hurriedly fetched the parlor bench so as to add to the two available chairs. "Can I get you fellows something to drink, some peach cider perhaps?" Dread, a device to delay the potential horror, rather than civility, precipitated the gracious offer.

"We're fine," said Wharton.

Thom joined Dinsmore on the bench. Angst bubbling within, Thom endeavored to display a calm façade. "So, uh...what brings you gents out this way?"

Wharton motioned to Winslow. "You wanna do the honors?"

Whether there was unease in Wharton's voice or it was Thom's imagination, his sense that their visit had distasteful ramifications amplified.

Winslow cleared his throat. "This has to do with the powder that was stored in Cooper's barrels."

The irksome subject was an anomalous elixir. Relief abounded. The worst of bullets, death of his dearest friend, had been dodged. But the disclosure suggested another bullet was about to strike. Thom swallowed hard. He could have used the drink he had offered his guests.

"A few days ago Pico came to me..."

The instant he heard his friend's name, Thom felt his eyes widen.

If Winslow picked up on the reaction, he gave little clue. Apart from a brief pause, he continued with his story. "It seems that a couple of days earlier Pico had been on his way to fish along the Konkapot about a half-mile west of Brewer's Mill when he chanced upon Ezra Jenkins and George Whitaker. Unseen, Pico observed the two talking. He heard some very intriguing things, including their intention to meet there again yesterday. Pico asked me to accompany him to observe the

411

meeting. He mentioned you were away in Westfield, expected home today. Well anyway...yesterday I went back there with him. We got there some forty minutes before the appointed hour. We hid and waited. Sure enough, Jenkins arrived, and minutes later, Whitaker. After confirming he hadn't been followed, Whitaker said he had nothing new to share. Jenkins told him he was working on a plan to make another Tyringham Patriot look like a spy. Whereupon Whitaker slapped Jenkins on the back and said: 'Brilliant, the way you told Webster you knew about the powder in Cooper's barrels, just when Dinsmore came out of my barn.'"

"I'm sorry, Thom," said Dinsmore. "At the time it...uh...looked real bad. Jenkins hooked me good. Made me think you were pretending to be one of us, so all the while you could feed the Tories with information."

Thom took a deep breath. "You telling me I'm in the clear?" His gaze moved over the three men. "That you no longer think I'm a spy?"

"That's exactly what we're saying," said Wharton. "And we're also saying...we're sorry. Mighty sorry for accusing you."

"Wow..." A plethora of thoughts reverberated in Thom's brain. A huge onus eased.

"The fact we have to be careful doesn't excuse what we've put you through," said Wharton. "We hope you'll forgive us."

A notion popped into Thom's head.

Wharton studied him for a moment. "You're reluctant to call it bygones. I can see it on your face, not that I blame you."

"No...That's not what I was thinking."

"What then?"

"Wendell—it's not your place to ask! The man's thoughts are his business." Winslow turned to Thom. "Ignore our rude shoemaker. You're under no obligation to satisfy his churlish curiosity, especially after the way we've treated you."

"It's okay. I...uh...was wondering whether I might be able to rejoin the militia."

"No need to ask," said Wharton. "That's already been discussed. Even Crane—he's the one who blackballed you from the Minutemen—acquiesced, though, unlike everyone else, his okay didn't come until after we damn near hammered his stubborn head on his anvil."

"Crane...I should have known," muttered Thom, just loud enough to be audible. He looked at Winslow. "And all along I thought it was you."

"Me?...Why?"

Thom felt his face flush, partly from the slur he had directed at Winslow, but more so from reluctance to remind everyone that Winslow had rejected him as a would-be son-in-law. "It was only a guess. Sorry."

"You, least of all, need to apologize," said Winslow.

"About the militia," said Wharton. "I have to clarify what I said. As far as we men in Tyringham are concerned, you're in...Unfortunately, I'm not sure we can make it happen."

"I don't understand." Thom feared his neighbors were about to renege on the good news.

"I assume you're aware that last month the Continental Congress named George Washington as Commander-in-Chief of the Continental Army. He took command this past week."

"I knew he had been named to the post, but not that he had actually taken command. But what does that have to do with me?"

"As yet we're unsure what effect it will have on our militia or exactly how individuals will be enlisted into the common army. From what we've heard, Washington has seventeen thousand men under his command in Cambridge."

"Seventeen thousand!" The number rang in Thom's head. "That's one hell of an army. It's surely bigger than what the British have here."

"For now...I guess," said Wharton. "But word has it, additional British troops are arriving every day."

"Yeah, last week when I was at the Hogshead," said Dinsmore, "a fellow passing through from Springfield—he seemed to know what he was talking about—claimed the British army totals fifty-six thousand, not to mention another eighteen thousand in the Royal Navy.[259] How many will be sent here is anybody's guess."

"One thing sure," said Wharton, "England won't give in without a helluva fight."

Thom's experience over several years in Tyringham had taught him that whenever conversation turned to politics or war, as it often did, unanimity was about as common as unicorns. But like most rules, there were exceptions that supposedly proved their contrary counterparts. Apparently Wharton's comment was such an exception. It drew a nod, along with voiced responses: "Ya got that right," and "No doubt about it." A brief silence ensued before Wharton suggested the three men take their leave. As Thom closed the door behind them, he pumped a fist into the air. Thanks to Pico, his days as a Tyringham pariah had ceased.

∿◯◯)))◯◯∿

Along with Pico, Thom stepped through the door of the Hogshead. Several days had passed since Wharton, Winslow and Dinsmore had invited Thom back into the community's good graces. It had been many weeks since he had last visited the tavern. Men between the ages of sixteen and thirty, including his closest friends, remained in Cambridge with the Minutemen and the militia, in what had become the Continental Army.[260] Thom looked around the popular hangout. It was much quieter than usual. Off to his left, Orville Crane sat with Captain John Brewer. In the adjacent booth, as well as a mid-room table, there were men Thom didn't recognize, most likely passing through on the Albany-Boston Post Road. In a booth to his right, Deacon Hale was seated with Darby Walters. Thom motioned Pico to another booth where they could relax alone. As they were about to sit, Deacon Hale called out, "C'mon. Why don't you join us?"

Thom hesitated. Hale was a fine gentleman, but Thom had little in common with the older man. Even less appealing was sharing a table with Darby Walters. Thom had nothing against Walters, but their only link was Juliette Chandler—Juliette Walters for nearly a year. Ever since the winter's day when Thom had tried to call on Juliette, he felt uncomfortable around Darby. And like Hale, Darby, who was several years older than Juliette, herself roughly fifteen years older than Thom, was from

414

a different generation. "Well...uh...thanks," said Thom, unable to find a decorous way to decline the invitation.

As the two men slid toward the wall, Pico seated himself next to Walters, and Thom moved in alongside Hale.

"Darby, you know Thom. Right?" said Hale.

"Sure, but I can't say I've met his friend."

"This is Pico," said Thom. "Been living with me for the best part of two years."

Walters extended his hand and shook Pico's. "Nice to meet you." He turned to Thom. "Glad to see you got cleared of being a Tory informant.

"I've got Pico here to thank. He's the one who caught Jenkins and Whitaker trying to frame me."

"Whitaker—that son of a bitch," said Walters. "One thing to be a Tory. Another to be a spy. Some folks wanna try him for treason. Tar and feather him,[261] and then let him rot in the Great Barrington Jail. It would serve him right." Walters looked Thom in the eye. "Be interested in hearin' how you feel about it, seein' as how the creep had folks talkin' such charges against you."

The possibility triggered mixed feelings. But Thom was reluctant to cast stones at the Yankee peddler. "You might better ask someone not in the middle of things."

"Mighty fair answer," said Hale. "Doubt Whitaker woulda been so generous if the shoe was on the other foot." He turned to Pico. "Folks here appreciate what you did, catching Whitaker. Were it not for you, he'd still be playing his underhanded game."

"I was just helpin' Thom. He's been real good to me. Gave me a home and—"

"The truth be known, I've gotten the long end of the stick. Pico helped me build my saltbox. There's not a better hunter or fisherman in Tyringham. And he's got more skills than...than Crane's got nails."

"Speaking of Crane..." Hale turned to Pico. "Did our dear blacksmith ever express regrets about the time you spent locked up?"

"Nah, but our paths rarely cross."

"Well, he shoulda gone out of his way to say something. Hell, he was screaming for your hide when, all along, his boy,

415

the little snot, was responsible. By any chance, did Elmer ever apologize?"

Pico simply smiled, his silence a definitive answer. Mary came to take their order, a trench of the nightly stew, along with their respective beverages of choice.

"Mary, the bill is mine," said Hale.

"Nice of you to offer," said Thom, "but we insist on paying our share."

"Nope!" Hale was emphatic. "Both of you are owed apologies. It's the least I can do." He refocused on Mary. "You've got your orders."

"Mighty kind of you," said Thom. "Anything new on the war front?"

"Last we heard there was no fighting," said Hale, "but yesterday we got word from Philadelphia that the Continental Congress sent communiqués to King George laying out our position...Maybe I should say...*positions.*"

"What do you mean—*positions?*"

"Just what I said. On July 5th the Congress sent King George an Olive Branch Petition."

"Don't tell me they're begging his pardon?" A clench of his jaw underscored for Thom just how upset the possibility made him.

"Not that bad," said Hale. "Despite expressing loyalty to King George, the Petition condemned the actions of his ministers and Parliament."[262]

"Sounds like a placating peace pipe to me."

"My first reaction too, Thom. But the next day the Congress followed it up with a 'Declaration of Causes and Necessity of Taking Up Arms.' Among other things, they threatened independence if our demands aren't met."[263] He gestured at Walters. "Darby here has some of the what-fors...Fill 'em in."

Walters drew a note from his pocket. "Reverend Bidwell had a copy of the document. I wrote down one of its key lines...It says that we're, and I quote, 'resolved to die free men rather than live as slaves.'"[264]

"If you ask me," said Hale, "that sends a clear message we're ready to fight."

"I'd say it does," said Thom, buoyed by the resolute stance. "You think King George might give in to our demands?"

"Sure," said Pico, his interjection garnering the full attention of the other three. "And no doubt Parliament will pay the colonists a shilling in tribute for each cup of tea they drink."

"Well put," said Hale.

Thom heaved a sigh. "Yeah...I guess my comment was a bit naïve."

"A bit?" Hale leaned back. "Were it not for the fact that Mary is yet to bring your ale, as well as our stew, I'd dismiss it as an inebriated impairment of logic. And speaking of Mary, where the hell is our food?"

⚬⚬⚬⚬

Seated in the parlor of Reverend Bidwell's home in his preferred spot, last row on the end (experience had shown that unlike him, most folks liked to sit up front), Thom felt comfortable; well, less uneasy than other times when he had attended Sunday meetings. Many moons had come and gone since he had joined his neighbors in the celebration of the Sabbath. In the interim war had broken out at Lexington and Concord, the Patriots had held their own at Bunker Hill, and the Continental Congress had sent a force of one thousand under the command of General Philip Schuyler to move on Montreal.[265] Thom's desire to get the most up-to-date information about hostilities was a motivating factor in his attendance at the meeting. Earlier when accusations that he was a Tory spy ran rampant, no way would he have made an appearance, not that he would have been welcome. Since he had been cleared, many had gone out of their way to be friendly, perhaps to make up for the injustice.

In the back of Thom's mind was the possibility Polly might attend the service. Roughly nine months had elapsed since Peter had died. Better judgment counseled that any hopes of rekindling a romantic relationship be nipped. Scars from his prior journey down that rocky road could become open wounds. But the chance to see her, a woman no longer spoken for, was

417

tempting. Her friendly smile, an innocent greeting to brighten his day, could do no harm. That's what Thom told himself. Nevertheless, the potential risks could not be denied, and trepidations stirred.

As it turned out, Thom's musings were nothing more than abstract conjectures. Wishful thinking never materialized. The last of the parishoners arrived, and Reverend Bidwell, standing tall behind his lectern desk, commenced the meeting. Polly was a no-show.

Since the hostilities with England had erupted, Reverend Bidwell, an activist supporter of the Patriot cause, had been devoting more of his sermons to the issues of war.[266] While his information was more reliable than the oft-embellished rumors and opinions that floated through Tyringham, Reverend Bidwell added little to the scuttlebutt Thom had heard at the Hogshead and Brewer's gristmill. The meeting, as usual, seemed interminable. But thanks to the friendly greetings of his neighbors, on balance, Thom was glad he attended.

"Good Sabbath, Thom," said Deacon Hale, moments after the final amen had been spoken.

"And good Sabbath to you, Deacon."

"Nice to see you here. The start of a trend, I hope."

"Maybe," said Thom, though he suspected otherwise.

"Care to join me in some cider?"

Thom welcomed the offer. With a noggin of the fermented drink scooped from the punchbowls arrayed in the Reverend's dining room, he felt more at ease.

"Shall we adjourn to the front yard?" said Hale. "That way we can leave room for others, not to mention take advantage of the sunshine." He gazed out the room's front window. "Can't believe tomorrow's the first day of autumn."

"Summer flies by far too fast." The cliché, which under other circumstances might have had Thom chiding himself, rolled from his tongue as easily as the fermented cider flowed the opposite way. He followed Hale to the nearby stone wall, noting the artistry with which it had been laid. Not wind, nor rain, nor snow would beat it down. Two centuries hence, long after many of the nearby trees had succumbed, the flat-stoned wall might well persist.

"Sure to be another tough winter...especially for our troops. Word has it, they're short on everything: powder, guns, rations, blankets, warm clothing, you name it." Hale poured a swallow down his gullet. "Come the close of December when enlistments end, it may be tough to fill the ranks. Word has it many want to return home, at least for the bitter winter months. Others, missing their families, want to stay there permanently." He glanced skyward before looking back at Thom. "You got any plans for the winter?"

"Oh...perhaps some woodworking...along with staying warm by the fireplace."

"A single fellow, like yourself, might want to think about enlisting."

The overture clarified why Hale had drawn Thom outside where they could be alone. He said, "I've been contemplating the possibility for several weeks."

"And?"

"Good chance I'll enlist."

Hale chuckled.

"Did I say something humorous?"

"No, I was laughing at myself. When I saw you arrive, I decided to approach you. Don't tell the Reverend, but much of the time I was thinking how I'd broach the subject. Turns out, I didn't need to."

"Well, I'm glad you did. It's nice to be asked."

Hale hesitated. "I've got another question for you, but if I'm...uh...out of line, stop me. Do you...uh...think your friend Pico might also want to enlist?"

Ordinarily Thom would have refused to speak for Pico, but past discussions allowed for an exception. "It's highly doubtful...at least for now." The frown that greeted the words prompted Thom to add, "Let me explain. From what he's heard, many Indians expect to remain neutral. Others are likely to choose our side, while some will go with the British. Before Pico picks up a gun—if he does, it will be with us—he wants to see the landscape. In the meantime, assuming I join the troops, he'll take care of my house." Thom gazed at the Reverend's saltbox. Doubtless the Reverend prized it. Thom valued his own as much. He inhaled the comfortable late summer air. The

Sabbath was a day to give thanks, and having a friend like Pico provided good reason.

# Chapter 26

As Thom tied Lodestone to the fence fronting the Hogshead, he eyed the horses tethered there. His survey confirmed what he knew. None of his pals, Richard Thorn, Paul Cooper and Johnny Woodstone, would be inside. They were all in Cambridge, part of the army under General Washington's command. Thom paused near the swinging wooden signboard that hung from the big post, a short distance from the entrance. Still emblazoned in big, carved, gold letters was: "HOGSHEAD INN," followed by "Good Food, Drink, and Lodging." But no longer did the crimson coat of arms of King George III occupy the bottom. In its place was the face of George Washington. The change was symbolic, but it was a lot more.

Thom strode toward the big oak door. A whinny halted him. Most times he could distinguish Lodestone's call, but with a fairly stiff breeze whistling about, he was unsure which of the several horses had neighed. Thom weighed the possibility that Lodestone might be counseling him to forgo his visit. The idea was absurd, especially given uncertainty as to the source. He looked around at the trees that bordered the clearing in front of the tavern. With November more than half over, apart from the few evergreens and some oaks bearing crinkled, rusty leaves, the timbers were bare. Their vibrant green foliage was a distant recollection. He turned back toward the Hogshead. The chums with whom he often enjoyed brews and jocund chitchat were also distant. Most men his age were in Cambridge. Presumably an older crowd, the kind that left Thom ill at ease, filled the tavern's tables. Did he really want to go in? He could climb back onto Lodestone and return to the sanctuary of his saltbox. With his vacillating brain in a quandary, his seemingly self-governing feet marched him to and through the doorway. Straight ahead in the center of the room sat John Kellogg, Zacariah Thomas and Jonathan Whapples. That they would invite Thom to join their table was unlikely, not that he would have relished the invitation.

Off to his right, strangers, typical folks passing through Tyringham, occupied two booths. Over to his left, Orville Crane and Wendell Dinsmore sat in another. Thom recalled the sign outside, not the wooden one, but the horse's whinny. He detested superstition, yet wished he had heeded the omen. He started to leave.

"Thom, where you going?"

Dinsmore's call could not be ignored. Thom turned, shrugging sheepishly.

"C'mon, we've got room." Dinsmore slid toward the wall.

Joining the shoemaker was fine, if only he weren't seated with the hardheaded blacksmith. Refusing the invite, especially with no explanation, would be boorish. Thom shuffled over to the booth and climbed in next to Dinsmore.

"Glad to have you."

"I appreciate your kindness, Wendell."

"How do," muttered Crane, as he grabbed his tankard and imbibed whatever it held.

"And good day to you." It was the first time Thom had been face to face with the blacksmith since his son Elmer had confessed to the fires that had consumed Dodge's barn and Mansfield's hay bales. Thom wondered if words of regret, even if short of a heartfelt apology, might be forthcoming.

"Orville and I were discussing the latest on the hostilities with England. Of course, these days that's mainly what folks talk about."

"Can you blame them?" said Crane.

Thom gazed across the table making eye contact with the blacksmith. Crane looked away, resorting to the security of his liquid refreshment. Mind-reading was not among the skills that Thom professed, but at that moment he would have bet cash—six shillings to be precise—that he could read Crane's thoughts. The blacksmith was thinking about the fires or the debt he had never repaid...or maybe both. On second thought, it couldn't be both. That would exceed Crane's minuscule mental capacities.

"Can you believe that damn King George?" said Dinsmore. "The bastard makes my blood boil. The Continental Congress sends him an Olive Branch Petition, and the mucker refuses to read it. If that weren't enough, he has the gall to issue a proclamation declaring us guilty of treason. And rather than righting our injustices, he claims we're in rebellion."[267]

"Well, if nothing else, it proves his true colors," said Thom.

"You got that right. And it's not the red of the Union Jack. More like the shade of the citrus he puts in his tea."

"You mean tan...from honey?" said Crane.

Dinsmore smacked his hands against either side of his head. "Citrus!...Lemon! Yellow! Nauseating, chicken yellow!" He heaved a sigh and turned to Thom. "What do you think about our invasion of Canada this past month?"

Thom preferred to remain non-controversial. "It's an interesting tactic."

"If you ask me, it's a smart move. We gotta protect the northern flank, plus it brings France into the equation. The way I see it, if we show strength in Canada, there's a good chance the French will come to our aid. They'd love to settle old scores with England, especially when doing so might expand their interests in this hemisphere." Dinsmore looked across the table. "Orville, any opinions about Canada?"

"From what I hear, it gets mighty cold there in the winter."

"I was referring to our invasion."

Crane shrugged. "What about it?"

Dinsmore turned to Thom. "That's what I like about Orville. Unlike some fellows who go off half-cocked, his views are carefully measured."

Across the table Thom observed no reaction. He suspected the blacksmith had taken the shoemaker's jab as a compliment. He also suspected that Dinsmore had asked for Crane's view as a source of humor, not because he was interested.

Dinsmore turned kitty-corner in his seat, so he faced more toward Thom. "Just when I got here, a fellow from Boston—he was on his way back home—told me that the British burned Falmouth last week.[268] Said they turned most of the town into rubble. You gotta wonder, how many more of our ports will feel the wrath of their navy?"

Regardless whether the question was rhetorical, Thom treated it as such.

"I guess we're lucky living way out here in the hinterlands. Far less likely battles will be on our soil."

423

Though Dinsmore's point had crossed Thom's mind, he hadn't voiced it for fear it might be deemed unchristian.

"General Washington is facing a daunting task trying to keep our army supplied." Dinsmore raised his brew but did not imbibe. "From what I hear, they're short on everything: guns and ammunition, clothing, camp equipment, food...all sorts of stuff. How can you fight a war, especially against the strongest army on the planet, when your troops lack the basics?" He shook his head. "Gonna get a whole lot harder once winter sets in."[269]

"You got that right." Thom signaled Mary to bring him a brew. "Filling the ranks won't be easy come the end of December, once the first enlistments end."

Dinsmore nodded. "Fighting a war takes money, not to mention strong leadership. Some folks may not approve, but like it or not, the Continental Congress has gotta take control."

Much as Thom understood the need for strong leadership, political philosophy ingrained during his days in Boston, as well as prior discussions, demurred. The Continental Congress was a group of delegates, largely chosen by self-appointed committees of safety and provincial assemblies, none of which had the authority to cede power to the Congress. Nor was there a document purporting to enumerate the powers of the Congress. How could such an *ad hoc* exercise of authority be ignored when the very issue that had brought the colonies to the battlefield was England's arbitrary use of power? Once the Congress began assuming authority, might it assume more? Where were the checks and balances? What were the limits? Like Parliament, could the Congress claim absolute power?[270] But Dinsmore was right. Fighting a war against the likes of the British army demanded not only unity, but also a well-equipped and well-organized force. Thom's brain put him on both sides of the fence.

"You seem hesitant. That mean you disagree?"

"It's not that," said Thom. "It's just that I get nervous when a central authority purports to empower itself."

"Damn. You lookin' for us to lose the war?" Dinsmore glanced across the table. "Even Orville knows we can't pussyfoot. Right?"

"Yeah...I guess."

"The Continental Congress is only doing what we requested. I understand our Provincial Congress here in Massachusetts specifically asked them to take control of the army in Cambridge."[271]

Thom hardly relished an argument, but the point ignored the threshold question: Did the Massachusetts Provincial Congress have the power to grant such authority to the Continental Congress, especially when the army at Cambridge included militias from numerous colonies. "I hear you, but—" Thom clipped his tongue. In the face of a war demanding pragmatics, Dinsmore would be deaf to theoretical pedagogy.

"But what?" Dinsmore folded his arms.

"Well...I understand that war has it exigencies, but it's not an excuse—"

"Excuse! You call resisting Parliament's enslavement an excuse?"

Thom swallowed hard. Past experience had schooled him in the folly of equivocation. Maybe it was best he yield. Across the table he caught a glimpse of Crane's smug grin. Allowing the dumb blacksmith, who had contributed nothing to the discussion, to gloat, was worse than a fight. Thom searched for a middle ground by which he could tactfully express his concerns without sparking Dinsmore's ire.

Before he found a way, Dinsmore said, "Do you...or do you not respect General Washington's authority as Commander-in-Chief of the colonial troops to set the parameters for waging this war?"

A simple yes would assuage the shoemaker's pique, but it would feed the appetite of the gloating blacksmith. "I'm sorry," said Thom, "but I believe your inquiry begs the question."

Dinsmore's face reddened. "Begs the question! What the hell does—" He halted just long enough to make certain his raised voice had not drawn the attention of other patrons. With voice lowered, but very firm, he said, "What the hell do you mean—'begs the question?'"

"Does the Continental Congress have the authority to appoint George Washington as Commander-in-Chief?" said Thom.

425

A dumbfounded expression painted Dinsmore's face. "They're the Continental Congress, aren't they?"

"Yes."

"So...they're in charge."

"Yeah, they're in charge." Crane folded his arms defiantly as he parroted Dinsmore's assessment.

Thom leaned forward and stared at the blacksmith. "Fine. Then be so kind to enumerate their powers."

Crane jerked back. He glanced at Dinsmore as if looking for the shoemaker to step in.

Thom kept his eyes trained on Crane. "Like Parliament, is their power absolute? Can they do anything they please? Tax us? Close our ports? Seize our land?"

Crane threw up his arms. "How the hell should I know?"

"You're the one who said they're in charge."

"Wendell said it first."

Thom shook his head.

"Orville...you're pathetic," said Dinsmore.

"Me?...Then you gotta be pathetic too, 'cause you said the same thing."

"Yeah, I did. But unlike you, I take responsibility for what I say." He turned to Thom. "Tell me why you object to the Continental Congress taking charge."

With Dinsmore seemingly more willing to listen, though unlikely to acquiesce, Thom said, "I agree with your basic premise. Hodgepodge groups of farmers can't fight a war against England. Having said that, I'm troubled. We're fighting this war on principle—our right to be free of arbitrary governmental authority. The troops over which George Washington has taken charge are militias from the several colonies of New England. They were established under the laws of those colonies. By what authority does the Continental Congress take control of those militias?"

Dinsmore's eyes narrowed. "The Continental Congress consists of delegates from the various colonies. Therefore, the Congress represents the colonies."

"Yeah," said Crane. "They represent—"

"Orville—Shut your mouth!" said Dinsmore. "Thom and I are trying to have an intelligent discussion."

426

Crane bristled.

Dinsmore ignored him, refocusing on Thom. "Do you disagree with my point that the Congress represents the colonies?"

"No...but that doesn't tell us their powers. Unless I'm mistaken, they were selected for the purpose of communicating the colonies' grievances to King George and hopefully gaining redress."

"Well, they're redressing those grievances."

Thom gave Dinsmore a look.

The shoemaker nodded. "I hear what you're saying. But we have a war on our hands. Someone has to take charge. If not the Continental Congress and General Washington, then who?"

"Frankly...I don't know."

Dinsmore heaved a protracted sigh. "That's not a reassuring answer."

"You're right," said Thom. He hesitated, as he attempted to bridge the gap between the demands of war and the limits on authority. A huge abyss divided principles and practicalities, and parsed words would build nothing more than a bridge of cards. Discretion, coupled with a sense that Dinsmore had given his argument a measure of respect, guided Thom back from the brink of the abyss. He reached for the brew that Mary had placed before him. As he took a swig, he glanced at Crane. If nothing else, the buffoon had been put in his place.

---

"Got a minute?"

Poised to drive his froe into a four-foot log, Thom turned and spotted Wendell Dinsmore coming up from behind.

"Sorry to interrupt your work, but our discussion yesterday left me unsettled. I'd like to revisit the matter...if you don't mind."

"Uh...okay." Thom's response contradicted his feelings.

"Nice piece of hickory," said Dinsmore. He pointed at the hardwood that stood atop a flattened tree stump. "Looks well-seasoned. Oughta burn real well."

427

Thom laid his froe onto the log. "Never can have too much firewood, what with our winters."

"You can say that again."

Thom would have if he thought it might avoid the subject that had occasioned Dinsmore's visit.

"I'd like to talk about yesterday."

"I...uh..."

"No, please hear me out first."

The prior evening, Thom had developed second thoughts about the position he had taken at the Hogshead. He preferred to offer words to defuse the situation, but Dinsmore had other ideas.

"When it comes to England and the war, I have strong feelings. Sometimes I'm a poor listener. Yesterday you made some good points—points that I didn't want to hear. Rather than give them credence, I lashed out. Don't misunderstand. I still believe the Continental Congress should exercise authority with regard to the war, but I owe you an apology. Legitimate arguments merit more than gruff outbursts."[272]

The unexpected contrition left Thom speechless.

"Does your silence mean my behavior offended you?"

"Just the opposite," said Thom. "I regretted what I said. With my cynical nature, I have an annoying habit of playing devil's advocate, even when I agree with someone. Believing as I do that our cause is right, I should have looked for ways to justify and define the authority of the Continental Congress, rather than attacking it."

"You know," said Dinsmore. "I suspect our views are a lot closer than we realized."

Thom nodded. His mind drifted back to the prior evening. What had seemed a huge chasm was a narrow fissure. Pig-headedness, coupled with deaf ears, had thwarted communication. Both he and Dinsmore had been guilty. Similar intransigence led nations to the battlefield. It was possible the split between the colonies and England illustrated the point. The musing had appeal, but the facts compelled Thom to reject it. The first colonists had left England searching for religious freedom. Parliament had not only denied them that, but with the passage of time, economic, social and political freedom as well.

The insurmountable divide demanded war. He said, "You're right. Frustration, more than real differences, led to our disagreement."

Dinsmore laughed.

Thom had no idea why.

"Don't mind me. Your mention of frustration made me think of Crane, the third member of our discussion yesterday. Any time Stonehenge skull is involved, it's bound to be frustrating."

Thom smiled. Badmouthing others, even Crane, was a practice he avoided. On the other hand, defending the Boeotian blacksmith was out of the question.

"Well, I'll let you get back to your work." Dinsmore started to leave but glanced back. "It was hard for me to come today. Pride, unmitigated pride—Reverend Bidwell often speaks about it—bridled me. But...with hindsight, I'm glad I did."

"Makes two of us," said Thom, unsure whether the shoemaker, already on his way, caught the comment.

⁓ೲ⎱⎰ೲ⁓

"I'll miss you," said Sarah.

"I'll miss you too." Thom gazed out the front window of Sarah's dining room where large flakes of snow, a brief squall, but an undeniable harbinger of what was to come, floated gently from the late November sky. "And I'll miss dinners with desserts like this." He gestured at the center of the table where Sarah had placed her fabulous rum-berry trifle, the elegance of which was exceeded only by its incredible taste. Beneath a coat of rich whipped cream, decorated with concentric circles of boysenberries, raspberries and blackberries with a half-plum in the middle, were four layers of rum-soaked sponge cake, each separated by a layer of whipped cream and one each of the aforesaid berries. "It seems a shame to spoil such a beautiful masterpiece," said Thom, as Sarah prepared to plunge her long-handled server into the dessert.

"If that's how you feel..." She drew her hand back.

"It's a shame, but..." Thom eyed the trifle. "Surviving without it would be unbearable."

429

Sarah smiled and dished him a helping fit for two. "Things will be awfully quiet around here without you."

"I'll probably be back shortly after the first of the year." Thom consumed his first mouthful. "You outdid yourself. It's delicious."

"Thank you." She served herself a portion, not half the size of his. "You really expect to be gone that long?"

"The trip north to Fort Ticonderoga will be quick, but bringing the cannons through the mountains is bound to be tough. At this point I don't know the details, but rivers and weather are certain to complicate the logistics."

"I take it you'll be part of the army."

Thom gagged on a bite of the trifle. "Not really." The puzzled look that greeted his eyes prompted him to add, "Even the leader of the expedition, Boston bookseller Henry Knox, is a civilian, though I understand he's likely to become a commissioned officer. Anyway, it'll give me a chance to help the cause now, rather than waiting until after the New Year when the current enlistments expire. The fact I'm a civilian won't matter."

"Do you know what route Knox plans to take from the Fort?"

"I'm not sure...but my guess, he'll go south to Albany, or maybe Kinderhook, and then head east to Boston. Altogether it's roughly three hundred miles."

Sarah got up from the table and went over to a map that hung on the wall adjoining the kitchen. "That would take him along the two perpendicular sides of a right triangle. A lot of distance could be saved by going directly from Ticonderoga to Boston, along the hypotenuse."

"I suppose...but from what I know, roads on much of that stretch are virtually non-existent." Thom joined Sarah at the map. "Whatever route he chooses, we'll have to cross the mountains, the Berkshires if we head south first, the Greens of Vermont if he opts for your route along the diagonal. Either way, it won't be easy."

"Once you get to Boston, any chance you might stay there with the army?"

"I can't rule it out." Thom returned to his seat, taking time to savor another bite, this from the boysenberry layer. "If Knox opts for the route south, the longer way, presumably he'll come through Tyringham. If so, I might leave the convoy at that point. A few more miles and he'll be out of the Berkshires. The rest of the trip should be easy, a comparative cakewalk. He won't need as many men."

"Well...whichever way you go, as soon as you get back, I'll expect you for dinner."

"A brigade of Redcoats couldn't keep me away." The words, flavored with rum and whipped cream and sponge cake and berries, streamed from Thom's tongue as mellifluously as the trifle flowed the opposite way.

A rap drew Thom's attention from one of three triangular shelves he was fashioning for the corner of his dining room. He put the wood aside and opened the door.

"Glad I caught you," said Issac Winslow. "I heard you're leaving tomorrow to join Henry Knox's expedition to transport the arms from Ticonderoga to Boston. Imagine you're pretty busy getting your things together for the trip."

"Actually, I was working on a shelf." Thom displayed a file he still had in hand. "Finished my packing and was ready to go two days ago." He stepped aside and gestured Winslow into the parlor. He slid a chair for Winslow closer to the hearth and, after tossing another log onto the fire, angled the bench along the wall toward the blaze. All the while he wondered about the reason for the visit. "Can I get you something to drink? I made a stout ginger beer the other day."

"Sounds good, but...I'll pass." Winslow gazed pensively at the fireplace where flames of amber and blue crackled.

Certain that Winslow had come with a particular purpose, Thom waited patiently.

"Some months back I sent a letter to England. I wanted to know the circumstances that had landed you in jail when you were a teen."

The comment had Thom recalling information Richard had passed along when Thom was still trying to discover who had blackballed him from the Minutemen. Whether his face

431

reflected the tightening of his jaw, Thom couldn't say; regardless, the disclosure displeased him.

"It's not like I meant to spy on you."

*Oh really.* This time Thom suspected that dipping brows were more demonstrative.

"Well—I guess I was checking you out. I...uh...needed to know, not that I don't trust you."

Thom managed to suppress a groan. Sarcasm was another matter. "So, what wonderful revelations did your investigation produce?"

"Please...don't get me wrong. I never intended to recant my earlier apologies. I have no qualms about your patriotism. You're a good citizen and neighbor."

The kudos invited a word of thanks, but Thom found them too hard to utter. "You didn't answer my question—what you learned from your inquiry."

Winslow nodded and reached into his pocket and pulled out a piece of paper. "The other day I received a letter from the constable where you were locked up. According to him you stepped in to defend a fellow who was being pummeled by the son of a local politician. The constable says the politician's son, not you, should have been jailed, but he had connections, and you didn't. I hope you at least got the best of him."

"I did...unfortunately."

"Unfortunately?"

"Yeah. If I'd been wiser, once I had protected the other fellow, I would have let the snot win the fight. Much as it would have bruised my ego, and maybe my jaw, it might have saved me a stint behind bars."

"Interesting assessment."

Thom waited a moment, still wondering about the purpose of Winslow's visit. "So, why the great interest in my past?"

"Well...before doing a one-eighty, I...uh...wanted to be certain about you."

"Am I finally okay?" That Winslow, even after his earlier apology, still had qualms, irked Thom.

"I don't blame you. I'd be annoyed if someone repeatedly questioned my conduct and integrity."

432

Thom glanced toward the front window. His demeanor bore the iciness of the outside chill; his temperature, however, more closely resembled the fire.

"I want to thank you again for what you did last year when you carried Peter home from the shores of Twelve-Mile Pond."

"In the long run it failed to benefit Peter."

"That's not true. As I've told you before, it let Polly say goodbye to Peter, and he to her."

"I suppose, but it would have been a darn side better had he survived."

"Well, yes...but..." Hands in his lap, Winslow fidgeted. "You know it's been a full year since Peter died?"

"Yes...I guess it has. Hard to believe how time flies."

"And that brings me to the reason for my visit."

*The anniversary of Peter's death.* Thom ran the thought through his head. Why would that bring Winslow to his door?

"For all these many months Polly has been holed up alone in her house. Yes, she goes to Sunday meetings occasionally, and from time to time she visits Brewer's gristmill, but for the most part she stays at her place. Many weeks she ventures no further from her door than her garden or barn. She's grieved long enough. It's time she starts living again." A hint of melancholy draped Winslow's voice. "Lord knows, I've tried repeatedly to draw her out." He looked Thom in the eye. "I believe you can do it."

The request was tempting, but bargaining with a devil offering a masochistic game of chess was not Thom's preference, especially knowing he was a pawn. And too, there was the possibility that Polly, the queen, had amorous designs on a king named Richard. Thom shook his head.

"You won't do it?" Winslow bore an incredulous expression. "I thought you'd welcome the chance."

Disbelief at the bizarre turn of events had Thom struggling to express his thoughts. "I...I can't deny that a part of me begs to say *yes.*"

"Then why?...I don't get it. What's the problem?"

Unable to maintain eye contact, Thom focused on the blazing wood that filled the fireplace. "The last time...back when you denied me Polly's hand in marriage, it took me a year to dig out from the depths. Much as I'd like to help Polly, no way could I risk such Hell again. Jail was far easier."

"You no longer have feelings for her?"

Thom bowed his head. "Yeah...I do." That was the point. Spending time with Polly would re-ignite those feelings, and having them unrequited would spiral him back into unbearable misery. "Deep in my heart, the yearnings remain. But that's where they need to stay."

"I understand your hesitancy, but given your feelings, I'm surprised you won't take the chance."

Easy for you to say. You won't have to bear the ineffable hurt.

"Much as I'm disappointed, I can't blame you. I have only myself to blame. I misjudged you, thinking you were a self-centered ne'er-do-well. You're anything but. You're industrious and kind. You willingly give of yourself to help others, and you have integrity. Had I judged you fairly in the first instance, I would not have opposed your marriage to Polly."

A possible new twist on what Winslow was saying emerged. "Are you suggesting that if Polly were willing to marry me, you'd give your blessing?"

"Absolutely. Did you think otherwise?"

Thom nodded, his reaction hardly indicative of his excitement. "All along I assumed you were simply looking for me to draw her out of her self-imposed asylum. That I might court her to be my wife was not part of the equation." A notion popped into Thom's head. Before coming, Winslow must have discussed the subject with Polly. Presumably she was on board. Fantasy was about to become reality. The impossible was about to occur. With flames dancing at the hearth, the commodious saltbox on Beartown Mountain blazed with euphoric warmth.

"Knowing that you'd have my blessing, does that change your willingness to call on Polly?"

"Absolutely," said Thom, echoing the identical word that had passed Winslow's lips moments earlier. "I assume you discussed this with Polly before coming here today."

Winslow froze, his blank countenance seeking refuge in the ever-changing hues of the translucent flames.

Silence, interrupted only by the crackling fire, resounded. Like the disintegrating wood, Thom crumbled with Winslow's hush.

"I...I knew if I asked, Polly would have prohibited me from coming."

Collecting his thoughts from amidst the ashes was a struggle. "If I hear you correctly, in the event I call on Polly, she'll likely turn me away."

Winslow shrugged. "Frankly, I don't know. I have no idea how she feels or if she is ready for any man to come into her life."

Even a remote possibility that Polly might be receptive to his advance was enticing. But what if hints that she had designs on Richard bore truth. Memories, tormenting souvenirs of an unbearable wintry depression, sounded alarms. Potential rewards were indescribable, but so too, the possible devastation. Regardless, Thom had committed to leave for Albany the next day to aid Henry Knox. Men, with loves of their own, had already given their lives for the cause of freedom. All along he had voiced his resolve, supporting the Patriots' cause. Young and vibrant, he could not turn his back on his countrymen. He would not go back on his word. "Come morning, I must join the men of Henry Knox and transport the cannons and armaments from Fort Ticonderoga to Boston."

"You won't call on Polly?"

Thom heaved a sigh. He slowly shook a lowering head.

"Well...I can't blame you. Truth is—the fault lies here. I judged you unfairly." Winslow got up and headed to the door.

Thom followed and opened the portal.

Winslow stepped outside but glanced back. "Perhaps when you return from your mission, you'll reconsider?"

Thom found it hard to speak. Thanks to the expedition with Henry Knox, he had escaped the conundrum of inconceivable reward and unbearable risk. "I don't know," he said. "I just don't know."

435

# Chapter 27

THOM ENTERED THE DINING ROOM carrying two toddies. He handed one to Pico and seated himself opposite his friend.

"It must have been quite a trip. I want to hear all about it."

Thom kicked back, putting his feet up onto one of the two trestles that held the table-board during meals. "It was a helluva venture. There were times when it seemed impossible, but Henry Knox was one determined man, the kind who doesn't give up. Whatever the obstacles, however harsh the conditions, he pushed onward. By the time I joined him on the 7th of December, a couple of days after he had arrived at Fort Ticonderoga, he had begun making trips with a gundalow, transporting the artillery to the head of Lake Champlain. Once there, we loaded the artillery on ox carts and dragged them down the portage road to the north end of Lake George."[273]

"Was the lake frozen?"

"Owing to its size and depth, not as yet. And that was fortunate. We were able to float the cannons down the lake, nearly thirty miles, using a flat-bottom barge and a bateau that Knox had acquired. By the 16th, all the weaponry had arrived at Fort George down at the southern end of the lake."

"So, that part of the journey went smoothly?"

"Relatively, compared to others. Of course, along the way, the barge ran aground, and we had a helluva time getting her free. Once we reached Fort George, we had it easy for a few days. But not Knox. He headed south to Albany, about sixty miles, to acquire teams and sleds to transport the cannons. A huge snowstorm, the best part of two feet, added to what was on the ground, saddled him with a tough go. Anyway, by January 1st, the sleds and teams of horses arrived at Fort George."[274]

"Give me a moment," said Pico, gesturing at the shrinking flames in the dining room fireplace. He added a log, an all-dayer, and threw on several pieces of kindling wood before returning to his seat. "Seems like the snow that made Knox's trip tough should have made it easier for the sleds."

"You'd think so...and in some ways it did." Thom sipped his toddy, as he recalled the details of the journey. "It certainly helped as we moved the sleds southward, especially because the roads, what there was of them, were racked with deep gullies. The snow helped fill them in. But in order to reach Albany, we had to cross the Hudson River. The blanket of snow kept the river from freezing. Knox, who had waited in Albany when the sleds and horses were sent north to get the cannons, brought in people to pour water to melt the snow in the hope it would expedite the formation of a frozen passage at Lansing's Ferry, near Halfmoon. Of all things, mild temperatures, the one time they were unwelcome, delivered a diabolical thaw.[275] All we could do was sit and wait. When we finally attempted the crossing, one of the heaviest cannons crashed through the ice. We shifted the crossing to a spot on the Mohawk. The ice was thicker there, but even so, another cannon broke through. Much as I hate to admit it, I began wondering if the expedition might best be left for spring and, at worst, destined to failure. Fortunately, Knox was less of a pessimist, not to mention indomitable. With the help of people from Albany, the impossible, at least in my mind, occurred. We recovered the cannons that went though the ice, made the crossing and, by the 9th of January, we were on our way southeast from Albany.[276]

A wide-eyed Pico stared at Thom.

"What's the matter?"

"It's only the 11th. You mean you moved the cannons all the way from Albany to here in only two days? That's incredible."

"Knox wasn't one to dawdle. He just plowed ahead. Once we left Albany, we headed southeast, about nine miles beyond Kinderhook. From there we went east, and by the 10th, we had reached the Massachusetts border."[277]

"But then you had to face the Berkshires."

"And face them we did. As Knox put it, by nightfall we had 'climb'd mountains from which we might have seen all the Kingdoms of the Earth.'"[278]

"So, where are the cannons now?"

Thom shrugged. "I'm not certain. Around Westfield...I guess."

"You're not gonna see them through to Boston?"

Thom reached for his mug, seeking a haven from the embarrassing question.

"Don't you want to see them delivered to General Washington?"

"Yes, but..." An image of the gratifying moment had Thom debating whether he should have resisted pressure to abandon the caravan as it passed Tyringham. "Knox wanted me to stay here. Finding others to take my place was easy."

"Didn't he..." Pico's voice trailed off, but his message, the possibility that Thom had been pressed to leave the march, was apparent.

"It wasn't like that." Unpleasant recollections of how he had been blackballed from the Minutemen stirred.

"So, why'd you leave?"

Feet still up on the trestle, Thom rocked his chair back onto its rear legs, nearly tipping over. "There was this fellow—John. We became good friends along the way. He told me about his life in Saratoga, and I told him about mine in Tyringham. After much conversation he suggested I leave the march to attend to my personal affairs. When I was reluctant, he went to Knox, who encouraged me to stay here in Tyringham." The mixed emotions that had surrounded his departure from the expedition echoed in Thom's brain. "When your Captain urges you to do something...you do it."

"It's not right...the way people treat you."

"No—you misunderstand. They were concerned about me. They were trying to help." The skeptical look that Thom observed across the table encouraged him to explain, but he preferred to avoid the matter. Though he knew that was not what Pico wanted, he doubted his friend would pry. Unlike most, who yielded to self-indulgent curiosity, Pico respected others' privacy. "Anyway," said Thom, as he skirted the issue, "once the caravan descends from the east side of the Berkshires, the remainder of the trip beyond the Connecticut and Westfield rivers to Boston should be easier. The worst is all behind them."

Visions of the harsh trip they had endured was replaced by an image of the cache that would be reaching the colonists' army. "It's a helluva stockpile that Knox will be delivering. Fifty-nine pieces in all. Forty-three brass and iron cannons, six cohorns, eight mortars and two howitzers.[279] Knox is convinced they'll enable Washington and his men stationed on the Dorchester Heights overlooking Boston to deliver a punishing blow to the British troops below. If he's right, the Siege of Boston, two-thirds of a year long, could cease to be a standoff. The Ticonderoga arsenal could send the Redcoats retreating to the refuge of their harbored ships."

⌇⟋⟋⟍⟍

Atop Lodestone, Thom wended his way from his saltbox down the Albany-Boston Post Road. With several days having passed since the last snowfall, traffic of horses, wagons and a few ox carts had packed much of the white powder, especially in the gullies carved by rolling wheels. Just beyond the intersection of Royal Hemlock Road, Thom drew Lodestone to a halt. He could turn around and head back to higher ground and the security of his saltbox. Two days had elapsed since he had returned home following the expedition to Fort Ticonderoga, and opportunities to venture forth to the quaint Cape Cod would be rife. He could let the matter await the arrival of spring when, with buds bursting under an ever-warming sun, emotions, enervated through the grim depths of winter, would vivify with the gurgling rush of theretofore frozen streams. In the context of pure abstraction, the logic of delay was impeccable. To the extent it purported to be a candid evaluation, it was nothing more than a patent rationalization. Postponement constituted a device to avoid the risks of a precarious undertaking.

Exposure to physical pain would have offered less of a deterrent than the threat of rejection and depression. Scars, memories buried deep within, could again grow raw, and even the most palliative salve would do nothing to alleviate the agony. The risks were inconceivable, but so too the potential rewards. The upshot, much like the "Law of Excluded Middle" that he

439

had encountered in his studies of philosophy, would be either Hell or Heaven, with no middle ground.[280]

Reins in hand, Thom drew Lodestone to a halt and looked in all directions. Barren trees both left and right, sullied snow under foot, and gray skies above portended misfortune. Beguiled and waffling, Thom sat frozen. Lodestone resumed a slow walk. Thom acquiesced, guiding his faithful stallion in the direction of the neat Cape Cod. Minutes later they pulled up in front of the house. Thom drew in several deep breaths. There was still a chance to turn around. He vacillated for a few moments before climbing down and tethering Lodestone to the white picket fence.

Thom inched toward the front door. He climbed the two stairs leading to the portal. He raised the swinging anchor of the nautical brass doorknocker but simply held it in a cocked position. He had previously been inside the Cape—just once—the day he had carried the direly ill Peter Blake from the ground adjoining Twelve-Mile Pond. Thom closed his eyes, envisioning what lay beyond the wooden door, a tiny foyer and stairway with a room on either side. Cold feet cajoled him to steal away. He took another deep breath and released the brass hinge, leaving it to suffer the obdurate whim of gravity. It clacked decisively.

Moments later Polly opened the door. "Why Thom—what an unexpected surprise. I heard you were away in New York helping transport cannons from Fort Ticonderoga."

"I was, but with some encouragement from my cohorts, I left the caravan as it passed through here on route to Boston."

"Come on in, out of the cold."

As she led him into the parlor, he took note of her beige cap and her brown, quilted linen petticoat, beneath which she surely had three or more to keep warm on the seasonably cold January day. Even in her plainest of everyday attire, she was exquisite. She gestured him toward the hearth to a Queen Anne chair with velvet seat and cabriole legs. She seated herself across the way on the turquoise silk-covered settee. "To what do I owe the pleasure of your visit?"

"Lodestone and I were—" Thom choked on the absurdity of his response. He forced himself to be direct. "Uh...some weeks back your father paid me a visit and—"

"My father?" Her brow rippled. "He never mentioned it to me."

The comment, no surprise, had Thom rethinking his approach. Unfortunately, time to chart a sagacious strategy was a luxury he lacked. "Well, he...uh...mentioned it had been a year since Peter's death, and...uh...after the funeral I never really stopped by to pay my respects...uh...that is, personally."

"Oh, it's nice of you to come, not that it was necessary."

Nerves, coupled with the appearance that he had all but fulfilled his avowed purpose, tempted Thom to express his condolences and gracefully leave.

"May I get you some warm cider?"

"No thanks." The instinctive reply was no sooner uttered than he realized the beverage would have provided an excuse to stay.

"I'm glad you came by."

The comment, almost as good as an invitation, kindled a wave of optimism.

"I too have felt remiss. After the funeral I should have visited your home and expressed my thanks. Were it not for you, Peter might have perished alone in the woods. No one should have to spend the last of his earthly moments that way. And thanks to you, I had the chance to tell him goodbye."

The appreciative words, though nice, dashed the excitement Thom had felt a moment earlier when Polly had voiced enthusiasm about his visit.

"I...I'm sorry Peter didn't fair better with his illness."

With a somber mien, Polly heaved a sigh.

The precisely sewn sampler of her countenance was familiar. Pain owing to the loss of her husband was stitched across her face. Perhaps it was time for Thom to depart. He had conveyed his sympathies, and she, her thanks. The visit could be labeled a success; nowhere near the success for which he yearned, but at least free of the horrific agony that rejection would bear. The perils filled his head. He remained uncertain whether she, not her father, may have quashed their relationship several years earlier. Even if she were not responsible, there had been hints her current affections lay elsewhere, perhaps with Richard. Thom's brain raced in self-debate. Fleeing was a double-edged sword. It could foster interminable regrets, never knowing whether his dream of dreams could have become reality. He blurted out, "I...I would like to call on you...if I may?"

"Court me?" Her eyes were wide, but her lips lacked the curvature of the enthusiastic smile he had hoped to see.

"Uh...yes, I'd like to court you again...if that's okay?"

She shook her head. "It's...it's not a good idea." In a soft and rueful voice, she added, "I'm sorry."

Whatever ache she may have experienced, it paled when compared to the pain precipitated by the dagger she had driven into his heart. "I understand," he said, his words the antithesis of what he felt. Reeling from the thunderous blow, he got up from his seat. "I...I should be going."

She followed him to the door. As he opened it, she said, "I appreciate your coming."

He nodded, unable to utter an audible response. The sound of the door closing behind him, like a coffin being shut, struck a painful note of finality. From the warmth of her hearth, he had stepped out into a desolate world. Mindlessly, filled with despair, he mounted Lodestone and rode off.

⁓⟋⟋⟋⟋⟍⟍⟍⟍⁓

One by one the agonizing days of January and February rolled past. Though less painful than the winter that ensued four years earlier when his marriage proposal had been nixed, it was a difficult time. Where Sarah had tried to distract Thom from his misery in 1772, Pico endeavored to do the same in 1776. Like the chores at Sarah's home that had helped Thom's mind travel halfway from Hell to normalcy, tasks at the saltbox provided a measure of escape. He had added a hickory mantle over the parlor fireplace and fashioned a fine dining room table whose curved lines and ogee edges bore a French provincial flavor. It was far more impressive than the chair with circular fold-down back he had previously contemplated. But what might have been exciting labors of love were riddled with emptiness. And then there were the nights, long hours of darkness in which his mind could not elude itself. The harder he tried to keep

Polly from his thoughts, the more she dominated them. Interludes of sleep, fitful at best, were interrupted with her image. Her place, as ever, was on a pedestal, one that grew higher as Thom sank lower. But unlike its predecessor, when the veto of his marriage had come as a total shock and he had crashed into a seemingly bottomless abyss, in 1776 Thom had approached Polly with lower expectations. He understood the risks, and that knowledge helped mitigate his pain. Regardless, that was little consolation. It was pain nonetheless.

It was the first Saturday after the vernal equinox, and tantalizing harbingers of spring, though far from ubiquitous in the Berkshire elevations, were breaking winter's stranglehold. Under an ever-higher sun, accumulated snow was transmuting into tiny meandering streams. In a matter of days the first crocus would poke its nose through the loamy earth, and robins, returned from warmer havens in the South, would chirp blithe melodies. Along with Pico, Thom sat in Sarah's parlor. A month had passed since he had ventured more than a few hundred yards from the confines of his saltbox. Preferring to free Sarah of the fuss associated with one of her magnificent dinners, not that she deemed them a burden, Thom and Pico had dropped by unexpectedly. Even so, her acquiescence to serve them nothing more than molasses cookies and a hissing-hot brandy flip was begrudging.

"Yesterday, when I was down at Brewer's gristmill," she said, "Deacon Hale passed on some interesting news from Boston." From her seat in the rocking chair that Thom had made, she looked him in the eye. "I don't imagine you hermits are up to date on such matters."

Pico gestured at Thom. "My friend here thinks the universe begins and ends with the plot we call home. Last week I tried to drag him to the Hogshead, but when a mule refuses to budge, a mule refuses to budge."

"He can be stubborn." Sarah brandished an outlandish grin.

Sensing he was outnumbered and that defensive posturing would fuel more gibes, Thom said, "Do you plan to leave us in the dark about the news from Boston?"

Sarah leaned Pico's way. "On top of obstinate, he's touchy too." She flashed another smile before looking back at Thom.

"The Deacon says those cannons you helped transport came in handy. They reached Boston fifty-six days after they left Fort Ticonderoga. Washington and his troops had a field day once they arrived. For almost a year the siege of Boston has been a standoff. Once the artillery was stationed at the Dorchester Heights, they began bombarding the British army in the city below. Sure enough, the Redcoats fled to Boston Harbor and the safety of their ships.[281] According to the Deacon, folks are starting to believe we can win this war."[282]

∽◌◐◑◌∼

Seated on the huge boulder located at the edge of the clearing some twenty yards from the southeast corner of his saltbox, Thom soaked in the rays of an inordinately warm early April midday. He had finished gathering scores of fallen twigs and branches, a process that enhanced the appearance of his property, while providing an ample supply of kindling wood for the next winter. He drew his head back and, gazing upward at a blue sky decorated with a few fair weather clouds, watched a white elephant approach the nebulous head of a dragon. The ephemeral forms slowly merged, leaving an undefined, ever-changing mass in their wake. Thom closed his eyes, contemplating the after-image of the amorphous sight. Life in the Heavens metamorphosed faster than on earth, but it was no more anomalous. In either realm prognosticating the future was a rash ride over a capricious course.

Amidst his reverie he thought he heard the call of his name. It was as if God were calling to him. A moment later he heard his name again, only this time it was apparent it had come not from the distant reaches of the firmament, but rather close by. He opened his eyes and saw Polly standing in front of him.

"I hope I didn't startle you."

"Uh...no...uh...not at all," he said, the jerky staccato of his cadence belying his words. He sat up from what was nearly a prone position on his back. "What brings you up this way?"

"I..." She broke eye contact, her discomposure arguably exceeding his. "The...uh...last time we spoke, at my house,

I...uh...thanked you for bringing Peter home where he and I could say goodbye, but my thanks to you were incomplete."

"Incomplete?"

She nodded.

"Where are my manners?" he said, as he started to get up.

"I'd rather we sit...and with such a big rock, there's plenty of room."

He moved over, and she joined him.

"What did you mean when you referred to your thanks as incomplete?"

"Just before Peter died, he begged that I not wallow in grief too long. Future happiness, a new love, would be, as he termed it, my gift to him. When I showed reluctance, he made me promise to try. Were it not for you, I would have never had his blessing, let alone entreaty, and without them I would have withdrawn into an ascetic shell. But thanks to you, I have not only the chance to find love, but also the obligation. My failure to express my appreciation was inexcusable."

Thom's heart sank. Her words lauding his kindness had punctured the spirits they were intended to lift. She was ready to find a new love. Perhaps she already had. And no doubt, Thom was not the lucky man. Back in January she had spurned his request to court her again. A quick assessment, and Thom was confident where her affections lay. The realization compounded his pain. Silent, aching, he stared into space.

"Your reaction confirms what I said. Not thanking you was inexcusable."

He shook his head. No sooner did he make the instinctive gesture than he realized he was encouraging her self-flagellation. "No, you misunderstand. I wasn't faulting you."

"Then what?"

"It's...it's..." Admitting he could not bear to hear her utter Richard's name was harder yet than the granite on which they sat. He sought solace knowing that his rescue of Peter was not in vain. He had freed Polly of shackles that would have barred her from future happiness. Thom would do anything for Polly. He told himself: *Your good deed is an immense gift not only to Polly, but also your dearest friend, Richard. Take pride that you have proved yourself a good man, far better than he who begot*

445

*you.* His brain's exhortations, their reasoned counsel, were compelling. Logic battled emotions. A part of him was happy for Polly and Richard. But for himself, there was pain. And the pain was excruciating.

"I came here to apologize. Instead I've distressed you." She drew in a deep breath and murmured to herself, "How can I say this?"

With Polly struggling as much as he, Thom glanced skyward. No animals floating above were there to help. And if the master of the Heavens had any advice, his message was lost in the vast beyond.

"Last evening my father stopped by and asked if at any time since last December you had tried to court me. When I told him you did, he said, 'And?' His reaction baffled me, and I responded, 'And what?'"

Befuddled, Thom had all he could do to suppress a redundant *And?* of his own.

"Then my father asked me what I had said to you, and when I told him I had turned you down, he responded with a dumfounded expression, after which he said, 'Why?'"

"You don't have to tell me. I know the reason."

"You do?"

"Yes...because you're in love with someone else."

Her eyes grew wide. "Someone else?"

Her incredulous look demanded that he explain himself. "You...you aren't in love with Richard?"

"Whatever made you think that?"

Thom searched his brain summoning the evidence. Richard had described her as the prettiest woman this side of the Connecticut River. The description, while accurate, proved nothing regarding her feelings for him...Jenkins had seen Polly and Richard walking along the Konkapot. Big deal. Jenkins was anything but credible. And when furnishing the gossip, he was trying to get under Thom's skin...Other evidence? Not really, apart from unfounded surmises...Add common sense to the equation—Richard would never stab Thom in the back—and the scenario became implausible. Still the facts, the logic, did not preclude the possibility that Polly was in love with another. Thom gazed at her, uncertain what to say.

Patient, as always, she appeared to await his explanation.

"I...uh..." Thom shrugged abashedly. "Uh, pretend I never mentioned Richard's name."

Polly smiled.

The warm expression, more powerful than words, mitigated Thom's discomfort, though hardly enough that he could aptly respond.

She waited several moments before reaching down, just below her neckline. She removed the top two straight pins fastening the top of the gown that lay under her red cape. She slid her hand into the opening and drew out a wooden busk.

With its two, small carved hearts, Thom recognized it as the one he had given her several years earlier.

"After you came to court me last December, I dug this out from the bottom of what was once my hope chest. No doubt I loved Peter, but you...you were the love of my life. With him gone a full year and with me still languishing in grief, I needed something...something to lift my spirits, if only symbolically. The busk you gave me filled the bill. I put it on and have been wearing it ever since."

A spark of hope flashed. But it made no sense. She had turned him away.

Almost as if she had read his mind, she said, "Your overture was welcome. But its inevitable consequences drove me to reject it. I assumed my father would never bless our relationship. To begin it anew, only to see it crushed again, was more than I could bear."

The disclosure reminded Thom of his own conversation in which he had erroneously assumed Polly's father had spoken to her before encouraging Thom to court her. Issac Winslow, knowing his daughter was languishing from the loss of her husband, did not want her to get her hopes up, only to suffer the pain of rejection. Exposing Thom to that risk was easier than his daughter. Thom leaned back onto his elbows, again taking in the sky. The clouds overhead had drifted away. Sun-filled, blue heavens prevailed. Thom turned to Polly as he searched for the right words to confirm her message.

Before he could phrase his thoughts, Polly leaned closer. The longing in her eyes, a mirror of his emotions, provided ample verification. An instant later their lips met. Moments before he had been gazing at the Heavens. With eyes closed, he could no longer see the celestial world. It mattered not. There in Tyringham, on a granite rock, Thom had found paradise. He was in Heaven.

# Bibliography

Abbott, Tim (blogging as Greenman, Tim). *Through the Berkshires with Henry Knox.* Posted 15 May, 2010. *Walking the Berkshires Blogspot,* 19 Sept. 2010 <http://greensleeves.typepad.com/berkshires//2010/05/through-the-berkshires-with-henry-knox.html>.

Adams Samuel. *The Rights, of Colonists, The Report of the Committee of Correspondence to the Boston Town Meeting.* 20 Nov. 1772. Retrieved from the Constitution Society website, 29 Nov. 2009 <http://www.constitution.org/bcp/right_col.htm>.

*Adonijah Bidwell. Wikipedia.* 9 Nov. 2009 <http://en//wikipedia.org/wiki/Adonijah_Bidwell>.

*All About Maple. Siloam Orchards.* 2 Aug. 2010 <http://www.siloamorchards.com/ALL%20ABOUT%20MAPLE.htm>.

American History, 1763-1783, Second Continental Congress. u-s-history.com. 28 Aug. 2010 <http://www.u-s-history.com/pages/h656.html>.

An Act Exempting for their Majestyes Protestant Subjects dissenting from the Church of England from the Penalties of certaine Lawes, 24 May 1689, 1 will. & Mar. c. 18. Wikipedia. 30 Nov. 2009 <http://en.wikipedia.org/wiki/Act_of_Toleration_1689>.

*American Colonial Customs and Traditions, Old Colonial Days and Ways, VI. School and Meeting House.* sonofthesouth.net. Maintained by McWhorter, Paul. 13 Nov. 2009 <http://sonofthesouth.net/revolutionary-war/colonies/colonial-ways.htm>.

*America's Best History – U.S. Timeline 1775. America's Best History* website. 5 Jul. 2010 <http://americasbesthistory.com/abhtimeline1770.html>.

Bachelor, Rosemary E. *What Was a Freeman in Colonial New England? suite101.com* website. 18 Dec. 2010 <http://www.suite101.com.com/content/what-was-afreman-in-colonial-new-england-a98295>.

*Baron de Montesquieu: A Short Biography. rigeib.com.* 24 Nov. 2009 <rigeib.com/thoughts/montesquieu/montesquieu-bio.html>.

Basic Information about Log Homes from Southern Cross Log Homes in East Tennessee, Truss Types. 19 Oct. 2009 <http://www.southerncrossloghomes.com/log%20homes/info.html>.

*Battles of Lexington and Concord. Wikipedia.* 13 Aug. 2010 <http://en.wikipedia.org/wiki/Battles_of_Lexington_and_Concord>.

Bernstein, Melvin H., Moderator. 8 January 2013. *Setting the Record Straight: The Worcester Revolt of September 6, 1774.* Massachusetts Society, Sons of the Revolution website. 8 Nov. 2013 <http://web.massar.org/setting-the-record-straight-the-worcester-revolt-of-september-6-1774/>.

*Bible, Deuteronomy.* Masoretic Text. Philadelphia: The Jewish Publication Society of America, 1917.

*Bidwell House Museum.* The Bidwell House Museum website. 1 Aug. 2009 <html://bidwellhousemuseum.org>.

Bidwell, O. C. *History of Berkshire County, Massachusetts.* New York: J. B. Beers & Co., 1885.

Bloy, Dr. Marjorie. *The Age of George III, The Coercive Acts. A Web of English History.* 27 Nov. 2009 <http://www.historyhome.co.uk/c-eight/America/coercive.htm>.

Bok, Hillary. Baron de Montesquieu, Charles Louis de Secondat, The Spirit of the Laws. Revised 20 Jan. 10. The Stanford Encyclopedia of Philosophy. 4 Oct. 10 <http://plato.stanford.edu/entries/montesquieu/>.

*Boston Pamphlet. Wikipedia.* (Citing Middlekauf, Robert. *Glorious Cause, The American Revolution 1763-1789*, p.223. rev. ed., New York: Oxford University Press, 2005). 28 Nov. 2009 <http://en.wikepedia.org/wiki/Boston Pamphlet>.

*Boston Tea Party. New World Encyclopedia* website. 27 Nov. 2009 <http://www.newworldencyclopedia.org/entry/Boston_Tea_Party>.

*Boston Tea Party Historical Society.* 14 Jan. 2012 <http://www.boston-tea-party.org/mohawkss.html>.

Burns, Edward McNull and Philip Lee Ralph. *World Civilizations.* Volume 2, New York: Norton and Co., 1958.

*By the King, A Proclamation For Suppressing Rebellion and Sedition.* Papers of the Continental Congress, 1774-1789, Item 152, Letters from Gen. George Washington, Commander in Chief of the Army, 1775-84, vol. 1, p.271. Records of the Continental and Confederation Congresses and the Constitutional Convention, Record Group 360; National Archives. Retrieved from National Archives website, 25 Nov. 2013 <http://www.archives.gov/historical-docs/todays-doc/?dod-date=823>.

*Cambridge and the American Revolution.* Cambridge Historical Society website. 7 Apr.10

<http://cambridgehistory.org/discover/Cambridge-Revolution/index.html>.

*Canada in the American Revolution*, Shmoop.com website, 2 Feb. 2016 <http://www.shmoop.com/american-revolution/canada-battle.html>.

*Christmas Celebration Outlawed.* Mass Moments, Multimedia Archive, Massachusetts Foundation for the Humanities website. 28 Sept. 2013 <httpp://www.massmoments.org/moment.cfm?mid=369>.

Colonel Ashley House, Sheffield, Berkshire Co., Massachusetts. 14 Nov. 2013 <http://www.josfamilyhistory.com/sheffield-ma.htm>.

Colonial America: The Simple Life, Early American Food and Drink. Colonial America: The Simple Life. 17 Dec. 2009 <html://colonial-american-life.blogspot.com/>.

*Colonial Gentlemen's Clothing: A Glossary of Terms.* Colonial Williamsburg website. 28 Dec. 2010 <http://www.history.org/history/clothing/men/mglossary.cfm>.

*Conciliatory Resolution. Wikipedia.* 5 Jul. 2010 <http://en.wikipedia.org/wiki/Conciliatory_Resolution>.

Cook, Don. *The Long Fuse, How England Lost the American Colonies, 1760 –1785.* New York: Atlantic Monthly Press, 1995. In *Parliament Hears Colonial Protest. suite101.com* website. 5 Jul. 2010 <http://www.colonial-america.suite101.com/article.cfm/parliament hears_colonial_protest>.

Cooke, Rollin Hillyer. *Historic Homes and Institutions and Genealogical and Personal Memoirs of Berkshire County Massachusetts.* New York: Lewis Publishing Co., 1906. Retrieved from *books.google.com.* 5 Oct. 2010

<http://books.google.com/books?id=EDzcGVZnIC&printsec=fr
ontcover&dq=Rollin+Hillyer+Cooke>.

*Cribbage Rules. www.cribbagesupply.com.* 5 Aug. 2010
<html://www.cribbagesupply.comcribbagerules.html>.

*DC Theatricks - British Redcoat Uniform. www.costume.com.* 8
Jan. 2011
<http://www.costume.com/sales/costumes/1776br.htm>.

*Declaration and Resolves of the First Continental Congress,
October 14, 1774.* The Avalon Project, Documents in Law,
History and Diplomacy. Yale Law School. 20 Oct. 2013
<html://avalon.law.yale.edu/18th_century/resolves.asp>.

DeSimone, David. *Another Look at Christams in the Eighteenth
Century* (Question #6). *The Colonial Williamsburg Interpreter.*
Vol. 16, no. 4, winter 1995-96. Reprinted Colonial Williamsburg
website. 28 Jun. 2010
<http://www.history.org/almanack/life/xmas/xmasqa.cfm>.

*Digital Collections – Splitting Froe or Frower.* Memorial Hall
Museum's *American Centuries* website. 23 Jun. 2010
<http://www.americancenturies.mass.edu/collection/itempage.jsp
?itemid=6536>.

Dooley, Rev. John, et al. *History of the First Congregational
Society in Monterey, Mass.* Great Barrington, MA: Courier Job
and Press, 1900. Retrieved from Internet Archive of American
Libraries, U. Mass., Amherst. 11 Sept. 2009
<http://archive.org/details/historyoffirstco00mont>

Earle, Alice Morse. *Home Life in Colonial Days.* New York:
The MacMillan Company, 1898. Retrieved from Internet
Archive of American Libraries, University of California. 20 Oct.
2013 <http://archive.org/details/homelifecolonial00earlrich>.

Eastman, Anne and Charles. *NH Years Of Revolution.* Profiles
Publications and NH Bicentennial Commission. 1976.

Retrieved from *seacoastNH* website. Robinson, J Dennis, editor. *Fort William and Mary, Tea Troubles. SeacoastNH.* 7 Apr. 2010 <http://www.seacoastnh.com/history/rev/willmary.html>.

Elverson, Virginia T. and Mary Ann McLanahan. A Cooking Legacy. New York: Walker, 1975. The Food Timeline: History Notes - Colonial America and 17th and 18th Century France, Breakfast , Lunch and Dinner? 12 Dec. 2005 <http://www.foodtimeline.org/foodcolonial>.

*Events of 1775. Wikipedia.* 28 Aug. 2010 <http://en.wikipedia.org/wiki/1775>.

*First Continental Congress. Wikipedia.* 30 May 2010 <http://en.wikipedia.org/wiki/First_Continental_Congress>.

Flags Over America - The Colonial Period, Pine Tree Flag 1686. americanrevolution.org website. 9 Jun. 2010 <http://americanrevolution.org/flags.html>.

Franklin, Benjamin (published under the pseudonym Richard Saunders). *Poor Richard's Improved: Almanack and Ephemeris, etc.,1753.* Retrieved from Gettysburg College website. 9 Dec. 2009 <http://public.gettysburg.edu~tshannon/his341>.

*George Whitefield (1714-1770). Calvinist, Evangelist and Revivalist. ReformationSA.org* website. 11 Dec. 2009 <http://www.reformationsa.org/articles/George%20Whitefield.htm>.

Grinsdale, Tom. *Eighteenth Century American Fowlers - The First Guns Made in America.* Retrieved from The American Society of Arms Collectors website. 15 Jan. 2010 <http://www.asoac/bulletins/89_grinsdale_fowler.pdf>.

*Gristmills.* Retrieved from the Baker Block Museum website. 15 Jun. 2010 <http:bakerblockmuseum.org/heritage/gristmill/gristmill.htm>.

Grizzard, Jr., Frank E. *Supply Problems Plagued the Continental Army from the Start.* Retrieved from H-Net Humanities & Social Sciences OnLine website. 9 Sept. 2010 <http://revolution.h-net.msu.edu/essays/grizzard.html>.

Hanson, Darryl. *The Massachusetts Revolution of 1774, The Colonists Response to the Coercive Acts.* 30 Aug. 2009. *suite101.com* website. 7 Apr. 10 <http://www.colonialamerica.suite101.com/article.cfm/the_mass achusetts_revolution_of_1774-0143897> (citing Raphael, Ray. *A People's History of the American Revolution.* New York: The New Press 2001, pp. 38-46).

Harper, Douglas. *Slavery in the North* website. 14 Nov. 2013 <http://www.slavenorth.com/massachusetts.htm>.

Hartman, Jon. *Into the Wood.* Daniel Boone Homestead website. 21 Nov. 2009 <homestead.org/oleyvalley.htm>.

History Myths Debunked, Myth #1: Houses didn't have closets in colonial days because people wanted to paying the closet tax, January 18, 2014, 26 Nov. 2014 <http://historymyths.wordpress.com/?=closets>.

Hunt, Agnes, Ph.D. *The Provincial Committees of Safety of the American Revolution* (Massachusetts). Cleveland OH: Winn & Judson, 1904. Retrieved from *books.google.com/.* 24 Oct. 2013 <https://www.google.com/search?q=Agnes+Hunt&btnG=Search =Books&tbm=bks&tbo=1>.

Hutchison-Whatley Letters. Encyclopedia.com. 27 Nov. 2009 <http://www.encyclopedia.com/doc/1G2-2536600541.html>.

*Intolerable Acts. New World Encyclopedia.* 27 Nov. 2010 <http://www.newworldencyclopedia.org/entry/Intolerable_Acts>.

*Iroquois Indian Tribe History. accessgenealogy.com* website. 4 Sept. 2010

<http://www.accessgenealogy.com/native/tribes/iroquioi/iroquois hist.htm>.

Jewett, Kenneth. *Gunne Versus Rifled Gunne in Colonial America.* 15 Jan. 2010 <http://kennethjewett.com/rifled-gun.html>.

*Jonathan Edwards and the Great Awakening in Colonial America.* Constitutional Rights Foundation website. 12 Dec. 2009 <http://www.crf-usa.org/bill-of-rights/bria-20-4-a.html>.

*Josiah Smith Tavern (Weston Places),* Weston Historical Society website, 16 Dec. 2013 <http://www.westonhistory.org/Extra-HTML-pages/Josiah-Smith-Tavern-Topic.html>.

Kraus, Melody. *Maple Sugaring: Native American Lore and History.* emmitsburg.net. 2 Aug. 2010 <www.emmitsburg.net/gardens/articles/adams/2010/maple_sugaring.htm>.

*Lath and Plaster. Wikipedia.* 19 Oct. 2009 <http://en.wikipedia.org/wiki/Lath_and__Plaster>.

*Law of Excluded Middle, Wikipedia,* 26 Nov. 2014 <http://en.wikipedia.org/wiki/Law_of_excluded_middle>.

*Letter from Governor Gage to the Earl of Dartmouth.* 27 Aug. 1774. Retrieved from American Archives, Documents of the American Revolution 1774-1776, Series 4, Vol. 1, Page 0741. Northern Illinois University Libraries. 13 Nov. 2013 <http://lincoln.lib.niu.edu/cgi-bin/philologic/getobject.pl?c.845:1.amarch>.

Lincoln, William. *History of Worcester Massachusetts, From its Earliest Settlement to 1836.* Worcester, MA: Charles Hershey, 1862. Retrieved from Internet Archive of American Libraries, The Library of Congress. 12 Nov. 2013 <http://archive.org/stream/historyofworcest00hers>.

Lionel, Henry and Ottalie K. Williams. *Old American Homes and How to Restore Them 1750-1850.* Garden City, New York: Doubleday and Co., 1946. Retrieved from Internet Archive of American Libraries. 1 Nov. 2009 <http://www.archive.org/stream/oldamericanhouse008982mbp/oldamericanhouse008982mpb_djvu.txt>.

Lossing, Benson J. *Our Country: A Household History for All Readers.* Vol. II. New York: Johnson Wilson & Co., 1875. Retrieved from Public Bookshelf website. 30 May, 2010 <http://www.publicbookshelf.com/public_html/Our_Country_vol_2/eventsfir_ed.html>.

*Mid 18th Century Club Butt Fowler Modified for Militia Usage,* Lodgewood Mfg. Ltd. website, 4 Nov. 2015 <http://www.lodgewood.com/Mid-18th-Century-Club-Butt-Fowler-Modified-for-Militia-Usage_c_238.html>

*Minutemen. Wikipedia.* 4 Nov. 2010, <http://en.wikipedia.org/wiki/Minutemen>.

Myers, Eloise. *A Hinterland Settlement, Tyringham, Berkshire County, Massachusetts.* Pittsfield, MA: Eagle and Binding Company, 1944. Reprinted Troy, NY: Troy Bookmakers.

*Native Americans of Columbia County New York, The Mohicans of Columbia County.* The Valatie Free Library website. 19 Sept. 2009 <http://www.valatielibary.org./mohicans.htm>.

Ohara, Robert J. *Why We Remember Lexington and Concord and the Nineteenth of April.* Robert J. O'Hara website. 13 Aug. 2010 <http://rjohara.net/gen/wars/Minutemen>.

Oliver Lynne. *The Food Timeline, Colonial American Tavern Fare.* The Food Timeline website, as updated 20 Jul. 2011. 31 Dec. 2011 <http://www.foodtimeline.org/foodcolonial.html>.

Palmer, Charles J. *Berkshire County, Its Past History and Achievements.* 1882. Retrieved from *eBooksRead* website. 27 Oct. 2009 <www.ebooksread.com/authors-eng/charles-j-charles-james-palmer.shmtl>.

Panshin, Cory. The Padget History of America from the Landing at Plymouth to the Events of the Revolution, The Revolution and After. 4 Nov. 2009 and 16 Dec. 2013 <http://enter.net/~torve/trogholm/geneal/history/historyD.htm>.

Perkins, Eric. *47ᵗʰ Foot in North America, 1772-1781. 47ᵗʰfoot.blogspot.com.* 8 Jan. 2011 <http://47thfoot.blogspot.com/2009/02/redcoat-uniforms-part-1-privates-and.html>.

Powder Alarm, Facts, Discussion Forum, and Encyclopedia Article. Wikipedia. 4 Apr. 2010 <http://www.wikipedia.org/wiki/Powder_Alarm>.

Pretzer, William S. *How Products are Made, Nails.* Vol. 2. madehow.com. 11 Nov. 2013 <http://www.madehow.com/Volume-2/Nail.html>.

*Quakers in Action, John Woolman. Quakers in the World* website. 16 Nov. 2013 <http://www.quakersintheworld.org/quakers-in-action/62>.

Raphael, Ray. Founding Myths: Stories that Hide Our Patriotic Past. New York: New Press, 2004.

Resolutions of the House of Burgesses of Virginia, Designating a Day of Fasting and Prayer, Tuesday the 24ᵗʰ of May, 14 Geo. III, 1774. UShistory.org website. 8 Oct. 2010 <http://www.ushistory.org/declaration/related/vsa65.htm>.

*Revolution Myth #5. thehistoricpresent.wordpress.com* website. 6 Sept. 2010 <http://thehistoricpresent.wordpress.com/?s=Revolution+Myrth+%235>.

*Rogers Rangers. Wikipedia.*18 Nov. 2010
<http://en.wikipedia.org/wiki/Rogers'_Rangers>.

Roueche, Berton. *Alcohol in Human Culture.* In: Salvatore P.
Lucia, *Alcohol and Civilization.* New York: McGraw-Hill, 1963
pp. 167-182. Retrieved from *Fun Facts, Puritans to Prohibition,*
of the *Alcohol, Problems and Solutions.* Website of Hanson,
David J., Ph.D. 14 Oct. 2009
<http://www2.potsdam.edu/hansondj/funfacts/PuritansToProhib
ition.html>.

*Rules of Cribbage.* American Cribbage Congress website. 5 Aug.
2010 <http://cribbage.org.rules/rule1.asp>.

Sage, Henry J. *United States History, Discovery and
Colonization 1550-1660, Colonial Period, The Puritans of New
England.* Sage American History website. 26 Oct. 2013
<http:/sageamericanhistory.net/colonial/topics/puritannewenglan
d.html>.

Samuel Adams: Summary and Analysis: Section 8: Committees
of Correspondence. sparknote.com website. 28 Nov. 2009
<http://sparknotes.com/biography/samadams/section.rhtml>.

Scott, John A. *Tyringham: Old and New.* Pittsfield, MA: Sun
Printing Co., 1905. Retrieved from Internet Archive of
American Libraries. Library of Congress. 12 Oct. 2009
<http://www.archive.org/stream/tyringhamoldnew00scot>.

Shelton, Jane DeForest. *The Saltbox House: Eighteenth
Century Life in a New England Hill Town.* New York: Baker
and Taylor, 1901. Retrieved from Internet Archive of American
Libraries. 4 Dec. 2009
<http://www.archive.org/details/saltboxhouseeigh00shelrich>.

*Smallpox Information.* Mount Sinai Hospital website. 4 Dec.
2013

<http://www.mountsinai.org/patient-care/health-library/diseases-and-conditions/smallpox>.

*Smallpox. Reference.com.* website. 10 Oct. 2010
<http://www.reference.com/browse/smallpox>.

*Smallpox Vaccine. Wikipedia.* 29 Nov. 2013
<http://en.wikipedia.org/wiki/Smallpox_vaccine>.

Smith, George F. *A Long Time Ago in Boston, Part III.* strike-the-root.com. Posted 10 Dec. 2003. 6 Oct. 2010
<http://www.strike-the-root.com/3/smith/smith17.html>.

Smith, Larry D. *A Chronology of the Revolutionary War, 1775 Liberty or Death. Mother Bedford* website. 5 Jul. 2010
<http://www.motherbedford.com/Chronology05.htm>.

Stone, Carol. Ways of the World. American Revolution: A Government Overturned in 1774. 7 Jul. 2009. Posted 18 Jul. 2009. The Geranium Farm: Ways of the World Blogspot. 8 Oct. 2010
<http://ways-of-the world.blogspot.com/2009_07_01_archive.html>.

*Sycamore Shoals. Wikipedia.* 9 Aug. 2009
<http://en.wikipedia.org/wiki/Sycamore_Shoals#Treaty_of_Sycamore_Shoals>.

*Tarring and Feathering.* HistoryWiz website. 13Nov. 2013
<http://www.historywiz.com/didyouknow/trringandfewathering.htm>

Taylor, Charles James. *History of Great Barrington (Berkshire County) Massachusetts.* Great Barrington, MA: Clark W. Bryan and Co., 1882. Retrieved from the Internet of American Libraries, U. Mass. Amherst. 9 Sept. 2010
<https://archive.org/details/historyofgreatba00tayl>.

*The American Revolution, The Battles of Lexington and Concord. The American Revolution.* 13 Aug. 2010 <http://www.theamericanrevolution.org/battledetail.aspx?battle=1.html>.

*The Battle of Ticonderoga.* School City of Hobart website. 28 Aug. 2010 <http://www.hobart.k12.in.us/cside/American%20Revolution/revwar/ticonder.htm>.

*The Boston Tea Party. patriotresource.com* website. 27 Nov. 2009 <http:www.patriotresource.com/amerrev/events/bostontea.html>.

*The Boston Tea Party.* The American Revolution Home Page website. 27 Nov. 2009 <http:www.americanrevwar.homestead.com/files/TEAPARTY.HTM>.

*The Coming of the American Revolution: 1764-1776.* The Massachusetts Historical Society website. 25 Sept. 2010 <http://www.masshist.org/revolution/index.html>.

*The Continental Congress. Sonofthesouth.net.* Maintained by McWhorter, Paul. 13 Sept. 2010 <http://www.sonofthesouth.net/revolutionary-war/political/continental-congress.htm>.

*The Dominy Craftsmen of East Hampton.* easthamptonstar.com. 25 Dec. 2010 <http://www.easthamptonstar.com/DNN/Archive/1998/981231/hist.htm>.

*The Energy Story.* Updated 22 Apr. 2002. *Energy Quest* website, California Energy Commission. 15 Jun. 2010 <http://www.energyquest.ca.gov/story/chapter12.html>.

*The Kings Broad Arrow, The White Pine Monographs.*
Northeastern Lumber Manufacturers Association website. 9
Oct. 2010 <http://www.nelma.org/Page-19.html>.

*The Knox Trail - History.* New York State Museum website. 11
Oct. 2010
<http://www.nysm.nysed.gov/services/KnoxTrail/kthistory.html>.

*The Life and Times of Benjamin Franklin, The Hutchinson
Letters Affair.* The Franklin Institute website, Resources for
Science Learning. 27 Nov. 2009
<http://sln.fi.edu/franklin/timeline/hutchin.html>.

*The Massachusetts Body of Liberties* (91). *The Harvard
Classics,* Vol. 43, Eliot, Charles W., Editor. New York: P.F.
Collier & Son, 1909-14. Retrieved from *Great Books Online*
website. 14 Nov. 2013 <http://www.bartleby.com/43/8.html>.

*The Massachusetts Constitution, Judicial Review, The Mum
Bett Case.* Updated 22 Dec. 2010. *mass.gov.* The Official
Website of the Commonwealth of Massachusetts. 17 Nov. 2013
<http://www.mass.gov/courts/sjc/constitution-slaver-d.html>.

*The 1902 Smallpox Epidemic. Historic Knightstown Inc.*
website. 29 Nov. 2013 <http://oldktown.com/?page_id=819>.

*The Price of Furniture in Colonial Philadelphia.* New England
Antiques Journal website. 25 Dec. 2010
<http://www.antiquesjournal.com/pages09/monthlypages/april09
/cost.html>.

*The Story of Maine, The Burning of Falmouth.* Maine Public
Broadcasting Network website. 25 Nov. 2013
<http://www.mpbn.net/homestom/p11falmouthburning.html>.

*U.S. History.* www.apstudynotes.org, 30 Nov. 2009
<http://www.apstudynotes.org/us-history/outlines/>.

*UShistory.org* website. 7 Oct. 2010 <http://ushistory.org/>.

United States, National Park Service. *The American Revolution, Lighting Freedom's Flame,* as updated 24 Dec. 2008. 30 Dec. 2011 <www.nps.gov/revwar/about_the_revolution/capsules_history.html>.

*Vocabulary Words for Colonial America.* Yale University website. 27 Sept. 2009 and 8 Oct. 2011 <http://www.yale.edu/ynhti/curriculum/units/1990/5/90.05.04.x.html>.

Weiss, Dr. Richard. *There Are More Old Drunkards Than Doctors.* Blanchard Colonial Tavern website, 31 Dec. 2011 <http://www.blanchardstavern.com/TavernLife.html>.

Winthrop, Mark. *Major John Pitcairn, Battles of Lexington and Concord.* The Henderson Island website, 13 Aug. 2010 <http://www.winthrop.dk/majpit5.html>.

Wirt, William. *Sketches of the Life and Character of Patrick Henry.* Philadelphia: James Webster, 1817. Retrieved from *Documenting the American South* website. 12 Nov. 2013 <http://docsouth.unc.edu/southlit/wirt/wirt.html>.

# Endnotes

[1] O. C. Bidwell, *History of Berkshire County, Massachusetts,* Vol. II, Chapter XXXI, *Town of Tyringham* (New York: J. B. Beers & Co., 1885) p. 606 et seq. "The first permanent settlers were Lieut. Issac Garfield, Thomas Slaton, and Jon Chadwick, who came in April, 1739. It seems, however, from a petition made to the Legislature February 8th, 1743, that Samuel Winchell, was living for a time in this place as early as 1735 or 1736...Capt. Brewer is popularly supposed to have been the first permanent settler, but in fact he did not move into the town until August, 1739." p. 607, 608.

[2] *Bidwell House Museum* website, 9 Nov. 2009 <http://www.bidwellhousemuseum.org>.

[3] Shelby Sebring, *Summer Intern Cracks the Reverend's Code, Bidwell House Museum* website, Archives, Newsletters, Fall 2012, 7 Jul. 2014 <http://www.bidwellhousemuseum.org>.

[4] Cory Panshin, *The Padget History of America from the Landing at Plymouth to the Eve of the Revolution, The Revolution and After,* 16 Dec. 2013 <http:www.panshin.com/trogholm/geneal/historyD.htm>. The tavern of Josiah Smith in Great Barrington should not be confused with the more famous Josiah Smith Tavern in Weston, Massachusetts, constructed in 1757, which still exists today. *Josiah Smith Tavern (Weston Places)*, Weston Historical Society website, 16 Dec. 2013 <http://www.westonhistory.org/Extra-HTML-pages/Josiah-Smith-Tavern-Topic.html>.

[5] Ray Raphael, *Founding Myths: Stories that Hide Our Patriotic Past* (New York: New Press, 2004) pp. 147-149. *Give me liberty, or give me death!* Last modified 6 Nov. 2013, Ask.com Encyclopedia, 11 Nov. 2013 <http://www.ask.com/wiki/Give_me_liberty,_or_give_me_death!>.

[6] Ibid., Raphael, who arguably is the foremost historian of Patrick Henry's famed speech, among others, stated: "These words are stirring indeed, but Patrick Henry never uttered them. The speech was invented many years later, based on distant recollections of those who were present at the time. Although we know people were moved by Patrick Henry's oratory on March 23, 1775, we have no text of what he actually said." *Founding Myths,* p. 147.

[7] Ibid.

[8] Ibid., p. 4.

[9] Ibid., p. 5. In exploring these myths, Raphael asks and answers the question: "Why do we cling to these yarns? There are three reasons, thoroughly intertwined: they give us a collective identity; they make good stories; and we think they are patriotic." However, Raphael argues against their perpetuation. "Our stories of national creation reflect the romantic individualism of the nineteenth century, and they sell our country short. They are strangely out of sync with both the communitarian ideals of Revolutionary America and the democratic values of today. The image of a perfect America in a mythic past hides our Revolutionary roots, and this we do not need." p. 6, 7.

[10] *Plessy v. Ferguson*, 163 U.S. 537 (1896).

[11] Rev. John Dooley et al, *History of the First Congregational Church in Monterey* (Great Barrington, MA: Courier Job and Press 1900) p. 7, retrieved from Internet Archive of American Libraries, U. Mass., Amherst, 11 Sept. 2009 <http://archive.org/details/historyoffirstco00mont>.

[12] Eloise Myers, *A Hinterland Settlement, Tyringham, Berkshire County, Massachusetts* (Pittsfield, MA: Eagle and Binding Company, 1944) p. 1. Reprinted by Troy Bookmakers (Troy, NY).

[13] Ibid., pp. 1,2. John Brewer, among the first settlers of Tryingham, who arrived in 1739, agreed to build a sawmill within six months and a gristmill within two and one-half years after his arrival. The Provincial Legislature (Great and General Court at Boston), which created the township in 1737, reserved a seventy-five acre lot for the mill, and the more than sixty proprietors voted a tax upon themselves of one pound, ten shillings to pay for it.

[14] *Colonial America: The Simple Life, Early American Food and Drink*, 17 Dec. 2009 <html://colonial-american-life.blogspot.com/>. The early American breakfast was termed a *bever* from old English meaning light meal. It typically consisted "of a mug of beer or cider, bannock or hot cakes, and a bowl of porridge, and often a cornmeal pudding called mush, pap, Indian pudding or hasty pudding. The pudding would be eaten with milk poured over it or maple syrup or molasses...Although today we think of oatmeal porridge, there were many kinds of porridges in colonial days. Suppawn, samp, hominy and succotash came from corn. Suppawn was a thick porridge of cornmeal

and milk cooked together. This was a favorite of the Dutch and southerners. Samp was a coarse hominy, made by crushing the kernels in the mortar, and boiling them up, and eaten cold or hot with milk or butter. A favorite in New England was bean porridge."

[15] Dooley, op. cit., p. 7, indicating a 1765 Tyringham census showed fifty-one homes housing fifty-five families and a total of three hundred thirty-five inhabitants.

[16] Town center was near the southern end of Royal Hemlock road. Myers, op. cit., p. 20. Royal Hemlock road, an old Indian trail and the first north to Hop Brook (North Tyringham), opened in 1743. Supposedly it got its name because of an "RH" carved on a tree. Though intended to identify the way to Hop Brook, it was misconstrued as Royal Hemlock because trees marked with an "R" were reserved for warships of King George.

[17] Consumption of alcohol in the eighteenth century colonies was widespread. Even breakfast included beer and various fermented ciders. Virginia T. Elverson and Mary Ann McLanahan, *A Cooking Legacy* (New York: Walker, 1975) p. 14. *The Food Timeline: History Notes—Colonial America and 17th and 18th Century France, Breakfast, Lunch and Dinner?,*12 Dec. 2005 <http://www.foodtimeline.org/foodcolonial>. "...[T]he average colonial consumed the unbelievable daily quantity of more than 3.1 gallons of liquids such as beer, hard cider, perry (pear cider), and mead (honey wine)..." Weiss, Dr. Richard, *There Are More Old Drunkards Than Doctors,* Blanchard Colonial Tavern website, 31Dec. 2011 <http://www.blanchardstavern.com/TavernLife.html>.

[18] "Taverns...were NOT known for good food. In fact, most people who ate there complained bitterly about the poor quality and service of the food...People were served together, and they could take as much as they wanted from communal bowls." Oliver Lynne, *The Food Timeline, Colonial American Tavern Fare,* The Food Timeline website, as updated 20 Jul. 2011, 31 Dec. 2011 <http://www.foodtimeline.org/foodcolonial.html#tavernfare>. "'Meals were served at a set time and fixed price...Many customers couldn't have cared less about the food; they came for news, good talk, and companionship.'" Ibid., quoting *America Eats Out,* John Mariani (New York: William Morrow, 1991) pp. 18-21.

[19] Elverson and McLanahan, op. cit.

[20] *Boston Tea Party, New World Encyclopedia* website, 27 Nov. 2009 <http://www.newworldencyclopedia.org/entry/Boston_Tea_Party> indicating: "In 1768, Hancock's ship, *Liberty*, was seized by custom officials, and he was charged with smuggling."

[21] Op.cit., blanchardstavern.com to the effect that New England rum was often smuggled to France and Spain. England tolerated such smuggling because it provided the colonists with gold that enabled them to buy English goods.

[22] *The American Revolution, Lighting Freedom's Flame*, United States, National Park Service website, as updated 24 Dec. 2008, 30 Dec. 2011 <www.nps.gov/revwar/about_the_revolution/capsules_history.html>. The *Declaratory Act*, enacted in March 1766, with the repeal of the *Stamp Act*, asserted Parliament's unlimited authority over the colonies. The *Stamp Act*, which had proved unenforceable, was repealed in an effort to save face.

[23] Bidwell House Museum website, op. cit.

[24] Ibid. Reverend Bidwell's 1784 death inventory indicated he owned a remarkable forty-eight chairs.

[25] Myers, op. cit., p. 35.

[26] Ibid., p. 1.

[27] John A. Scott, *Tyringham: Old and New*, (Pittsfield, MA: Sun Printing Co., 1905) p.10, retrieved from Internet Archive of American Libraries, Library of Congress, 12 Oct. 2009 <http://www.archive.org/stream/tyringhamoldnew00scot>.

[28] Op. cit., Bidwell, History of Berkshire County, p. 606.

[29] Ibid., pp. 606, 607.

[30] Scott, op. cit., pp. 10, 11.

[31] Myers, op. cit., p. 25, indicating: "After the minutes of town meeting [sic] in 1773, there is a notation stating the school house burned on March 5, 1773. Thus went the first school house in Tyringham—like so many of those early buildings." As to the cause of the fire, the text gives no indication that it was ever determined. The school was located on Lot #43, not far from town center.

[32] Ibid., identifying him as the Tyringham school teacher.

[33] Bidwell, History of Berkshire County, Massachusetts, op. cit., p. 608.

[34] Ibid.

[35] Scott, Tyringham, op. cit., p. 9-11.

[36] Jon Hartman, *Into the Wood,* Daniel Boone Homestead website, 21 Nov. 2009 < homestead.org/oleyvalley.htm>.

[37] History of the Bidwell House, Bidwell House Museum website, op. cit.

[38] Edward McNull Burns and Philip Lee Ralph, *World Civilizations,* Vol. 2 (New York: Norton and Co., 1958) p. 31.

[39] Ibid.

[40] Baron de Montesquieu: A Short Biography, 24 Nov. 2009 <rigeib.com/thoughts/montesquieu/montesquieu-bio.html>.

[41] Hillary Bok, *Baron de Montesquieu, Charles Louis de Secondat, The Spirit of the Laws,* revised 20 Jan. 10, The Stanford Encyclopedia of Philosophy (Fall 2008 Ed.), 4 Oct. 2010 <http://plato.stanford.edu/entries/montesquieu/>.

[42] The motivating force behind separation of church and state in France and the American Colonies was not exactly the same. In France, where the church had long wielded its power, the goal was to free the state of the church's controlling hand. The people rebelled seeking a more secular society. In contrast, so many of the early colonists had fled England to gain the freedom to practice their religion. The Pilgrims or Congregationalists of Massachusetts illustrate this point. For them separation of church and state meant removal of the state's exercise of control over religion. These differences between France and the United States persist to this day. France places a bit more weight on preventing the church from regulating secular affairs than does the United States which in turn adds more weight to the free practice of religion. Of course, both aspects of separation of powers persist in each nation, and the difference is merely the amount of emphasis given to these aspects.

[43] Rogers' Rangers was an "independent company of colonial rangers attached to the British army" that was organized by Major Robert Rogers. The light infantry conducted "reconnaissance and special operations. *Rogers' Rangers,* 18 Nov. 2010 <http://en.wikipedia.org/wiki/Rogers'_Rangers>. In 1756 a band of Stockbridge Indians joined Rogers' Rangers to fight the French invasion from Canada. The Stockbridge Indians, a western

Massachusetts tribe, also supported the Americans in the Revolutionary War. *Native Americans of Columbia County New York, The Mohicans of Columbia County,* The Valatie Free Library website, 19 Sept. 2009 <http://www.valatielibary.org./mohicans.htm>.

[44] Rollin Hillyer Cooke, Editor, *Historic Homes and Institutions and Genealogical and Personal Memoirs of Berkshire County Massachusetts,* Vol. I, pp. 24, 25 (New York: Lewis Publishing Co., 1906), retrieved from Google Books, 5 Oct. 2010 <http://books.google.com/books?id=EDzcGVZnIC&printsec=frontcover&dq=Rollin+Hillyer+Cooke>.

[45] *Minutemen, Wikipedia,* 4 Nov. 2010 <http://en.wikipedia.org/wiki/Minutemen>.

[46] Burns, World Civilizations, op. cit., p. 276.

[47] *Quakers in Action, John Woolman, Quakers in the World* website, 16 Nov. 2013 <http://www.quakersintheworld.org/quakers-in-action/62>. John Woolman, 1720-1762, was an abolitionist Quaker who wrote essays and spoke throughout the colonies against slavery. He refused to buy goods or wear clothes that were the product of slave labor. He died on October 7, 1772 in York, England from smallpox.

[48] Douglas Harper, *Slavery in Massachusetts, Slavery in the North* website, 14 Nov. 2013 <http://www.slavenorth.com/massachusetts.htm>.

[49] *The Massachusetts Body of Liberties* (91), *The Harvard Classics,* Vol. 43, Edited by Charles W. Eliot (New York: P.F. Collier & Son 1909-14), retrieved from *Great Books Online* website, 14 Nov. 2013 <http://www.bartleby.com/43/8.html>.

[50] Douglas Harper, *Northern Profits from Slavery, Slavery in the North* website, 14 Nov. 2013 <http://www.slavenorth.com/profits.htm>.

[51] Colonel Ashley House, Sheffield, Berkshire Co., Massachusetts, 14 Nov. 2013 http://www.josfamilyhistory.com/sheffield-ma.htm>. In the eighteenth century the Sheffield home of John Ashley was reputed to be the "oldest complete house in the Berkshires," and the county's "center of social, economic and political life."

[52] The January 12, 1773 Sheffield Declaration was "so nearly in the language of the subsequent Declaration of Independence of 1776 that the latter might seem to have been copied from it. And as the resolution was drawn up by the celebrated Theodore Sedgwick, even

then, as afterwards, prominent in National Councils, it is not impossible that there may have been a close relationship between the two. This appears to have been the first, or very nearly the first, public action of the kind in the whole land." Charles J. Palmer, *Berkshire County, Its Past History and Achievements* (n.p., 1882), p. 7. Retrieved from *eBooksRead* website, 27 Oct. 2009 <www.ebooksread.com/authors-eng/charles-j-charles-james-palmer.shmtl>.

[53] In 1781 Theodore Sedgwick, author of the Sheffield Declaration (see note 52, *supra*), brought a lawsuit under a newly enacted Massachusetts statute on behalf of one of John Ashley's slaves, Mumm Bett, seeking her freedom. After prevailing in the lawsuit, Mumm Bett, the first to win such freedom in America, changed her name to Elizabeth Freeman and worked for the balance of her life as a domestic servant in the Sedgwick household. When she died, she was buried in the Sedgwick family cemetery, along with Theodore Sedgwick, whose legal career included more than a decade as an Associate Justice of the United States Supreme Court. *The Massachusetts Constitution, Judicial Review, The Mum Bett Case*, updated 22 Dec. 2010, *mass.gov*, The Official Website of the Commonwealth of Massachusetts, 17 Nov. 2013 <http://www.mass.gov/courts/sjc/constitution-slavery-d.html>.

[54] Verdigris is copper acetate. Henry Lionel and Ottalie K. Williams, *Old American Homes and How to Restore Them 1750-1850*, (Garden City, NY: Doubleday and Co., 1946) p.205, retrieved from Internet Archive of American Libraries, 1 Nov. 2009 <http://www.archive.org/stream/oldamericanhouse008982mbp/oldame ricanhouse008982mpb_djvu.txt>.

[55] History of the Bidwell House, Bidwell House Museum website, op. cit.

[56] After more than two and one-half centuries the remarkable, mortar-free arch at Reverend Bidwell's home remains intact and can still be seen at the Bidwell House Museum in Monterey, Massachusetts, *Ibid.*

[57] Myers, A Hinterland Settlement, op. cit., p. 35.

[58] Ibid., p. 25.

[59] Rosemary E. Bachelor, *What Was a Freeman in Colonial New England?*, *suite101.com* website, 18 Dec. 2010 <http://www.suite101.com.com/content/what-was-afreman-in-colonial-

new-england-a98295>. When it came to voting in colonial New England, it mattered whether one was a *freeman, freeholder,* and/or an *inhabitant. Freeman,* those who had taken the *freeman's* oath to defend the Commonwealth and not plot overthrow of the government could vote to elect magistrates and deputies. A freeman, generally one being indebted only to God, could vote to elect magistrates and deputies. A *Freeholder,* an individual who "by grant, purchase or inheritance, was entitled to share in all the common and undivided lands" of the community, could vote at a meeting of freeholders. There were other more general meetings where inhabitants were also entitled to vote. In all cases, however, only men could vote. *Freeman (Colonial), Wikipedia,* 25 Jul. 2011 <http://wikipedia.org/wiki/Freeman_(Colonial)>.

[60] American Colonial Customs and Traditions, Old Colonial Days and Ways, VI. School and Meeting House, sonofthesouth.net website, maintained by Paul McWhorter, 13 Nov. 2009 <http://sonofthesouth.net/revolutionary-war/colonies/colonial-ways.htm>.

[61] Myers, op. cit., p. 25.

[62] Ibid., p. 35.

[63] Ibid., p. 8.

[64] Hutchison-Whatley Letters, Encyclopedia.com, 27 Nov. 2009 http://www.encyclopedia.com/doc/1G2-2536600541.html>.

[65] Ibid.

[66] In May, 1773, Parliament removed certain taxes on tea that had caused its price to rise, as a result of which tea had piled up in warehouses and the stock price of the East India Tea Company had fallen from L260 to L160. However, Parliament did not remove the three-pence Townshend import tax applied in the colonies. George F. Smith. *A Long Time Ago in Boston, Part III,* posted 10 Oct. 2003, strike-the-root.com website, 6 Oct. 2010 <http://www.strike-the-root.com/3/smith/smith17.html>.

[67] History of the Bidwell House Museum, Bidwell House Museum website, op. cit.

[68] *Boston Pamphlet. Wikipedia* (Citing Middlekauf, Robert, *Glorious Cause, The American Revolution 1763-1789,* p.223. rev. ed., New York: Oxford University Press, 2005), 28 Nov. 2009

471

<http://en.wikepedia.org/wiki/Boston Pamphlet>.

[69] *The Kings Broad Arrow, The White Pine Monographs*, Vol. XXVII, Num. 1, Northeastern Lumber Manufacturers Association website, 9 Oct. 2010 <html://w.nelma.org/files/File/Monographs/Broad%20Arrow.pdf>.

[70] Boston Pamphlet, officially known as The Votes and Proceedings of the Freeholders and other Inhabitants of the Town of Boston, In Town Meeting assembled, According to Law, pp. 42,43, retrieved from The Coming of the American Revolution 1764-1776, The Massachusetts Historical Society website, 25 Sept. 2010 <http://www.mass.hist.org/revolution/doc-viewer>.

[71] Ibid., Appendix No. 1, The Message of the Town of Boston to the Governor, p. 37.

[72] An Act Exempting for their Majestyes Protestant Subjects dissenting from the Church of England from the Penalties of certaine Lawes, 24 May 1689, 1 will. & Mar. c. 18, Wikipedia, 30 Nov. 2009 <http://en.wikipedia.org/wiki/Act_of_Toleration_1689>.

[73] While it has often been said that colonists did not have closets because their homes were taxed based upon the number of rooms and closets counted as rooms, the so-called "closet tax" is a myth. See *History Myths Debunked, Myth #1: Houses didn't have closets in colonial days because people wanted to avoid paying the closet tax*, January 18, 2014, 26 Nov. 2014 <http://historymyths.wordpress.com/?=closets> stating: "Taxes varied widely from colony to colony and later from state to state, but research has turned up no examples of a tax on closets in any of the thirteen colonies."

[74] Lionel, Old American Homes, op. cit., p. 130.

[75] *Adonijah Bidwell, Church Life and Business, Wikipedia*, 9 Nov. 2009 <http://en//wikipedia.org/wiki/Adonijah_Bidwell>.

[76] See note 14, *supra*.

[77] *New Testament*, I Peter, Chap. V, Verse 8.

[78] Basic Information about Log Homes from Southern Cross Log Homes in East Tennessee, Truss Types, 19 Oct. 2009 <http://www.southerncrossloghomes.com/log%20homes/info.html>.

[79] Benjamin Franklin (published under the pseudonym Richard Saunders), *Poor Richard's Improved: Almanack and Ephemeris, etc.,*1753, retrieved from the Gettysburg College website, 9 Dec. 2009 <http://public.gettysburg.edu˜tshannon/his341>.

[80] Myers, A Hinterland Settlement, op. cit., p. 35.

[81] Bidwell, *History of Berkshire County,* Massachusetts, op. cit., p. 607.

[82] Franklin, Poor Richard's Improved, op. cit., p. 15.

[83] Lionel, Old American Homes, op. cit., p. 146.

[84] Myers, op. cit., p. 20, 21.

[85] George Whitefield was a dynamic evangelical preacher who, during the *Great Evangelical Awakening* of the 18th century, preached an average of twelve times per week to crowds that at times exceeded twenty thousand. Not a scholar, but a communicator of the Gospel, with Calvinist views he urged spellbound audiences to be reborn accepting Jesus into their lives. *George Whitefield (1714-1770), Calvinist, Evangelist and Revivalist,* Reformation SA.org website, 11 Dec. 2009 <http://www.reformationsa.org/articles/George%20Whitefield.htm>.

[86] Jonathan Edwards was a so-called *New Light* evangelical preacher, part of the 18th century *Great Awakening* that challenged the growing secular way of life in the colonies with the need to be reborn and accept Jesus into one's life. His famous sermon *Sinners of an Angry God* implored a return to the Bible. *Jonathan Edwards and the Great Awakening in Colonial America,* Constitutional Rights Foundation website, 12 Dec. 2009 <http://www.crf-usa.org/bill-of-rights/bria-20-4-a.html>.

[87] Lionel, op. cit., p. 211.

[88] An H hinge resembles the letter *H* with the portion that is attached to the door resembling the letter *I*. The H&L hinge is similar, except the portion attached to the door resembles the letter *L*. See Horton Brassie website, www.horton-brassie.com, 7 Oct. 2010 <www.horton-brassie.com/store/hinges/handforged/hhinges>.

[89] The designation of nails as two-penny, four-penny, etc., came from England and referred to the price per hundred nails. Thus, 100 two-penny nails cost two pence, 100 four-penny cost four pence, etc. Today the term *penny* relates only to a nail's length, not its cost. Ten-penny nails are three inches long. From ten-penny down to two-penny, length

decreases by .25 inch per penny. Above ten-penny there is no such pattern. William S. Pretzer, *How Products are Made, Nails,* Vol. 2, madehow.com, 11 Nov. 2013 <http://www.madehow.com/Volume-2/Nail.html>.

[90] "Slat-back chairs were arguably the most common type of the period. Sixty-one are listed in accounts between 1796 and 1818, at prices from four to six shillings." *The Dominy Craftsmen of East Hampton,* easthamptonstar.com, 25 Dec. 2010 <http://www.easthamptonstar.com/DNN/Archive/1998/981231/hist.ht m>. But fine furniture, e.g., a desk with serpentine drawers, ogee edges, decorative pediments and dentils, etc., could cost ten or twenty pounds. *The Price of Furniture in Colonial Philadelphia,* New England Antiques Journal website, 25 Dec. 2010 <http://www.antiquesjournal.com/pages09/monthlypages/april09/cost.h tml>.

[91] Alice Morse Earle, *Home Life in Colonial Days,* (New York: The MacMillan Company, 1898) p. 103, e-text of the reprint by the Berkshire Traveler Press, Stockbridge, MA, 1974, retrieved from BE Book website, www.myebook.com, 7 Oct. 2010 <myebook.com...free_ebook/earle-alice-morse...ebooks/home-life-in-colonial-myebook7983pdf>.

[92] Ibid., p. 113, 114.

[93] In colonial America spinach or salad was termed sallats; cucumbers, cow cumbers; and vinegar, sweetened vergi. *Vocabulary Words for Colonial America,* Yale University website, 8 Oct. 2011 <http://www.yale.edu/ynhti/curriculum/units/1990/5/90.05.04.x.html>.

[94] Colonial America: The Simple Life, Early American Food and Drink, 17 Dec. 2009 <html://colonial-american-life.blogspot.com/>.

[95] Jane DeForest Shelton. *The Saltbox House: Eighteenth Century Life in a New England Hill Town* (New York: Baker and Taylor, 1901) p., 117, retrieved from Internet Archive of American Libraries, U. of Cal., 4 Dec. 2009 <http://www.archive.org/details/saltboxhouseeigh00shelrich>.

[96] George F. Smith, A Long Time Ago in Boston, Part III, op. cit.

[97] Ibid.

[98] A scarf joint is made by notching or grooving two pieces of wood so they overlap and fit tightly together. Lionel, *Old American Homes*, op. cit., p. 106, 107.

[99] Scott, Tyringham, op. cit., p. 9.

[100] *Native Americans of Columbia County New York, The Mohicans of Columbia County,* The Valatie Free Library website, www.valetialibrary.org, 19 Sept. 2009 <http://www.valatielibary.org./mohicans.htm>.

[101] Ibid.

[102] Charles J. Palmer, *Berkshire County, Its Past History and Achievements* (n.p., 1882), retrieved from *eBooksRead* website, 27 Oct. 2009 <www.ebooksread.com/authors-eng/charles-j-charles-james-palmer.shmtl>.

[103] George F. Smith, A Long Time Ago in Boston, Part III, op. cit.

[104] In the pioneering society, where manual labor was the norm, lawyers were held in low regard and often viewed as windbags or troublemakers. Individuals frequently avoided lawyers, handling their own cases. *U.S. History, Chapter 5: Colonial Society on the Eve of Revolution, 1700-1775,* AP Study Notes website, 30 Nov. 2009 <http://www.apstudynotes.org/us-history/outlines/>.

[105] George F. Smith, op. cit.

[106] Samuel Adams: Summary and Analysis: Section 8: Committees of Correspondence, sparknotes.com website, 28 Nov. 2009 <http://sparknotes.com/biography/samadams/section.rhtml>.

[107] *Christmas Celebration Outlawed,* Mass Moments, Multimedia Archive, Massachusetts Foundation for the Humanities website, 28 Sept. 2013 <httpp://www.massmoments.org/moment.cfm?mid=369>. David DeSimone, *Another Look at Christmas in the Eighteenth Century* (Question #6), *The Colonial Williamsburg Interpreter,* vol. 16, no. 4, winter 1995-96, reprinted Colonial Williamsburg website, 28 June 2010 <http://www.history.org/almanack/life/xmas/xmasqa.cfm>.

[108] Eighteenth century men always wore waistcoats (a vest, but with sleeves termed a *jacket*). They came in all qualities of silk, cotton, wool and linen and could be adorned with tassels, embroidery, lace, etc. They replaced the longer doublet in the early part of the century. Cravats, a neckcloth, were also standard ware even for laborers. The

ends sometimes had lace, embroidery or knots. Stockings, generally knit, came up to the knees where breeches ended. *Clocks* or *clocking* were embroidery on the ankles. *A Colonial Gentlemen's Clothing: A Glossary of Terms*, Colonial Williamsburg website, 28 Dec. 2010 <http://www.history.org/history/clothing/men/mglossary.cfm>.

[109] *Bible, Deuteronomy*, XXXIV, 1-12.

[110] Pumpkin. *Vocabulary Words for Colonial America*, Yale University website, 27 Sept. 2009 <http://www.yale.edu/ynhti/curriculum/units/1990/5/90.05.04x.html>.

[111] *The Coming of the American Revolution, 342 Chests of Tea Into the Sea, Boston Gazette and County Journal*, 20 Dec. 1773, The Massachusetts Historical Society website, 8 Jan. 2010 <http://www.mass.hist.org/revolution/doc-viewer>.

[112] Boston Tea Party Historical Society website, 14 Jan. 2012 <http:/www.boston-tea-party.org/mohawkss.html> citing Grinde, Donald A. and Johansen, Bruce E., *Exemplar of Liberty; Native America and the Evolution of Democracy* (1991). Symbolism, not disguise, was the primary reason the Sons of Liberty dressed as Mohawk Indians for the Boston Tea Party. At the time the "Mohawk image was emerging as an emblem of liberty..." Some units of the Sons of Liberty had already used the image of an Indian when protesting. To this day the Massachusetts State Seal, designed by Paul Revere, still bears an Indian at its center.

[113] *The Boston Tea Party*, The American Revolution Home Page website, 27 Nov. 2009 <http:www.americanrevwar.homestead.com/files/TEAPARTY.HTM>.

[114] Tom Grinsdale, *Eighteenth Century American Fowlers – The First Guns Made in America*, The American Society of Arms Collectors website, 15 Jan. 2010 <http://www.asoac/bulletins/89_grinsdale_fowler.pdf>. The photograph of the Club Butt Fowler on the cover of this book is credited to Danielle Stavio, Lodgewood Mfg Ltd. As indicated on Lodgewood's website, it "was built by master builder Steve Krolick" with attention to every "historical detail." *Mid 18th Century Club Butt Fowler Modified for Militia Usage*, Lodgewood Mfg. Ltd. website, 4 Nov. 2015 <http://www.lodgewood.com/Mid-18th-Century-Club-Butt-Fowler-Modified-for-Militia-Usage_c_238.html> also indicating as follows: "These fowlers were popular in Massachusetts from the 1750s

through 1800 and were used by Militiamen in the French and Indian War, Revolutionary War, and the War of 1812." They were popular "as hunting guns" and "many militiamen used their personal guns during their military service."

[115] Kenneth Jewett, *Gunne Versus Rifled Gunne in Colonial America*, Kenneth Jewett website, 15 Jan. 2010 <http://kennethjewett.com/rifled-gun.html>.

[116] *Lath and Plaster, Wikipedia*, 19 Oct. 2009 <http://en.wikipedia.org/wiki/Lath_and__Plaster>.

[117] "The bulk of the tea cast overboard at the Boston Tea Party was a [C]hina variety called bohea named after a hill in China but no longer available." Weiss, op. cit., <http://www.blanchardstavern.com/TavernLife.html>.

[118] Scott, Tyringham, op. cit., p. 10.

[119] Melody Kraus, *Maple Sugaring: Native American Lore and History*, Town of Emmitsburg website, 2 Aug. 2010 <http://www.emmittsburg.net/gardens/articles/adams/2010/maple_sugaring.htm>. *All About Maple*, Siloam Orchards website, www.siloamorchards.com, 2 Aug. 2010 <http://www.siloamorchards.com/ALL%20ABOUT%20MAPLE.htm>.

[120] *The Life and Times of Benjamin Franklin, The Hutchinson Letters Affair*, The Franklin Institute website (Resources for Science Learning), 27 Nov. 2009 <http://sln.fi.edu/franklin/timeline/hutchin.html>.

[121] George F. Smith, *A Long Time Ago in Boston, Part III*, op. cit. Smith describes the reaction to Hutchinson's handling of the Boston Tea Party as follows: "The *Gazette* published a front page attack on Hutchinson, saying he had 'committed greater public crimes than his life can repair or his death satisfy.' Hutchinson wanted to go to England, at least until conditions settled, but Andrew Oliver, his lieutenant governor, was ailing and unable to replace him. In early March, Oliver died, and his enemies turned his funeral into a boorish affair by giving three cheers as his casket was lowered into the grave. England recalled Hutchinson and replaced him with General Thomas Gage as acting governor. Soon after, five thousand Redcoats arrived and turned Boston into an armed garrison."

[122] Ibid.

[123] Ibid.

[124] Ibid.

[125] Cory Panshin, The Padget History of America from the Landing at Plymouth to the Events of the Revolution, The Revolution and After, 4 Nov. 2009 <http://enter.net/~torve/trogholm/geneal/history/historyD.htm>.

[126] Rev. Adonijah Bidwell was a patriotic supporter of the cause of Independence. It is believed his sermons often focused on freedom. He penned "them in a cryptographic code to disguise the language", perhaps to protect himself against claims of treason. *Adonijah Bidwell, Bidwell the Patriot, Wikipedia*, 1 Aug. 2009 <http://wikipedia.org/wiki/Adonijah_Bidwell>.

[127] Resolutions of the House of Burgesses of Virginia, Designating a Day of Fasting and Prayer, Tuesday the 24th of May, 14 Geo. III, 1774, USHistory.org website, 8 Oct. 2010 <http://www.ushistory.org/declaration/related/vsa65.htm>.

[128] Ibid.

[129] On the front (south) wall of the dining room of the Bidwell House is a Brass Lantern clock, circa 1745, "made in Lavenham, England and attributed to a clockmaker Thomas Watts." *Bidwell House Museum – Lantern Clock*, Bidwell House Museum website, 1 Aug. 2009, <http://www.bidwellhousemuseum.org/Articles/newsletter2000_clock.htm>.

[130] Dr. Marjorie Bloy, *A Web of English History, The Age of George III, The Coercive Acts*, www.historyhome.co.uk, 27 Nov. 2009 <http://www.historyhome.co.uk/c-eight/America/coercive.htm>. In law *Mandamus* is an order from a court commanding a lower court or administrative body to perform an act. In England it was originally a royal prerogative.

[131] Ibid.

[132] Earle, *Home Life in Colonial Days, op. cit.,* pp. 496, 497. "Every inn had a name, usually painted on its swinging sign-board, with some significant emblem. These names were simply repetitions of old English tavern-signs until Revolutionary days, when patriotic landlords eagerly invented and adopted names significant of the new nation. The scarlet coat of King George became the blue and buff of George Washington; and the eagle of the United States took the place of the British lion."

[133] *U.S. History, Chapter 7: The Road to Revolution 1763-1775,* AP Study Notes website, 30 Nov. 2009 <http://www.apstudynotes.org/us-history/outlines/chapter-7-the-road-to-revolution-1763-1775>.

[134] Bloy, op. cit. Under the *Peace of Paris* at the end of the Seven Years' War, Canada became a British colony and subject to British law, including provisions that discriminated against Catholics.

[135] Samuel Adams, *The Rights, of Colonists, The Report of the Committee of Correspondence to the Boston Town Meeting,* 20 Nov. 1772, retrieved from the Constitution Society website, 29 Nov. 2009 <http://www.constitution.org/bcp/right_col.htm>.

[136] Bloy, op. cit.

[137] Jewett, *Gunne Versus Rifled, op. cit.* Rifled guns, with rifling grooves that held powder residue, were slower to load and, thus, less capable as an infantry weapon. However, they were accurate to 150 yards and could fire smaller calibers, thereby helping to conserve what was a limited supply of lead.

[138] Instructions for the Deputies appointed to meet in GENERAL CONGRESS on the Part of this Colony, By the Virginia Convention of 1774, UShistory.org website, 7 Oct. 2010 <http://www.ushistory.org/declaration/related/instr.htm>. In the instructions to their Deputies, the Virginia Convention, while strongly expressing their grievances against Parliament and General Gage, took a more conciliatory position vis-à-vis King George. The Instructions state: "[W]e desire that that they will express, in the first place, our Faith and true Allegiance to his Majesty King George the Third, our lawful and rightful Sovereign; and that we are determined, with our Lives and Fortunes, to support him in the legal Exercise of all his just Rights and Prerogatives. And however misrepresented, we sincerely approve of a constitutional Connection with Great Britain, and wish most ardently a Return of that intercourse of Affection and commercial Connection that formerly united both Countries, which can only be effected by a Removal of those Causes of Discontent which have of late unhappily divided us."

[139] Bloy, op. cit. But see *Intolerable Acts,* New World Encyclopedia website, 27 Nov. 2010 <htttp://www.newworldencyclopedia.org/entry/Intolerable_Acts> to the effect that claims that the Quartering Act allowed the billeting of troops

in private homes was a myth. It only allowed quartering "in uninhabited houses, courthouses, barns, or other buildings."
[140] Instructions for the Deputies appointed to meet in General Congress etc., op. cit.

[141] See note 24, *supra.*

[142] "The first Meeting House was situated on the brow of a hill in a field south of the old Carrington House which was the first Manse, still standing in Monterey...It was a windswept, bleak spot. There is some question as to whether the building was ever quite finished. Town meetings were held there but in winter they more often adjourned to the house of John Chadwick or widow Beulah Jackson, Innholder." Myers, op. cit., p. 10. "These were a rugged people who settled on this hilltop, faithful to their church, heedless of the weather, on Sundays they filled the pews with only the minister's fervent expostulations and their footstoves to keep them warm. They were progressive too, for about 1774 they decided to take up the 'body seats and make pews in their place.'" Ibid. at p. 10.

[143] Darryl Hanson, The Massachusetts Revolution of 1774: The Beginning of the End of British Rule in North America. August 30, 2009, suite101.com website, 4 July, 2010 <http://colonial-america.suite101.com/article.cfm/the_massachusetts_revolution_of_1774> citing Raphael, Ray, *A People's History of the American Revolution* (The New Press 2001), pp. 38-46.

[144] Charles James Taylor, *History of Great Barrington (Berkshire County) Massachusetts* (Great Barrington, MA: Clark W. Bryan and Co., 1882), p. 232, 241, 242, retrieved from Internet Archive of American Libraries, U. Mass., Amherst, 9 Sept. 2010 <http://www.archive.org/details/historyofgreatba00tayl>. "The people knew no court, recognized in the judges no authority, but insisted that they should leave town which they did. David Ingersoll, Esq., of Great Barrington was taken into custody by the Connecticut men and carried to Litchfield County and imprisoned." Taylor, p. 232.

[145] Ibid.

[146] An historic stone monument outside of the Great Barrington Town Hall bears the inscription: "NEAR THIS SPOT STOOD THE FIRST COURT HOUSE OF BERKSHIRE COUNTY ERECTED 1764. HERE AUGUST 16, 1774 OCCURRED THE FIRST OPEN

RESISTANCE TO BRITISH RULE IN AMERICA." *First Open Resistance to British Rule & Berkshire County Courthouse,* posted 13 July 2013, *Waymarking.com* website, 8 Nov. 2013 <http://www.waymarking.com/waymarks/WMHTMB_First_Open_Re sistance_to_British_Rule_Berkshire_County_County_Courthouse_Gr eat Barrington_MA>. Other locales might lay claim to the first act of open resistance. For example, the Boston Tea Party, December 16, 1773, was earlier, but the tea was privately owned by the East India Company, albeit a monopoly established by British governmental authority. While the issue could be viewed as one of semantics, Berkshire County has considerable justification for its claim, and there is no doubt that the events at the Courthouse in Great Barrington constituted a significant revolutionary steppingstone.

[147] Hanson, op. cit.

[148] Anne and Charles Eastman, *NH Years Of Revolution, Profiles Publications and NH Bicentennial Commission* (1976), retrieved from the *SeacoastNH* website, Dennis J. Robinson, Editor, *Fort William and Mary, Tea Troubles,* 7 Apr. 2010 <http://www.seacoastnh.com/history/rev/willmary.html>.

[149] Panshin, The Revolution and After, op. cit.

[150] *Cambridge and the American Revolution,* Cambridge Historical Society website, 7 Apr. 10 <http://www.cambridgehistory.org/discover/Cambridge-Revolution/index.html>.

[151] Eastman, op. cit.

[152] See note 139, *supra,* suggesting that no occupied private homes were actually commandeered under the Quartering Act.

[153] Eric Perkins, *47ʰ Foot in North America, 1772-1781, 47ʰfoot.blogspot.com,* 8 Jan. 2011 <http://47thfoot.blogspot.com/2009/02/redcoat-uniforms-part-1-privates-and.html>. *DC Theatricks - British Redcoat Uniform,* www.costume.com, 8 Jan. 2011 <http://www.costume.com/sales/costumes/1776br.htm>. Each British regiment had a distinctive color for the facings that covered their coats, lapel collars and cuffs.

[154] Colonial America: The Simple Life, Early American Food and Drink, 17 Dec. 2009 <html://colonial-american-life.blogspot.com/>. Suppawn was a thick porridge of cornmeal and milk, and gruel was

what people ate when they were so poor they had to water down their porridge to make it last.

[155] Weiss, Dr. Richard, *There Are More Old Drunkards Than Doctors*, *op. cit*. A syllabub, also spelled sillabub, can be served as a drink or, with extended shaking, solidified as a dessert. Its key ingredients are wine, cream and lemon. Other ingredients, such as juice or nutmeg, may be added.

[156] Powder Alarm, Facts, Discussion Forum, and Encyclopedia Article, Wikipedia, 4 Apr. 2010 <http://www.wikipedia.org/wiki/Powder_Alarm>.

[157] Cambridge and the American Revolution, op. cit.

[158] Powder Alarm, Facts, Discussion Forum, and Encyclopedia Article, Wikipedia, 4 Apr. 2010 <http://www.wikipedia.org/wiki/Powder_Alarm>.

[159] Ibid.

[160] Ibid.

[161] In a letter, dated August 27, 1774, to Lord Dartmouth in London, General Thomas Gage stated: "By the plan lately adopted, forcible opposition and violence is to be transferred from the town of Boston to the country...it is very high, also, in Berkshire County, and makes way rapidly to the rest. In Worcester they keep no terms; openly threaten resistance by arms; having been purchasing arms; preparing them; casting balls, and providing powder; and threaten to attack any troops who dare to oppose them. Mr. Ruggles, of the new Council, is afraid to take his seat as Judge of the Inferior Court, which sets at Worcester, on the 7th of next month; and I apprehend that I shall soon be obliged to march a body of troops into that township, and perhaps into others, as occasions happen, to preserve the peace." *Letter from Governor Gage to the Earl of Dartmouth,* 27 Aug. 1774, retrieved from American Archives, Documents of the American Revolution 1774-1776, Series 4, Vol. 1, Page 0741, Northern Illinois University Libraries, 13 Nov. 2013 <http://lincoln.lib.niu.edu/cgi-bin/philologic/getobject.pl?c.845:1.amarch>. See also, William Lincoln, *History of Worcester Massachusetts, From its Earliest Settlement to 1836* (Worcester, MA: Charles Hershey, 1862), retrieved from Internet Archive of American Libraries, The Library of Congress, 12 Nov. 2013 <http://archive.org/stream/historyofworcest00hers> at p. 88: "A body of about six thousand men assembled on the invitation of the committee of

correspondence, on the 6th of September, and blocked up the passage to the Court House. The Justices of the Inferior Court of Common Pleas were compelled to make a declaration in writing, that they would not attempt to exercise their authority, or appear officially, in opposition to the will of the people...No trials were had, or judgments rendered, until July, 1776, when the courts were again opened under the new government."

[162] The Massachusetts Revolution of 1774: The Beginning of the End of British Rule in North America, suite101.com website, 4 July, 2010 <http://colonial-america.suite101.com/article.cfm/the_massaxchusetts_revolution_of_1774>. The documented militiamen from 37 Worcester towns totaled 4622. Melvin H. Bernstein, Moderator, 8 January 2013, *Setting the Record Straight: The Worcester Revolt of September 6, 1774,* Massachusetts Society, Sons of the Revolution website, 8 Nov. 2013 <http://web.massar.org/setting-the-record-straight-the-worcester-revolt-of-september-6-1774/> citing Ray Raphael, *The First Revolution: Before Lexington and Concord* (New York: The New Press, 2002).

[163] Ibid., Setting the Record Straight; Raphael, The First Revolution.

[164] See *Tarring and Feathering,* HistoryWiz website, 13 Nov. 2013 <http://www.historywiz.com/didyouknow/trringandfewathering.htm> to the effect: "Tarring and feathering was successfully used as a weapon against the Townshend Duties (including the tea tax which led to the Boston Tea Party)." One member of Parliament "argued that 'Americans were a strange set of people, and that it was in vain to expect any degree of reasoning from them; that instead of making their claim by argument, they always chose to decide the matter by tarring and feathering.' Fearing that the practice was getting out of control and was harming their image, Boston leaders called a halt to the practice. Elsewhere in the colonies, it persisted as a way to intimidate and punish Loyalists."

[165] Scott, *Tyringham,* op. cit., p. 25.

[166] Panshin, The Revolution and After, op. cit.

[167] Henry J. Sage, *United States History, Discovery and Colonization 1550-1660, Colonial Period, The Puritans of New England.* Sage American History website. 26 Oct. 2013 <http:/sageamericanhistory.net/colonial/topics/puritannewengland.html>.

[168] Benson J. Lossing, *Our Country: A Household History for All Readers, Vol. II, The Events of the First Continental Congress of 1774* (New York: Johnson Wilson & Co., 1877), an excerpt contained in and retrieved from Public Bookshelf website, 30 Mays 2010

&lt;http://www.publicbookshelf.com/public_html/Our_Country_vol_2/ev entsfir_ed.html&gt;. In the fall of 1774, even as the drums of possible war began to beat, few in the colonies expected a declaration of independence.

[169] Powder Alarm, Wikipedia, op. cit.

[170] Ibid.

[171] *Minutemen, Wikipedia*, 4 Nov. 2010 &lt;http://en.wikipedia.org/wiki/Minutemen&gt;.

[172] A doublet is a "jacket of cloth or leather, usually with sleeves and open down the front". *Vocabulary Words for Colonial America*, Yale University website, 8 Oct. 2011 &lt;http://www.yale.edu/ynhti/curriculum/units/1990/5/90.05.04.x.html&gt;.

[173] Carol Stone, Ways of the World, American Revolution: A Government Overturned in 1774, 7 Jul. 2009, posted 18 Jul. 2009, The Geranium Farm: Ways of the World Blogspot, 8 Oct. 2010 &lt;http://ways-of-the world.blogspot.com/2009_07_01_archive.html&gt;.

[174] Ibid.

[175] Agnes Hunt, Ph.D., *The Provincial Committees of Safety of the American Revolution* (Massachusetts), (Cleveland OH: Winn & Judson, 1904), retrieved from *books.google.com/.*, 24 Oct. 2013 &lt;https://www.google.com/search?q=Agnes+Hunt&btnG=Search=Book s&tbm=bks&tbo=1&gt;.

[176] Ibid.

[177] Ibid.

[178] Powder Alarm, Wikipedia, op. cit.

[179] Lossing, Our Country, Vol. II, op. cit.

[180] Ibid.

[181] *The Coming of the American Revolution 1774-1776, The First Continental Congress, Introduction*, The Massachusetts Historical Society website, 31 May 2010 &lt;http://www.masshist.org/revolution/congressl.php&gt;.

[182] Lossing, op. cit.

[183] *The Kings Broad Arrow, The White Pine Monographs*, Vol. XXVII, Num. 1, Northeastern Lumber Manufacturers Association

website, 9 Oct. 2010
<html://w.nelma.org/files/File/Monographs/Broad%20Arrow.pdf>.

[184] Flags Over America – The Colonial Period, Pine Tree Flag 1686, americanrevolution.org website, 9 Jun. 2010 <http://www.americanrevolution.org/flags.html>.

[185] The Kings Broad Arrow, op. cit.

[186] Ibid.

[187] A vaccination for smallpox was developed by Edward Jenner in 1798, and smallpox was eradicated by the World Health Organization as of 1977. New Light preacher Jonathan Edwards (See note 86, *supra*) succumbed to an experimental smallpox inoculation in 1758. *Smallpox Vaccine, Wikipedia,* 29 Nov. 2013 <http://en.wikipedia.org/wiki/Smallpox_vaccine>. An effective treatment for smallpox was never found. As many as thirty percent of those infected died of the disease. *The 1902 Smallpox Epidemic, Historic Knightstown Inc.* website, 29 Nov. 2013 <http://oldktown.com/?page_id=819>. When one became infected with smallpox, "the virola virus, after an incubation period of about two weeks a sudden onset of flu-like symptoms would occur." To similar effect, see the Mount Sinai Hospital website indicating: "Symptoms usually occur about twelve days after exposure...**Early symptoms include:** •High fever •Fatigue •Severe headache •Backache •Stomach pain •Fatigue (sic) •Sore throat •Nausea and vomiting •**Delirium**" (emphasis added). *Smallpox Information,* Mount Sinai Hospital website, 4 Dec. 2013 <http://www.mountsinai.org/patient-care/health-library/diseases-and-conditions/smallpox>.

[188] *Smallpox. Reference.com* website, 10 Oct. 2010 <http://www.reference.com/browse/smallpox>.

[189] Water-powered gristmills date back centuries to as early as 19 B.C. *Gristmills,* Baker Block Museum website, 15 Jun 2010 <http://www.bakerblockmuseum.org/heritage/gristmill/gristmill.htm>.

[190] Ibid. See also, *The Energy Story,* Chapter 12: *Hydro Power* (updated 22 Apr. 2002), *Energy Quest* website, California Energy Commission, 15 Jun. 2010 <http://www.energyquest.ca.gov/story/chapter12.html>.

[191] A splitting froe or frower is a simple construction tool used to make "workable forms out of raw wood." Typically with a handle and barrel,

each about a foot long and at right angles, at the bottom of the barrel is a blade, an inch or two wide, which, with a mallet, is driven into a piece of wood, thereby splitting the wood. *Digital Collections – Splitting Froe or Frower*. Memorial Hall Museum's *American Centuries* website, 23 Jun. 2010 <http://www.americancenturies.mass.edu/collection/itempage.jsp?itemi d=6536>.

[192] Seasoned wood has about "20 - 25% moisture content, while unseasoned wood can have up to 45% moisture content...Pound for pound all wood has approximately the same BTU content," but seasoned hardwood is roughly twice as dense as softwood and, therefore, an equal volume of hard burns twice as long as soft. *Firewood Hints*, Padgett Chimney and Fireplace website, 10 Oct. 2010 <http://chimkc.com/firewood>.

[193] Eastman, NH:Years Of Revolution, op. cit.

[194] Paul Revere rode up to Portsmouth passing the information along. (This should not be confused with Paul Revere's more famous ride which occurred on April 18, 1775 in connection with the battles of Lexington and Concord.) Another Patriot, John Langdon, rounded up the group that attacked Fort William and Mary.

[195] Powder Alarm, Wikipedia, op. cit.

[196] Charles J. Taylor, History of Great Barrington, op. cit., pp. 282-286.

[197] Ibid.

[198] Lossing, *Our Country, Vol. II,* op. cit. Lord Dartmouth was given the unenviable task of sending a letter to the colonies expressing the King's displeasure with the Second Continental Congress set for May of 1775 and urging them to use their "utmost endeavors to prevent such appointment of deputies" for the Congress. The letter was deemed a "bull without horns."

[199] *Declaration and Resolves of the First Continental Congress,* October 14, 1774, The Avalon Project, Documents in Law, History and Diplomacy, Yale Law School, 20 Oct. 2013 <html://avalon.law.yale.edu/18ᵗʰ_century/resolves.asp>.

[200] Lord Chatham, also known as Lord Pitt, the Earl of Chatham. Larry D. Smith, *A Chronology of the Revolutionary War, 1775 Liberty or Death, Mother Bedford* website, 5 Jul 2010 <http://www.motherbedford.com/Chronology05.htm>.

[201] Ibid.

[202] *First Continental Congress, Wikipedia,* 30 May 2010 <http://en.wikipedia.org/wiki/First_Continental_Congress>.

[203] Larry D. Smith, op. cit.

[204] Ibid.

[205] Myers, *A Hinterland Settlement,* op. cit., p. 25, stating: "After the minutes of town meeting [sic] in 1773, there is a notation stating the school house burned on March 5, 1773. Thus went the first school house in Tyringham—like so many of those early buildings."

[206] *Conciliatory Resolution, Wikipedia,* 5 Jul. 2010 <http://en.wikipedia.org/wiki/Conciliatory_Resolution>.

[207] Ibid.

[208] Don Cook, *The Long Fuse, How England Lost the American Colonies, 1760 -1785* (New York: Atlantic Monthly Press, 1995), source for *Parliament Hears Colonial Protest,* retrieved from *suite101.com* website, 5 Jul. 2010 <http://www.colonial-america.suite101.com/article.cfm/parliament_hears_colonial_protest>. During the first few months of 1775, Benjamin Franklin had quietly tried to work out a peace plan with several members of Parliament including Lord Richard Howe. Franklin sought repeal of laws passed without American representation. His one concession was to pay for the Boston Harbor tea, which he offered to do himself. When his efforts proved fruitless, after he learned of his wife's death, he returned home to America where he penned the following letter to William Strahan: "You are a member of Parliament and one of that Majority which has doomed my Country to destruction. You have begun to burn our Towns and murder our People. Look upon your Hands! They are stained with the Blood of your Relations. You and I were long Friends. You are now my Enemy and I am, Yours, B. Franklin."

[209] *America's Best History - U.S. Timeline 1775,* America's Best History website, 5 Jul. 2010 <http://americasbesthistory.com/abhtimeline11770.html>.

[210] *Rules of Cribbage,* American Cribbage Congress website, 5 Aug. 2010 <http://cribbage.org.rules/rule1.asp>. *Cribbage Rules,* Cribbage Supply.com website, 5 Aug. 2010 <http://www.cribbagesupply.com/cribbagerules.html>. The English poet John Suckling is credited with creating the game of Cribbage in the early

seventeenth century. James Masters, *The Online Guide to Traditional Games*, 1997, 13 Oct. 2013 <http://www.tradegames.org.uk/games/Cribbage.htm>.

[211] See note 155, *supra*.

[212] After Patrick Henry delivered his famous *Give Me Liberty or Give Me Death* speech on March 23, 1775, the crowd was reputed to have lept from their seats shouting, *To Arms! To Arms!* However, re-examination of the circumstances calls the details of the speech and reaction to it into question. See New World Encyclopedia website, 5 Aug. 2010 <http://www.newworldencyclopedia.org/entry/Patrick_Henry> as follows: "Problematically, the text of Henry's famed speech did not appear in print until 1817, in the biography, *Life and Character of Patrick Henry* by William Wirt. Although Wirt assembled his book from recollections by persons close to the events, some historians have since speculated that the speech, or at least the form with which is familiar today [sic], was essentially written by Wirt decades after the fact." Citing Ray Raphael, *Founding Myths, Stories That Hide Our Patriotic Past*, New Press, (2004). See note 6, *supra*.

[213] Myers, A Hinterland Settlement, op. cit., p. 25.

[214] Ibid., pp. 7, 8.

[215] Indians in the Revolution, Answers.com website, 10 Aug. 2010 <http://www.answers.com/topic/indians-in-the-revolution>.

[216] Ibid.

[217] *Indians and the American Revolution, theamericanrevolution.org* website, 9 Aug. 2010 <http://www.theamericanrevolution.org.ind1.html>.

[218] *Sycamore Shoals, Wikipedia*, 9 Aug. 2009 <http://en.wikipedia.org/wiki/Sycamore_Shoals#Treaty_of_Sycamore_Shoals>.

[219] Earle, Home Life in Colonial Days, op. cit., pp. 19, 20.

[220] Charles J. Taylor, *History of Great Barrington,* op. cit., p. 232, stating: "The battle of Lexington was fought on the 19th of April, 1775...Doubts have been expressed as to the reception of the news of the battle on the 20th, and some have deemed it impossible. But the Pay Boll [*sic*] of Captain William King's company of Great Barrington Minute men shows that they marched on the 21st."

[221] Mark Winthrop, *Major John Pitcairn, Battles of Lexington and Concord*, The Henderson Island website, 13 Aug. 2010 <http://www.winthrop.dk/majpit5.html>.

[222] *The American Revolution, The Battles of Lexington and Concord*, American Revolution website, 13 Aug. 2010 <http://theamerican revolution.org/battledetail.aspx?battle=1>.

[223] Ibid.

[224] Ibid. See also *American Revolution: The Battle of Lexington and Concord*, Library Thinkquest website, 13 Aug. 2010 <http://library.thinkquest.org/TQ0312848/boflandc.htm?tql-iframe>. But see Ray Raphael, *Founding Myths: Stories that Hide Our Patriotic Past*, op. cit., casting doubt whether Colonel John Parker actually made the famous declaration.

[225] Ibid., Library Thinkquest website.

[226] The American Revolution, The Battles of Lexington and Concord, op. cit.

[227] Ibid.

[228] Ibid. See also, Robert J. Ohara, *Why We Remember Lexington and Concord and the Nineteenth of April*, Robert J. O'Hara website, 13 Aug. 2010 <http://rjohara.net/gen/wars/minuteman>.

[229] Ibid. American Revolution website.

[230] Ibid.

[231] Charles J. Taylor, *History of Great Barrington*, op. cit., p. 233-235, indicating that the rolls in Boston of the Massachusetts Secretary of State show in Book 12, Rolls 149, that of the forty-five Great Barrington and Tyringham men in Captain William King's company who marched to Boston on April 21, 1775, twenty-eight enlisted on May 8, 1775 for service until the end of the year, while the others returned home. Of the forty-five the following were from Tyringham: Samuel Brewer, Lieut., Joel Walker, Sergt., Henry Smith, Levi Wheelock, Peter Fuller, More Bird, Jonathan Dyke, Nathan Hale, Martin Langton, Jonathan Chapin, Daniel North, Abijah Markham, 2nd Lieut., Samuel Graves, John Chadwick, Jr., Sergt., Amose Curtiss, John Brown and Asa Allen.

[232] *Battles of Lexington and Concord, Wikipedia*, 13 Aug. 2010 <http://en.wikipedia.org/wiki/Battles_of_Lexington_and_Concord>.

[233] American Revolution website. *op. cit.* A large militia force that arrived from Salem and Marblehead might have cut off British Commander Hugh Percy's path to Charleston had not American Colonel Timothy Pickering halted his men on Winter Hill allowing the British to complete their retreat. Pickering claimed he feared such a beating of the British troops would result in all-out war but subsequently tried to blame his decision on orders from above.

[234] Winthrop, *Battles of Lexington and Concord*, op. cit., indicating: "When they arrived back in Boston some 32 hours after the battles, the King's troops had lost 73 killed, 174 wounded and 26 missing while the Colonials lost 49 killed, 39 wounded and 5 prisoners."

[235] *Siege-of-Boston*, Timelines website, 25 Aug. 2010 <http://timelines.com/1775/4/19/siege-of-boston>.

[236] Larry D. Smith, Chronology of the Revolutionary War, retrieved from the Mother Bedford website, op. cit.

[237] Cook, The Long Fuse, op. cit.

[238] *Conciliatory Resolution, Wikipedia,* 5 Jul. 2010 <http://en.wikipedia.org/wiki/Conciliatory_Resolution>.

[239] Ibid.

[240] Larry D. Smith, *op. cit.,* indicating that the *New England Trade and Fisheries Act* became more popularly known as the *New England Restraining Act.*

[241] *American Revolution: Conflict and Revolution 1775-1776,* The History Place website, 28 Aug. 2010 <http://www.historyplace.com/unitedsates/revwar-75.htm>.

[242] *The Battle of Ticonderoga,* School City of Hobart website, 28 Aug. 2010 <http://www.hobart.k12.in.us/cside/American%20Revolution/revwar/ticonder.htm>.

[243] Ibid.

[244] Ibid.

[245] Colonial America: The Simple Life, A Bit About Furniture, 17 Dec. 2009 <html://colonial-american-life.blogspot.com/>.

[246] Earle, Home Life in Colonial Days, op. cit., p. 103.

[247] "The early colonialists [sic] made alcoholic beverages from, among other things, carrots, tomatoes, onions, beets celery, squash, corn silk, dandelions, and golden rod [sic]." Berton Roueche, *Alcohol in Human Culture.* In: Salvatore P. Lucia, *Alcohol and Civilization* (New York: McGraw-Hill, 1963) pp. 167-182, retrieved from *Fun Facts, Puritans to Prohibition,* of the *Alcohol, Problems and Solutions* website of David J. Hanson, Ph.D., 14 Oct. 2009 <http://www2.potsdam.edu/hansondj/funfacts/PuritansToProhibition.html>.

[248] Shelton, *The Salt-Box House*, pp. 90, 91.

[249] *The American Revolution - The Battle of Bunker (Breed's) Hill, theamericanrevolution.org* website, <http://www.theamericanrevolution.org/battletail.aspx?battle=5>. Whether American Colonel Prescott chose Breed's Hill rather than Bunker hill because the former was better situated in relation to the British warships or erroneously fortified it owing to the darkness of night or due to a mapping mistake, the battle of Bunker Hill actually took place on Breed's Hill. Regardless, when 2,300 British troops arrived the next morning, they "were stunned to see Breed's Hill fortified with a 160-by-30-foot earthen structure."

[250] Most every child learns in school that Commander Prescott (or Israel Putnam) ordered his men to hold fire "till you see the whites of their eyes." Ray Raphael makes a strong argument that this storied quote is the product of romanticized legend rather than fact. *Founding Myths, op. cit.,* p. 157-171. Raphael points out: "None of the Revolutionary era historians—William Gordon, David Humphreys, John Marshall, or Mercy Otis Warren—mentioned anything about the 'whites of their eyes' command." p. 167. Objectivity, coupled with logic, gives credence to Raphael's conclusion. Waiting to fire until the whites of the eyes of the oncoming British troops became visible would seem a foolhardy, self-destructive tactic.

[251] Earle, Home Life in Colonial Days, op. cit., p. 218.

[252] The American Revolution - The Battle of Bunker (Breed's) Hill, op. cit.

[253] *Second Continental Congress,* United States History website, 28 Aug. 2010 <http://www.u-s-history.com/pages/h656.html>. *The Second Continental Congress - May 5, 1775,* School City of Hobart website,

28 Aug. 2010
<http://www.hobart.k12.in.us/cside/American%20Revolution/revwar/tic
onder.htm>.

[251] Hunt, The Provincial Committees of Safety, op. cit.

[255] *Events of 1775, Wikipedia,* 28 Aug. 2010
<http://en.wikipedia.org/wiki/1775>.

[256] *Iroquois Indian Tribe History, accessgenealogy.com* website, 4 Sept.
2010
<http://www.accessgenealogy.com/native/tribes/iroquioi/iriquoishist.ht
m>.

[257] Ibid.

[258] Franklin, Poor Richard's Improved Almanack and Ephemeris, op.
cit., p. 17.

[259] *Revolution Myth #5, thehistoricpresent.com* website, 6 Sept. 2010
<http://thehistoricpresent.wordpress.com/2009/06/24/revolution-myth-
5-america-had-no-chance-of-winning-the-war>.

[260] *Minutemen, Wikipedia,* 4 Nov. 2009
<http://wikipedia.org/wiki/Minutemen>.

[261] See note 164, *supra.*

[262] Second Continental Congress, United States History website, op. cit.

[263] Ibid.

[264] American Revolution: Conflict and Revolution 1775-1776, The
History Place website, op. cit.

[265] *Canada in the American Revolution,* Shmoop.com website, 2 Feb.
2016 <http://www.shmoop.com/american-revolution/canada-
battle.html>.

[266] Bidwell House Museum website, 6 Nov. 2013
<http://www.bidwellhousemuseum.org/index.php/bidwell-connectyion-
to-revolutionary/war/>. In an article entitled *Bidwell Connection to the
Revolutionary War,* which appears on the Bidwell House Museum
website, Wilma Heckendale Spice, a fourth great-granddaughter of
Rev. Adonijah Bidwell, states that "documents clearly indicate Rev. Adonijah's
patriotic Revolutionary War activities: For four years in a row, Rev. Adonijah
Bidwell lent his entire salary to the town, so the town could pay the soldiers. He
sold beef to the army. He later lent the town another 60 pounds so they

could pay the army. (And it is doubtful that the town ever was able to repay what they owed him.)"

[267] *By the King, A Proclamation For Suppressing Rebellion and Sedition,* Papers of the Continental Congress, 1774-1789, Item 152, Letters from Gen. George Washington, Commander in Chief of the Army, 1775-84, vol. 1, p.271; Records of the Continental and Confederation Congresses and the Constitutional Convention, Record Group 360; National Archives, retrieved from National Archives website, 25 Nov. 2013 <http://www.archives.gov/historical-docs/todays-doc/?dod-date=823>.

[268] *The Story of Maine, The Burning of Falmouth,* Maine Public Broadcasting Network website, 25 Nov. 2013 <http://www.mpbn.net/homestom/p11falmouthburning.html>. On October 18, 1775, four British ships attacked and burned the port of Falmouth, Massachusetts. (The site of the attack was what is today Portland, Maine, not to be confused with either Falmouth, Massachusetts or Falmouth, Maine of today.) British Commander Lt. Henry Mowatt afforded the residents an opportunity to escape before the bombardment commenced. By the time it ended, two-thirds of the town was in ruins.

[269] Frank E. Grizzard, Jr., *Supply Problems Plagued the Continental Army from the Start,* The American Revolution website, 9 Sept. 2010 <http://revolution.h-net.msu.edu/essays/grizzard.html>.

[270] Second Continental Congress, Wikipedia, 28 Aug. 2010 <http://en.wikipedia.org/wiki/Second_Continental_Congress> quoting Cyclopedia of Political Science, Political Economy, and the Political History of the United States, Vol. I, 274.4 (Maynard, Merrill and Co., 1899) as follows: "The appointment of the delegates to both these congresses was generally by popular conventions, though in some instances by state assemblies. But in neither case can the appointing body be considered the original depositary of the power by which the delegates acted; for the conventions were either self-appointed 'committees of safety' or hastily assembled popular gatherings, including a small fraction of the population to be represented, and the state assemblies had no right to surrender to another body one atom of the power which had been granted to them, or to create a new power which should govern the people without their will."

[271] The Massachusetts Provincial Congress sent a letter to the Continental Congress requesting that the latter take control of the army

at Cambridge. *The Continental Congress*, sonofthesouth website, op. cit., 13 Sept. 2010.

[272] The dilemma regarding the scope of the central government's power has continued throughout our nation's history and persists today. Both liberals and conservatives play both sides of the fence. Liberals have welcomed a broad construction of the Commerce Clause in order to facilitate an agenda of progressive legislation, perhaps best illustrated by the New Deal. Conservatives cry out for strict constitutional construction until it conflicts with their agenda. Biblical principals suddenly take precedence over constitutional dictates such as separation of church and state. Such is the natural consequence of a broadly worded flexible document that was the product of compromise. That is not to suggest that a detailed and restrictive document would be preferable. To stand the tests of time in an ever-changing world, especially one with a diverse population, flexibility is necessary.

[273] *The Knox Trail - History*, New York State Museum website, 11 Oct. 2010 <html://www.nysm.nysed.gov/services/KnoxTrail//kthistory.html>.

[274] Ibid.

[275] Ibid.

[276] Ibid.

[277] Tim Abbott, blogging as Tim Greenman, *Through the Berkshires with Henry Knox*, posted 15 May 2010, *Walking the Berkshires Blogspot*, 19 Sept. 2010 <http://greensleeves.typepad.com/berkshires//2010/05/through-the-berkshires-with-henry-knox.html>.

[278] *Ibid.* See the actual diary text at *The Coming of the American Revolution 1774 - 1776*, Henry Knox Diary (20 November, 1775 - 13 January, 1776), p. 24, The Massachusetts Historical Society website, 25 Sept. 2010 <http://www.masshist.org/revolution/doc-viewer.php?item_4638mode+nav>.

[279] The Knox Trail — History, op. cit.

[280] The first formulation of the *Law of Excluded Middle* was in Aristotle's *On Interpretation* in which he indicated that given two contradictory propositions, one must be true and the other, false. *Law of Excluded Middle*, *Wikipedia*, 26 Nov. 2014 <http://en.wikipedia.org/wiki/Law_of_excluded_middle>.

[281] Ibid.

[282] Tim Abbott, *Through the Berkshires with Henry Knox*, op. cit., summing up the impact of Knox's fifty-six day trek as follows: "Whether the siege guns really forced the British to give up Boston or provided them with a ready excuse to do so is open to conjecture, but there is no doubt that the fact of their arrival gave a boost to patriot arms that they would not enjoy again until the following Christmas, when Washington and Knox crossed the Delaware to surprise the Hessians at Trenton." Less than four months after the British left Boston, on July 4, 1776, the colonies declared their independence from England. The artillery Henry Knox captured at Fort Ticonderoga was ammunition that helped bring that about.